# DREAMS BIGGER THAN HEARTBREAK

# DREAMS BIGGER THAN HEARTBREAK

## CHARLIE JANE ANDERS

TOR
TEEN

A TOM DOHERTY ASSOCIATES BOOK

NEW YORK

DREAMS BIGGER THAN HEARTBREAK

Copyright © 2022 by Charlie Jane Anders

Edited by Miriam Weinberg

A Tor Teen Book
Published by Tom Doherty Associates
120 Broadway
New York, NY 10271

www.tor-forge.com

Tor® is a registered trademark of Macmillan Publishing Group, LLC.

The Library of Congress Cataloging-in-Publication Data is available upon request.

ISBN 978-1-250-31739-1 (hardcover)
ISBN 978-1-250-85838-2 (signed)
ISBN 978-1-250-31738-4 (ebook)

Our books may be purchased in bulk for promotional, educational, or business use.
Please contact your local bookseller or the Macmillan Corporate and Premium
Sales Department at 1-800-221-7945, extension 5442, or by email at
MacmillanSpecialMarkets@macmillan.com.

First Edition: 2022

Printed in the United States of America

0  9  8  7  6  5  4  3  2  1

*For Annalee, who gave me a ride on their starship*

# DREAMS BIGGER THAN HEARTBREAK

# PROLOGUE

■

(27.8.33.12 of the Age of Despair)

Princess Evanescent (*she/her*) knows her ship is under attack before the crew does. She flinches awake, as if a pleasant dream just went sour all at once.

Her moss-covered Yarthin face twists into a mixture of sadness and amusement under her glimmering crown, and she speaks into a slender flower twining around the nearest lacquer screen, next to her brocaded chair.

"All hands, this is Princess Evanescent. The *Questionable Decency* will be boarded by the Compassion shortly. They've sent their flagship, the *Unity at All Costs,* and thus I am afraid we are very much outgunned. Please abandon ship. I will greet our guests alone. It has been my honor to journey with you. Goodbye."

A moment later, alarms and crewmembers both start screaming as the assault begins.

A young Scanthian attendant named Orxyas (*he/him*) appears in the doorway. "Your Radiance, come with us. Please. Or you and I could switch places. I could stay, and you could . . ."

The princess shakes her head. "I'm their primary objective, and they will not be easily deceived. This will end badly for me, but it needn't for you. I imagine they'll let you depart in peace, so long as I remain."

Orxyas starts to protest anew, then just bows his head and takes his leave.

The air rings with the sound of alarms and the frenzy of the crew—who are still trying to fight an unwinnable battle, in spite of the princess's orders. Then all of the evacuation modules launch, and the ship goes quiet.

Princess Evanescent takes one last bite of Zanthuron coral. She plays a few poignant notes on her qhynqhun, a musical instrument with a long curved neck and a flat body.

A sharp crack rings out.

Footsteps approach.

The princess rises to greet her visitors.

Princess Evanescent is seized by heavily armed people in matte black armor with a red slash across their chests. They drag her through the gold-dappled walkways of the *Questionable Decency* as her slippered feet try in vain to touch the ground.

The *Unity at All Costs* stretches so far above and below, it appears endless. Princess Evanescent takes in every detail of the echoing superstructure studded with crooked spikes. Here, in the heart of the Compassion's power, she is alone—except that she's never alone, even for a moment, because she is a princess.

The soldiers carry the princess to a room full of prismatic clouds that scatter dark rainbows everywhere. Her resolve—to show no fear—evaporates as they deposit her in front of an apparatus with a dozen bent legs and a long sharp drill.

Her breath comes faster and shallower.

"You know what I want," says a treacly sweet voice.

"I know who you are," the princess says. "Kankakn. The founder of the Compassion, and its self-styled spiritual leader. As to what you want? I cannot say."

"I've come to take your crown," says Kankakn (*she/her*). "For this process to work, I must peel away everything you are. I will unchoose all your choices, unthink all your thoughts—until all that remains of you is a weeping husk. You will be lower than all the misshapen creatures your Royal Fleet has striven to protect."

The Compassion soldiers lift the flailing princess and carry her toward a set of restraints, facing the sharp blade on legs.

"Don't!" the princess shouts. "Don't do this. The Firmament and the Royal Fleet have only tried to help, to bring peace—"

"My poor child, try to clear your mind," Kankakn says. "Let me remove your crown without causing you too much suffering."

Acolytes in cream-colored robes shove Princess Evanescent's limbs into restraints, and she seems to reach a decision.

"Petals in a deluge," she says in a low voice. "Sparks in a whirlwind."

The crown atop her head catches on fire. Wisps of smoke waft into the air, and delicate filaments crumble and smolder.

Kankakn sees too late, and rushes forward. "No! No, you pampered fool—"

One of the acolytes tries to seize what's left of the crown and comes away howling, with a burnt hand.

Princess Evanescent smiles. Her scalp is on fire, the remains of her crown turning into a wreath of golden smoke.

A few heartbeats later, the princess's head is utterly consumed by flames.

Hey Rachael, I'm going to let you off the hook right now. You don't need to be the glue anymore.

You did it. You brought us all together, you kept us going when we traveled into the hot sweaty armpit of death. You made us a family, and you saved all of our lives.

Let us take care of you for a change. Please.

This isn't like eighth grade, when I decided I was going to be your bodyguard, and I went around staring down Walter Gough and Lauren Bose, until you told me I was embarrassing you. Nobody thinks you can't take care of yourself, we just want to be there for you. The same way you've been there for all of us.

The rest of us are making our scary beautiful fantasies come true. Me, Damini, and Yiwei are learning so much at the space academy—and I thought I knew every weird fact already. Kez looks so good in those trainee ambassador threads, I can't even stand it. When Kez makes it back to Earth and leads everyone into the light, there are going to be Kez T-shirts and posters and TikToks and movies, and I can't wait. And Elza? She's going to blow everyone's mind at the Palace of Scented Tears.

We're all becoming our best selves—thanks to you.

Every now and then, I have to stop and look at my life, and I can hardly believe that I'm here, in the greatest city that's ever existed. (Don't worry, not gonna subject you to me singing *Hamilton* off-key again.) It's not the life I used to dream of, back home on Earth. It's better.

I only wish you hadn't paid such a high price.

Or there was something the rest of us could do to help you pay it.

I would go back into the stankiest part of death's armpit, if there was a chance of helping you get back what you've lost.

# 1.

## RACHAEL

Rachael Townsend used to have a mighty superpower: anything she saw, she drew. She traveled from world to world, and sketched every mind-blowing vista.

Until she woke up from a coma, and the one thing that gave meaning to her life was gone.

This is the most outstanding sight Rachael has ever seen—and it's wrecking her heart.

Rachael's boyfriend, Wang Yiwei, lies across her bed wearing nothing but his blue Space Underpants, which fit like a glove because they were made for him specifically. (Yiwei's muscles look even more cut after a couple weeks of Royal Space Academy training.) His lovely brown eyes are full of warmth, though he's probably getting a cramp from staying in the same position for so long, with his leg bent and his chin resting on one hand.

Rachael has never felt so helpless in her life.

"I'm sorry," she says yet again. "I'm trying. I'm trying so hard. I just . . . can't."

"You're fine." Yiwei smiles bigger. "Take all the time you need."

Rachael perches on the edge of the bed and tries to put on a brave face.

In between her and her half-naked boyfriend is a plastiform pad and a pile of lightpens and styluses.

She picks up a stylus and tries to put the outline of Yiwei's spiked hair and square jaw on the page. This used to be so easy. Just . . . turn what you see into a shape. Light and shadow, texture, colors, all of it.

Rachael's stylus touches the page, and . . . nothing. Her mind freezes. She loses concentration.

"It's okay," Yiwei says. "I can hold this pose forever."

Something is hollowing Rachael from the inside, eating away at her willpower. Her self-esteem.

*Who am I, if I can't do the one thing I was always good at?*

"You are giving me lots and lots of inspiration," she tells Yiwei. "Just not the kind that turns into drawings on a page."

"Relax," he says. "Nobody but you and me here."

This time, Rachael picks up a lightpen. For a moment, muscle memory takes over, and she can feel the picture take shape. Turning vision into execution—but as soon as the lightpen touches the page, it's gone.

She lets out a roar of frustration and throws the lightpen at the wall. Xiaohou picks it up with one of his little front legs and tries to drum on the floor until Yiwei tells the musical robot to cut it out.

"You can stop," she tells Yiwei. "We're done here."

Xiaohou looks up and warbles a few bars of Rachael's favorite K-Pop song by Blackpink, like the robot wants to cheer her up. She glares at his round opaque metal face, with its gumdrop eyes and pouty little snaggletooth mouth. His little ears wiggle. The music stops.

Yiwei hasn't broken out of his pose. "Don't give up yet. We barely got started."

Rachael is already putting away her art supplies, with a throatful of sour. "No point bashing my head against the wall. There's something seriously wrong with me."

"Your brain got jacked by that doomsday machine," Yiwei says. "None of us could have done what you did, and of *course* it took a toll on you. I bet the aftereffects will wear off eventually."

Rachael shakes her head. "If it was going to wear off, it would have."

The best brain experts from a hundred planets did every test *twice,* and they all said there was nothing they could do. Rachael used the art-making part of her brain to control an ancient superweapon at the head of a butterfly made of starlit threads—and now, every time she sets out to create art, her brain tries to connect with that weapon, and she freezes.

She'll probably never make art again. This is killing her.

"Everyone owes you a debt that's impossible to calculate." Yiwei maintains eye contact with Rachael as he puts on his Space Pants. "You saved all our lives—not only me and the other Earthlings, but everybody, everywhere. You're the galaxy's number-one hero."

Whenever Yiwei says things like that, it's like he's lowering a huge weight onto the space between her shoulder blades.

Rachael steps out of the Royal Academy dormitory (where she's sharing a suite with Tina and Damini) and winces. She would give *anything* to be able to draw this skyline.

Off in the distance, she can see the curved crystal fingers of the Palace of Scented Tears, the walls of the Wishing Maze, the multicolored lights of Gamertown, and the truthspike at the center of the Space Academy campus. More walkways crisscross underneath the one she stands on, as far down as she can see.

The whole city is at her fingertips, thanks to the blue-and-white-striped puff that floats next to her. Her Joiner has little googly eyes and a slanted grin, and it bounces when it delivers a new message.

*JoinerTalk, Damini to Rachael:* Rachael, everyone at the academy wants to meet you!!!! You're famous! In a good way, I promise. Can I bring some kids over to the dorm later???

When Rachael gets a "text" from one of her friends on her Joiner, the words appear in a cloud that only she can see. But also? She kind of "hears" their voices in her head, and "sees" their faces, like living emojis, in her mind's eye. When she replies, she sometimes forgets to smile back.

Wentrolo, the main city in Her Majesty's Firmament, has 150 million people living in it, from a few thousand planets. Everybody has a place to live, because the buildings are constantly changing shape. (Today, a bunch of the nearby buildings are shaped like ampersands, but a few days ago, they were teardrop-shaped.) There's no money—you can get anything you want for free, as long as you help other people occasionally.

Even if all you want is just to hide from everyone.

Stuff Rachael thinks about when she's hiding out in her room and *not* making art:

1. I hope my parents checked on Tina's mom. Maybe the three of them are better friends now?
2. What if someone farted in the middle of the Javarah Smell Ceremony?
3. If I had all my old *Supernatural* AU fanfic with me, I could publish it on the JoinerShare and nobody would know what it was based on. A whole bunch of aliens would think I invented Sam and Dean, and they always worked together at a truck-stop diner.
4. Even though we're all here together, I miss the other Earthlings so much.
5. If I stare at the wall long enough, I can see patterns in the tiny cracks.

Wentrolo feels like a small town most of the time. Rachael only sees the neighborhoods she's interested in, and she has her Joiner set to maximum privacy, so nobody notices the "war hero" walking among them.

Most of the time, anyway.

Right now, a familiar voice comes from behind her.

"Honored Rachael Townsend!"

She ignores the shouts. Instead, she gazes down at a family of Javarah who are playing with their kids, one level below. Adult Javarah look like fox-people, but their kids are shiny and blue, with no fur yet.

"Esteemed Rachael Townsend! Please wait up!"

Here comes Senior Visioner Moxx (*he/him*), a large Ghulg (with tusks going up the sides of his face past his eyes). The left sleeve of his cranberry-colored uniform scrolls with his medals and commendations from the Royal Fleet, under an insignia that reads WE GOT YOUR BACK. He strides toward Rachael, as if he's about to take command of a planet.

The sight of this swaggering warthog-man brings back memories of high school. Moxx isn't going to fat-shame Rachael or throw her stuff in the trash, but his body language is way too familiar.

"Gracious Rachael Townsend, may you walk in gentle sunlight and sleep under bright stars." That's how a Royal Fleet officer greets a civilian in the Firmament.

Rachael knows the correct response, but she only gives him a tiny nod.

"You haven't been responding to my messages!" Moxx grimaces, making his tusks lift up to his neon-red hair. "We want to give you the Royal Fleet's highest commendation, the white half spiral, for your role in the Battle of Antarràn."

Sometime in the past few months, people started talking about the Battle of Antarràn. Rachael prefers to call it "that time we got trapped in a mausoleum and a bunch of people died for no reason."

"There'll be a ceremony, and you will deliver a speech. Everyone will attend," Moxx says.

*Ugh. Hard pass.*

"Why am I the one getting an award?" Rachael stammers. "I bet Tina would *love* the white half spiral. Or Damini, or Elza."

"You're the one who actually saved us all." Moxx fidgets. "Additionally, your friends are enrolled in the Royal Academy, the princess selection program, and the ambassador program. It wouldn't be appropriate to single out any of them."

Rachael's stressing out, which is when the headaches start.

Moxx is still talking. "You are the only one who's ever communicated with the Shapers. I mean, uh . . . the Vayt. You told us that they warned you about some terrible threat. Something that we don't know how to fight is coming for us. Everyone is more scared than they want to admit. We need your help!"

And with the headaches come glimpses of . . . something. A terrible presence scritches at the underside of Rachael's brain, leaving an impression of distorted flesh, glistening like lukewarm soup—things no human was ever meant to see. Rachael can almost hear them shriek, the way they sometimes do in her dreams.

Rachael always had a little voice in her head feeding her anxiety, telling her that everything was already ruined. Now that voice has a personality of its own, and it's the people who took away her ability to make art. The Vayt.

"I told you everything I know," Rachael mutters. "I don't exactly get a clear message from the Vayt, and the connection only goes one way."

She takes a breath, and then another, until the headache fades.

When Rachael wasn't being examined by doctors to figure out why she can't do art anymore, she was getting prodded by experts trying to understand the Vayt, the mysterious creatures who rigged the entire galaxy to put human-shaped people on top. The weapon Rachael controlled was part of the Vayt's plan to protect against some mystery threat to everyone, everywhere—all she knows is, the danger is already here, and time is running out.

So they attached brain-gargoyles to Rachael's head (she still has bite marks on her scalp). She spent a day doing Aribentoran poetic meditation, where she tried to doubt everything. She went inside a smoke-cocoon. She even got a hug from a one-eyed Oonian cuddle-priest who was *way* too handsy.

Damini keeps fretting that Rachael could suffer serious damage if she tries too hard to dial in to these nightmares.

"I was thinking," Moxx says, "you could try going into what the Javarah call the urrl zatkaz. It is a type of restorative coma."

Rachael sighs. "Do you really think it'll do any good?"

Moxx has the worst poker face in the universe. His tusks go sideways and his big eyes unmistakably say *nah*. But he stammers, "It's . . . worth a try. We have to try everything."

"One coma was enough for me. Sorry."

"It's not entirely like a coma," Moxx says. "I did some research and found the Earth term 'spa day.' You never know, maybe this will—"

Rachael flicks her left ring finger. Xiaohou responds by doing a happy backflip and blasting some CrudePink music.

She walks away, with Xiaohou on one side and her Joiner on the other. Xiaohou has gotten upgraded so many times, he no longer has any visible speakers or cameras, and he looks more like a metal monkey. He can actually swing by his tail.

*JoinerTalk, Rachael to Tina:* ugh moxx again. this time he wants to put me in another coma, for funsies

*JoinerTalk, Tina to Rachael:* this is NOT what the Royal Fleet is about. We do not force people to undergo medical experiments

*JoinerTalk, Tina to Rachael:* do you need me to come down there? i can ditch school

*JoinerTalk, Rachael to Tina:* nah i got this

"Honored Rachael Townsend!" Moxx shouts over the CrudePink. "Please don't turn away." He rushes after her. "You must understand! The galaxy is at a breaking point, and we need answers!"

Rachael walks on, and the CrudePink gets louder. It's that song about getting burned to nothing by a supernova and then your fried atoms coast through space for a billion years, until they drift down to a planet and become part of someone's lunch, and they choke on your billion-year-old ashes. Super catchy.

"We've had teams of scientists examining the Vayt machine in the Antarràn system," Moxx yells. "And nobody has been able to connect with it the way you did. It's completely shut down."

*Not my problem.*

"Gracious Rachael Townsend, please!" Moxx shouts.

Rachael does another hand signal, and her Joiner summons a barge, which glides right next to her. A moment later she's flying over the city, and Moxx is a tiny speck.

## Joinerguide: Life in Her Majesty's Firmament

Welcome to Wentrolo, a stunning achievement in urban design. Right at the center of the Glorious Nebula, Wentrolo is the capital of Her Majesty's Firmament, resting on top of an oval made out of pure starstone. We have everything we could ever need, including our own private sun.

Around half a million people arrived in Wentrolo on the same day you did, but don't worry: this city keeps growing to make room for everybody.

There's *so much* to see here. There's the Palace of Scented Tears, where the queen and her Privy Council help to decide the fate of worlds. Tourists aren't allowed inside the palace, but you can explore the outside, not to mention the beautiful Peacebringer Square, and the Wishing Maze—which might just change your life. Elsewhere, there's the Royal Space Academy, the majestic Royal Command Post, and the Garden of Starships. But also! You can play every game in Gamertown, get anything you might need in the Stroke or the other shopping districts, or learn about the traditions of a hundred different worlds in their separate neighborhoods.

But don't feel overwhelmed! The device you hold in your hand, that little ball of fur looking up at you right now, is your key to finding your way around this city. Your Joiner will help you to locate whatever you need, and you can also decide just how much city you're ready to handle at any given time.

You don't need money, or any other sort of device, as long as you've got your Joiner. Your fuzzy friend will follow you around like a pet. In exchange for all this abundance, your Joiner might occasionally ask you to do favors for other people: like if someone needs help moving furniture, or delivering something, you'll be asked to lend a hand. Here in Wentrolo, we all help each other—and we're so happy to see you here.

# 2

.

Rachael almost heads to the Slanted Prism, her favorite arcade in Gamertown. She's gotten hooked on *WorstBestFriend*, a game where you try to create an evil imaginary friend who tears down your self-esteem. (Rachael's fake friend is named Chloe—she's blond and adorable and totally sadistic.)

> **JoinerTalk, Yiwei to Rachael:** miss u! we just had a class in cycle theory
> **JoinerTalk, Yiwei to Rachael:** all about how to break cycles of violence and create peaceful cycles instead. So so cool!

But that conversation with Moxx weighs on her mind. Plus, she stares at the shape-shifting cityscape and imagines never being able to draw any of this. Art wasn't something Rachael *did*, it was who she *was*.

So Rachael uses her Joiner to ping her best friend.

> **JoinerTalk, Rachael to Tina:** Hey. I'm finally gonna do it. I need moral support.
> **JoinerTalk, Tina to Rachael:** "moral support" is totally the name of my next starship. meet u there!

Now Rachael's committed. She steers her barge in the direction of the Wishing Maze.

Tina has somehow gotten taller than the last time Rachael saw her—at least six-foot-four—and her skin is a brighter shade of violet. Plus she's started wearing jewels in her cheeks and jawline, so she looks a lot more like Captain Thaoh Argentian, the Makvarian hero she was cloned from. (Long story: Rachael and Tina were best friends back on Earth, but then Tina turned out to be an alien clone who was left on Earth as a baby.) Tina's uniform looks a lot like Moxx's, except it's paler (because she's a cadet) and instead of ranks and honors, her left sleeve displays a bloodred oval from that one time when she disobeyed orders. Her right sleeve displays one of the best pictures Rachael ever drew: out-of-control wildflowers.

The moment Rachael sees Tina, she feels better. Tina offers her a hug and she says yes, and then she's embracing her bestie and babbling about her random ideas for comics. For a heartbeat, Rachael can pretend the two of them are back home, heading inside the 23-Hour Coffee Bomb to eat donuts and doodle in the last booth on the left under the big speaker.

As they walk across Peacebringer Square toward the entrance to the Wishing Maze, Rachael tells Tina more about Moxx's plans to give her a medal and put her in a coma (maybe not at the same time). "I don't want to be anyone's savior, I want to lock myself in my room for a year and not speak to anyone. Even Yiwei. Even you."

Rachael glances up at Tina, anxiously. Tina's friendly expression looks the same as always, though her face is a different shape and there are jewels over her dimples.

"I know!" Tina says. "It's not just that you're missing a creative outlet. It's more like, making art was your safe place where you could recharge your batteries, when people got to be too much. Right? And you don't have that anymore, at least not right now. So of *course* socializing is going to be tough, even when it comes to the people you're closest to."

Best friend: the person who gets you when no one else does.

"It's okay to be messed up by what you went through. Nobody's expecting you to be suddenly fine," Tina adds.

Rachael feels some of the tension drain from her neck, her wrists, her spine.

The two of them get lost in the Wishing Maze, where the walls are at least twenty feet tall, made of a stone that looks like granite.

"I feel like a bad girlfriend," Rachael says. "Yiwei is having this awesome life at the academy, and I'm holding him back. And . . . remember Lou?"

Tina has to think for a moment, then she nods. Lou was the sculpture guy with the great eyebrows who had a whirlwind romance with Rachael at art camp, the summer after ninth grade. They were madly in love, for five weeks.

"We were great for each other at camp, because we shared all this camp stuff, and we went through this intense camp experience together, and I feel like I just said the word 'camp' a hundred times. Our relationship only made sense in those nasty cabins." Rachael always feels self-conscious mentioning her exes because Tina never had a real relationship until Elza.

"You and Yiwei did *not* go to art camp together," Tina says. "You crossed the galaxy and had each other's backs in a hundred life-or-death situations. All six of us are bonded for life."

"Yiwei got to know me at my best, is the point." Rachael stops trudging

and stares at her pale shadow on the wall. "And now I'm . . . not. At my best."
She rocks on her feet for a moment, thinking of the revolting voice in her
head, sliming her thoughts. "And meanwhile? His ex, Jiasong, is a turbo-
genius who helped him start a half-robot rock band. I could never live up to
that."

Tina snorts. "Whatever."

Dead end. They turn and retrace their steps. The shadows lengthen.

"All I want," Tina says, "is to do what you did for me: remind you you
don't have to be anyone, or anything, other than Rachael Townsend."

Rachael's shadow stiffens. She can't talk, and then she can. "Yeah.
Except . . . who I am is kind of a moving target."

"That's okay too." Tina's smile has gotten bigger, along with everything
else.

They're definitely close to the center, where wishes can maybe come true.

"I think we're almost there," Rachael says.

Rachael's feet are sore by the time they find the statue at the heart of the
Wishing Maze: Untho Kaash, a skull-faced Aribentor who was the founder
of Her Majesty's Firmament. She pulls out the wafer she got from an artisan
in the Stroke, and writes on it: "I wish I could make art again." Just writing
those words makes her want to ugly-cry.

Tina raises a big purple thumb.

Rachael reaches up to Untho Kaash's skull-face and sticks the wafer inside.

A moment later, it's gone. He ate it!

Someone is watching Rachael and Tina from the nearest bend of the
Wishing Maze. The stranger waves at Rachael—then ducks around the corner before she can get a good look at them.

Tina and Rachael rush after this mystery person and catch sight of
them rounding the next turn. Rachael almost knocks over a sunflower in a
smock, who hisses at her to watch where she's going.

Another turn, another glimpse of the stranger disappearing from view.

"You go left," Tina says. "I'll go right."

Rachael nods and veers left, but she doesn't see her stalker. Until she
notices an opening in the wall that you can only see if you're looking right
at it. The opening leads to a junction, where the stranger is looking right at
Rachael. They're a Javarah—a fox/cat-person—with an elegant furry snout.
And on top of their head sits . . . a tiara? With glowing lights rippling and
flowing directly inside this person's skull.

The queen. Rachael has been chasing the queen around the Wishing
Maze.

She lowers herself to one knee. "Your . . . your, uh, Radiance?"

The queen grins and waggles her ears, like she's trying not to laugh at Rachael's courtly manners.

She points to a hand-painted red box on the ground next to her, and vanishes. Like: poof!

Tina runs up, panting, and she gapes at the look on Rachael's face.

It's true! I see you all the time—though I still miss you like a fiend when we're not hanging out.

There's a hologram of you in the entry hall of the Royal Space Academy, looking metal AF. Gritting your teeth, white-knuckling your fists. You're right next to the renowned Smaa the Monntha—and two spaces down from the legendary Thaoh Argentian.

Before you say it . . . sure. There's a part of me, a teeny smidgen, that wishes it was me there. But then everybody would be looking to me for answers instead of you—and I would probably pretend to have some, and it would be a whole disaster. Right?

It's weird here. Fun, but weird.

The academy is the size of a small city, with these huge mustache-twirls out front, and a courtyard with the super-tall truthspike. And a ton of classroom buildings—and out back, there's the Garden of Starships. Rows of wriggly spreeflowers grow between a dozen newly built ships, waiting to take off and fly somewhere.

This two-year program is designed to start out by teaching us history, going back to the Seven-Pointed Empire, which ruled most of the galaxy for ages and then collapsed. And then there were years of chaos until something new came along: the Royal Fleet. We're supposed to get a common understanding of the past, and build from there.

But the Royal Fleet is shorthanded, and the garden is bursting with the new ships they're frantically building. So instead of learning the basics first, they're throwing us at the wall right away. We've spent hours in the simulator, practicing how to dive out of a spaceship into a planet's atmosphere.

I keep hearing that the war with the Compassion is going downhill. Our big ships can't be everywhere at once, and the smaller ships are getting pasted. The leader of the Compassion, Kankakn, is stepping up to take charge of the fight, and people don't even mention her without lowering their voices.

At least Damini is having the time of her life. She's made a new friend: this girl named Zaeta, who has ninety-nine eyes in between little fish scales, and the weirdest cutest laugh. Zaeta is the only person I've met who loves danger *and* weird puzzles as much as Damini.

Soon we're going to start learning to do combat, and I'm . . . gonna have a problem. I made everyone promise I wouldn't have to fight, but I shoulda known it'd never be that easy. The top brass at the academy, like Wyahaar and Barthanoth, keep grumbling that they have to make a special curriculum for me. Plus whenever I see that hologram of Captain Argentian, her smoky gaze gives me a soul-rash. Which is why I look two spaces over, instead. At you.

Can't wait to help you figure out that red box, and why the queen wanted you to have it. Maybe we can work on it after school today? Slanted Prism. I'll get the snah-snah juice!

# 3.

Gamertown always messes with Rachael's eyes at first.

Her barge descends past a dozen towers, blaring with candy-colored lights. Holographic gameplay swirls around the rooftops and cartoon icons run around under a skyline dominated by the crimson curlicues of the nearby Royal Space Academy. Even with Rachael's Joiner set to "maximum introvert" mode, the shouts of a half-million players and spectators still ring out, and she can smell the fried Scanthian parsnips and bottles of snah-snah juice that everybody uses to fuel marathon gaming sessions.

*Ugh, the more I see this place, the more I need to draw it. Wish things would stop looking like a dream all the time.*

Like every other neighborhood in Wentrolo, Gamertown changes its layout and architecture to make room for more and more visitors. But Rachael's main hangout, the Slanted Prism, always looks the same.

*JoinerTalk, Yiwei to Group:* Rachael where are you? everyone else is here.
*JoinerTalk, Kez to Group:* i'm already on my fifth snah-snah juice!

On the outside, the Slanted Prism looks like a chunky box turned sideways and resting on one corner, with walls made out of mirrors that refract the light into rippling colors. A ramp leads through a big arch, and then you're on the inside, where the tilted walls shine like mirrors, catching the light from a hundred games of *Ringforge, YayJump!,* and Rachael's favorite, *WorstBestFriend.*

Everybody sits on floating cushions, or invisible chairs. Groups of people cluster together around their own holographic gameplay.

Rachael makes her way through the big front area, where some of the game noises remind her way too much of being on an actual starship under attack. Then she reaches one of the private rooms, with undulating walls that look like marble, and finds her friends from Earth sitting around a large holographic sun: Kez, Tina, Damini, Elza, and Yiwei.

They're playing *RingForge:* everyone tries to be the first one to build a ring around a star. And Yiwei is winning.

"I am so sexy right now, I can't stand it," Yiwei roars. "I heard if you win three games in a row, you get a dancing-sun tattoo that everyone can see through your clothes. It's going to look so tough."

Kez hoots and then knocks a planetoid out of orbit, shattering part of Yiwei's crystalline ring structure. "Whoops. I'm sorry, were you using that?"

Yiwei curses and vows revenge for this heinous act of sabotage.

Today, Kez is using she/her pronouns. She came out as gender-fluid a while ago, and now she has a new, rotating set of pronouns. Rachael would be anxious about screwing up and hurting Kez's feelings—except that the EverySpeak makes it impossible to use the wrong pronoun by mistake. Even if you did misgender Kez, the EverySpeak would treat this as a miscommunication and make sure that nobody else heard it.

Damini leans way over to the left to swerve her ringbuilder ship, and drags a whole ton of space dust into her ring. "Hah!" She's wearing her long black hair up, over her round laughing face, with a dash of red between her eyebrows.

Tina notices Rachael standing in the doorway, and pauses the game. "Hey, Rachael," Tina says.

"Oh, hi!" Kez leaps to her feet. She's wearing her new trainee ambassador uniform, a million strands of gold crisscrossing her entire body, from neck to knees, over a white tunic. All of that gold sets off her high cheekbones and wide dark eyes. She's styled her hair into twists, and she looks ready to negotiate a peace treaty between a dozen planets.

All the Earthlings surround Rachael, chattering and asking questions, and it's actually . . . nice. They're not a crowd, they're family. The big crimson sun flickers in the middle of the room, surrounded by five half-finished rings.

"You met the queen!" Damini says. "Was she gorgeous? I bet she was gorgeous."

"I'm not jealous you got to meet the queen," Tina says.

"I hope you put in a good word for me." Elza laughs.

"And she gave you a present!" Kez says.

"I'm not jealous at all," Tina says.

Rachael pulls the red box out of her satchel and shows it to everyone. In the light of the holographic sun, she can see all the little brushstrokes from whoever painted it, and the little flourishes carved into the sides and top.

"It's beautiful," Damini says. "Is it a puzzle?"

"No idea," Rachael says. "I don't know how to work it."

Damini finds a hidden catch and the box opens to reveal a scene inside a single room. A Makvarian family: three parents with purple skin and jewels on their faces, fussing over a newborn baby. There are tiny nubs in two of the four corners, and when Damini plays with them, the scene shifts, and the baby is suddenly a toddler and the three parents are older.

"Here, let me try." Yiwei adjusts the little nubs again. The toddler grows up before Rachael's eyes, until they're an adult.

This box contains every single moment in that baby's life.

"How did somebody make this?" Damini turns the box over and over. "It's not holographic. I can't find a mechanism."

"According to my Joiner, it's called a layered panopticon, because you can see the story from every angle, and every point in time," Kez says. "Are you sure you want to be messing with this? You're still recovering from the last time you did the Royal Fleet's dirty work for them."

Kez grew up with a control-freak dad who put tons of pressure on her to be perfect and wanted her to join the family business, making weapons and high-tech surveillance gear, so now all she wants to do is help people make peace instead of joining an alien military.

"This is different. I think." Rachael can't keep her eyes off the box and the tiny people inside. "I asked for help with my art problem, and this was the answer."

"I'll see what I can find out when I go to the palace," Elza says. Then she raises her hands to her face, swaying a little. "Oh, I'm going to the palace soon! I need to sit down." She plunks herself down on a flying pillow, and Tina fetches her some snah-snah juice.


Now that Rachael knows how the box works, she spends hours poking at it, alone in her room. Somehow this thing contains the story of a whole life, lived inside a single room: love, joy, sadness, grossness, longing, despair, hope.

The longer Rachael plays with the layered panopticon, the more she learns about the person whose birth and death are the beginning and end of the story. One time she "peels" to a moment where this protagonist is a teenager, and they're kissing someone else, with their unlaced shirt sliding down off one shoulder.

She flips ahead, and these same two lovers are standing over what looks like a corpse.

The whole thing looks handcrafted, but what kind of hand could do *this*? And why would the queen give it to her?

Did the main character of this story-in-a-box murder someone? With the help of their lover? What was that body doing at their feet?

How the hell do you pack so many scenes into this one tiny box? Every time Rachael asks how the box works, Tina rattles off more jargon. But Damini responds: "It's art. Which means it's kind of magic, right?"

## Journeyguide: So You Lost a Loved One in the Abduction. Why Did This Happen?

The Abduction. The Reaping. Whatever name you prefer, this was a defining trauma for a whole generation.

We watched in horror as glowing windows opened up in midair, and streaks of pure energy grabbed our loved ones, on every planet where humanoids live. Our friends, our family members, were twisted into horrifying shapes, and then pulled inside some kind of nightmare space, to be lost forever. Anyone who wasn't present has seen the recordings. There's not enough therapy in the universe.

How could this have happened? Who could have done such a thing?

We soon realized this was the answer to a mystery we'd been trying to solve for a long time: the mystery of the Shapers.

When you look at the most advanced species in the galaxy, they all have one thing in common: the same basic shape. Two arms, two legs, and one head on top (usually with two eyes, two ears, and two nostrils.) For a very long time, we all believed that this was natural: humanoids were just better at everything, and that's why we ruled the galaxy.

Then, about forty NewSuns ago, we learned the truth. Someone with unthinkable power had given us two-legged people an unfair advantage, long before any of us were recording our history. These mysterious people traveled around and whenever they found creatures with a humanoid shape, they provided help and support. When they found people who were shaped differently, with more than two legs (or tentacles or slimetrails instead of legs), they sabotaged and ruined them—or just wiped them out altogether.

This was the greatest crime in history, and every wealthy planet had benefited from it.

So who were these ancient fiends? For a long time, we knew nothing about them. We called them the Shapers, and we believed that they looked like us (two legs and all). And they had evolved into a higher form— become gods!—and they wanted to help us evolve as well. That was a comforting fairy tale that we liked to tell each other.

The truth was much darker.

At the same time that the Abduction was happening on so many worlds, the Battle of Antarràn was raging. From the survivors of that battle, we learned the truth: the so-called Shapers were actually called the Vayt. They were nothing like us, at all, and they hadn't helped our ancestors because they wished us well.

The Vayt were losing a war, an eternity ago, against an enemy that we still know nothing about. So they devised some sort of ultimate weapon, made out of living bodies as well as technology—and this weapon needed billions of humanoid bodies as raw material. At the Battle of Antarràn, this weapon was activated for a brief time.

So when you think about that vision of people being crushed into unnatural shapes and then pulled into a sickening void, remember that the people who created that weapon were afraid of something even worse.

# 4.

—drowning choking nothing but greasy chills flooding her nose and mouth—all life, everywhere, dead and forgotten—too late too late, death is coming—

Rachael wakes with a lurch, and for a moment the thunder in her chest and the shallow fast breaths in her ears drown out everything. Then she closes her eyes and gets a grip. Just another nightmare.

Another useless warning from the Vayt.


Rachael has never seen Kez (*she/her*) look so powerful. Kez always used to seem twitchy, neurotic—but now she holds her head high, even with the higher gravity in the Irriyaian Quarter, and she strides forward as if she's thrilled to be settling a family squabble. It's part of her ambassador training: before you can make peace between worlds, you need to practice mediating neighborhood disputes.

"Every day I get to do some good for somebody," Kez tells Rachael as they stroll through the twisty snaggly streets. "If only my father could see me now. He would be *furious*."

Rachael nods. She's barely spoken two words so far, but Kez doesn't seem to mind that she's having one of her extreme introvert phases.

All the buildings are made of a shimmering rock that looks like quartz, and the sunlight looks a bit redder than elsewhere in Wentrolo. Almost everyone else here is Irriyaian: tall, bulky, with bony studs coming out of their bald heads and necks, and colorful tiger stripes on their skin.

She can't resist thinking about how she'd capture all of this, if she still had that power. The best angle to show the whole sprawling scene, the direction the light should come from. Her head starts to throb again—she cannot handle any alien visions right now. She closes her eyes and tries to think about Kez's new gig instead.

"The only bad part is when people serve up some microaggressions." Kez sucks in air through her teeth. "Which is . . . often. They look at me and see a 'lesser humanoid.'"

"That sucks." Rachael can't hear the phrase "lesser humanoid" without hearing Marrant sneer at her and her friends on the worst day of her life.

"It really does." Kez shakes her head. "Everywhere you go, there are hierarchies within hierarchies. You and I are at the top of one heap, simply because we have two arms and legs, but we're also at the bottom of a different heap. It's weird, but also strangely familiar."

"Because you were part of the upper class back home," Rachael murmurs.

"Right. Except that everyone went out of their way to make me feel unworthy, because I was a second-generation immigrant. It does your head in."

Rachael beams up at her. "You're going to go home and become the most important person in human history. Those jerks can suck it."

"They can. They really can."

Kez obsessively checks the directions on her Joiner. Left, right, around the hairpin corner, and at last they arrive at a house made out of a curved slice of polished stone, in the old style of Irriyaian architecture (according to Kez). An older Irriyaian, with gnarled head-spikes, sits on a long bench in front of a window shaped like a peacock.

Kez holds up her golden medallion and says, "Mediator-in-training Kez Oduya, here to see Renna the Nahhi. Ummm . . . the light of reason shines where our vision fails."

Renna the Nahhi (*he/him*) is the old dude on the bench, and he's spitting mad over a floatbeast that's belonged to his family for generations.

The floatbeast, named Vha, used to hover over Renna's house like a big balloon made of flesh, and provide cooling shade and delicious bloodmilk. But then Vha split into three smaller floatbeasts, which happens sometimes. One of those three smaller floatbeasts went missing for ages, until at last it turned up—and it had become part of another floatbeast, belonging to a lady called Jyiri the Nahhi. This is the kind of thing that would have led to duels and face-painting, back in the day.

"Vha would never have abandoned me, even after splitting apart," Renna grumbles. "Jyiri the Nahhi must have used powdered floatbeast extract to lure Vha into breaking into pieces, so she could steal the most precious part of the beast: the hindquarters."

"So Jyiri insists that your floatbeast just divided up on its own," Kez says. "And its—uhhhh—its butt just randomly drifted over to her farm and became part of her floatbeast, before she even knew what was going on."

"She would say that. She lies about everything. She's been scheming to take what's mine since we were in school." Renna slaps his bench, his big fish eyes glaring. "I want her to return Vha's hindquarters to me, and I want payment for my emotional suffering and distress."

Kez listens to all of Renna's bellyaching as if this were a vitally important controversy. But she does keep pointing out, gently, that you can't tell where Jyiri's floatbeast Reo ends and the piece of Vha begins.

Rachael would not have the patience for this, not in a million years.

"Can I arrange a meeting between you and Jyiri?" Kez asks at the end of Renna's tirade. "So the two of you can try to work this out in person?"

Renna sputters for a while, but finally agrees. "Allow me to do you a service in turn: when you travel back through the Irriyaian Quarter, avoid the main gate. There could be some unpleasantness that you might wish to avoid." He flashes a toothy grimace.

Kez just shrugs and ushers Rachael out of there.


As they walk back down the steep slope toward the main part of the Irriyaian Quarter, Rachael whispers, "So how exactly are you going to resolve their dispute? There's no way Renna's getting his floatbeast butt back. Right?"

Kez nods. "Yeah, but this isn't about a floatbeast at all. It's about the stuff Irriyaians always obsess over: respect, status within the Nahhi nation, and control over land. Jyiri can give Renna some clippings from her snah-snah vines, and they can invite each other for dinner. And when Jyiri's floatbeast breaks into pieces, Jyiri can give a piece to Renna. Simple enough, really."

"You're good at this," Rachael says.

They're right near the main gate, which Renna told them to avoid. Spiky reeds grow out of the top of the arch.

Rachael can hear voices coming from near the gate, like the shrieking of banshees. Plus a loud crack, over and over, that could be some kind of alien drum or actual violence.

Kez tenses up, like this is bringing back horrible memories, and steers Rachael toward one of the side entrances. They take side streets until they're on one of the main streets, with a clear view of what's happening back at the main gate.

Irriyaians wearing black clothing are shouting something—it's more a roar than a slogan. A few aliens (including a couple of "lesser humanoids") try to come through the gate, but they get grabbed and thrown on the ground by the mob. Rachael doesn't see what happens to them after that. Rachael and Kez sneak a bit closer.

**JoinerTalk, Kez to Group:** uh, i hate to bother you all in the middle of what i am certain is something v important

**JoinerTalk, Kez to Group:** but you might want to come and have a look at this

*JoinerTalk, Tina to Group:* i'll be there as soon as i can
*JoinerTalk, Yiwei to Group:* i'm on my way right now

"This shouldn't be allowed to happen here," Kez mutters. "I thought this was a safe place. I thought—"

Then she stops. And stares.

Near the gate is a big structure that looks like a black cake topper. In front of it stands an Irriyaian, facing the mob, wearing a black jacket . . . with a familiar red slash painted across the chest.

"They took our people," the person with the red slash shouts, loud enough to hear over the music. "Someone pulled our friends, our co-parents, our children, into holes that appeared out of nowhere. They were stolen, screaming for their lives, and lost forever. Nobody is doing anything. We need stronger leadership. Scratch that, we need leadership."

"What the hell," Rachael says. "Are they . . ."

". . . recruiting people to join the Compassion?" Kez says. "Yeah. But that's not the worst part."

Rachael finally gets a good view of the apex of the cake topper.

A hologram shows a recording of a Irriyaian—a kid, younger than Rachael—shouldering a ginormous weapon and shouting, "For freedom! For Irriyaia!" The kid shoots at some fire-breathing monsters, and they're torn into bloody chunks. The kid's shoes are spattered with brightly colored blood and guts.

Rachael stares at this young action hero: ripped clothes, gritted teeth, glaring eyes. And then she realizes who it is.

Yatto the Monntha.

The gentle soul who made Rachael feel at home when she'd just left behind everything she ever knew. Who told her that there is no greater valor than to create beauty.

"This must be one of the action movies that Yatto starred in when they were young," Kez says.

This is way more violent than Rachael expected: Yatto shoots into a swarm of fire-breathing creatures, so their bodies are all torn apart and pieces land everywhere.

Tina comes running up. "Are you okay? What's happen—" She follows Rachael's gaze, and her jaw falls open. "Is that . . . ?"

"'Fraid so," Rachael says. "The Compassion are using Yatto as a mascot."

"They said those movies celebrated the ugly past," Kez says, "when Irriyaia dominated the rest of the galaxy as part of the Seven-Pointed Empire."

Rachael sways on her feet. Tina helps her to lean against the nearby wall. She keeps remembering the fire in Yatto's eyes as they fake-murdered a bunch of creatures.

Tina whispers in Rachael's ear. "Listen, I think something is coming. Something really bad." She glances at the video of young Yatto, shooting a red-hot burst out of their cannon. "I don't think the queen gave you that box just to help you out with your problem. I think we need to solve that puzzle soon, before it's too late. For all of us."

Rachael pulls the red box out of her satchel and stares at it again.

It's still just a box, full of love and murder. And no answers.

Hey cutie. You're sleeping in my bed, and instead of lying next to you I'm recording this, because I can't sleep and I'm an eternal uber-dork. You might notice this message waiting on your Joiner when you wake, but I hope you don't open it until you get to the Palace of Scented Tears.

Still not sure how much we'll be able to communicate while you're in the selection process, and I want you to be able to see me telling you how much you mean to me.

Here are some things I could never tell you face-to-face:

I'm scared all the time.

I feel like I'm never going to be enough. Like I can never be the person everyone needs me to be. Even after everything we've been through, I can't trust that I'll know what to do when things get hard.

I miss my mom. I miss the Lasagna Hats. I even kind of miss my cruddy high school. I have all these fantasies about taking you home and showing you where I grew up. I want you to show me around São Paulo, too. I want to dance to Brazilian funk with you until we get lost in the beats and the feeling of the crowd moving around us.

I'm scared if I ever make it home to Earth, people will freak out at the sight of a giant purple girl, and call the police. Or animal control.

You know what I'm *not* scared of? I'm not worried that you'll let anyone down, or that you won't seize your dreams with both hands. I know you'll outsmart all the haters, and the princess selection program will never know what hit it. You have such a beautiful ferocious heart, I don't question you'll be a star.

I don't know if you'll get to be a princess, because life is weird. I'm living proof that things don't always work out the way they're supposed to—but I know you will keep growing into your power.

Soon you're going to wake up and I'm going to walk you over to one of the hundred golden doorways that will open up to let in all the kids who want to become princesses. The whole thing is designed to look intimidating, but you'll ace this, and I'll stay with you as long as I can.

Soon, everything will be different. I'll be a seasoned cadet in the Royal Space Academy, and I'll probably be better at saluting and doing math in my head. I'll be wearing my new uniform, which makes the ones we were wearing on the *Indomitable* look like worn-out pajamas.

And you'll have been hanging out inside the palace, rubbing elbows with the people who run the galaxy.

We'll both be closer to the people we were meant to be. I can't wait for the new me to meet the new you.

I love you, Elza. There, I said it. I never want to stop saying it. Love you love you love you.

Oh, damn, you're waking up. I gotta go. Byeeee!

# 5.

## ELZA

Elza would have sworn her heart was crushed into such a tiny space, she could never pry it open again.

But then she fell in love at first sight. Twice.

First, with an obnoxious girl in a ripped space suit who dropped out of the sky.

And then with the Palace of Scented Tears.

Elza stands in the Royal Receiving Room and feels something open all the way up inside her, like wonder is flooding into every tiny nerve and capillary. She soaks up every detail.

A million crystal wings flutter and shift overhead. The walls are made of spun sugar that catches the light and looks like it'd crack at a single touch. Attendants bustle around the room, wearing colorful clothes made of some fabric like silk, and everything in here is alive—if you talk to anything in the palace, it'll talk back.

But the reason Elza loves this place is because it feels like a library, crossed with a hackerspace, crossed with a Candomblé terreiro. (Except her terreiro back home was smaller and more joyous, with everyone dancing and singing in white lace and colorful African fabrics, the air rich with lavender and abô, plus the smell of acarajé frying in the kitchen.) This is a place of celebration and a storehouse of knowledge. A place where all your questions will be answered . . . or at least, replaced by better questions.

This room is half the size of a futebol field, and it contains a few thousand people: a tiny fraction of the hundred thousand candidates in the princess selection program. Music comes from everywhere—somehow it's impossible to hear and also a total earworm. The air smells fragrant and warm, like a summer day, or like the candles they used to light in the Parca de Republica on Sundays.

Elza is about to cry her foolish eyes out. Maybe at last she's found a beauty so complicated, it'll swallow any ugliness you bring to it, leaving no trace.

Every instinct urges her to run and hide, find a crawl space and make herself as small as possible. Anything to avoid making herself a target for all these beautiful people who wish her no good. She still remembers when she was living on the street in São Paulo, when she kept running from the alibā and the travequeiros and the predators, and she learned the hard way never to be too exposed.

Elza looks up, and sees the queen herself standing at the front of the room, on a staircase that has no beginning and no end. Just . . . stairs, in midair.

The queen is a fox-faced Javarah in her mid-thirties, and she's wearing a cloud funnel that goes from her torso to her legs. Somebody turned a hurricane into a piece of clothing. The crown on her head is more like a cluster of haloes, which keep shifting as they connect her brain to the Ardenii, the supersmart computers at the heart of the Firmament. With that "crown" on her head, the queen knows everything it's possible to know, all at once.

Elza nearly dies of envy, looking at that rig.

Then the queen speaks to Elza, personally.


"Elza," she says. "You are the first person from Earth to enter this palace, and we could not imagine a better person to represent humanity."

"Um," Elza mutters. "Thanks. Umm, Your Radiance."

"Your acquaintance is a prize, Elza from Earth." The queen's smile widens and her ears curl forward.

Elza checks out the people standing nearby, including some species she's never seen before—they're all talking to the queen in muffled voices. Everyone in this room is having a one-on-one conversation with Her Radiance at the same time. Elza would love to know how this works. Is it telepathic, like the EverySpeak, which can translate any language? How do you generate enough bandwidth *and* keep every one of these sessions secure?

Elza gets so deep into obsessing, she's startled when the queen carries on talking to her. "Do you still wish to put yourself forward as a candidate to be our next princess?"

For a moment, Elza thinks about saying no. She wanted to see the queen for herself, and get inside the Palace of Scented Tears, and now she's done both those things. This could be her last chance to bow out.

But it's too late—Elza's already swept away by longing.

For as long as she can remember, she's dreamed of two things: being surrounded by real timeless beauty, and outsmarting this vicious universe. And here's a chance to do both.

"Yes," Elza says. "I do. I want to put myself forward."

"Very well," the queen says. "Then we have two questions for you. One personal, one theoretical."

Elza tries to do a curtsey, but it comes out as a clumsy samba move. "Ask me your questions, Your Radiance."

"Excellent!" The queen claps her hands. She keeps going back and forth between "little girl getting her first bicycle" and "ancient super-genius who knows all the secrets."

"Here's your personal question: Are you sure you are not merely doing this because Tina expects you to?"

Elza stops and stares, because that's the last thing she ever expected Her Radiance to ask. And for a moment, Elza can't think of what to say.

A little while ago, Elza was curled up in Tina's arms, in her Earth-style bed at the Royal Space Academy dorm. Strong arms holding her, warm sweet breath on her face. Tina had grown so tall, Elza could nestle into her side and feel protected.

"Wouldn't it be funny if you become a princess and I'm still a cadet?" Tina murmured. The Space Academy takes two NewSuns, and the princess selection only takes one—so whatever happens, Elza will finish her schooling before Tina. "I would have to do ten kinds of curtseys every time I saw you."

"That's one of a hundred things that scare me," Elza said. "I've gotten really good at multitasking my fear."

"Don't be scared," Tina said—then caught herself, because Elza had asked her not to say things like that anymore. "I mean, sure. Of *course* it's natural to be scared. You're putting yourself out there and trying out for one of the biggest prizes in the galaxy. Maybe *the* biggest."

"Not helping." Elza nudged her.

"Just saying, there's no shame if you don't make it. And if you *do* make it, I can be your consort! Plenty of princesses have had consorts before."

"What if I decide to bow out?" Elza stared at the red arched dorm-room ceiling.

Tina pulled away enough for Elza to look into her big limpid eyes, with dark purple pupils that contain swirls of blue and white. "Elza. I will be proud of you no matter what, even if you decided to do nothing but play *YayJump!* for the rest of your life."

"Thank you," Elza whispered. "I do want to try out as a princess, more than anything. But . . . sometimes, I feel like if I don't laugh at fear and throw myself feetfirst into the unknown, you'll be disappointed that I failed to live up to the Tina Mains standard. Even if you pretend it's all good."

"Sweetie," Tina said. "You're not the only one who is multitasking fear.

But I believe in you—and I've already watched you rock out, under way worse pressure than this. That palace is so not ready for you."

Elza leaned forward and kissed Tina on her full mouth, grabbing her dark purple-black hair with one hand and pulling her closer. This could be the last time they were together for ages, and Elza could never get enough of Tina's scent, her warmth, the impossible generosity of her heart.

Elza shakes her head. "Tina encouraged me. But this is my desire. I want this more than anything."

"Very well." The queen looks pleased. "Here's the second question: If the Grattna designed their own computers, what would their code look like?"

*That's* a question Elza has no idea how to answer.

The Grattna are a species with three of everything: three arms, three wings, three eyes, three lobes of their brains. So they don't think in terms of opposites, the way creatures with two hands do. They believe there are always three choices in any situation, and three sides to any conflict. Sort of like how Portuguese has words for "this," "that," and "that over there."

But every computer Elza has ever seen is based on two choices: ones and zeroes. Even the Ardenii, if you dig down to their original programming.

"Umm . . ." Elza stammers. Her mind has gone blank.

The queen widens her eyes, like *take your time*.

Elza tries to rewire her entire understanding of computers in a few seconds, face-to-face with a woman wearing a storm and a halo. In a normal computer, everything begins with a yes-or-no question. But what if you could choose "maybe," or "both"? Elza thinks of the three-headed thistle, the Grattna symbol she used to wear on the right sleeve of her Royal Fleet uniform.

"You'd never be able to close anything off," Elza stammers. "It would . . . it would just keep expanding. Three choices, leading to three more choices, forever, like ternary logic. I don't know how it would compile, but it would be beautiful, like a wild vine."

Elza looks up to see if the queen is still smiling—but she's gone.

Elza sees nothing but a rippling cream-colored wall. All around her, aliens blink and stare into space, like they've all ended their own conversations with Her Radiance.

If Elza'd had a few seconds longer, maybe she could have come up with a real answer, instead of blurting out parts of her process. Her stomach curdles. What if she's already blown this chance?

"Well," says a skull-faced Aribentor next to Elza. "That was fun. I got asked a question with no real answer."

"Me too," says another Aribentor. "That's how they're going to send most of us home."

Elza feels a little better, hearing that everyone else also had a hard time answering the queen.

"You never know." Elza smiles at them. "If a question has no right answer, that also means it has many answers that are *almost* right. Maybe the point of the test is how you deal with it."

"We weren't talking to you." The first Aribentor glares—which is every bit as terrifying as it sounds: eyes bugging out of sockets.

"Yeah," the other Aribentor says. "I don't know what species you're supposed to be, but keep your opinions to yourself."

Elza turns and walks away from them, with her face burning.

She looks around the room. All the Aribentors are standing with the other Aribentors. And the worm-faced Undhorans, also standing together. Ditto with the moss-covered Yarthins, and the pile-of-rocks Rosaei.

She's all on her own, surrounded by cliques.

Elza used to live on board a starship called the *Indomitable,* where people from a dozen worlds lived and worked together, and everyone was friends. Somehow it never occurred to her that here in the Firmament, people would only want to hang out with their own kind.

"Watch where you're going," one of the Javarah says to Elza when she almost bumps into them. Then the Javarah says to their friend, loud enough for Elza to hear: "I don't know why they bother to let these lesser humanoids in here." The Javarah's ears are arrowheads aimed at Elza's face.

Elza trips over herself, trying to get away from the mean fox-person, and almost knocks over an alien plant. Everybody in this giant space is staring at her.

Then she hears Tina in her head: *That palace is so not ready for you.* And she thinks of the slogan everybody used to say back home: Travesti não é bagunça. (Which means something like, "Don't mess with travestis.") She raises her head and keeps her face neutral.

She's Elza Monteiro. She's faced down armies and stared into the face of pure evil. She may or may not win a crown—but before she leaves this palace, everyone will know her name.

It's only been a day since I saw you, but it feels like a lifetime and a half. I can't concentrate on all the antimatter-for-breakfast simulations they have us running, because I'm too busy daydreaming about your first day inside that palace.

Yiwei and I are hanging out a lot, and Yiwei is teaching me about music and robots. But I barely see Damini at school anymore, because she's spending all her time with her new friend Zaeta—who's only the second person from her planet, Wedding Water, to join the Royal Fleet.

Zaeta and Damini keep pushing each other to do more and more death-defying stunts, like Zaeta convinced Damini to climb the truthspike in the courtyard. A hundred feet up, no handholds, everybody screaming and cheering. I was running around on the ground with an ion harness, ready to catch her if she was about to go splat.

Wedding Water is one big snowball half the year, and near boiling the other half, so Zaeta's people lay their eggs before the big freeze, and then find them again during the big thaw. Nobody can ever find their own eggs, so it's normal to raise someone else's kids, and these literal found families go into space together. It's a huge taboo to travel into space with anybody but your family members, so Zaeta got a lot of grief for wanting to come here on her own.

Also, Zaeta's people, the Tuophix, have this thing called the vunci, which is a friendship so intense you share *everything*. They don't usually do it with outsiders, but Damini is super obsessed.

Speaking of friends . . . I've done some digging. Yatto took a leave from the Royal Fleet after they got injured, and nobody knows where they went. Annnd . . . looks like Yatto's old action movies are being used as a major recruitment tool for the Compassion everywhere, especially in places where a lot of Irriyaians live. It's going to break their heart.

That's everything going on with me. Cannot wait to hear all about your first day of school!!! See you soon. Right?

# 6

.

Elza tries to give everything in the palace one last look as she walks out, in case this is the last time she sees all of it. The little stone bridge over a river whose reflection shows you your sweetest fears, the ballroom with the undulating shimmery strands growing out of the floor, all the cartoon creatures on the walls that whisper to her as she passes by.

She still hasn't heard whether she passed the queen's test, and she can't stop fidgeting and doing math in her head. All she wants is to explore this palace until she knows all of its secrets.

Elza's lime-green Joiner must have been blocked from receiving any outside messages while she was inside the palace—because it blows up as soon as she steps outside into Peacebringer Square and breathes the warm, sweet air. Most of the messages are from Tina.

> *JoinerTalk, Tina to Elza:* Hey baby girl, did u meet the queen yet?
> *JoinerTalk, Tina to Elza:* If they try to feed u any of those Undhoran funnel breakers, don't eat any part except for the crispy ends
> *JoinerTalk, Tina to Elza:* those are safe for human stomachs.
> *JoinerTalk, Tina to Elza:* Also, don't forget to smile. U have the cutest smile! <3 <3 <3
> *JoinerTalk, Tina to Elza:* U could be a princess by the END OF THE WEEK if u give them a taste of the dimples

Whenever Tina does something to make Elza feel safe and loved, she flashes on the people back home who told her they'd *consider* dating a White travesti, but a Black travesti was only good for "diversão."

Elza wants to run to wherever Tina is, to tell her all about her first day. But her Joiner is insisting that her presence is still required inside the palace. When Elza scrolls down, she sees a note that says there aren't a hundred thousand princess candidates anymore—there are a thousand. And Elza's name is on the list.

Elza sits by herself at dinner and ignores all the cliques talking around her.

And then her new bedchamber bombards her with questions. "What kind of sleeping surface do you prefer? I could provide you with an Earth-style bed, with or without curtains around it. Do you prefer to sleep in silence? Or gentle background noise, or music? How do you want your walls decorated?"

"I don't know," Elza says again and again. "I don't need anything fancy. I don't care."

To this day, Elza never takes for granted she'll have a bed to sleep in. She tries to keep her back to the wall, she always has an escape route in the back of her mind, and she doesn't trust peace and quiet.

"I only want you to be as comfortable as possible." The bedroom sounds peevish.

The only times Elza has slept well, since her parents kicked her out of their split-level house in Alto de Pinheiros, have been when she's been scrunched up next to Tina. There's nothing this room can do to make Elza feel better, if she's not allowed to stay with her girlfriend.

"Give me my cabin on the *Indomitable*," Elza says at last—because that's the next best thing.

A second later, Elza's bedroom has transformed. The gold-leaf decorations on the walls and ceiling are gone, and so are the big fluffy bed and the diamond-studded bathroom. Instead, she's in a space so tiny she can stretch out her arms and touch the walls. There's a small workstation, a single tea-cup chair, a web of bedding, and a primitive bathroom with some grungy nozzles. She can hear the whoosh of starship engines, and smell the musty recycled air.

It's ridiculous, giving up all that luxury for this gross old box.

But as soon as Elza's back in her old cabin, she feels herself relax. Except now she keeps expecting alarms to blare, letting her know the ship is under attack *again*.

"This is perfect," Elza says. "Thank you."

---

### Joinerguide: What Is the Queen's Privy Council?

Wentrolo is the center of Her Majesty's Firmament and the home of the Palace of Scented Tears . . . but who is Her Radiance? And why do we have a queen?

It's pretty simple, really. When you think about it, a galaxy is a really big place. Any one planet contains more secrets and mysteries than you could hope to understand if you lived a thousand lifetimes. So multiply that by a hundred thousand civilized planets, and you've got a nearly limitless number of things that are on fire, or could burst into flames at any moment.

Nobody can keep track of all those situations. But the queen can, because her brain is plugged into the Ardenii, the ancient supercomputers that see everything on countless planets. The Ardenii share all of their awareness with the queen (and a portion of it with the princesses). And the queen, in turn, gives advice and ideas to her Privy Council.

So who are the Privy Council? They're representatives of all the powerful and civilized worlds, including Aribentora, Irriyaia, Ooni, Javarr, Scanthia Prime, and so on. The queen cannot give orders to the council, but they take her advice seriously—and in turn, they can't tell any individual planet or nation how to run its business, but they can offer help and support where it's needed.

And the Privy Council's decisions are carried out by the Royal Fleet.


In the morning, Elza finds a white gown folded on her teacup chair: empire-waisted, flared skirts, lacy sleeves. Plus there are some new shoes, and a packet of cosmetics. The dress reminds her of the white clothing she used to wear at the Ile Axé Omo Oxo Ibalatan terreiro, when she would visit with her friend Fernanda sometimes—Elza was always so scared to do the wrong thing, and Fernanda always told her to relax and listen to her body and to the pai de santo.

Elza puts everything on, and almost doesn't recognize the sophisticated court lady she sees in the holographic "mirror." She can't resist twirling and giggling.

After breakfast in a bright-walled hospitality area—perfect little tarts—Elza goes back to the room with the crystal-wing ceiling, where the thousand remaining candidates are gathering. Yet again, everyone stays with their own kind. The hulking Irriyaians are a wall Elza can't see over, and the Aribentors are a skeleton forest. A few Makvarians, who look like Tina, hang out in one corner, chattering.

Everyone has their back turned to Elza.

Reminds her of the hackerspace where she slept on a rickety cot in the storeroom. The way Mateus asked her trick questions whenever she walked by, or João accused her of stealing anytime a USB drive or tiny piece of gear went missing. Everyone excluded Elza from their hackathons and games, when they weren't begging her for help with coding. They knew she was desperate for a safe place to stay.

But she's still in the palace—and most of the kids who dismissed her yesterday are gone.

And you know what? None of these entitled jerks ever hacked the onboard computers on a knifeship while genocidal monsters were trying to break down the door.

So she looks past the cliques, and thinks: *What would Tina do?* She's pretty sure Tina would look for the other outcasts in the room and team up with them.

Elza spots one. She marches up and introduces herself to a six-legged beetle, two meters long—with nine eyes organized in a W shape around a mouth full of smoke and hooked teeth. "My name is Wyndgonk, and my pronoun is *fire*. I'm from Thythuthy." As usual, Elza somehow *knows* this person has a nonstandard pronoun thanks to the EverySpeak, even though it breaks Portuguese grammar in a dozen ways. (She's pretty sure the pronouns in a lot of these alien languages don't work the same as in most human languages. Maybe instead of being about gender, they let you know someone's status, or job, or affiliation.)

As Wyndgonk speaks, a burst of dark smoke sprays out of fire mouth, nearly getting soot on Elza's white dress.

Elza sees another kid standing alone: a furry blue-gray creature with a round head surrounded by seven fleshy petals, and a sleek long body with five hyperactive arms/legs. Plus a face that cracks open, revealing a mouth with several glistening dark blue globs inside. She walks over and introduces herself.

"I'm glad someone's having fun. Flenby's wine, this is a sour-faced group. You'd think we were waiting to be taken out and shot, not getting a chance at glory and wisdom. My name's Gyrald." Gyrald's pronoun is *they*.

"Nice to meet you." Elza doesn't know whether to try and shake hands.

Gyrald spits on the floor in front of her—their spittle is red, with yellow foam on top—and says, "My great pleasure."

Elza spits too, right near Gyrald's hooked toes, and says the pleasure is all hers.

"Finally, someone with manners," Gyrald says.

Wyndgonk spits too, and one of the flowers between the paving stones bursts into flames.

"I can't believe one of the humanoids is condescending to speak to us. We'll try not to embarrass you too much." Wyndgonk is one of the most sarcastic people Elza has ever met—and not just because everything fire says is a literal burn.

"It's true. You don't want to be seen with Wyndgonk or me," Gyrald says. "You'll ruin your chances."

"I'm a 'lesser humanoid.'" Elza shrugs. "So you probably shouldn't be seen with *me*."

"Oh, yeah?" All nine of Wyndgonk's chocolate-chip eyes squint. "How many planets do your people have?"

"Uhh . . . one?"

"*One* planet?" Gyrald does a double take. "Seriously?"

"Yeah. We've barely visited our own moon."

"You're right, that is embarrassing." Wyndgonk snorts with laughter, sending puffs of smoke upward. "Did your people get confused and aim your ships at the ground instead of the sky?"

Wyndgonk's people, the Thythuthyans, have spread across a half-dozen stars, in places that were too hot for anyone else to survive. The Vayt screwed up Wyndgonk's planet a long time ago, but the Thythuthyans were able to adapt to a super-hot, toxic atmosphere by learning how to grow food in the noxious clouds.

Gyrald's civilization, the Flavkin, spread out across their solar system and a couple others, using ships they'd copied from the spores of the nectar-stalks that covered their world. That meant there were millions of Flavkin living elsewhere when their planet got wiped out by a comet—and the Royal Fleet didn't do a damn thing to prevent this disaster.

"My people sent me to learn how things are supposed to work around here, so next time maybe we'll know how to ask for help and actually get it," Gyrald mumbles. "The universe rewards those who believe in kindness."

"How exactly does the universe reward anyone?" Wyndgonk grumbles.

"We're here, aren't we?" Gyrald's mouth splits open wider, which Elza thinks is their version of a smile. "We're the luckiest people we know."

Elza notices one more outcast: a humanoid, with grayish skin and a single eye in a long slit, like the ship's doctor on board the *Indomitable*. An Oonian.

Tina told Elza there are only a thousand Oonians alive at any given time, so it makes sense there would only be one of them in the princess selection program.

Gyrald and Wyndgonk both recoil when Elza wants to go say hi to the Oonian. The Oonians used to rule most of the galaxy as part of the Seven-Pointed Empire, along with the Irriyaians, the Makvarians, the Aribentors, the Javarah, the Undhorans, and the Scanthians.

"They might be on their own," Wyndgonk growls, "but that Oonian would definitely *not* be happy to associate with us."

Elza catches another glimpse of the Oonian's big lonesome eye, staring at the ground. It's not her problem . . . right?

Their head instructor shows up: an Undhoran (slimy, face covered with tubes) named Senior Councilor Waiwaiwaiwai (*she/her*). Her voice rings out: "Congratulations on reaching the semifinals. Now the real challenges begin."

Everyone's Joiner pops up with a hectic schedule of classes and activities, from "first jewel" to "last jewel." Most of the class names make no sense, like "ambiguation." Or "pinwheel."

The next elimination round is a few days from now. Half the people in this room will be gone.

"Enjoy the fancy palace bedroom while it lasts." Wyndgonk belches smoke. "I'm not even sure I still *want* to be a princess, after what happened to Princess Evanescent."

"Hold on," Elza says. "Something happened to one of the princesses?"

"See for yourself," Wyndgonk says. "This video got leaked on the Joiner-Sphere a while back."

Wyndgonk holds up fire Joiner, and a moment later, Elza is watching a Yarthin in a crown, struggling in the clutches of two Compassion soldiers. A sugary voice says, "I will unchoose all your choices, unthink all your thoughts."

Gyrald shudders. "That's Kankakn. The Compassion's founder. Flenby's tears, I can't watch this next part."

By the time Elza gets to the part where the princess's crown self-destructs, she's covering her face with her hands. A cold sickly feeling creeps back into her guts—she hasn't felt this dread since Antarràn, but it feels all too familiar.

Elza wants to say something, but there are no words. And Waiwaiwaiwai is still talking.

"The queen was hoping to speak to you again," grumbles Waiwaiwaiwai. "But she was called into an urgent meeting of the Privy Council to hear testimony from an eyewitness to the Battle of Antarràn."

*Tina.* They must have brought Tina to the palace—or maybe Rachael, Yiwei, or Damini.

If Elza could hear Tina's voice right now, she could start to forget the image of the blazing crown. She's filled with a craving so intense it's like a hunger pang.

"Okay. So how do we sneak into a council meeting?" Elza asks Wyndgonk and Gyrald.

They both gape at her.

# 7.

"You've got to be kidding." Wyndgonk groans.

"Are you *trying* to get kicked out of the program?" Gyrald says.

"You can stay here if you want." Elza slips away from the crowd without looking back.

That soft voice keeps replaying in her mind, saying *sparks in a whirlwind*.

She sneaks down a long trellised walkway around a courtyard ringed with flowers that turn their heads to watch her pass, and through a candlelit hallway that gets narrower and narrower.

"You're going the wrong way." Gyrald stamps a hooked foot. "If we're going to get in trouble, we at least ought to get somewhere."

Elza and Wyndgonk follow Gyrald until they walk onto a balcony overlooking a chamber that looks like a luxury hotel, with a silver floor that slants upward at one end. A few hundred humanoid aliens in fancy costumes gossip on the main floor, and virtual cartoon creatures scurry around them. Six aliens in fancy dresses and crowns stand on the raised part of the floor—these must be the princesses. On the other side of the room, six musicians play thunderous chords.

How can all these people chatter about politics and pointless drama, when they all must have seen that recording of a woman turning to gold and bone? Why aren't they all hushed, staring at the floor? Despairing?

"They don't care," Wyndgonk says, as if fire read Elza's mind. "They haven't cared for a long time, if they ever did."

The queen has just arrived at the top of the raised platform. This time she's wearing a model city, with little vehicles and train tracks zooming around her torso.

Everything goes so quiet Elza can hear feet scuffling below her. Soon she'll be looking down at Tina, or maybe Rachael.

"Friends, we welcome your company, as always. But this time, you have not come to attend to our augury." The queen's courtesy is as bitter as spoilt milk. "A monster has come among us, a monster who used to be one of you. His compatriots only recently took Princess Evanescent from us. And yet, you all demanded to hear his report. So be it. But we shall not stay to listen."

The queen turns and disappears behind a curtain of white petals, without looking back.

The entire room gasps, and whispers come from every corner. The queen probably isn't supposed to ditch a council meeting.

Elza's mind spins until everything suddenly makes too much sense—and then she spies a face she hoped she'd never see again.

Short blue-black hair, milk-white skin, smirking thin lips, blazing dark eyes.

*Marrant.*

He walks into the room, with restraints on his wrists and his ankles, and two Royal Fleet officers guarding him. Still, he swaggers as if he owns the place. And then he looks right up at the balcony where Elza and her friends are hiding. She's sure he sees her.

Marrant looks Elza in the eye, and winks.

## From the Transcript of Thondra Marrant's Address to the Queen's Council, 67 Days Before Newsun

I wish all of you the brightest starfields and the fastest ships. Councilors, Courtiers, Princesses. Your Radian—

*Marrant turns and notices that the queen has left the council chamber. He sighs.*

It seems I must offer my good wishes to the queen in her absence. Pity. I was looking forward to meeting her, after all the time I spent with her predecessor.

No matter. I'm here to tell you what I saw during the Antarràn incident, since I am the only surviving witness—apart from a few young people, whose accounts have proved unreliable and feckless. I have been struggling to make sense of what I saw, and still I struggle. Even the supposedly all-seeing Ardenii have no answers to offer.

*Marrant looks around the room.*

I can tell that you are all frightened.

But not half as frightened as you ought to be.

*Audience chatters with disbelief.*

You experienced the Abduction—mutilated bodies, displaced family members—but you did not witness where it started from.

If you had seen what I saw, you would be paralytic with terror. I, myself, remain terrified, and I have seen so many other abominations over my long career.

The Shapers—the Vayt, they call themselves—saw us as nothing more than raw material for their war machine, to use against . . . someone.

We were used, we were *violated*, as part of a final strike in a long-ago war, and we still do not understand why. We believed that the Vayt recognized our innate superiority as humanoids, and that they intended for us to inherit their legacy.

We were all wrong. They saw us as cannon fodder.

There is only one way to respond to this crime: every humanoid, every advanced world, must join together now. Forget this pointless war between the Royal Fleet and the Compassion. This was an attack on every humanoid, and all of us must join together to respond.

*Audience erupts into shouts and hissing and loud arguments.*

We don't have the luxury of blame. We don't have time to fight each other. It's time to grow up and face reality, together.

I saw with my own eyes what that ancient machine was doing with the people it stole from their homes: they were being girded for war. There could be other machines out there, other experiments that could ensnare all of us.

Whatever the Vayt were so afraid of, it's still out there. I think it's coming for us.

We don't know how soon, and we don't know how to prepare.

*Audience goes silent.*

One word comes up over and over, in my studies of Vayt lore: the Bereavement. Some weapon, perhaps, or a plague. Something that will kill us all, without any warning.

History will judge us based on how quickly we cast aside our petty concerns and focus on this danger.

We can still be the protectors and explorers that we always told ourselves we were. The choice is up to all of you.

*One audience member stamps their foot. Then another, and another, until the applause becomes deafening.*

---

*JoinerTalk, Tina to Group:* i can't i just can't

*JoinerTalk, Tina to Group:* he had that whole room in the palm of his melty-hatey hand

*JoinerTalk, Tina to Group:* Marrant

*JoinerTalk, Elza to Group:* the speech was worse in person. hologram does NOT do it justice

*JoinerTalk, Yiwei to Group:* i need to punch a few hundred people in the face

*JoinerTalk, Yiwei to Group:* i know, i know, violence isn't always the answer

*JoinerTalk, Kez to Group:* I don't get it

*JoinerTalk, Yiwei to Group:* but i wish i had a hundred rocket fists right about now

*JoinerTalk, Kez to Group:* I seriously don't get it, he caused this huge disaster but they're still listening to him

*JoinerTalk, Tina to Group:* when things get scary & confusing, that's when everyone craves certainty

*JoinerTalk, Tina to Group:* and Marrant is good at sounding like he's on top of things

*JoinerTalk, Rachael to Group:* I'm sorry! i'm sorry i'm sorry i'm sorry

*JoinerTalk, Yiwei to Group:* this is NOT YOUR FAULT

*JoinerTalk, Damini to Group:* nobody thinks this is your fault

*JoinerTalk, Tina to Group:* yeah srsly please stop apologizing

*JoinerTalk, Rachael to Group:* the more you say it's not my fault the more i think it must be

*JoinerTalk, Rachael to Group:* everybody is counting on me to have The Answer

*JoinerTalk, Rachael to Group:* and when i don't come up with it, they turn to that vàávillurn instead

*JoinerTalk, Tina to Group:* starting to regret teaching you to cuss in Aribentor

# 8

.

## RACHAEL

Rachael's parents met in medical school, but her father dropped out to open a tattoo shop, while her mom became a doctor. People acted like she was too good for him, or he was too childish for a grown-up job. In sixth grade, Rachael came home choking back tears from something Walter Gough had said about her weight, and her dad gave her hot chocolate.

When the cocoa was gone, Rachael asked, "Don't you get sick of people giving you side-eye all the time?"

"Nah." Jody scoffed through his graying beard. "People always want to feel like part of the in-group. You can be a full-blown war criminal and get invited to a fancy dinner in Washington, but god forbid you ever wear the wrong shirt. It's a waste of time to worry about trifling people."

Rachael sits in the corner of the Slanted Prism, by the spectral light of a paused game, and glowers at the red box. She keeps hearing Marrant in her head, calling her "unreliable" and twisting everything around. And then, the applause of councilors who just wanted to be part of the in-group.

For the first time in ages, Rachael is feeling something other than sorry for herself: pure, cloud-of-murder-hornets rage.

"Maybe if we can solve this damn box, it'll lead us to something we can use to wipe that smirk off Marrant's face," Rachael says to Damini. "Or maybe we could do some more research on the Vayt, because Marrant said he had been studying their lore, right? We were studying it too, why don't we know everything he knows?" She can hear herself spiraling, feel the blood in her face. "We used to be the people who found all the answers."

"Please don't let Marrant get in your head, okay? Because that's what he does, he plays upon your worries and anxieties, like when I first met him." Damini fingers the red thread around her wrist.

Damini's new friend Zaeta comes over with some snah-snah juice, and then hesitates. "If the two of you want to be alone, I can . . ." Zaeta has bumpy fins going down her back and flipper-arms, and ninety-nine eyes peek out between the pearlescent scales on her face.

Rachael feels way too awful to socialize. But she can tell Zaeta is nervous about hanging with Damini's other friends.

So she just nods. "Pull up a chair. I was just looking at this." She hands the red box to Zaeta, who shows a mouthful of needle-y teeth.

"Oooh. I've heard of these things." Zaeta examines the box with her wiggly frond hands.

"I just—" Brain made of murder hornets. "I thought we had won. I thought we beat him, and now—"

"Let's talk about something else for a moment." Damini points at the frozen hologram next to Rachael. "What's this game?"

"Oh." Rachael stares until she can focus on something besides spiraling. "It's *WorstBestFriend*. That's Chloe, she's my made-up frenemy. I miiiiight be kind of addicted."

Rachael braces for Damini to judge her for playing such a toxic game— she can't explain why she likes it, except it's a little taste of poison that helps her to feel okay—but Damini being Damini, she only asks a dozen questions about gameplay and scoring. Rachael shows Damini how to increase Chloe's sarcasm and dial back her passive-aggressiveness, until Chloe is saying, "What is the actual story of your *face*?"

"Frustration!" Zaeta is still poking at the red box.

"What?" Rachael says.

"I tried to push this box forward in time, and it just . . . stops." Zaeta shows Rachael a scene at the end of the main character's life: they're embracing one person but staring at another, who stands alone.

"I think that's the end of the story," Rachael says.

"Umm, no," Zaeta says. "There's more, but it won't go any further."

"Let me try." Damini takes the box from Zaeta.

Chloe the evil friend watches them, laughing.

"Zaeta's right," Damini says. "There's another part, but it's jammed so you can't get to it."

"Jammed," Rachael says. "Like, on purpose?"

"Maybe," Zaeta says.

Rachael feels her chest tighten, watching Damini fiddle with the mechanism. If anything happens to this box . . .

"Got it!" Damini laughs. "And yes, it was definitely blocked on purpose. Let's see what they were trying to hide."

Damini nudges the box gently, past the point where it was stuck. And . . . the main character is lying on a high-tech bed, mobbed on all sides by machines (like when Rachael was in a coma). People come and go, but the protagonist stays, out cold.

Then a funeral: white silk flutters in the middle of the box. A few people slouch, holding tiny flames. Hanging on the wall of the box is an emblem: a stringy creature with a dozen mouths. The main character is absent, as if this is their funeral.

"So the person whose story this is . . . died?" Damini says.

"Maybe?" Zaeta blinks half her eyes. "The box could be their memorial."

"Except there's more," Rachael says. She takes the box from Damini and pushes past the funeral, to the final scene: the main character hunched over, alone.

"Confusion," Zaeta sputters. "I don't know how funerals work here, but on Wedding Water, people don't usually walk around afterward."

"Pretty sure that's the way funerals work everywhere." Rachael gazes at the hero of this little story.

All alone, because everyone thinks they're dead.


Yiwei shows up a while later, and Rachael's heart does a flip, like some gravity-warping starship maneuver. She jumps out of her chair in time for Yiwei to offer a hug. The fret-calluses on his left fingertips brush the back of her neck, and it's pure magic.

"Who's your friend?" Chloe asks. "Is he available? Could he *be* available if I leaked all the nudes I stole from your phone?"

Yiwei rolls his eyes and ignores Chloe as usual. Rachael pauses the game.

Damini chatters about the person who survived their own funeral—then stops and stares at Yiwei's cadet uniform. "Oh. You . . . changed your sleeve."

"Oh, yeah, I did." Yiwei peels away from Rachael and shows off his right arm: a picture of Captain Othaar from the *Indomitable,* with some lines of the captain's poetry about doubt and impermanence. "I wanted to do something to honor him."

Damini makes a face like she's tasting stomach acid. "Oh. Sure. I think it's . . . it's great that you're doing that."

Yiwei looks at Damini, and she looks away. The silence between them goes on so long the air feels swampy.

"Captain Othaar deserves to be remembered," Yiwei says in a low growl. "There's been enough applause for monsters lately, we owe it to ourselves to celebrate our heroes."

"Dearly wish I could," Damini mutters.

Damini was there when Marrant killed Captain Othaar. Which means she got hit with the full effect of Marrant's death touch, and now she can't think about Othaar without a flood of vicious thoughts.

Zaeta wraps her flipper-arms around herself, like she's uncomfortable getting caught in the middle of . . . whatever this is.

Rachael finally speaks up, barely audible over all the game noises. "Marrant took so much from all of us. I can't stop thinking about him."

"If I ever see him again, I'm going to kill him," Yiwei says. "I know Tina wouldn't approve, but I don't care."

Damini shakes her head. "He's not worth it."

"Every day he's walking around and convincing people to trust him, he's spitting on the memory of our friends," Yiwei says. "He's more dangerous than ever."

"We'll defeat Marrant the same way we did last time," Damini says. "By using our minds. Everywhere we look, there's collateral damage from a war that was fought before any of our ancestors were born. We need to make sense of it before Marrant does."

"I'm in." Rachael reaches out a hand, and Damini clasps it. "Maybe I can be your research assistant."

"Sounds good! Let's spend some serious time in the archives very soon." Damini glances at Zaeta, who nods. Then Damini glances at her red-and-yellow-swirly Joiner. "We should get going. We have a combat simulator session coming up."

Then it's just Yiwei and Rachael (plus Chloe).

Rachael goes back to the red box. When she looks up, Yiwei is staring at her with an expression she can't read at all.

". . . What?" Rachael says.

"It's not fair," Yiwei says. "I wish you didn't have to be the one who hears these monsters in your dreams. I wish I could take that burden away from you. But you've been chosen by fate, and you know what? You saved us once, and you can do it again."

Ouch. The murder hornets are back, along with a swarm of anxiety wasps.

"You're actually saying I'm a chosen one, like it's my job to save everyone." Her voice is so tiny she's not sure it carries over the video-game sounds. "That's almost as bad as Marrant saying that I'm feckless or whatever."

Yiwei looks at the portrait of Captain Othaar on his right arm. "I'm saying that Marrant is wrong, and he shouldn't underestimate you. Us."

Those starship-somersault feelings are like a distant memory. Rachael feels gross.

"Just because I got stuck with nonsense bad dreams doesn't mean I have some heroic destiny," she mumbles. "You want to put Captain Othaar on a pedestal? Go ahead, but treat me like a person."

"What is up with you?" Yiwei's eyes are wide and his lip trembles.

Things are starting to make sense. When Yiwei first met Rachael, she was bursting with creativity—and she was teaching him all about life on board the *Indomitable*. She exuded confidence and artistic fever, and now she's an unartistic mess.

She should let him off the hook. Rip off the Band-Aid. He'll be sad for a minute, but then he'll probably be relieved.

Rachael opens her mouth to tell Yiwei they should be friends for now, but she's lost all the words. Her floating chair wobbles.

Then she looks down and notices something: the room inside the red box has a window. And you can look through it, at the outside world.

# 9.

Rachael rushes out of the Slanted Prism, looking at everything through the red box's window. Once she's outside, she spins in a slow circle, looking at the cityscape. Until . . . something lines up.

"I can't believe I didn't see this before." She shows Yiwei.

The light from Wentrolo's artificial sun shines through the window and makes shadows of the three tiny people inside the box . . . and the shadows form an arrow, pointing away from the Palace of Scented Tears and the academy, toward a neighborhood Rachael never noticed before.

"This way." Rachael leads Yiwei along the walkway, keeping one eye shut and the other eye peering through the window.

*Of course.*

The artist who made this box designed it so anyone who found it could always return it to its creator.

Yiwei scrambles to keep up as Rachael rushes past alien families and artisans offering their wares. She can feel him right behind her, still stewing about the things she said a moment ago.

The arrow leads Rachael to the wall of some Yarthin cultural center, and she has to go three walkways over and around.

Xiaohou plays some chase music, full of wah-wah guitar, high hats, and kettle drums.

Yiwei stops and curses. "What the—"

Right in front of Rachael and Yiwei is a symbol the EverySpeak refuses to translate, because it's too offensive.

It's painted next to a holo-display that shows the Royal Fleet launching ships into the void, like dandelion seeds. The obscene symbol melts the wall, exposing the greasy struts and pipes under the surface, and it smells like dog poop. Rachael has to pull her shirt up over her face.

"What kind of person lives in paradise and goes around ruining everything?" Yiwei spits.

Rachael says the answer without thinking: "An artist."

She follows the arrow past the stinky graffiti, up onto a rooftop, down to another walkway, and through a park full of flowers taller than redwoods.

They arrive at another Royal Fleet recruiting ad. A hunched-over figure, wearing a cauliflower-shaped puff over their head and shoulders, is spraying another foul-smelling symbol onto the runny wall.

The arrow points right at the vandal, and then disappears.

"Hey!" Yiwei shouts. "What are you doing? Why are you messing up that wall?"

The kid drops their high-tech spray paint and runs.

Rachael and Yiwei chase the graffiti artist, but they're too fast—sprinting along the wall over a garden, then ducking through a low opening and sliding down to another walkway twenty feet below. Rachael is getting a stitch in her side.

By the time they get to the bottom of the chute, the graffiti artist is disappearing into a mosh pit of Scanthians.

Rachael wastes some breath to shout, "Please come back! We just want to talk to you."

This kid looks back and sees the box in Rachael's hand. They turn and run away, even faster.

"Xiaohou," Rachael says. "Follow that person and let me know where they end up."

Xiaohou looks at the graffiti artist and blurts out a little hunting song, like "Dah dah dah DAH!" Then he jumps out of Yiwei's bag and takes off, scampering along the railing of the walkway.

A moment later, Rachael has lost sight of both the robot and the tagger.

*JoinerTalk, Kez to Group:* I keep trying to find out what's happening on Earth

*JoinerTalk, Kez to Group:* The Royal Fleet hasn't sent a ship anywhere near, since we left

*JoinerTalk, Kez to Group:* An extreme long-range imaging probe picked up something that \*might\* be weapons being deployed in orbit

*JoinerTalk, Kez to Group:* there are no ships going anywhere near Earth rn

*JoinerTalk, Kez to Group:* and I need to show up as an ambassador from an advanced society, not just some kid

The vandal is living inside a garbage vent, at the bottom of an ampersand-shaped building. Their lair is a weird mixture of stuff, including a piece of a starship hull and a couple of those teacup-shaped chairs that they have on starships. But also some Yarthin wall hangings, and an old food converter, and one of the flower-shaped beds that some people use here. Everything is ancient and coated with grease.

"Let me do the talking," Rachael whispers. Yiwei nods, though she can still feel the hurt feelings coming off him in waves.

Xiaohou burbles happily on the floor of the graffiti artist's hideaway.

"I've never seen a robot quite like you," the vandal says to Xiaohou. Then they look up and notice Rachael and Yiwei standing in the entrance. "Oh. You again."

Rachael feels shy as usual, even though she told Yiwei to make space for her to talk. She sits down on the floor next to the robot and the tagger.

"I found your box." Rachael holds it up.

"There is no way you just 'found' that box," the kid says.

They remove their head-covering, revealing blue-gray hair and a purple face pinched by wrinkles. Not a kid, after all. An elderly Makvarian.

"Oh," Rachael says. Then, in case her response was rude, she blurts out: "My name is Rachael and my pronoun is *she*. I'm from Earth. This is Yiwei, his pronoun is *he*."

"Nyitha. *She*." Nyitha looks at Yiwei. "So, an academy cadet, huh? You still have that glow." She snorts. "I'm not drunk enough to be keeping company with an idealist."

Yiwei stews in silence, because he promised Rachael he'd let her do the talking.

Nyitha turns back to Rachael. "*Now* will you tell me who gave you that box?"

"Umm. The queen?"

Nyitha curses in five different languages.

"I don't understand why someone who could create something as beautiful as this box would go around making gross messes," Rachael says. "And why you're living in a trash chute, when there's enough good housing for everyone."

"I'm living down here because it is damn impossible to stay off the grid in utopia," Nyitha says. "I tag those symbols because people here are living in comfort, and meanwhile on ten thousand other worlds, people are hurting, and the Royal Fleet isn't—"

Yiwei bristles. "I've seen people in the Royal Fleet give their lives to help others."

Nyitha shrugs. "Still not drunk enough." Then she turns back to Rachael. "I thought I had destroyed all these boxes a long time ago. But of course if anyone could find one, it would be the queen. Why is Her Radiance so interested in some girl from Earth, anyway?"

Rachael clutches the red box to her chest, because she can't bear the thought of Nyitha destroying it. But also, she tells Nyitha the whole story.

"Hmm." Nyitha frowns. She leans forward and spits in Rachael's eye.

"What the hell was that?" Rachael wipes spittle out of her eye, and stumbles to her feet, backing away a little.

"Oh, just taking some neurological readings." Nyitha swishes her own spit around her mouth. "Your eyes are connected to your brain, after all." She swallows the saliva she was holding in her mouth and then stares up at Rachael. "Have you tried drawing with your eyes closed?"

"What? No. How would that even—"

"You say your brain keeps trying to connect with that doomsday machine, instead of letting you make art. But you can use your hands for other things, correct? You can put on your own shoes. So perhaps this is about the connection between your eye and your hand." Nyitha sighs theatrically.

Yiwei starts to ask a question. Nyitha shushes him without taking her intense sea-blue eyes away from Rachael.

"Very well. This will probably kill me, but I suppose I have no choice, if the blood-forsaken queen sent you. I'll do it."

"Do what?" Rachael stammers.

"I will be your new art teacher."

Nyitha offers both her hands.

Rachael only hesitates for a moment before clasping them with both of hers.

I know you're getting these messages. Why won't you answer?

Listen, I get it. Your planet, Irriyaia, was pretty evil back in the day, when it was part of the Seven-Pointed Empire. I know about the camps, the people who were forced to mine asteroids, the magnetosphere siphons. A lot of your people still feel not-so-secretly nostalgic for the bad old days, and they turned you into a symbol, when you were too young to know any better.

I had a heroic vision dropped on my head when I was a kid too. Letting go of that dream was the hardest thing I've ever done, and I still don't know who I am without it. Now I see Captain Argentian every day at the academy, staring at me. She looks disappointed.

But you were one of the people who helped me to understand that we get to choose who we are. We don't have to let some legacy define us, or anybody else's expectations. We can make our own way.

I just saw a speech by the Compassion's founder, Kankakn, going viral on the JoinerSphere—because apparently they won't censor anything people want to post on there. And meanwhile, a huge riot just happened on Irriyaia. Thousands of screaming Irriyaians put on the red slash and dragged any "aliens" they could find into the street to beat them bloody. They were holding up holographic images from your old movies.

Please respond when you can. The only thing that can stand up to the fake Yatto is the real Yatto.

And we miss you.

# 10

.

Rachael sits on top of a skyscraper, with a view of the entire Wentrolo sky-line stretching endlessly in every direction, but she can't see the ground. It's only scary if she thinks about it. This view reminds her of when she stood on a balcony at Rascal Station and drew the entire space-city.

She wants to drink in every last detail—but Nyitha plunks a helmet down on her head, and everything goes dark. "How's that?"

"I can't see anything. There's a visor blocking my eyes."

*What the hell, Obi-Wan?*

Rachael is definitely about to plummet to a messy death.

"Mmm. How about now?"

Now Rachael sees yellowy outlines. "Umm . . . a little?"

"Your species has such feeble eyes. I'm blocking out almost every fre-quency of visible light. How is this?"

Ow. Bright red light flare. Rachael closes her eyes, but it still burns. "Make it stop makeitstop!!!"

The light turns pale orange.

"Perhaps if we filter some wavelengths, we could trick your brain into getting past whatever is making you freeze up." Nyitha stops, like she's pondering. "Take your shoes off."

"My what?"

"Your shoes! Take them off. You can't draw with your hands, let's try your feet."

Rachael reaches down, fumbling, and unstraps her cadet-style shoes.

Nyitha sticks something between the big toe and second toe (index toe?) on Rachael's right foot. A stylus.

"This is ridiculous," Rachael says.

"I'll keep changing the colors, and you draw whatever you see with your foot." She makes this sound totally reasonable somehow.

Another adjustment, and everything goes turquoise.

Rachael tries to make some marks with the stylus, but her foot starts to cramp.

"Come on, you can do better than that."

Hard to concentrate, when Rachael's convinced she's about to go splat. Why couldn't they have done this experiment on the ground? Nyitha's "cruel senpai" act is working Rachael's last nerve.

Now everything's leaf-green.

Rachael slashes at the "page," trying to capture the zig-zag skyline.

"Forget about skill," Nyitha says. "Forget craft, forget all about mastery. Just concentrate on how it feels."

How does it feel? Sore, spasmy. The stylus falls out of her toe-grip and she hears it roll away.

Rachael makes a sound between a roar and a groan. She tugs at the helmet, but it won't come off.

The world is a gray haze.

The helmet slides off Rachael's head. Sunshine hits like a floodlight, and she has to cover her eyes until they adjust.

Nyitha picks up the pad that Rachael "drew" on with her foot, and shows her a big squiggle.

"Look at this energy, this fire." Nyitha points at the center, where a bunch of lines collide. "You made a piece of art—and that means you can make more."

Rachael stares at the ugly scribble. "This is garbage. It's not a good picture, it doesn't say anything. It won't make anybody feel better, or feel *anything* worthwhile."

"And you think it's your responsibility to make people feel better?" Nyitha snorts like a horse. "This is going to be a good deal harder than I expected."

Rachael doesn't know whether she wants to cry, or yeet Nyitha's cruddy helmet off the roof. Instead, she pulls her shoes on, grumbling.

"Enough." Nyitha holds out one big purple hand to help Rachael up. "Let's go."

"Where are we going?"

"To steal some art supplies."

This is the first time Rachael's ever seen Nyitha smile, and it's kind of terrifying. Her round sky-blue eyes have this gleam in them, and her teeth look way too big.


Nyitha picks the lock on a gray door that displays a picture of a rock with an open mouth and saber teeth over the words FIRMAMENT SECURITY.

Rachael can't understand why they need to steal. As long as you have a Joiner, you can have anything you want for free—you only have to be willing to help people occasionally, like when Rachael did some errands for a nice old Aribentor lady.

"I don't need a Joiner, and I don't care to do anyone else's dirty work," Nyitha mutters.

Rachael is about to ask how Nyitha can survive in this city without a Joiner—and then she hands Rachael two of them.

One of the Joiners is crimson with electric-blue streaks, and the other is yellow with white spots. Rachael's Joiner perks up, like it's found some friends.

"Here's where you come in," Nyitha says. "When I hit this next lock, every Joiner in the neighborhood will demand that its owner come and investigate, plus Firmament Security will swarm here. Unless you help me confuse the system."

Rachael's about to become an outlaw. She can't imagine what Yiwei would say.

She doesn't hesitate. "What do I do?"

The Joiners are so cute—two fuzzy balls with googly eyes—and they look up at Rachael like they're asking, *Are you our new friend?*

Nyitha hands Rachael a piece of barbed wire.

"Wire them together, so they get stuck in a feedback loop. The barbs stick right in."

*Now* Rachael hesitates. "I don't want to hurt them."

"They're not alive, and they don't feel pain. They're basically phones. Did that word get translated as something that makes sense?"

Rachael feels like she's about to torture two adorable puppies.

"Listen, Rachael." Nyitha looks away from the lock she's picking. "You need to see things for what they really are. Not the surface. Not the fake image someone put there to manipulate you. I know you know this."

Nyitha knows exactly the right buttons to push. Rachael grits her teeth and jams the spiky ends of the barbed wire into the two Joiners.

The Joiners go from happy chirps to crying-baby-bird hoots.

"Perfect," Nyitha says. "Don't let them get away."

The critters wriggle and squirm. Barbed wire jabs her palms.

"I can't hold on much longer!"

Rachael's going to have to change her alignment. Chaotic neutral? Lawful evil?

Then she thinks about the Vayt, the monsters who invaded her dreams and stole her gift, and squeezes those critters harder. *Go ahead and squeak. You'll find no mercy here.*

Nyitha gets the door open. "Keep watch."

The next few moments crawl by. The Joiners are having a meltdown, and Rachael's hands are sore, and people keep getting closer, and she's going to be put in space jail forever.

Nyitha comes out with an armful of tech that looks scary familiar.

Rachael was expecting paint, or crafting supplies. But this is starship guts.

"What do you need those for?"

"What do you think?" Nyitha cackles.

They run away, leaving two sad furballs crying on the ground.

*JoinerTalk, Tina to Rachael:* hey i'm in the middle of my space first aid class but i got some free time this afternoon if u wanna hang

*JoinerTalk, Tina to Rachael:* they wont let me take any classes related to space combat

*JoinerTalk, Tina to Rachael:* which turns out to be almost ALL the classes

*JoinerTalk, Tina to Rachael:* space first aid is a trip—u wouldn't believe what we do instead of mouth-to-mouth.

*JoinerTalk, Tina to Rachael:* or maybe u would. u were a space medic, after all!

*JoinerTalk, Rachael to Tina:* i wish we could hang

*JoinerTalk, Rachael to Tina:* i'm busy being terrorized by Nyitha

*JoinerTalk, Rachael to Tina:* starting to miss the brain-gargoyles tbh

*JoinerTalk, Tina to Rachael:* is she messing with u???? i will come over there and beat her up

*JoinerTalk, Tina to Rachael:* nonviolently i mean

*JoinerTalk, Tina to Rachael:* i will beat her up with nonviolence

*JoinerTalk, Rachael to Tina:* it's fine. she just . . . she is big on the tough love

*JoinerTalk, Tina to Rachael:* ugh.

*JoinerTalk, Tina to Rachael:* lemme know when ur done, i will buy you scanthian parsnips and snah-snah juice.

*JoinerTalk, Rachael to Tina:* it is a plan. the plan is made.

*JoinerTalk, Rachael to Tina:* all hail the plan, planner of worlds!!!

"Seriously?" Rachael stares upward. "This has been here the whole time and I never noticed it?" They're on the outskirts of the Yarthin neighborhood, and the oxidation-ceremony chimes echo around her. (Yarthins worship rust. It's a whole thing.)

The psychic wall is at least fifty feet tall and a hundred feet wide, made of some kind of soft pink stone, covered with bloodred moss and vines.

"You probably don't see a lot of things, because you've turned up your Joiner's privacy filters to keep anyone from bothering you," Nyitha says. "It cuts both ways."

Rachael doesn't bother to flag the irony of Nyitha saying this stuff when she hides out in a garbage vent.

At times, Rachael hopes she doesn't end up like Nyitha: bitter, burned out, cranky, alone. Then a moment later, she'll look at Nyitha and see a survivor, someone who's seen some shit and is still out here cracking jokes. And maybe there are worse ways to turn out.

"So how does this work?" Rachael doesn't take her eye off the red-streaked wall.

Nyitha's eyes sweep the area. "We made it here at the right time, so we have the Wall of Dreams to ourselves. All you do is stare at it and form a picture in your mind's eye."

"And any image in my mind appears on this wall?" Rachael is sure she's going to visualize something obscene, or way too personal.

"It requires a lot of concentration. You have to really want to share an image," Nyitha says. "This will help us figure out if your problem is with your mind's eye, or the connection between your brain and your hands."

Rachael stares at the wall, fists white-knuckle tight. She tries to bring an image to her mind, but her breathing is too loud.

"What if . . . what if losing my art is just the price I have to pay? For saving everyone at Antarràn. For hearing the Vayt in my head. What if I'm supposed to let go of my dreams, for the good of everyone?"

"There's no such thing as 'supposed to,'" Nyitha says in a gentle voice. "You're allowed to fight for the things you care about. You cannot let anyone turn you into a hero, when all you want to do is draw cartoons. Now quit stalling."

Rachael slows her breathing. Her head doesn't hurt, the Vayt aren't sliming her thoughts. She can do this.

The clearest, most potent image Rachael can summon is the moment she almost broke up with Yiwei. It pops back into her head: Yiwei biting his lip, hunching forward a little bit, with his hands resting on his knees. His face stained five different colors by the light of nearby games. She can't stop wondering if she should have let him down easy.

Rachael tries to beam this scene onto the wall. She can feel it happen: the echoes of sadness and guilt make the details more vivid, she remembers the strong lines of Yiwei's jaw and his shadowed eyes.

But when Rachael looks up, there's nothing on the wall but a gray smudge, with fraying edges. It's a giant mural of dryer lint. She concentrates, but the smudge gets smudgier.

"Tell me what is happening right now," Nyitha says in a low voice. "Are you hearing the Vayt?"

"No," Rachael mutters.

"Do you feel any alien influence? Anything unusual?"

"No. I just . . . I just can't. The picture won't come together."

"Huh. Okay." Nyitha slaps her own left shoulder. "It was worth a try. Listen, though: I will not quit until we solve this. The queen sent you to me, and that means I will do anything in my power to make you whole again."

Rachael feels so exhausted she can barely think, and now the headache is starting after all. The Vayt crawl inside her head, somewhere between a memory and a bad idea. *Doomedalldoomed.*

"Thank you," Rachael manages to say. "You're the best art teacher I've ever had."

"I would hate to see the other ones. Come on, I'll buy you some opera candy."

Rachael follows Nyitha, and only looks back one time at the Wall of Dreams. The smudge disintegrates into a swarm of gray flakes.

# 11

.

The Royal Command Post looms over the Wentrolo skyline: a ginormous winged serpent made of chrome. A whole crowd of fancy-pants aliens inspects Rachael, in the black gossamer dress she got at the Stroke.

They would only let one cadet bail on the academy to accompany Rachael to this ceremony, and Yiwei really wanted to come. Rachael feels like blowing chunks, but she takes comfort in Yiwei's hand on hers. Fret-callus magic!

And then Yiwei has to ruin it.

"This is a good thing," Yiwei says in her ear. "People want to honor you. It's good to be recognized for the sacrifices you've made."

Rachael wants to say she didn't make any damn sacrifices, she was just in the right place at the wrong time. But she can't find the words.

"I'm glad everyone else is seeing how incredible you are," Yiwei says.

Why is it when Tina tells Rachael she's incredible, Rachael feels a warm glow—but when Yiwei does it, she feels gross? As if he's putting pressure on her.

Rachael hasn't had a real conversation with Yiwei since she almost told him they should be friends. She hasn't even told Tina about her near-breakup experience. How can two people mean so much to each other—like, so much that there's an invisible cord tangled all around their ribs and their blood vessels, connecting them to each other—and yet not see each other? At all?

Lately Rachael's been spending every waking moment with Nyitha, except for when she accompanied Damini and Zaeta to the archives to see if the Vayt might've left any more rocks like the Talgan stone lying around. (No luck yet.)

As soon as they get through security, an older Undhoran approaches, face-tubes clutching each other in distress. "Rachael Townsend, please, I need to know. My wafran, he was everything to me, he went inside one of those shining holes and vanished, can you tell me where he went, please? I'm beg—"

Rachael stares, no idea how to answer. Some guards tug her elbow and escort her inside the hall.

Moxx greets Rachael, along with a bunch of other Royal Fleet brass, and they lead her and Yiwei into an auditorium full of people. Which looks . . . exactly like an auditorium back on Earth, except the stage levitates. Moxx steps up to the podium first, to announce that they're giving Rachael the white half spiral for her valor and blahblahblah.

That's when it hits Rachael: she really is supposed to give a speech. She shuts her eyes so tight she could be wearing Nyitha's helmet again. Yiwei squeezes her hand and leads her forward.

*You cannot let anyone turn you into a hero, when all you want to do is draw cartoons.*

Rachael is going to walk up to that podium, and her head will explode in front of everyone. Wet brain-fragments spattering the first five or six rows.

A power drill is going through her forehead. And . . . here come the Vayt. Her mind floods with bubbling sewage. Slippery skin, wet with slime, slowly rotting away. *Alltoosoonalldoomed.*

Moxx gestures for her to come up to the podium.

She can't move. Her legs tremble.

"Go ahead," Yiwei whispers. "You deserve this."

Yiwei keeps trying so hard, part of her wishes he'd just give up.

Everyone stomps their feet and shouts her name.

The Vayt show her more visions of decay. *Allwilldiesoon.*

Moxx hands her a heavy chunk of stone, like alabaster, carved in the shape of a spiral cut in half, attached to a square base. She hands it to Yiwei.

"Enjoy your special moment," Moxx whispers as he prods her forward. "And afterward, we must discuss another option for accessing the information in your brain."

Rachael's limbs go from wobbly to stiff.

She gets it now. This exhausting spectacle is Moxx's attempt to butter Rachael up. He thinks if they give her a medal in front of all these bigwigs, she'll be so pathetically grateful, she'll agree to . . . something. Something worse than the brain-gargoyles.

The podium is right here. There are so many things she wants to yell, but she can't word right now. Every time she blinks, she sees squelching rotten meat. The Vayt say, *wetriednowaydoomed.*

Moxx nudges her. Yiwei's eyes sparkle. The Vayt show her the death spasms of a small creature turned inside out.

Rachael leans on the podium and croaks out five words: "It was a team effort."

Then she turns away, feeling shaky as hell.

———

Moxx and the rest of the brass lead Rachael and Yiwei onto a platform that shoots upward, and they step out into the inside of the winged serpent's head. The city skyline gleams in the light of the fading sun.

At last the small talk ends, and Moxx waves for everyone to sit in teacup chairs. "Honored Rachael Townsend, we must ask, have you learned anything new from the Vayt?"

Rachael shakes her head. Nothing but the same old nightmares and migraine spurts, no matter how hard she tries.

Her headache has faded, but the after-throb is still there.

"There's one thing we haven't tried," rumbles Dr. Thyyrpoah (*he/him*). "A procedure that involves opening your skull and removing your brain. Temporarily. We would put it back, with no ill effects whatsoever." He fidgets as he says the last part.

Rachael turns to Yiwei, sitting next to her, and he gives her a helpless look.

Moxx says, "You are a hero of the Firmament. We would not do anything to hurt you."

"But we must ask one more thing." An Oonian bats one huge eye in the corner. They didn't bother to introduce Rachael to that person, or maybe she missed it.

Moxx and the other bigwigs keep glancing at the wall to the left of this chamber.

Like there's something important on the other side.

Rachael has a gut-wrenching suspicion as to what (or who) they're checking on.

"None of this is my fault," Rachael mutters, almost too quiet for anyone to hear. "Blame that clown Marrant. He's the one who set off an ancient weapon that he had no idea how to control."

When she says that name—Marrant—they all stare at the wall. Anxiously.

Is he here right now? Creeping on Rachael, behind some kind of high-tech one-way mirror?

Rachael would bet anything the answer is yes.

She gets up and walks over to the wall. The smooth white surface ripples with light, like mother-of-pearl.

"What's going on?" Yiwei is still sitting down.

She gestures at the wall and whispers: "Marrant."

"She's figured it out," a familiar voice sneers from behind the wall. "No point in hiding anymore, I suppose."

The wall vanishes. Rachael is face-to-face with the man who murdered her friends and made her life hell. He's dressed in a nice gray suit, with cuffs on his wrists that aren't attached.

Rachael is barely aware she's muttering to herself. Her migraine comes back.

"Hello, Rachael." Marrant beams, as if he wasn't just telling everyone at the palace how *unreliable* Rachael was.

Behind Marrant, a couple of Royal Fleet grunts look a little panicked, because maybe they were supposed to keep an eye on him.

"We've never properly met, though we're connected in so many ways." Marrant's eyes are dark suns, impossible to look at.

Here come the monster thoughts. The Vayt hiss without making a sound.

"I've spent half my life studying the Vayt lore, and I'm so close to understanding them. You could provide the last piece of the mystery," Marrant purrs. "We have so much to offer each other, if you could just see past your hatred for me."

She can't she can't, her head is full of blood.

Rachael's anxiety spikes, and the Vayt rush in to feed on it.

"It's time to put aside your personal issues," Marrant says.

Yiwei steps forward, scowling. Rachael has never seen him like this: his arms and legs shifting into an aggressive stance, shaking with rage.

"What are you doing here?" Yiwei says to Marrant. "After what you did, you should never see sunlight, from any sun, ever again."

"Cadet Wang, stand down," Moxx hisses. "Thondra Marrant is advising us—"

Yiwei ignores him. "See this face on my sleeve? Remember Captain Othaar?"

Marrant nods.

"Stand down, Cadet," says the Oonian.

Yiwei doesn't stand down. Rachael watches as a bloodred oval fades into view on his left sleeve—because he just disobeyed a direct order.

"I swore if I ever saw you again, I would kill you," Yiwei says.

"I can't be killed, not with ordinary weapons. Panash Othaar learned the hard way. I understand why you might hate me, but we have bigger problems."

Yiwei isn't carrying a weapon with his dress uniform. He looks around for something he can use to end Marrant.

Another red oval appears on Yiwei's sleeve. And then another. And another.

"I'm offering you the chance to be the hero that everyone thinks you are," Marrant says to Rachael. "Don't let your petty anger ruin everything."

Marrant raises his hand, and fear snakes through Rachael's veins. If he so much as brushes one fingertip against her face, she'll melt into a foul sludge, and nobody will remember they ever liked her.

Rachael's stomach curdles. Her migraine blossoms like a poison flower. *Destructionsuffering soontoosoon.* Rachael calls out to Tina in her mind, and her Joiner sends a message automatically.

*JoinerTalk, Rachael to Tina:* help please help i'm trapped he's here MARRANT I'M TRAPPED

Something hits Marrant in the side of the face.

Rachael's award—the white half spiral—lands on the mosaic floor with a *thonk.* Rachael turns to see Yiwei still in a throwing stance.

A gash in Marrant's porcelain face dribbles purply-red blood.

"So you *can* be hurt," Yiwei says to Marrant. "That's really good to know."

Marrant scowls and his dark eyes blaze with pure violence—then he puts his cloying smirk back on.

Now Yiwei's left sleeve has fifteen or sixteen red dots on it, in a big circle.

"Rachael, stop and listen." Marrant holds one hand to his bloody face. "I know you want to do the right thing."

Something about that phrase, *do the right thing,* pisses Rachael off so much she snaps out of her paralysis. She turns and walks away from Marrant, from all of those dirtbags.

"This conversation is not over," shouts Moxx. "Cadet Wang, escort Rachael Townsend back to us. She's a vital strategic asset. We cannot allow—"

Rachael's already halfway to the elevator. Yiwei rushes to catch up with her. Her Joiner is flipping out.

*JoinerTalk, Tina to Rachael:* what's going on are u okay?
*JoinerTalk, Tina to Rachael:* please say something where are u? i can come to u
*JoinerTalk, Rachael to Tina:* i'm safe, we had a run-in with marrant, tell u everything soon

In the elevator on the way down, Yiwei curses under his breath. His chest heaves, his face is flushed, and his fists are still tight.

Rachael feels like she just ran an obstacle course in the rain.

"This whole time." Yiwei looks at the picture of Captain Othaar on his right sleeve. "This whole time, I believed I was doing something good by following in his footsteps. I would have given my life to those people, the same way he did. But now . . ." And then he sees all of the red dots on his left sleeve, and chokes. "Oh."

"You didn't notice?" Rachael says. "They were giving you those demerits the whole time you were standing up to Marrant."

"They're not demerits, they're a badge of honor," Yiwei says, still trembling. Then he realizes. "Oh. I threw your award. It's still on the floor up there. I'm so sorry. You deserve—"

"You found the perfect use for that thing." Rachael's heart suddenly goes from tiny to massive, like a Cydoghian eggburst. "Let's go chug some snah-snah juice and play *Matterstrike*. I need to blow something up."

Yiwei finally relaxes enough to let Rachael hold his hand.

But out of the corner of her eye, she catches Yiwei studying the ovals all over his left sleeve, and shaking his head. Like he just had his soul wrecked.

You heard about Rachael, right? They brought her to the Command Post and leaned on her to donate her brain to science. And Marrant was there, because he's "consulting" with them. Everything is upside down and backwards and messed up.

I don't want to freak you out, but something happened. A couple things, I guess.

They let me take part in a space-walk simulation, because that's not strictly combat, and there was . . . welp, it only lasted maybe twenty or thirty seconds, I don't know how long. I screamed my head off and nearly blew chunks and started to black out, basically like the puke-a-thon at the county fair back home. Everyone said it was an accident—sometimes the gravity gets spinny, and that's life, and I didn't actually lose any fingers.

But I heard some of the other cadets laughing, and they stopped when they saw me.

Don't worry. After the *Queen Pux* and Second Yoth and Antarràn, this is nothing. But *please* watch your back inside the palace, especially if they bring Marrant there again.

The other thing that happened? It's complicated.

I went to see Dr. Thyyrpoah, and he offered me something. A treatment, kind of. A way to make a real difference—like, maybe Rachael would never have to worry about their brain-snatching ways, and we could kick Marrant to the curb. I could actually . . .

Ugh. Never mind.

I can't do this. You've got enough to worry about already.

Delete. I mean, cancel message.

*JoinerGram not sent.*

# 12
.

## ELZA

When Elza spent one night sleeping in the doorway of an office building in São Paulo, she calmed her mind by looking for patterns in everything: the cars racing past, the lights on the buildings, the traffic lights, the police cars, the songs playing on the satellite radio in the restaurant two doors down. She tried to create algorithms in her head, in the space between waking and dreaming.

Now here she is, wearing a red dress with puffy sleeves, an open back, and a big bow at the base of her spine, made of something like satin. She's on the other side of the galaxy, and they have all the algorithms she used to dream of.

Elza is staring at an alien computing language, and her brain fizzes. She's missed this feeling so much.

Waiwaiwaiwai stands at the front of the long chamber, dotted with pods of workstations. She tosses bubbles of information at the students, and Elza feels like every one of her dreams is coming true before her eyes. (Except when she remembers Marrant winking at her, and before that, the vision of a crown made of smoke.)

"I don't understand any of this." Gyrald pokes at their pad with the light-pen held in one hooked claw.

"Me neither." Wyndgonk scoots fire big beetle shell closer.

"I think it's like if you're trying to describe the growth of a tree, and the flight paths of all the birds and insects that visit it," Elza tells Gyrald and Wyndgonk. "Sort of like a fractal, but simpler. And more complicated, at the same time."

Next to figuring out unfamiliar code for herself, Elza's favorite thing is teaching other people to understand it. Seeing someone's confusion turn into confidence always gives her a thrill, like when she unlocks some achievement herself—only warmer.

"I thought we'd be learning the secrets of the universe, not solving riddles," mutters Gyrald.

"I think this *is* how we learn the secrets of the universe." Elza points at one section, over her forehead. "Look at this: it's sort of recursive, but the answer changes each time."

"Stop cheating!" says a skull-faced Aribentor sitting nearby named Naahay (*she/her*). Elza's pretty sure this is one of the kids who hassled her on the first day. "Or if you're going to cheat, do it more quietly. I'm trying to concentrate here."

"We're not cheating." Elza feels the hairs on the back of her neck stand up. "We're just trying to make sense of it."

"We're supposed to be competing," says Naahay. "Not working together."

"Nobody told us it's against the rules to cooperate," Elza says.

"What's going on back there?" Waiwaiwaiwai's face-tubes are tied in knots.

"Nothing," Elza says.

"Nothing," Wyndgonk rumbles.

"These three were being disruptive!" Naahay points at Elza and her friends.

Elza doesn't have to guess which of them Waiwaiwaiwai will listen to—the three outcasts from nowhere planets, or the spoiled kid from Aribentora.

"Please take this seriously," Waiwaiwaiwai hisses. "Or I'll be forced to remove you."

Elza is burning up inside. She wants to storm out of there—but she looks at the ribbons of poetry-code, and her new friends, and her red dress, and takes a breath.

Yearning and curiosity are like two gusts of the same fragrant wind. Elza wants this too much to let anything ruin her chance, so she closes her mouth and shows Naahay her sweetest expression.

That night, Elza thrashes around in her tiny crew quarters, getting tangled up in the webbing. She should have stuck with a nice bed after all. Every time she starts to drift off to sleep, Marrant winks in her dreams, and she snaps awake again. He's breathing down her neck all the time, whispering: *Everything you are, everyone who cares for you, it can all be taken away with one caress.*

At last, she gets up and throws on some clothes (the closest thing to jeans and a sweatshirt she's found here) and wanders out into the palace.

*This place is supposed to have all the answers, right? So let's go get some answers.*

Elza circles up and up until she reaches the level with the council chamber and the classrooms and the big courtyard.

Someone whispers behind her. She turns around, tensing for Waiwaiwaiwai or someone else telling her she's not supposed to be in this part of the palace. But it's just some vines clinging to the wall, discussing the latest scandals.

As she gets deeper into the palace, flowers turn their heads to watch her pass, and tiny winged creatures float around her head. A bright green frog leaps onto a window ledge at the far end of this vine-covered walkway, puffs out their neck, and hops away.

Everything in this palace is watching, and listening.

Which means she can talk to it.

She stares at a cartoon-faced flower, which is peppermint pink-and-green. "You're part of the user interface of the palace."

"I have a face," the flower says. "And we're interacting right now. But I'm not sure you're a user."

"How do I get root on this place?" Somehow this seems like a reasonable question at the equivalent of three in the morning.

"My roots run very deep." The flower grins. "You can't dig that far."

"I need to understand. About Marrant, and the Compassion. How do I access your data archives?"

The flower seems to think, then one leaf points in the direction of a dark hallway.

"Thank you."

Inside the cloistered hallway, the light comes from tiny sconces at floor level, and Elza casts a huge shadow on the arches above.

At the other end, one symbol glows on the floor: like a ball of string with twelve mouths. Elza steps on the symbol with both feet, and a ramp opens, leading into the darkness.

At the bottom of the ramp sit two young Makvarians, wearing cadet uniforms, next to a racetrack. A bullet-shaped car screams past, followed by another and then another. On the other side of the track is a wall with a viewport showing stars and wisps of superheated gas.

They're on a starship so vast it has its own racetrack on board.

"I feel like I made a mistake," says one of the Makvarians to the other.

"You did not make a mistake," the other one says. "You just have to give it a chance."

Elza doesn't recognize Marrant until she hears his voice. He's young—a teenager—and his face has a healthy purple glow, instead of pasty baby-doll skin.

"I listen to you talk about it, and you're so proud, and full of big plans, you're going to have a gold oval on your sleeve before too long," Marrant's friend says. "When you say, 'With a will,' it's like your uniform is wearing a uniform."

"Of course I'm proud, Aym. I had to work hard to leave home and make it here, but so did you." Marrant looks so handsome and charismatic Elza almost can't remember how much she hates him. "But listen, greatness recognizes greatness. I will never apologize for striving to be the best of the best, and that's how I know that you are also meant for exaltation."

Aym. That name keeps bugging Elza. Until she remembers: this was Marrant's wife. The woman who died when Marrant blew up a planet and his life.

"Did you ever visit Vartnth? Don't feel bad, nobody ever does," Aym says. "It's right there in the Makvarian midworld, with the ice desert on one side and the edge of the swamplands on the other, and when the sun comes out, it's a special occasion. The whole town is so old-school and high-watch, I grew up knowing everybody else's business. Wentrolo was the first city I ever saw, and tears of my ancestors, I felt so tiny."

Marrant's smile is warm and not at all creepy. "If it makes you feel any better, I'm from Typfid, and Wentrolo still made me feel like a speck."

"I'm just saying. I don't even know if I really wanted to join the Royal Fleet, or if I just wanted an excuse to leave home. I don't have your whole righteous ambition thing."

"You seem plenty righteous to me. Remember in Wentrolo, when I caught you asking your Joiner if there were more people you could help out?"

"Yes, because I was raised high-watch. That's just what we do in Vartnth."

"Most people would have left home and rebelled. You left home and stayed true to your values."

Aym doesn't say anything, just watches the bullet-shaped cars zip past, against a backdrop of stars.

Marrant sees someone and his face brightens. "I know who can help. Thaoh. Thaoh! Come here."

Tina comes walking over.

No, not Tina.

She holds herself differently and she laughs like she's never gotten hurt. And her right sleeve displays Makvarian opera notations, instead of Rachael's flowers.

"Oh, hey," Not-Tina says to Aym. "I'm Thaoh, *she/her*. Long-lasting friendships and short-lived grudges."

"Wild parties and no early wakeups," Aym replies. "I know who you are. You're Thondra's best friend, and you've been avoiding me."

Thaoh looks adorably flustered. "I have not! Why would you—I have not been avoiding you!"

"I keep trying to find a way to say hi to you, and you just disappear."

"Oh. I, uh. I just didn't want to intrude, you two just started dating."

Marrant leans forward. "Yes, and I want my new girlfriend to get to know my best friend."

"Right, right. Sorry. I'm . . . I'm still finding everything on this ship." Thaoh squirms. "And I don't approve of people associating only with their own kind. We're all one crew, we should act like it."

Aym scoffs. "You can hang out with the two of us without forming some kind of Makvarian super-clique."

"Really," Marrant says. "Like right now, we need your input. Aym was just saying she's having second thoughts."

Thaoh looks at Aym. "About—?"

Aym gestures at the huge ship around them. "About this. The Royal Fleet, all of it. All of my parents warned me that I could lose myself out here, so far from the sunlit path."

Thaoh sits down next to Aym. She looks so much like Tina, Elza gets a stab of jealousy for a moment.

"Aym, right? Aym, listen. The way I look at it, I didn't leave Makvaria behind, because it's inside me. And I'm still on the sunlit path, I'm just finding my own way. Except now, I belong to a bigger family, including not just the Royal Fleet but everyone who needs our help, on a hundred thousand planets. We're all in this together."

"See?" Marrant beams. "I knew Thaoh would have a good answer."

"Yeah, that actually helped." Aym locks eyes with Thaoh. "But you better hang out with us more often, or I'm going to worry that you don't approve of Thondra dating me."

"Oh, no worries on that score," Thaoh says. "I'm just glad he found someone who'll take him."

The three figures fade away, leaving Elza staring at an empty hallway. *What did I just watch?*

# 13

.

When they call first jewel and Elza rolls out of her bed-webbing, her eyes are so bleary they burn. She can barely figure out how to put on the black A-line dress the palace left for her.

It's elimination day.

When Elza gets to her first class, the History of the Firmament, all of the other students stare into space, like they didn't sleep either. Gyrald and Wyndgonk don't try to talk to Elza, after the warning they got from Waiwaiwaiwai.

Elza finds herself sitting next to the one-eyed Oonian, Robhhan (he/him). He shakes his big square head and whispers to her: "I'm sorry you got in trouble for helping other students. That sucks."

"Thanks," she whispers back.

"I'm almost relieved I'm going to be eliminated," Robhhan says. "I don't know what I'm doing here."

Elza doesn't get a chance to respond before their teacher, a fox-faced Javarah named Kyaxiz (she/her), starts talking. Everyone shushes.

Nobody's bothered to explain what test they'll use to eliminate people. Maybe Elza scrubbed her teeth the wrong way this morning.

The class ends. "Nice talking to you. Maybe we'll meet again someday," Robhhan mutters to Elza. Then he trudges away, and the back of his neck turns dark blue with stress.

Elza loses track of time as the classes go by. Some of them are fun, like the coding classes. Some of them are confusing, like this strange game that's sort of like capoeira and sort of like tennis. And then there are the etiquette classes, where she has to move without making a sound, or hold still, or balance something on her head.

Right before her final class, Elza gets a message on her Joiner: she's being summoned to a special meeting. She looks around the room, and half the other candidates have also gotten messages.

"Guess we're eliminating the dead weight," Naahay says.

Everyone screwed with Elza when she lived at the hackerspace in São Paulo—like she couldn't leave food in the refrigerator or someone else would use it as a snack during a coding marathon, and people used her cot for activities that left weird stains or smells, because it was public property. So she should be used to this.

She wants to curse under her breath when she walks out into the covered walkway with the chattering vines. But she holds herself upright and takes slow, shallow breaths. Does her best to act like a princess. She belongs here, as much as anyone, and she's going to make them all see.

Travesti não é bagunça.

Elza's Joiner leads her to a sort of drawing room with elegant furniture and heavy emerald-green curtains covering the walls. She tries to memorize every detail, in case this is her last moment in the palace.

"Ah! There you are," says a voice behind her.

Elza whips around to see someone in the doorway.

Tall, elegant, posture like a supermodel. Head cradled by a silvery lattice: a crown, though not as grand as the queen's.

Elza's heart rocks like a boat on choppy waves. She's standing in front of a princess.

When Elza was little, she learned all about Princesa Isabel, the "Redentora," who signed the Golden Law that ended slavery in Brazil. Elza couldn't help daydreaming of a magical lady in fairy skirts, who waved a scepter and made all the shackles fall away. Eventually, Elza understood better: enslavement had ended because enslaved people had fought for their own freedom for years, rising up and burning their fazendas—and the struggle was far from over.

Now Elza is face-to-face with a real princess, and all those magical-lady fantasies race back into her head, tinged with saudades, and the kind of pure hope that only children feel.

"My name is Princess Constellation." As usual, Elza knows that Princess Constellation uses *she/her* pronouns without having to be told. "I'm here to 'evaluate' you." Princess Constellation is an Irriyaian, like Yatto the Monntha, except her skin is a brighter yellow, and her stripes are more green than blue. She's wearing a heart-stopping dress: a sky-blue fantasia with sequins that wink at Elza.

Elza tries to do a curtsey and nearly knees herself in the face.

"Your acquaintance is a prize, Elza."

"Uh, nice to meet you," Elza says with a way-too-dry mouth. She can't remember the last time she cared this much what a total stranger thought of her.

"New meetings are never nice." Princess Constellation sounds reproachful, like she caught Elza in a lie. "Meeting someone for the first time is terrifying, or strange, or boring, or exhilarating. But niceness? Is reserved for old enemies."

"Um, okay."

The thing about "old enemies" makes Elza think of Marrant. The queen didn't want him in the palace—but they brought him here anyway. So is the queen just a figurehead? All those history lessons, and she still doesn't understand how things work here.

"Last night you ventured into the lower palace, where we hide the memories that clash with our décor. You're so young, you're full of future, but you preferred to slum it in the past." Princess Constellation's laugh isn't musical, the way Elza expected—instead, it's obnoxious, full-throated.

"Nobody told me I couldn't go down there," Elza protests.

"You must be quite busy, if you visit every place that nobody has told you not to go."

The princess's big round eyes seem like they can see Elza's whole life, in one instant. She wants to run and hide, but she makes herself stand and make eye contact.

Princess Constellation smiles, and so do all of her sequins. "Another question: back on your own world, you wrote your own encryption software for your phone. If your right index finger touched the phone's sensor for a moment, the phone's contents would be erased with seven layers of randomness. Why do such a thing, when this could easily happen by accident?"

Elza shrugs. "The first thing the police would do if they arrested me is force me to unlock the phone with my fingerprint. I was a paranoid kid."

"Paranoia is beauty." Princess Constellation half twirls, like she just heard her favorite song. "Paranoid people see more possibilities than everyone else. The realm of the probable is a drab place with gray walls."

"You think it's so great that I'm paranoid?" Elza says. "Bringing Marrant into the palace is making my paranoia jump up and down like a starving dog. Doesn't it bother you? His friends killed a princess. *That's* why I went into the lower palace last night."

"You were angry, and you craved more information. Anyone else would have chosen to remain angry and ignorant." She tilts her head. "Have you ever eaten a grasshopper? I understand it's one of the main foods on your planet: a creature that makes the grass hop."

Elza is bracing herself for another test, like when the queen asked her about the Grattna. The anxiety is making her neck and jaw throb.

"You keep asking me questions with no good answers," Elza says.

"The only questions worth asking are the ones with bad answers! Like the riddle of the Vayt. We still do not know what they feared so intensely, and how long we have until that threat comes to our door. Fear will tear us apart: world against world, heart against heart. The Compassion is spreading like a sickness, and soon there will be fevers everywhere. I wish we had a few more NewSuns to teach you how to dream with accuracy."

This is it, the rejection. Elza suddenly feels drained, like she's been working so hard to hold on to hope, and now she can let go. "So just to be clear. You're saying I don't get to be a princess?"

Princess Constellation chuckles again. "Perhaps you should find out what being a princess means before you decide you are so eager to claim that mantle. But no. I am saying your schooling may need to take a more unconventional form." She reaches out one hand. "Teach me to dance."

"Excuse me?"

"Teach me to dance." She lifts her gossamer skirt with her free hand. "I will never teach you anything, Elza Monteiro, I will make you teach me, because I am a greedy bitch and you are a natural teacher. Your mind is engaged when you are teaching, more than at any other time. So you are from henceforth my Royal Dance Instructor."

Dizziness hits, like Elza's blood vessels suddenly pack more oxygen—she's about to faint—then it passes and she's back to being a raw nerve.

"Um, okay. I need some music." "Bang" by Anitta starts playing—one of the most-played songs on Elza's phone. "Um, can I touch you, your, uh, Your Radiance?"

"Yes, of course."

Elza puts her hand on the princess's waist, and cannot figure out whether she's being tested right now. Or if the princess is . . . flirting with her?

"Oh, so you want to move your hip that way, uh, and try to hear the downbeat, that snare sound. Do you hear it?"

Elza sways cheek to cheek with Princess Constellation, while Her Radiance whispers about things that are happening right now. "On Undhorah IX, a child was just born after the most difficult labor in their history, they had to add seventeen parents before the child was ready to come out. The Grattna just completed their factory for building more ships like the one you helped them steal. In the Uncharted Domain, a planet that the Royal Fleet has never visited has invented a new word for that feeling when you're dying of curiosity about the person you know best."

Elza can't keep up with all the information—and meanwhile, the princess moves with the precision of a professional samba dancer.

"You're an excellent teacher," she says when the music stops. "My Royal

Dance Instructor." She cocks her head. "I should go. Marrant has departed the palace and returned to his cell."

"Wait. He was here? Again?" Elza takes a step back. "Were you only trying to keep me out of the way while he was here? Was that all this was?"

Princess Constellation is already leaving. "I miss the days when I could do an action with only one purpose. Lately I require at least seven reasons for each move I make. We will dance again soon."

And then Elza is alone, more confused and torn up than ever.

After a few more classes, Elza sits by herself in the hospitality area, eating some delicious food she doesn't know the name of. (She's pretty sure the palace won't let her eat anything poisonous.) Her mind churns over her encounter with Princess Constellation. The dancing, the riddles, and the way the princess said, *Anyone else would have chosen to remain angry and ignorant.*

That sounded like . . . encouragement.

After dinner, Elza goes back to the lower palace, where all the hidden memories live. At the bottom of the ramp, she can make out two figures: Aym and Young Marrant.

They're sitting together on the hull of their starship, the HMSS *Indivisible*, with a view of the candy-colored Glorious Nebula. At the heart of the nebula, Elza can just glimpse the towers of Wentrolo, like shiny pinpricks.

"Took a bit of effort to get them to create an air pocket around this part of the hull. Let's just say I'm going to be pulling a few extra maintenance shifts." Marrant chortles. "Annnnd you won't believe what I went through to get these." He reaches into a box and pulls out a bunch of star-shaped flowers the color of ripe oranges.

"How—!" Aym shrieks and puts her elbows together across her chest. "Paquaras only grow in exactly the right soil, it's impossible, I haven't seen them since I left Vartnth. I can't believe!"

Marrant winks, the same way he did when he spied Elza hiding in the council chamber. "I have my ways. But when was the last time you tasted this?" He pulls out a little white boat full of glistening reddish-brown pearls.

"I can't even." Aym tastes one of the pearls and actually moans with happiness. "You didn't have to do all of this just because I'm homesick."

"Oh, I'm just getting started." Marrant keeps pulling things out of his box, and with each new surprise, he waits for Aym to exclaim with delight and amazement. Elza can't help noticing that after the fourth or fifth cool thing, Aym starts to get tired of cheering. "And in a few metacycles," Marrant says, "I've arranged for us to play a round of wardlock."

"You really don't have to do all this," Aym protests.

"It's nothing, I swear." Marrant's eyes are pretty in the starlight: blue flecked with yellow. "I just want to show you how extraordinary I think you are."

Aym blushes deep purple and reaches for some ruby-colored drink. She and Marrant both drink from the same cup at the same time. It's only creepy if Elza thinks about the person Marrant has become now.

The scene fades, and Elza turns to leave. But another scene appears almost immediately: Aym and Thaoh Argentian, sitting in a crowded parlor in Gamertown, with cups of snah-snah juice and a bowl of salty xargar shells between them. They must be on leave from the *Indivisible*.

"Never seen Thondra so happy," Not-Tina is saying. "He's got this bounce in his step." Instead of her uniform, she's sporting an outfit that would look great on Tina: an iridescent tunic that covers one shoulder, and mesh pants.

"I've never met anyone like him. He's not just charismatic or whatever—he makes me feel more alive," Aym says. "Like anything is possible, like this could be the moment when the whole universe changes, and we'll be right at the center of it."

Thaoh just smiles and chugs snah-snah juice.

"It's just . . . maybe not everything needs to be a special occasion, you know?" Aym lowers her voice. "My life is already plenty adventurous. Sometimes I just want to flop out and binge some light-dramas."

"Thondra Marrant does not do easygoing," Thaoh giggles like a little kid. "If you need someone to just drink Yuul sauce and complain with, my cabin is always open."

Aym smiles and leans forward, hands on the table. "That would be nice."

"I mean, I'm not *charismatic* or anything. I can't make comets fly through your hair, the way *certain people* can."

"Oh, you're plenty charismatic." Aym leans until her face is kissing distance from Thaoh's. "The difference is, you always leave me wanting more."

Thaoh blinks, startled, and pulls back a little. "Thondra is lucky to have you."

"Thondra doesn't 'have' me. Nobody does. I belong to myself. And I don't really believe in dating just one person—I'm from Vartnth, remember? We don't exactly do monogamy there." Aym's expression softens a little. "I just left home for the first time, and I don't even know who I want to be yet. I want to try everything."

Thaoh reaches out her hand, and Aym takes it. "I really, really like you. But I can't do anything to hurt Thondra. Listen, if you really want to open up your relationship, you should talk to him first."

"And then . . . would you be open to this?" Aym indicates their clasped hands with a flick of her eyes.

"Um. Maybe? I guess we'd have to see."

"You're blushing!" Aym laughs so hard she knocks a glass of snah-snah juice onto the floor, and then she's on her hands and knees, mopping.

The playback fades out, leaving Elza in a dark basement again. She can't help feeling a flush of jealousy, watching a stranger flirt with her girlfriend.

*Aff. This isn't Tina, it's fine.*

# 14
.

Tina's left cheek and eyelid are a much deeper purple than usual, and she keeps clutching at her left arm. And stealing a peek at some tiny object inside her bag.

When Elza asks what's up, she says "nothing" and looks away.

They're exploring the Makvarian district, breathing the aromas of steamed meat-spores and opera candy. The concave walls have images of the ice desert and Typfid, Makvaria's biggest city—which is so tall it reaches the edge of the atmosphere. Tina steers Elza toward this walled garden that's supposed to be the closest thing to breathing the air of the home-world she's never visited.

"What's going on with you?" Elza says to the back of Tina's head.

Nothing.

"Hey." Elza tries again. "I get enough secrets and riddles and desubi-cação at the palace. I need you to talk to me."

"It's complicated," Tina mumbles at last. "Don't know where to start."

"Start anywhere." Elza uses her gentlest "teacher" voice, even though she wants to yell. "Start on the outside and work your way into the center."

"Turns out being a pacifist at a military academy is not the secret of super-popularity." Tina won't make eye contact. "Especially when people know I inherited the skills of a legendary fighter, and I'm choosing not to use them. Even Damini doesn't talk to me anymore, because she's part of the cool pilot group, plus she's always with her new friend. And . . ."

Tina seems like she's about to say something else, but then she doesn't.

"And what?"

"Nothing. Everything is messed up."

Seeing Tina crouched over—haunted—Elza wants to wrap her up in love and protect her forever. But she's still hiding something.

"So they're bullying you to try and pressure you to give up on your vow of nonviolence?"

"Yeah. I mean, it's always an 'accident.'" Tina sighs. "S'funny. I used to be the person the bullies were afraid of."

"You should tell the people in charge."

"They know. They don't care."

"You can protect yourself without being violent, right?" Elza stares at Tina's clenched jaw. "Something else is on your mind. What's going on?"

"It's nothing. It's just . . . it's nothing." Tina puts on a weak smile. "I'm still wrapping my mind around the idea that Marrant's wife had the hots for Captain Argentian. I thought I already knew everything." Tina talks and talks, not leaving any space for Elza to interrupt. "We should get some opera candy. Oh, wow, I've heard of these comb-shaped ones, they're sweet at first and then super bitter."

Elza ignores the glistening red comb in Tina's hand. "You're scaring me. Please, please talk to me."

Tina puts down the comb and sighs. "I'm okay. Really. After everything we've survived, a few pranks are nothing."

Elza almost gets up and just walks out without saying another word to Tina. "You promised. You promised we would share everything." Hot face, burning eyes, a million spiky thoughts screaming inside her head. "I can't do any of this, if I can't trust you. There's no way you can be my consort, if you won't tell me what's going on with you."

"I don't want you to worry—" Tina protests.

Elza just stares at the crumbling wall behind Tina's head. When she looks back at her girlfriend, Tina is fingering some lump on the side of her explorer bag.


*JoinerTalk, Elza to Damini:* what is wrong with you?

*JoinerTalk, Damini to Elza:* excuse me?

*JoinerTalk, Elza to Damini:* why aren't you keeping an eye on Tina?

*JoinerTalk, Damini to Elza:* Tina can look after herself. she's . . . she's Tina.

*JoinerTalk, Elza to Damini:* I know you've got some new friend who you spend all your time with

*JoinerTalk, Elza to Damini:* and you're living all your pilot dreams

*JoinerTalk, Damini to Elza:* you don't know what you're talking about

*JoinerTalk, Elza to Damini:* Tina needs you—she's your roommate and your classmate

*JoinerTalk, Elza to Damini:* she's been there for you

*JoinerTalk, Elza to Damini:* and i know she's hiding something

*JoinerTalk, Damini to Elza:* it's a yellow rock

*JoinerTalk, Damini to Elza:* she's hiding a yellow rock

*JoinerTalk, Elza to Damini:* what is it?

*JoinerTalk, Damini to Elza:* don't know yet. but i'm working on it. i do not turn my back on my friends

*JoinerTalk, Damini to Elza:* you should know that by now

*JoinerTalk, Damini to Elza:* and i cannot resist a mystery

*JoinerTalk, Damini to Elza:* speaking of which . . . we need to figure out what Marrant is up to

*JoinerTalk, Elza to Damini:* leave that part to me

# 15

.

Princess Constellation stops in the middle of learning the ijexá, a dance that Elza's parents adored before she was born, and murmurs in Elza's ear. "They've brought Marrant here to live at the palace so he will be available to consult with the council. I did not want you to think I was keeping this from you. The queen is furious and refuses to speak with her own councilors. Here, eat this."

She hands Elza a stale cookie, or at least that's what Elza thinks it is.

After Elza finally swallows the leathery dough, she tries to ask Princess Constellation more questions about Marrant. Such as, why does anybody care what that jerk thinks, just because he used to be important around here? Why can't the queen order everyone to toss him in a cell?

But Princess Constellation responds to all of Elza's questions with random facts about all the worlds where nobody can hear sounds, at least the way we understand them—but those worlds still have music, and dancing. "No matter what you love, there will always be countless other people who think you're loving it the wrong way."

Marrant is meeting with the Privy Council yet again, and this time the queen and all of the princesses are absent. Marrant wears a bright blue tunic made of something like silk, with a tiny red slash across his right breast. Elza crouches in one of the observation galleries, out of sight, and grits her teeth as Marrant says, "If I hadn't activated that machine at Antarràn, none of you would even know about the Vayt. You should be thanking me."

Elza remembers Tina saying that Marrant could never admit his mistakes—like, after he wrecked an entire planet and killed his wife, he kept insisting it was someone else's fault.

The council meeting breaks up and Marrant is led away by two Undhoran palace attendants wearing armor, with cloudstrike guns at their sides. The guards chat breezily, only keeping one eye on their prisoner—because what's he going to do, here in the palace, where everything is watching all the time?

Elza slips out of the balcony and follows Marrant and his guards from a safe distance. The guards start leading Marrant back to his bedchamber, but he gives them his most charming smile and says, "If you don't mind, I would prefer to stroll a little longer, after so long in a cell."

The three of them pass through cloisters and walkways, past a little stone bridge over a river whose surface ripples with scary beautiful visions. They pass a ballroom with undulating shimmery strands growing out of the floor. Marrant finds little excuses to reach out and touch the walls with his fingertips, super casually.

Except the fourth time he does it, Elza is sure: he's probing for something. Some weakness in the holograms, some cracks in the foundation.

She's going to be late for her last few classes before the next elimination. That ache in her jaw and neck flares up when she even tries to imagine what they could throw at her next.

Marrant finds some excuse to lead the guards past the same spot in the palace three times, like he's noticed something there and he wants a closer look. Elza realizes: this is close to where the floor has been opening up to let her into the past. Is Marrant trying to find his way down there?

Elza stares at the moss-covered stone walls, covered with cartoon lizards, and tries to see what Marrant saw. Then she looks away and realizes: Marrant is gone. His guards are still there, face-tubes wiggling as they share some private joke.

The sickly stench hits Elza before she hears Marrant moving behind her.

"I don't appreciate being spied upon," Marrant says in Elza's ear.

She's gotten so used to the puppyish young Marrant, the sight of the malevolent older version startles her when she turns around. His face is a whole different shape, disturbingly perfect except for one fresh scar on his cheek, thanks to Yiwei. She can't quite meet his stare.

"Show some respect. I'm a princess-in-waiting, and you're in my house." Elza tries to take the ice in her bone marrow and put it into her voice. To talk like a princess, in spite of the tremolo in her voice.

"A change is coming. I won't be a prisoner soon, and this palace won't protect you much longer." Marrant's smile gets thinner and his eyes glint. "Already, you're not as safe here as you think you are. And do you really think that spying on me will reveal something that the all-seeing eyes of the Ardenii missed?"

Then Marrant turns and walks back to his guards, who only just noticed that he was gone.

Once the three of them have walked away, Elza lets the steel out of her spine. She slumps over, leaning against the wall, heaving and gasping with her hands over her face. Marrant's voice keeps replaying in her head: *You're not as safe here as you think you are.*

A hand comes down on her shoulder.

No, not a hand—a fleshy, leafy growth.

"Flenby's sweat, what do you think you're playing at?" Gyrald hisses. "Following that world-killer around the palace? From what I hear, you die if you touch any part of his skin, and then nobody will care that you're dead."

Elza swallows. "I've seen him do it."

"Then you should know better." Gyrald drags her farther away from Marrant's bedchamber. "You're trying to become a princess, and princesses are known for their discretion and tact."

"I'm so sorry I'm offending you with my un-princess-like behavior." Elza snorts. "I'll try harder to cross my ankles when I sit, and use the correct spoon."

"You misunderstood me," Gyrald flutters their petals. "A *real* princess would wait until the next time Marrant goes out, and then break into his room."

Elza cackles. "It's a date."

Elza is nearly late for ambiguation class. They're learning to spot patterns in random blocks of letters, numbers, and shapes—and then, to break those patterns. The first person to notice a pattern gets a star, but so does the first person to find the outlier that proves the pattern isn't real. This is usually her favorite subject, because it's a fun game, but not today.

When class finally ends, Elza sneaks away with Gyrald and Wyndgonk, plus Robhhan the Oonian tags along.

Marrant's bedchamber is on the opposite side of the palace from Elza's, past the vine-covered walkway and an open-air courtyard full of strange birds and a honeycomb of crawlways. The two Undhoran guards perch on high chairs, like barstools, in front of a plain orange door. Elza and her friends huddle around the corner, just out of sight.

"What are we doing?" whispers Robhhan, and Wyndgonk shushes him with a tiny puff of fire.

"We're spying on Marrant," Gyrald whispers. "He wants to kill all of my people. What's left of us after the comet strike, anyway."

"You can't trust Symmetrons." Wyndgonk scowls with all nine eyes. "Present company excepted, I guess."

"Thanks." Robhhan winces. His eye looks weirdly big, over a normal-sized nose and mouth.

They sit in silence, apart from the echo in Elza's head that goes: *A change is coming.*

Every once in a while, the guards shift around, and they hear a sound that might be Marrant coming out, but nothing happens.

It's tenth jewel—almost time for one of those ridiculous dinners. Everybody dresses up, and cartoon creatures style your face and hair, and then you eat twenty tiny dishes using skewers and twizzle-spoons.

"Maybe we should give up," Gyrald whispers.

One of the guards, an Undhoran, examines their Joiner and says, "It's time."

The guard knocks on the door, and Marrant comes out, wearing a baby-blue suit. The guards whisper to Marrant, and then all three of them are gone.

Elza counts to ten, then sneaks over to the orange door. Her heart is thundering.

She's never seen a lock like this one—a blank white rectangle—and she has no idea how to open it.

"Well," Wyndgonk rumbles, "this was fun. Let's go eat."

Gyrald looks up at the ceiling and spreads their petals. "Hello, palace. We're supposed to be learning. Right? And there's some stuff on the other side of this door that could be very useful to our education. Can you help us out? Please?"

A cartoon animal, like a bolo mouse, pokes its head out from the wall, right above the door. It studies the four of them for a moment, then ducks back inside.

The door clicks open, a few centimeters.

Inside, there's a bed-web, like in Elza's quarters, and a small bathroom, and an alcove where Marrant's clothes float on holographic racks. The four of them rush inside and rummage through everything.

A tiny workstation includes a carved replica of the Talgan stone and holographic scans of all the carvings on the buildings at the head of the Butterfly. Seeing this stuff again makes Elza feel sick to her stomach, but it's nothing new.

Wyndgonk is patting all the walls and floors with fire claws. "Anything Marrant wants to hide won't be on his workstation, where anyone could access it."

"In here." Robhhan is inside the bathroom, where he pokes at the tiny collection of cleaning nozzles. Something clicks, and a tiny compartment opens up.

Inside, there's a tiny box. Jackpot. The box contains a map of Irriyaia, with some markings all over it, all around the capital, Mauntra City. "Whatever Marrant and the Compassion are planning, it involves Irriyaia," Elza breathes.

Also inside the box: some handwritten notes. Most of them are Marrant's notations about the Vayt language. He divided it into two groups: the older markings, which are more complex and include a lot of symbols about living on a planet, and the later stuff, which is simpler and often features this one symbol that looks like a hexagon, with a smaller hexagon inside. Next to that symbol, Marrant wrote one word: "bereavement."

"But what *is* the Bereavement?" Elza asks out loud.

"That's what we're all desperate to figure out, before it's too late," says a familiar voice.

Princess Constellation is standing in the doorway.

"You're out of time," she says. "Marrant is on his way back, and you're late for dinner, my Royal Dance Instructor."

# 16

## RACHAEL

Rachael and Tina stopped talking to each other back in seventh grade because Tina started acting weird(er). First Tina decided not to invite anybody from school to her birthday party, and then she spent all her time lurking near the skater pit with her hood over her face, scowling at anyone who came close. Rachael tossed out the fancy pencils Tina had given her, and took detours at school so she wouldn't have to walk near her ex-friend.

The two of them almost stayed apart for good—except that Tina's mom asked Rachael's dad to give Tina a ride home from some school thing. Tina sat in the back seat next to Rachael, staring out the window like the fast food drive-thrus had personally attacked her. When they got to Tina's house, she sat there, not getting out of the car, while Rachael's dad got out and talked to Tina's mom in front of their apartment building.

The silence grew awkward, even by Rachael's standards. Was Tina going to stay in Rachael's dad's hatchback forever? Did Tina not realize they'd arrived at her place? At last, Tina blurted to her own reflection, "I found out something and I can't deal and it's bigger than anything and I wish I could tell you but I can't."

"You can, though," Rachael whispered. "You actually can tell me. I'm good at being told things."

That was the night that Rachael found out Tina was an alien. Tina had only just learned the truth herself, on her thirteenth birthday.

So Rachael knows what it looks like when Tina is holding on to a mind-eating secret. Tina has the exact same haunted expression now—only bigger, because everything about her is larger than life now. Tina has a day off from the academy, so she's tagging along with Rachael, and if there were judges scoring Tina on brooding, she'd get tens across the board.

One thing's certain: Rachael's not going to be the one to break the silence. It's been seventeen days since the white half spiral ceremony, and Rachael has said a dozen words total, to anyone.

After she got back from the Royal Command Post, Rachael locked herself in her room for a week, and only ventured out to grab some flap-hoppers or use the Earth-style bathroom. Yiwei sat at the foot of her bed playing music while Rachael clutched her own knees. She kept replaying *My wafran, he was everything to me,* and then the blinding lights and speeches. And Marrant, close enough to end her.

Everybody has been super patient with Rachael, handling her like a bitey cat. Tina kept whispering to Damini and Yiwei to let Rachael come out of hermit mode in her own time.

Rachael still isn't ready to deal with people again, but she got sick of hiding in her room. And she misses Nyitha.

Tina runs her index finger and thumb over a lump in the side of her bag whenever she thinks Rachael isn't looking. And she favors her left leg when she walks.

Their barge lands at the end of the Stroke, miles away from both the Palace of Scented Tears and the academy. There's Nyitha, waiting on the edge of an open-air market where creatures sell Day-Glo balls of booze and protein blobs that are spicy enough to melt your face off. Music comes from everywhere.

Over Nyitha's head, a fluttering canvas pops up with messages like, "ARE YOU SURE YOU DON'T ALREADY KNOW?" and "YOU HAVE PERMISSION TO MAKE YOUR OWN MESS."

Nyitha gets on Rachael's nerves at least half the time—but seeing her teacher, Rachael feels as if the sun just came out. She stops obsessing about Marrant and all the rest, and amazingly, hope rushes in to fill the empty space in her mind.

The art teacher scowls. "Ugh. I told you I did not want to meet any of your other friends, and you immediately—" She stops. And stares at Tina. "Great hunger of sages. You look exactly like her. I cannot believe . . . Do you have any of her memories at all?"

"Umm. Not really? It's complicated."

Rachael turns to Nyitha. "Did you *know* Captain Argentian or something?"

Nyitha rolls her head. "I saw her. You could hardly avoid seeing her. They do love a hero around here."

"So I've heard." Tina slumps, like something is wearing a groove into her shoulders.

Nyitha shrugs. "Okay, then. Let me introduce you to some of my friends."

Nyitha leads the two of them to a plain gray wall and bangs on it. "Open up. It's me." The wall topples forward—like Nyitha knocked it down with the force of her personality.

She leads Rachael and Tina into a circular space with a smoked-glass ceiling and walls covered with what looks like blue velvet and deep-stained mahogany. Aliens are lounging on sofas, armchairs, and floating cushions, nursing globes of liquor. An artist salon!

"Everyone, this is Rachael. She's an artist too, from a planet called Smudge. She's young, which means she remembers the stuff that we all forgot as we got older, so *be nice.* I'm sure you can remember how annoying it was to be young and able to remember things. Or perhaps you've forgotten."

The people in this room are a mix of humanoid and non-humanoid, super-glam and barely-bothered-to-get-dressed.

Nyitha whispers to Rachael: "I can introduce you to everyone here, but if that stresses you out, we can skip it."

Nobody's ever offered Rachael the chance to skip a whole introduction before. She decides it'd be worse to be surrounded by people she doesn't know.

"I guess I'd like the introductions."

Tina lurks in the background, checking out the whole space, while Nyitha introduces Rachael to the other artists.

Samnan (pronoun: *zeii*) is a three-foot-wide crystal who floats in midair. Samnan is in love with a cloud named Givti, who floats over the palace, in service to the queen. Givti doesn't know that Samnan exists—literally, Givti can't see the wavelengths of light that Samnan is visible on. So Samnan's art is all about trying to get Givti's attention.

There's a fox-faced Javarah named Cinnki (*he/him*), who creates portraits of his friends who died too young—and the portraits grow old in real time, thanks to a special moss. Cinnki isn't allowed to create art back on Javarr, because he's from the wrong tribe, or "clade"—only the three ruling Javarah clades get artist privileges.

Then Rachael meets Wendas (pronoun: *they/them*), a hedgehog-like Scanthian, who does this art form called pick-pitch—it's like a tapestry where the threads are alive, and they change depending on the emotions of the person standing nearest to them.

Finally, there's a Kraelyor (five eyes, two mouths, kind of sluggy) named Kfok (pronoun: *she/her*). "All of my art is aimed at letting the Symmetrons know I exist, and I'm not going anywhere." She makes firegrams— messages made of flame—to get the Royal Fleet's attention. They've locked down her Joiner, so she can't get art supplies anymore.

It's the same with almost all of them. Even Wendas is breaking the rules of pick-pitch, so they've been told to stop doing it.

"Nobody will let us make our art." Cinnki's ears curl sideways. "The only one who supports us is Nyitha."

Tina comes back from exploring the rest of the cozy space, beaming. If Rachael didn't know her so well, she'd think everything was all Jolly Ranchers and sunshine.

"How do you like my art salon?" Nyitha asks her.

"It's fantastic. Except . . . I think you ought to check the hydrogen up-take and make sure your gravitators are aligned before you try to fly any-where."

"Wait, what?" Rachael stares at her friend. "You're talking about this place as if it was a starship."

"It is! It's pretty sweet, too." Tina laughs. "Have you actually taken it into space yet?"

"Not yet." Nyitha shrugs. "But I think the time is coming soon. Thondra Marrant is back—and now *you* show up on my doorstep. Too many blood-forsaken ghosts walking around lately."

This cute sitting room looks totally different, now that Rachael knows this is the heart of a ship.

And then it sinks in: Nyitha could be leaving town soon. Going millions of miles away. That hopeful sunbeam fades, leaving her colder than ever.

Tina's smile vanishes as soon as they leave the starship salon, and she stoops again.

"Listen, you know you can tell me anything." Rachael can barely hear herself speak. "I'm good at being told things."

"If there was anything to tell, you'd be the first." Tina pastes her smile back on, and makes a big show of checking out some of the face-melting spicy protein blobs.

# 17.

Elza cannot get the hang of *WorstBestFriend*. She keeps making her fren-emy *too* mean—like Paola wants to put floatbeast poop into Elza's snah-snah juice. Elza adds more and more selfishness, gatekeeping, and micro and macro-aggressions, until Paola becomes a monster.

"Whoa," Rachael says. "She's supposed to be a bad friend, not an actual enemy."

"I don't see the distinction," Elza says.

Everyone else in the *WorstBestFriend* corner at the Slanted Prism pipes up with suggestions and ideas. (The one unwritten rule of *WorstBestFriend* is, the players all help and support each other.) One girl named Vovovovo of-fers to give Paola a competitive streak, like she has to upstage Elza at parties.

"I don't think this game is for me," Elza says.

"I find it comforting, because dealing with living people can get kind of scary." Rachael shows off Chloe, and she does a little twirl.

Instead of playing, they stroll around Gamertown and soak in the at-mosphere of a hundred thousand gaming sessions. Every parlor has ho-lographic pop-ups showing real-time gameplay, including something that looks more like a sport, with four players throwing yellow blobs at each other on a holographic court.

Elza holds her head high and doesn't fidget as much as she used to—and her face keeps lighting up, like she *knows* stuff.

"I'm worried about Tina," Elza says in Rachael's ear. "You've known her longer than anybody."

As Elza talks, everything inside Rachael clenches tighter.

Tina's getting bullied, or hazed. Bad enough that she got really messed up. She keeps staring at this tiny stone when she thinks nobody is looking. Something is gnawing at her.

"Tina shuts down when I ask her what's going on," Elza says.

The pieces are falling into place, and Rachael hates the picture.

"She's your girlfriend," Rachael says.

"But she's *your* best friend. You two share everything. At least that's what I thought."

"We do. We did." Rachael gets a mental image of Chloe laughing at her. *Who's the bad friend now.* "Here's what I think: Tina figured out who she *doesn't* want to be—like, she won't fight anymore. But she hasn't gotten to the part where she knows who she *does* want to be."

Elza winces. "So how do we get her to talk to us?"

Rachael stares at a life-size hologram of an Undhoran wrestling with a giant amoeba.

Tina told her she didn't need to be the glue anymore. Elza is asking her to be a whole supersize tube of extra-strength epoxy, and she can't recharge her batteries the way she used to. If anybody deserves a break from dealing with other people's crap, it's Rachael.

But she has a flash of Tina buying her a donut at the 23-Hour Coffee Bomb a couple years ago, after Lauren Bose posted that gross meme about her. That donut had sprinkles *and* frosting *and* chocolate filling, and she can still taste it in her mind's taste buds, and that leads to hearing Tina's voice saying, *Screw the haters, you are a star.*

"We're going to need everyone," Rachael says. "We can't do this without the others."

Elza nods. Her neck is twice as long as it used to be. "Earthlings."

"Earthlings." Rachael holds out her hand and Elza clasps her own around it.

Rachael shows up early for the Earthlings-minus-Tina gathering in the back room of the Slanted Prism. Damini and Elza are already sitting on a couch, looking at a bunch of holographic bubbles, floating in midair.

"There you are," Elza says. "Take a look at what Damini found."

"Is it the Vayt?" Rachael scoots closer. "Did you find more of their writing?"

"After what Elza found in Marrant's room, I went back and did some more digging, and yes, there is more Vayt writing," Damini says. "We just weren't looking in the right place. Zaeta helped me to realize that we should be looking for more stellar notations, like on the Talgan stone."

"I copied all of Marrant's notes on the Vayt language," Elza chimes in. "There's this one symbol that he thought was important." She shows Rachael a picture of a double hexagon.

"The most important thing is, we're all working the problem together," Damini tells Rachael. "This is not on you."

"Part of me wishes I never had to think about the Vayt again, but that's impossible. And maybe I can't move forward until I understand why they built that machine." Rachael looks at her friends. "Thank you. For all of this. I—" Sudden case of frog-throat. "I don't know where I would be without both of you."

"I know exactly where I would be without you," Elza says to Rachael. "You never need to thank me for anything."

Rachael gets lost in the Vayt carvings, as if she could find some explanation for why they took a piece of her soul if she just stared hard enough.

The next person to show up is Kez (*they/them*), followed by Yiwei. Everyone chatters about nothing for a few minutes, and then a heavy silence falls.

Damini is the one who speaks up. "So. I hardly see Tina at the academy, because we're in different tracks."

"I see her around. She's definitely hiding something." Yiwei gives Rachael a thirsty look, because he's been giving her space since the white half spiral thing, and now she's clearly engaging with people again. Rachael needs to find a way to stall him for a few more days, until she can figure out what she even wants to say to him.

What if she never again has an open heart? She can remember what it used to feel like, to coax out the connections between people, to make strangers into family. Long ago, another life.

"I keep getting sent to mediate tiny local disputes, which means getting people to admit what's actually bothering them," Kez says. "Especially the bloody Irriyaians, who have this fiendishly complex system of clan honor and prenthro. It's a mess. Ganno has been trying to explain it to me."

"Ummm," Damini says. "Who's Ganno?"

"Oh. Sorry." Kez gets flustered and looks down at their hands. "Ganno the Wurthhi. He's my . . . well, we're not using labels. We've gone on a couple of dates, I suppose."

Ganno has canary-yellow tiger stripes and a godlike brow, judging from the pictures on Kez's Joiner.

"Irriyaians don't exactly do romance, but they do like to have fun," Kez mumbles.

"How much fun are we talking about?" Elza raises an eyebrow.

"Umm." Kez has never looked this bashful before. "More fun than I've ever had before in my whole life?" They wave their hands, like *let'schange-thesubject*. "Soooo . . . anyway. I've found the best way to get people to let their guard down is to use their own cultural traditions."

"So if we want Tina to tell us what in the thousand flaming lakes is bothering her, we need to get her to do some Makvarian stuff?" Yiwei's started using the "thousand flaming lakes" thing lately, since he heard some aliens say it.

"Except . . . Tina still doesn't have much connection to Makvarian traditions." Elza looks at Rachael. "We could try to find something from back home."

Rachael tries to think of something—like, what if they could do a *Masked Singer* marathon? But nobody brought any *Masked Singer* videos from Earth. By now, they probably revealed who the gerbil was.

"I've got an idea." Damini rubs her hands together. "Why don't we use the NewSun festival?"

NewSun is like Christmas and New Year's and Thanksgiving rolled into one, plus Damini has started referring to it as "Space Diwali." You get together with everyone you've ever loved or might love in the future, and you all sit in the darkness together, singing and lighting candles. People exchange vows, give out gifts, take lovers, start feuds, make resolutions . . .

. . . and confess their deepest secrets.

"Damini, you're a genius," Elza says. "I definitely do not tell you that enough."

"I'm doomed to be unappreciated in my own time." Damini giggles.

"Yeah, this is perfect," Rachael says. "Let's invite everybody. We'll make it a party. A totally fun, chill, happy party, in which we will lean on Tina to spill whatever garbage she's been keeping to herself."

"This is going to be the best NewSun ever." Yiwei laughs, then looks at his Joiner and realizes they only have seven days to plan a party.

All five of them start sending out frantic messages.

# 18

.

The last few days before NewSun are darker than the dead of winter back home. Rachael stumbles along the walkways, and she almost steps on Xiaohou a couple times. Maybe the old sun is already burnt out and running on fumes—or maybe they dialed it down on purpose, to get people hyped for the festival.

*JoinerTalk, Kez to Group:* okay so we're not supposed to drink snah-snah juice
*JoinerTalk, Kez to Group:* there's a drink whose name i cannot pronounce, but it's basically "blackout wine"
*JoinerTalk, Kez to Group:* you toast with it after the sun goes out
*JoinerTalk, Yiwei to Group:* i don't drink alcohol
*JoinerTalk, Damini to Group:* me neither
*JoinerTalk, Kez to Group:* it's not exactly wine i guess?? it warms you, without being intoxicating
*JoinerTalk, Elza to Group:* i think i can score some snacks from the palace
*JoinerTalk, Tina to Group:* palace snacks!
*JoinerTalk, Tina to Group:* i bet they have nhaa cookies! i know all about them but i've never tasted them
*JoinerTalk, Rachael to Group:* Cinnki the Javarah made tons of this super-sweet paste called vwvooth
*JoinerTalk, Tina to Group:* we're going to party like it's . . . [checks notes] the ninth year of the Age of Despair.
*JoinerTalk, Tina to Group:* doesn't have such a great ring to it tbh

When NewSun comes around, everybody gets together on a flying barge, floating over Gamertown under a pink-tinged gray sky. Damini obsesses over making every last detail perfect—like, black draperies hang over one side of the barge, reddish-gold draperies on the other. And she'll release a swarm of glow-mites at the exact right moment, for everybody who can't be here, like Govind and Uncle Srini and everyone else's friends and family back home. Everybody wears jet-black clothing. "Reminds me of the Goth phase I went through when I was fourteen," Damini says.

When Rachael arrives, the only other ones on the barge are Damini and Zaeta. Damini is telling Zaeta about the epic unshakable friendship between Lord Krishna and Lord Arjun.

"On Wedding Water, our friendships are—what's the right word?—inseparable," Zaeta says. "Like, if I hadn't left home when I did, I don't know if I would've been able to. If you're friends with someone for long enough, you get so that you know what they're going to do before they do it. That's called vunci, when that happens."

"It sounds *amazing*." Damini's eyes are as big as saucers, and full of sparkle.

"Is it like a psychic bond?" Rachael leans forward, fascinated. "Or chemical? Or just being really in tune with someone emotionally?"

"It's a little of everything." Zaeta looks cheerful, except the eyes on the right side of her face are twitchy. "Most outsiders are scared to death of it."

"I don't get why," Damini says. "If you know what you're getting into, then you should be fine, because everything is always about informed consent, right?"

According to Damini, Zaeta's eyes are divided into three groups. The top layer, near her forehead, express what she's thinking—like, the way she thinks she ought to feel, not the way she *does* feel. The eyes on the left side of her face express the hopeful, joyful part of her, the part that reaches out for connection with other people. And the right side is the scared, worried, angry part of her that second-guesses everything and wants to push everyone away. When she's really happy, or really sad, all ninety-nine of her eyes look the same.

Now Zaeta is explaining about seven-paragon, a game they play on Wedding Water—part puzzle, part contact sport, part religious ceremony.

Rachael watches the two of them chattering together, and it's kind of amazing: Damini found someone who gets her. She only hopes Damini doesn't end up getting hurt. Again.


Yiwei shows up next, full of weird facts about the enormous star-factory where engineers toil constantly, building the next sun. As usual lately, when Rachael sees him, her heart is a damn eggburst—huge/tiny/huge/tiny. Why can't she just feel one way about her boyfriend?

Cinnki the Javarah climbs on board and tells them all about a bunch of artists who are saving their biggest, most colorful art to unveil in the moments after the sky blazes with a brand-new light.

Elza arrives from the palace looking like a supermodel, in a cloak of black feathers with shiny black beads mixed in, over a shiny black tunic and leggings. She brings two other princess candidates with her: a big fire-breathing beetle named Wyndgonk (*fire/fire*) and a five-legged, petal-faced creature named Gyrald (*they/them*).

Kez (*they/them*) arrives with their new boyfriend Ganno the Wurthhi (*he/him*), who is distractingly good-looking. Strong jawline, intense gray-green eyes, powerful shoulders and arms.

"I know you," Yiwei says to Ganno. "You were a guest lecturer in our class on cycle theory. You were the one who told us all about how to break a cycle of violence and turn it into a cycle of peace."

"Right!" Ganno claps his hands. "That was fun. I'm still a student, but they thought I could talk about all the activism I was doing on Irriyaia, with the Cup Full of Cups. That's our, uh, anarchist collective. Did that last phrase make sense in your language?"

Everybody nods. "Yep," Yiwei says.

"Totally," Elza says.

Rachael's surprised the academy wanted an actual anarchist to come talk to one of their classes. But this is the Royal Fleet in a nutshell: they're creepy brain-snatchers, and they're also peaceful helpers.

Kez brought some blackout wine, which Ganno says is designed to strengthen your eyes, so you can see your friends after the light is gone.

Tina is the last one to show up, wearing a black sleeveless dress that shows off her powerful shoulders and long legs. Everyone goes quiet for a moment, and the gathering darkness suddenly feels thick enough to swim in. Tina stares at everyone, flustered by the silence.

Rachael pats the seat next to her and whispers, "We saved you a seat." Tina plunks herself down.

Slow, sad music comes from all around them. Rachael can make out the voices of the people on the next barge over, giving speeches about gratitude and regret. Everybody scoots closer together, because maybe this'll be the time when something goes wrong and the city never gets its light back.

"I can't tell if the sun has gone out yet." Rachael squints.

"There's still plenty of light." Wyndgonk, the nine-eyed giant insect creature, vents an orange fireball. "Your human eyes are weak, is all."

"So sick of people telling me my eyes are weak," Rachael grumbles.

"I can barely see my own hand, and I've got Makvarian eyes," Tina says.

Rachael feels Yiwei and Tina on either side of her. She doesn't feel any colder, but it's still hard to fight the instinct to huddle for warmth.

"Back on Wedding Water, we have massive celebrations when our planet freezes solid, and again when the water starts to boil," says Zaeta. "The big freeze is a time to get closer to your old friends and family, but the steam-time is when we go out and find new friends, when we're already losing our winter skins. I always liked the steam-time best." She wraps her flipper-claw around Damini's hand.

"We need another name for our group," Rachael says. "We can't call ourselves Earthlings anymore, not without excluding all our new friends."

"Oh," says Gyrald. "Oh, Flenby's river, wow."

"You don't have to change the name of your group," Zaeta says.

"Yeah. We do," Yiwei says to her. "You're one of us now. If you want to be."

Nobody can think of a name. The Screwups? The Outcasts? The Champions of Suck?

"We'll think of something," Tina says.

The sun goes into its death throes, sputtering and giving a few last incandescent bursts. Cheers erupt from every rooftop and barge and public square.

Damini pours the blackout wine into glasses and passes it around.

"Drink up, everyone," she commands. "I'm by your side, in the dying of the light."

Everybody joins the toast: "In the dying of the light."

# 19
.

When the sun goes all the way out, it's hard to miss. The darkness goes from shroud to blanket, and Rachael can't see a few inches ahead. A whooshing sound hurts her ears, as the sun vents the last of its plasma.

People start singing all over, in a thousand languages at once: *We're all still here. We haven't lost each other. We haven't forgotten ourselves.* Xiaohou hums along.

Yiwei and Tina each take one of Rachael's hands. Everybody else is holding hands too, or whatever they have to hold.

Elza whispers, "I never liked darkness. I always slept with a night-light when I was little."

"Just a little while," Tina whispers back. "I got you. Hang in there."

Candles flicker to life in the distance: in the plazas, on the walkways, and on every barge and balcony. Sweet candle smoke fills the air, making Rachael's head swim. On their barge, Damini lights some clay diya lamps that she made herself.

Nearby, Ganno whispers to Kez, "You're still beautiful."

"I must have misheard," Kez mumbles. "I could have sworn you called me beautiful. Nobody's ever. My whole life. Nobody's even called me easy on the eyes."

"You're not easy on the eyes," Ganno protests. "What an odd phrase that is. You're the most difficult sight my eyes have ever lit upon. I can't get enough of your face. I could stare forever and still be struck anew."

The people sing, *I won't let go of you.*

Everybody on their barge huddles in silence. Someone hands Rachael a cup with more wine in it, and she tosses it back. She feels warmer, but not tipsy.

"Feels like we'll never see sunlight again," Elza says. "I really need to hear all your voices right now."

"What do we talk about?" Tina asks in a small, un-Tina-like voice.

"This is the moment when we're supposed to share a secret or confess something," Rachael says. *Please let this work please let this work.* "Doesn't have to be anything huge, but . . . when you're sitting in the dark and the sun has gone out, that's a good time to open up to your friends."

*Come on, Tina, that's your cue.*

Long, cringetastic silence—which feels ten times longer since there's nothing to look at.

"I went and talked to Explorer Instructor Wyahaar, and I told him I'm dropping out of the academy," Yiwei says.

"What?" Rachael whips her head around, even though she can't see him. "I thought the academy was your dream."

"So did I. It shattered into a million dreamy pieces. But maybe it's good, I'll have more time to work on my music again. I can learn more CrudePink songs."

Rachael squeezes his hand tighter.

"My teacher said she's leaving town soon, right after she promised not to quit until she found a way to help me," Rachael says in a low voice. "Everybody wants me to be someone I'm not, and I feel like I'm suffocating, and I can't deal with people wanting me to be their hero or their . . . their girlfriend. I can't be anything to anybody right now, I just can't."

Yiwei lets go of her hand.

"Why didn't you say anything?"

"I tried, I really tried," she says. "Let's talk later, okay?"

"Okay." He sounds like he's on the edge of tears.

Another long, crushing silence. Rachael feels cold again, like the wine just drained out of her. She can feel Yiwei shrinking in on himself.

"Well, I found out I'm still really good at making powerful enemies." Elza sighs. "And the next elimination from the princess selection is going to narrow the list down to fifty candidates. There's no way I'm surviving that."

Now Gyrald is talking in a hushed voice, but Rachael is busy cursing herself. The whole time she's known Yiwei, he's only ever tried to be there for her, and she just reached out and smushed him when he was already in a bad place. The worst thing is, part of her feels *relieved.*

Other kids start sharing their secrets—except for Tina. Wyndgonk growls about everyone who treats fire like a giant bug.

"I hate the way everyone treats me at the academy," Zaeta says. "I was willing to risk making myself sick to leave home so I could learn to fly a starship, and everyone treats me like *I'm* a disease, just because I look different, and they're paranoid about the vunci. Like they think if they even talk to me for a moment, they'll be stuck in a psychic bond with me forever."

"Screw those people," Damini says. "They don't deserve your time."

"Turns out I loathe ambassador training," Kez says. "I thought it would be a dream come true, but it's been the worst. My boss Anthanas finds fault with everything I do, and I have to mediate disputes between people who see me as a 'lesser humanoid,' and it's driving me nuts."

Ganno squeezes Kez's hand. "Peace is a bitch."

Everybody *but* Tina is spilling their guts, and Rachael just destroyed her relationship for nothing. Rachael feels chilled to the bone.

Someone squeezes Rachael's hand. "What's wrong?" Tina says in her ear.

"What?" Rachael says. "We're sitting here in pitch darkness and I wasn't making a sound and how did you know—"

"We've been friends a long time," Tina says. "Plus, Makvarian eyes, remember? What's bothering you? Is it the Vayt?"

"No . . ." Rachael can barely get words out. "It's—it's you."

"Me? What did I—"

"You've been keeping something from all of us," Elza says.

"What do you—" Tina sputters. "I don't—"

"We care about you," Kez says. "Like, a lot."

"We need to know what's going on," Damini says.

"And you thought if you threw a big NewSun party, I'd . . ." Tina's voice breaks. "You did all this to get me to . . . You did all this for me." She makes tiny choking sounds. Rachael can feel her tremble. "I'm sorry. I should have told you."

The singing in the distance gets louder. Someone on the roof of the Slanted Prism is laughing, or crying, or both at once.

"They called me into Dr. Thyyrpoah's office," Tina says, almost too quiet to hear. "And he offered me a chance to make a real difference."

Everybody stares at Tina, waiting for the other shoe.

"Not as me, though," Tina says. "As *her.*"

"Captain Argentian?" Damini says.

"Wait," Rachael protests. "The memory restoration failed. I was there."

"There's still a way," Tina says. "They gave me this tiny rock, called a Ruglian mindstone. All I have to do is hold it up to my forehead, and Captain Argentian is back—all the way back. There's just one catch."

Everyone stares.

Elza is the first to speak. "Oh. Oh . . . no. Not that."

"What are you—" Damini says. And then she gets it too. "Oh, that's a *huge* no."

"No to the five billionth power of no," Kez says. "All of the no in the universe, concentrated in one super-dense, ultra-hard nugget of *No.*"

Rachael was sure she couldn't feel any worse. Oops.

Yiwei snaps out of the daze he's been in for the past few minutes. "What do you mean? What is it?"

"Tina would be erased," Damini says. "They could restore Captain Argentian, with all of her memories and everything. But only by getting rid of Tina completely."

"That's not going to happen," Elza says. "Captain Argentian never wanted to be brought back in the first place. She definitely wouldn't want this. And you promised you wouldn't turn yourself into a sacrificial goat again without talking to all of us first."

Tina's been stewing on this by herself, when Rachael's been right there.

When Tina said, *You don't need to be the glue,* what she really meant was, *You're too fragile to burden with any of my problems.* Tina didn't think Rachael could handle a two-way friendship anymore.

"But what if . . . what if she's the only one who can save everyone?" Tina says. "Something terrible is coming and all we can see is its shadow. The Compassion is stronger than ever, and the Vayt keep telling Rachael that we're all doomed, and what if I have to live with knowing that I could have done something?"

"We are not about to let that happen," Kez says. "We will figure this thing out."

"You should throw that rock away," Damini says.

"I know," Tina says. "I just . . ." She trails off.

"You promised," Elza says. "You made so many promises, and the first chance you get, you—" She curses in Portuguese, or maybe it's Pajubá. "I can't believe after everything you said, you haven't changed. I thought you had grown up and stopped being . . ."

Tina moves in the dark, and then Elza says, "Don't touch me."

Rachael, too, can't help pulling away from Tina. Now both her hands are free.

Everyone on the ground and the rooftops starts counting down, like New Year's Eve.

When they reach zero, a thunderclap rings out, and the sky fills with light. Warmth soaks into Rachael's skin and she's dazzled for a moment, then her eyes adjust and she sees her friends again. All the people on the roof of the Slanted Prism cheer, like they just got a second chance at life.

But on the barge, Rachael's friends stare at each other with haunted expressions on all their faces, human and otherwise.

Everything dazzles Rachael as the newborn sun reflects off countless mirrors and metal surfaces. The city has colors and textures Rachael never noticed before. (*Wish I could draw thiiiiiis!*) The fresh sunbeams hurt a little, like everything else that nourishes her soul.

Music erupts from everywhere, a joyous pounding rhythm that goes chachacha WOMWOM chachacha POW. Xiaohou comes to life: drumming, hooting. Everywhere Rachael looks, people jump up and down, swinging each other around, holding on tight.

Voices sing, *Everything is brand-new, forgive yourself, everything is new as long as you have light in your heart.*

Everybody on Rachael's barge is still stunned. Tina is covering her face, while Elza refuses to look at her. Yiwei is turned away from Rachael, cradling Xiaohou.

Worst. Party. Ever.

Rachael knows she should say something to Tina. She even knows what she ought to say: *I get it. You didn't share this with us before because we would have told you to throw that rock away, and you're scared you might need it. People are so shook, they're turning to Marrant for answers, and you? You could give them someone better to turn to. I do get it. I do. But erasing yourself shouldn't be an option. And I really thought we were past keeping secrets.*

But knowing what to say and being able to say it are two different things.

# 20

.

Yiwei and Rachael sit barefoot on Rachael's bed, next to Xiaohou (who's remixing the NewSun anthem). Her window spews sunlight, even with the high-tech shade mostly closed.

". . ." Yiwei looks at the huge shadows on the wall. "We need to talk."

"Okay. Let's talk." Rachael doesn't know what to say next.

Yiwei is wall-gazing, waiting for her to speak, and the distant NewSun festivities sound like every high school dance that Rachael sat across the street from. She's still frozen.

If Rachael could draw one stick figure, she *might* have the spoons for a relationship conversation. But she already started it, in front of all their friends.

The only thing Rachael can say is the worst thing she could say. "I almost broke up with you."

"You . . . what?" His face is bright red and she can feel him tremble. "When?"

"A month ago. I felt trapped, and I couldn't bear to keep disappointing you, and I . . . I thought we should take a break." The words hurt to say, and saying them somehow makes Rachael feel worse, not better.

"What . . ." Yiwei hears the scream in his own voice, and takes a breath. "What did I ever do to make you think I was disappointed in you?"

"Everything! You kept telling me I was a hero and, and, a freaking savior, which is the *last* thing I ever wanted to be. And I saw you obsessing about Captain Othaar all the time, and his heroic legacy. There's no way I could live up to any of that. I felt like you wanted to put me on a pedestal, instead of just letting me be messed up." This all made sense in Rachael's head, but it sounds ridiculous now that she's said it out loud.

Yiwei hides his face in his hands for a moment, then looks up. "You're right," he says slowly. "I think . . . you need a friend more than you need a boyfriend right now."

Rachael's heart is stained with some thick heavy tar that leaves a coat all over her insides. Her head is fogged up, she feels lost in a bad dream.

"Okay. Sure." She can barely breathe, like a slow-motion panic attack.

She doesn't feel like she tore away a piece of herself—more like she was already tired, and now she's even more tired, and she can just glimpse how terrible she'll feel about this in a little while.

Yiwei gets off the bed and reaches for his shoes, then he stops. "No," he says. "I'm not done with this conversation. Did you get mind-reading powers? Because otherwise, the only way you get to know what I'm thinking is if you *ask me*."

Rachael stares at her ex-boyfriend's beautiful face, which she'll never caress again. His cheeks are slick with tears, and Rachael realizes her face, too, is hot and smeary. She didn't even realize, but she's actually choking on tears.

"I've been trying to be there for you. The last thing I wanted to do was make you feel worse. I've watched you struggling, I've seen how hard it's been, and I wanted you to know I believe in you. And this whole time, you've been feeling . . ."

"I'm sorry," Rachael manages to say. "I'm—"

Rachael's own voice interrupts her: "Social interaction alert."

It's coming from her door.

Takes Rachael a moment to realize this is the sound she programmed as the doorbell to her bedroom.

"Go away," Rachael says.

Her own voice responds, louder this time: "Social Interaction Alert!"

Rachael gropes for her Joiner and pulls up a hologram of Tina, still in her black dress from the NewSun festival, standing outside, looking scared.

For a moment Rachael thinks Tina's here to apologize for not telling her about her big secret. But she knows Tina's expressions too well. This is something else.

"Hey." Rachael pulls herself together, and gets the door open. "What's up?"

"You need to go," Tina says. "Right now."

"What?"

"They're coming. Moxx and the rest of the Royal Fleet brass. They decided they can't wait any longer, and there's too much at stake, so they're going to scoop out your brain." She bites her lip. "Zaeta found out and managed to warn us."

Damini comes running into the common room. "Rachael! Why are you still here? They'll be here any moment!"

"Let me get my shoes."

When Rachael turns back, Yiwei is holding her shoes out to her. "Let's go."

Rachael looks around her bedroom—she barely has time to throw some clothes, her one old sketchpad, and Xiaohou into a bag. (Xiaohou whistles as he falls between two shirts.) Then she's following Tina, Damini, and Yiwei out of the dorm room.

A moment ago she was burning down her relationship, and now the rest of her life is on fire, and it feels like a terrible justice.

The four of them hurry down the long hallway, away from the main entrance.

Moxx steps out in front of them, flanked by a whole squad of Firmament Security officers in shiny helmets and light armor with the Joyful Wyvern on their chests.

"Esteemed Rachael Townsend, come back," Moxx calls out. "We don't want to have to turn this into a forcible imprisonment."

"I'll stall them." Tina turns and runs toward Moxx and his pals before Rachael can reply.

"Stop!" Moxx charges forward.

Tina blocks the hallway with her arms and legs.

"Cadet, out of our way," Moxx barks. "Captain Argentian would understand that we have to make sacrifices—"

Damini and Yiwei hustle Rachael around the corner and down the ramp that goes down in a tight spiral.

"Too bad for you Captain Argentian's not here," Tina says, and then Rachael can't hear her voice anymore.

Damini grabs Rachael's arm and stops moving—because more footsteps are ringing out, in front of them and behind them. They're trapped.

"Remember all those times we hoverbooted off the top of the administration building?" Damini has that gleam in her eye that usually means she's about to risk breaking every bone in her body.

"Um, yeah," Yiwei says. "But we don't have any boots, and there's no way out from here."

Damini points at her own feet, which are currently wearing hoverboots. "I'll get Rachael to safety, while you make a distraction. Don't let them see you. You're in enough trouble already."

"Okay," Yiwei says. And then he doesn't move.

Rachael feels suddenly shy in front of Damini. She mumbles, "We'll talk later."

"Count on it," Yiwei says.

Rachael is terrified, running on pure adrenaline. But there are a hundred other feelings trying to claw their way to the surface, and she knows she's not going to enjoy any of them when they hit. (If she's still alive when that happens.)

She nods, with a huge effort. "Okay," she says.

"Go!" Yiwei's pulling the ceiling apart with his bare hands, climbing up into some kind of service crawlway, giving them one last wave before he disappears.

Security officers appear at both ends of the hallway, yelling and running. Damini sticks out her tongue at them.

Then Damini opens a tiny side door that leads to the laundry facility, where you can put your clothes in the molecular scrubber, and she tears the panel off the inner wall, revealing a vent that's open to the air.

"Come on," Damini says. "This'll be fun!"

Damini leans out the vent, until she's hanging by a few fingertips on the ledge, a hundred feet above the plaza. She activates her hoverboots with a finger-snap and gestures for Rachael to climb into her arms.

Rachael hesitates. "Do you always wear hoverboots, like all the time?"

Damini shrugs. "I don't sleep in hoverboots. At least, not *every* night? I don't think."

The Security forces burst into the laundry room, brandishing stun weapons.

Rachael jumps into Damini's arms, and holds on tight as they rocket straight up.

Rachael and Damini ascend until the dorm, and the campus, look tiny. Someone throws an ion harness and Damini barely dodges it, then she's swooping and banking away from the academy and all the shouting.

Rachael hears a cymbal crash, loud enough to split her ears even from this distance, and then the whole dorm building vibrates—the outer walls start to play this one CrudePink song about dancing in the debris of a crashed starship. THE WHOLE BUILDING IS A SPEAKER NOW. A VERY, VERY LOUD SPEAKER.

Yiwei's distraction. Right on time.

*My ex-boyfriend.* Rachael can't stop rehashing their conversation as she zooms through the air.

"We made a friend," Damini says.

Their "friend" is a robot attack craft that looks like a tiny version of the *Skin of Our Teeth,* their old ship. The robot races toward them, closing the distance even when Damini darts around the knotty buildings and under the walkways.

Damini's eyes gleam. "Finally, a challenge."

They come within a couple inches of wiping out on a flying barge, and Rachael has to shut her eyes. *Not going to scream. Not going to scream.*

The attack drone launches some kind of missile. Looks like an ugly red spike, sounds like a snoring giant.

"Damn. Are they trying to kill us?" Rachael yells in Damini's ear.

"Nah, that's a showstopper missile. If it hits us, we'll be frozen until they can come get us. But it's not going to hit us, because this is me we're talking about. Hang on tight."

Rachael clutches at Damini's waist as she amps up her hoverboots. A swing-wing slices through the air right over them, and nearly takes their heads off. Damini chatters about everything she's learned at the academy—including all the different ways of looking at physics—as she flies through the upper loop of one of those ampersand-shaped buildings.

"You see, different planets learned about astrophysics in very different ways, depending on where they were in the galaxy, and what they could see of the cosmic background radiation," Damini says. "Oops, watch out, this is going to be a close one." She giggles as they swerve around the expanding side of an apartment building that's in the middle of changing its shape.

Rachael wishes she'd gotten a helmet somehow.

The showstopper missile is right behind them. Damini can't possibly outrun it, and she's still busy chattering about how the smoke turtles of Pyha think about light and time and gravity. And how the so-called objective truth depends on where in the universe you stand.

And then the missile hits, with an ear-jangling *plorp* noise.

Rachael braces for the impact, the feeling of everything grinding to a halt. Then she realizes: they're still going. Behind them, the missile has left behind a bright orange bubble of timelessness, surrounding a few Aribentors who were having an argument on their balcony. One of them is stuck in the middle of raising a skeleton hand to make a point, while another one is frozen in mid-retort.

"Ha," Damini says. "That'll teach you to shoot missiles at me. OK, let's find a safe place to lay . . ."

She trails off.

They pass through the gap between two buildings, and run smack into five more Firmament Security attack craft, closing in on all sides.

A second later, the air is full of red darts.

"Eep. Too many missiles!" For a second, Damini looks like a scared kid who's way out of her depth.

Then she smiles with one corner of her mouth, and flicks her thumb.

The hoverboots turn off.

Damini and Rachael fall out of the sky. Balconies and walkways and gardens and NewSun displays and barges whiz past, until they turn into a colorful blur.

Please write back when you get this. Please. I need to hear from you.

Please.

I don't know if you're not responding because you're at the palace with no Joiner reception, or if you're ghosting me. But I'm really scared. Everything went to hell way too fast, and I don't understand.

Right after our tragic NewSun party, the Royal Fleet came to seize Rachael's brain by force. This is not what I thought the Royal Fleet was about. I still don't know if Rachael escaped in one piece, but I'd put any money on Damini getting her to safety.

I'm sorry I didn't tell you about the mindstone. I wanted to, a bunch of times, but every time we hung out, we were celebrating how much you were crushing it in the princess selection program. I never wanted to ruin any of those dates.

I promise I'm not going anywhere. I want to keep getting on your nerves until we're both weird old ladies. We'll live in a big house on an asteroid somewhere, with a dozen flout-skitters running around and shedding rainbow fur everywhere. I'll collect every fluff-pile and learn to knit, so I can make you a fuzzy blanket with every color ever.

I'm scared something has happened to you, especially after what just went down with Rachael. We were all together at NewSun, and then suddenly everyone was scattered in a million directions, and I'm terrified I'm going to lose you. I love you so much.

Please get back to me when you get this. I just need to know you're alive and you don't hate me. Please.

# 21
.

## ELZA

Elza is getting another makeover while she practices shooting a gun.

She feels the cloud chamber fizz inside the cloudstrike weapon, and she tries to aim at the holographic target on the other side of the big open-air courtyard. Meanwhile, a will-o'-the-wisp with a cartoon face is fluttering around, painting tiny streaks of silvery blue across her eyes. The palace has decided she's going to be beautiful *and* super-tough, at the same time.

She shoots—and the beam hits a few centimeters away from the target. She curses and nearly messes up her makeup.

"Try to relax," says the tiny fluff that's painting her face. "It'll help your accuracy *and* make my job easier."

*Relax?*

Tina has been carrying around a stone that could erase her, for *months,* and didn't bother to tell Elza. After all those speeches about sharing everything and being there for each other.

And Marrant is still here in the palace, close enough that Elza can almost smell the noxious flesh-melting stench of his skin. And lately, when Elza fantasizes about becoming a princess, her imagination immediately goes to Princess Evanescent.

The terrible part is, Elza still loves both Tina and the palace. She has a fire inside her rib cage that never goes out, and when she thinks of Tina's eyes, or all the moments when she learns to break patterns while wearing a velveteen dress, she can feel that little flame rise up. Part of her wishes she could douse that flame, because it hurts to care this much about a person and a place when they keep letting her down.

You have to fight for the things and the people that give you meaning, and part of that means fighting to make them better. Even though it would be so much less exhausting to expect nothing from them.

Elza learned at her terreiro: the feeling of unconditional acceptance and joy washing over her whole skin as she danced and touched the orixás. That feeling came from being connected to her ancestors, who had pre-served their culture—disguising the orixás as Catholic saints, hiding their rituals in plain sight. When something moves you, you have to keep it alive at all costs.

Today is the day: the big elimination. All but fifty of the five hundred remaining candidates are about to wash out of the program. Including Elza, probably.

The gun throbs in Elza's hand and she can't aim, and meanwhile this fuzzball keeps flying right in front of her eyes.

"Can you just—can I just do one thing at a time, please?" Elza snaps. "Can I shoot the gun now and *then* get the makeover?"

"You have syllogism class right after this." The flying puff sounds annoyed. "And you came to the wrong place, if you only want to do one thing at a time. Princesses need to be able to do several things at once. Always."

"It doesn't matter. I'm getting sent away today."

"Well, if that's true, then you ought to look damn good walking out of here," the puff says.

Elza groans and concentrates on shooting the gun without hitting any more walls. And she tries to find a way to hold on to that flame inside her, in spite of everything.

Elza stands under an archway that's so narrow, the sides graze against her lace-covered arms. "That's perfect," Princess Constellation says. "Stay like that." She always tells Elza to do weird poses and eat random crap, and never gives a reason.

"Have you ever dreamed about forgetting a dream?" the princess asks.

"This is probably the last time we're going to see each other," Elza says. "They're going to eliminate me in a few jewels."

"Oh, you've learned to see the future? Please teach me!"

"You can't put in a good word for me?"

Princess Constellation doesn't bother to answer this time. Elza already knows the answer is *no*.

Apparently the princesses can't interfere with the selection program—any more than the queen can kick Marrant out of the palace.

"Did you know they gave my girlfriend a rock that would destroy her?" Elza says. "Of course you did, you know everything. Thanks for warning me."

Princess Constellation doesn't answer. She stares off into space, not even blinking.

Then she hands Elza a cake that's an exact replica of the palace. "Eat this."

"How do you deal with it?" Elza asks Princess Constellation.

"Deal with what?" She holds out the palace-cake until Elza takes it.

"People thinking you're . . . I mean, the way you talk, and act, the fact that you're always hearing voices nobody else can hear. And half the things you say make no sense."

"Only half?" She laughs. "One must try harder. One really must."

"How do you stand having people think you're . . ."

"Mad?" She pours a milky liquid into a red cup and offers some to Elza. "Sanity is vastly overrated. Sanity is music without syncopation, dancing without stumbles."

Elza bites into the cake, and it tastes like chocolate and first kisses and cherries and the first beautiful day of spring.

"Back on Earth, when I was . . ." Elza chokes on cake for a moment. "When I was living on the street. I only spent a couple months couch-surfing and sleeping rough before I found the hackerspace, but it felt like forever. And I put so much into not letting anyone see I was falling apart. Even though I was— the rejection, and the way people looked at me, were getting under my skin. But I could never let it show, or people would have treated me even worse."

"You've answered your own question. A princess can get away with a little strange behavior, much more easily than a child with no home. If you attain a high enough status, then normality is whatever you say." She eats a bite of the cake. "One does so enjoy these architectural confections."


Elza walks outside the palace to breathe, and her Joiner bursts with a hundred missed messages. Most of them are from Tina, and she can't look at those right now. But Kez and Yiwei are saying Rachael had to run for her life from the Royal Fleet—Damini sent a signal to let everyone know she's safe, but nobody knows where she and Rachael are now.

Then there's something else.

*JoinerTalk, Kez to Group:* Oh no no no. This is . . . no, I can't believe.

*JoinerTalk, Tina to Group:* Wait, what happened? Is it Rachael?

*JoinerTalk, Kez to Group:* It's Irriyaia. It's . . . oh god.

*JoinerTalk, Kez to Group:* Poor Yatto. This is going to kill them.

*JoinerTalk, Elza to Group:* What happened to Irriyaia?

Before Elza's friends can answer, she hears a gasp next to her. Robhhan stands nearby staring at his Joiner, which has a 3-D hologram of the clan-meeting chamber in Mauntra City.

All of the leaders of Irriyaia's different nations are having some kind of emergency meeting. One of them, Zinyat the Wurthhi (*he/him*), is giving a speech about all the refugees from other planets that Irriyaia has taken in lately. "It's time we took care of our own."

Everyone in the room cheers and stomps their feet.

"We face a danger we can't understand, and the Firmament has been asking too much of us, for much too long," growls Enday the Nahhi (*she/her*).

Another figure steps up to one of the lecterns in the meeting chamber: a fox-faced Javarah, whose artificial "fur" looks different than usual, glimmering and casting rainbows around the space. "Thank you for inviting me here," says a voice that sounds familiar. "The Compassion only wants to lift you up and free you from carrying so many lesser creatures on your shoulders."

They keep talking, and Elza can't place where she's heard that voice before.

Until someone says the name "Kankakn," and she remembers. This is the founder of the Compassion, who captured Princess Evanescent and tried to steal her crown.

"I know this is a difficult choice." Kankakn shows fangs. "But you are putting your own people first."

"Then it's decided," says Enday. "As of two days from now, Irriyaia will be officially departing from Her Majesty's Firmament and the Royal Fleet. Instead, we will be the first world to become part of the Compassion."

They keep talking. All unsanctioned aliens will be required to leave Irriyaia, especially non-humanoids and lesser humanoids.

The Compassion will establish military bases on Irriyaia.

Royal Fleet personnel have two days to leave the planet, or be considered enemy combatants.

From now on, Irriyaia fights for the humanoids.

The last thing Elza sees is someone holding up a big hologram: Yatto the Monntha, aiming a superstream cannon at the sky, as everyone in that chamber goes berserk.

# 22
.

A princess stands in front of the five hundred remaining candidates inside the receiving room with the winged ceiling, but it's not Princess Constellation.

"My name is Princess Nonesuch, and my pronoun is *she*. I'm here to banish most of you from the Palace of Scented Tears." Princess Nonesuch is a Yarthin—her skin is covered with a kind of moss—wearing a dress made of a hundred mirrors. "The reality is, almost none of you is worthy to stand inside this room, because your minds are weak and easily distracted."

Elza is still shivering, trying to pull herself together. Everyone around her keeps whispering about Irriyaia.

"Well, this is it," Wyndgonk grumbles. "We'll have to stay in touch on the outside."

"You never know," Elza says—even though she does know.

She wants to stand straight like a princess, but she can't resist huddling, hands in her armpits.

"I can't go home if this fails." Gyrald sighs. "Nobody on Draay will welcome me if I don't bring back some assistance in recovering from that comet strike. It's been a generation, and we're still suffering."

Elza stares at the beady dark eyes and globby mouth inside Gyrald's petals. They always seem so cheerful and laid-back, she never would have guessed they were so desperate.

"Please be quiet," hisses Robhhan. "I'm trying to listen."

"Being a princess is more than glamour and ceremony," says Princess Nonesuch. "It requires discipline, which is why I've devised a test for you all. You will each be granted a small share of the Ardenii's higher awareness, and you must solve a logic sphere."

That doesn't sound so hard. Solving a puzzle, with the help of the greatest computers ever?

Elza pushes the Compassion and Irriyaia out of her mind. She's got this handled.

"The test begins now," says Princess Nonesuch.

Elza's hands are holding a logic sphere, which is divided into thirty-six diamond shapes, each with a symbol on it. She starts looking for some pattern to the symbols . . .

. . . and then her mind floods with garbage.

On Irriyaia, someone is tearing a small Kraelyor away from their parents—the child wails and shrieks, while a hologram of Yatto the Monntha cheers and shouts slogans about cleansing the world of alien filth. On Makvaria, a young thont has stumbled while climbing the White Tower of Yeshka, and is falling to ser death *right now.* An elderly Grattna named Wendup is dying of old age, knowing her two partners will not be there to meet her when she goes to the godparents, because they died in the Antarràn system, far from home.

This is not at all like the thing Tina talks about, where she has the knowledge of Captain Argentian in her head. It's a thousand times worse.

Elza doesn't just *know* stuff, she *experiences* all of this suffering and injustice, somewhere deep in her bones and tendons. She can't do anything to help any of these people, but she can't look away. Is this what it's like for Princess Constellation, all the time? Or are they deliberately showing her the worst, to throw her off her game?

Elza tries to focus on all the symbols, but her mind is cracking like a rotten egg.

"Ugh I can't do this," she says out loud.

"Good," Naahay says, standing nearby with her own sphere. "About time you realized."

Naahay sounds like João, back at the hackerspace.

"Screw you," Elza says.

She tells herself: *I'm doing this for all of those suffering people. I need to shut them out now, so I can help them later.* She tries. She focuses on the sphere and ignores everything.

She wishes Damini was here, because Damini always rocks at puzzles.

On Vandal Station, a Pnoft is being torn to shreds, right when they were about to become a real person.

Okay. So one of these symbols is clearly "not," meaning whatever you put it next to is negated. And this other symbol is like an asterisk, meaning every possible variation of something is allowed. But . . . there's one symbol that has both "not" and "everything" connected to it. Which makes no sense: How can something be not allowed, and also allowed in every situation?

The only way to solve this puzzle is to embrace contradictions.

A whole starship full of refugees has blown up. They're getting sucked into space, crying for help. She can see their silent screams, as if she were right there.

Elza finds it: the one symbol that makes sense of the rest. She's sure, in her guts if not her brain.

Then the Ardenii show her one last thing.

Tina slouching on the edge of her bed, staring at her golden rock.

Elza falls apart. She can't do this. She can't move or think. Can't even see straight, too many tears.

She wipes her eyes clean, and reaches out for that symbol, the solution, with her index finger.

Princess Nonesuch calls out, "Time's up."

Elza's logic sphere vanishes before she can touch the right symbol.

"Wait," Elza says. "I was about to—"

The flood of horrors is gone from Elza's mind.

"Too late," Princess Nonesuch smirks. "Anyone who didn't finish is eliminated."

Naahay smirks. "Too bad for you. I finished mine ages ago."

Elza stares at that skull-face, boasting about mastering a puzzle while being forced to witness all the misery, all the death, happening everywhere. This was a test that only a monster could be proud of passing.

And now she knows why Princess Constellation said, *Perhaps you should find out what being a princess means, before you decide you are so eager to claim that mantle.*

Elza wants to throw Naahay's scorn back in her face—but she just feels drained, as if she's been lifting a mountain over her head. The only person she wants to yell at is herself.

So she turns and walks away.


*I don't know where I'm going to sleep tonight.* The thought hits like a lightning bolt.

After Elza's parents threw her out, she slept a few times on the street, but also in an abandoned building that had transformed into a cortiço for everyone to live in. She kept applying to stay at the shelter at Casa Florescer, plus Fernanda let her sleep in the closet of her tiny studio in the Lúz a few times, until things went bad between them. When she thinks back to that time before the hackerspace, she only remembers feeling cold and alone.

Everyone says there are no unhoused people in Wentrolo, and that always sounded like paradise to Elza. But now she has no clue how to find a place. Maybe she can stay with Tina, but they're not supposed to allow guests in the academy dorm—plus Elza can't see Tina right now.

She wants nothing more than to stride out of the palace with her head high. She can't wait to get out of this place and tear off this empire-waisted ballgown and cry for a few days.

But when she's halfway to the big entrance chamber, with the winged ceiling, she stops.

She can't do anything about Naahay's arrogance, or Princess Nonesuch sneering at her when she almost solved an impossible puzzle, or all the tiny ways everyone has let her know she doesn't belong. But Marrant? She can still do something about.

Elza sneaks across the palace to Marrant's room—and the orange door is wide open. The room is totally empty. No guards, nothing.

"What the hell," Elza says out loud.

Everything is gone, including the bed and all the furniture. The secret compartment inside his bathroom holds nothing. No sign anyone was ever here. "Palace! Do me one last favor, please. What happened to Marrant?"

No response. Maybe the palace doesn't care about her anymore, now that she's no longer a princess candidate.

"Come on," Elza says. "I'm not asking for another chance at princess status. Where is Marrant?"

The bolo mouse pokes its head out from the wall. "Are you sure you want to know? Because if you know the answer, it becomes your responsibility."

Elza nods. "Tell me."

"Very well." The bolo mouse shrugs its little shoulders. "He's gone. Escaped. Somebody sent away his guards and overcame the palace watchfulness protocols. The palace was never supposed to hold prisoners to begin with."

"Do you know who let him go?"

The bolo mouse considers for a moment, then shrugs its tiny shoulders. "I can't answer that question. Goodbye, Elza from Earth."

The mouse vanishes, leaving Elza alone in an empty room.

# 23

.

*If you know the answer, it becomes your responsibility.*

That sounded like a warning. But maybe the not-a-mouse was also offering encouragement? Elza has spent enough time studying—time to light some fires.

Princess Constellation is nowhere to be found. Elza has been sending her messages like, "Marrant escapes on the same day Irriyaia joins the Compassion? Not a coincidence."

She can't leave until she gets to the bottom of this.

Every time Elza sees the palace guards, or attendants, or any of her former teachers, she has to shrink behind a pillar or arch or curtain until they're gone. Of course the palace knows she's still here, but it hasn't bothered to tell anyone else—which has to be a good sign, right?

Elza ends up back down in the basement of secrets. "Please," she whispers. "I know I'm not a student anymore, and I can't stand the idea of owing favors to a building. But I need to understand about Marrant and the Compassion, and how they got started."

A moment later, a figure fades into view in the darkness of this crypt: Marrant, when he was young and craggy-faced.

He's in a part of Wentrolo that Elza has never seen before—it looks sort of like the Stroke, where Elza has gone to "buy" presents for her friends. Rows and rows of market stalls are shrouded by curtains that keep turning into sheets of water, and then back into cloth.

Something catches Marrant's eye: a rippling symbol that comes in and out of focus as the curtains turn watery. He stares for a moment, then follows the curtain to a secluded spot with a dozen cushions bathing in golden shafts of light.

Sitting among the cushions is a tall Javarah with a long fox-muzzle and expressive ears.

Marrant's mouth twists. "You're not a Makvarian dry-root sage. That symbol was false advertising."

The Javarah's ears stand straight up. "The symbol is designed to look like whatever your spiritual tradition is. If you'd been an Aribentor, it'd have been a few lines of poetry. Also, I have telepathic shields in place, to ensure that only those who really need me can find me."

"And . . . why exactly would I need you?"

The ears go in opposite directions. "I can't tell you why that symbol spoke to you, but perhaps you're having a spiritual crisis. Only you can name the reasons. I merely offer to help. My name is Kankakn" (*she/her*).

Elza feels dizzy for a moment, starved for air.

She's standing right in front of the woman who killed Princess Evanescent and tipped Irriyaia over the edge into xenophobia.

Marrant is still talking. "I'm going to report you on my Joiner. You're luring people into your creepy pillow cave under false pretenses."

"They're never going to let you be happy," Kankakn says. "Everything here is designed to make you feel close to a greatness that can never be yours. The palace, the Royal Fleet, all of it. The moment they glimpse your true mettle, they will try to destroy you."

"So. You're a spiritual teacher who spreads the gospel of resentment." Marrant makes the scornful noise that Elza remembers from when he was trying to kill her friends.

"I am not seeking students or disciples, I'm starting a movement." Kankakn spreads her palms face up, as if to show she has nothing to hide. "We're going to fix everything that's wrong with this place. We're going to give people their dignity back. Nobody will ever again decide what is best for everybody else, or force you to wear yourself out helping creatures who can't be helped."

"I see." Marrant purses his lips. "And what exactly is this movement called?"

"We're still settling on a name. I was thinking, 'the Compassion.'"

"Sounds very therapeutic." Marrant makes that sound again, and Elza can't help flinching. "Sorry, I already belong to something much better."

"You will never be valued as you deserve, if you stay on this path." Kankakn tilts her ears forward. "You'll learn the hard way. It's already happening, or you wouldn't have followed that symbol and found me. The Royal Fleet will always try to turn you into a servant of the weak. And the people in your life will always be threatened by your accomplishments."

"I can't possibly imagine why you haven't found anyone else to sit on all these cushions. Goodbye." Marrant turns on one heel and walks away.

The scene shifts to Marrant back on board the *Indivisible,* talking to Aym.

Elza tries to listen, but someone is coming up behind her.

Senior Councilor Waiwaiwaiwai looms over her shoulder. "Ex-candidate.

You were instructed to leave the Palace of Scented Tears. Why are you still here?"

Elza feels nothing but despair, but she forces a cheerful look onto her face.

"I'm leaving in a moment. I want to see the rest of this. It's the best novela ever."

"You're leaving now. Come on."

Elza almost gets up and follows Waiwaiwaiwai. But she doesn't have to obey anymore.

A ghostly Marrant is saying something to his girlfriend, some romantic declaration.

"I want to talk to Princess Constellation," Elza says. "I'm not going anywhere until I get to talk to her one more time."

"She has more important things to do than speak with a rejected candidate in the secondary node selection program." Waiwaiwaiwai bristles.

"You heard me," Elza says—not to Waiwaiwaiwai, but to the palace. "I'll leave quietly, as soon as I talk to Princess Constellation."

"Palace attendants are on their way down here, to remove you by force." Waiwaiwaiwai snarls.

She won't get upset. She won't give them anything. She might not be princess material, but she can keep her face on.

Then another figure appears next to Waiwaiwaiwai—tall, with a glowing crown.

"Please give us a moment," Princess Constellation says to Waiwaiwaiwai. "I'll see that Elza arrives in the correct place."

Waiwaiwaiwai bows. Her eyes look calm and blank, but her face-tubes are torqued on either side of her cheekbones. "Very well, Your Radiance."

Elza is alone with the princess, probably for the last time.

"Let's not talk down here." Princess Constellation looks around the cellar. "I never like to spend too much time in the past. It has a way of seeping into everything, and then I have to take a dozen baths to get my timeline clean again."

Elza follows her up the ramp as the vision of Aym and Marrant fades away.


"So this is it," Elza says to the back of Princess Constellation's bald head. "I'll never teach you to dance again. Whatever you were trying to say with all your riddles, I'll never get to understand."

Princess Constellation doesn't answer, just leads Elza deeper into the palace.

Bad enough she has to leave the palace with nothing, especially on the same day that Irriyaia switched sides and the Royal Fleet came for Elza's friend. But to leave without some sign that Princess Constellation saw something special in her, that the princess chose to mentor Elza for a real reason, will wreck her. Is this a pathetic thing to ask for? Some sign that all this mattered? Maybe, but Elza still craves it.

"You and the other princesses, you see every awful thing, on a thousand worlds," Elza says. "And all you ever do is sit around in exquisite couture, eating cake."

Still no answer.

Elza can't find the words to describe this feeling—it's like being in love, and not knowing if the other person loves you back. A trembling, yearning need, in every breath she takes and every moment she feels the warm fragrant air currents of the palace move across her skin. Elza wants to shut down, to stop caring, but then she remembers the way Princess Constellation looked at her and said, *Teach me to dance,* and something inside her leaps with joy and anticipation. As if her brain's reward system is messed up beyond reason.

"Why don't you go to Irriyaia and find out what the Compassion's up to, before it's too late?" she says to the back of Princess Constellation's head. "Take action for a change."

Princess Constellation turns toward Elza. Her smile is so gentle it knocks Elza back on her heels.

She leads Elza into a chamber she's never seen before, where the walls and ceiling are made out of wind chimes.

"Why do you think we have all this?" Princess Constellation gestures at the tinkling walls, but also the whole palace. "What is all of this finery in aid of? Why do we need a queen, and princesses, and attendants?"

Elza wants to say, *I don't care anymore.*

But that would be a lie, and she wants to tell the truth in this moment.

"They taught us in history class," Elza says. "The Royal Fleet started as a simple peacekeeping force, and meanwhile, the founding planets decided to develop fancy computers that could warn them about threats. And over time, the computers became so smart, they could think for themselves, and nobody could understand them anymore, so they needed the queen to speak for them."

"You told me *how* it happened." Princess Constellation frowns. "But I asked *why.*"

"Why? Uh." Elza looks around this clanging, singing chamber. "People are scared of anything they don't understand. They want a living face to talk to. They always fear that smart computers will go all *Terminator* and kill everyone, even though that makes no sense."

"That's a piece of the truth." Princess Constellation reaches out and pokes a single crystal among the thousands hanging from the ceiling, so it rings a high, clear note. "But also . . . people fear knowledge. Knowledge is hard, and grotesque, and messy, and it eats away at whatever you believe in. We cannot travel across the stars and keep worlds safe and well fed without knowledge, but nobody has to like it."

"So . . . all of this is designed to make knowledge seem beautiful, when it's actually ugly?"

Her face lights up. "My Royal Dance Instructor. I knew I had chosen wisely."

Elza can't help it: her heart does a twirl. She had no idea how much she needed to hear the princess say those words.

"I would be pleased to welcome you on board my starship." Princess Constellation pokes again, and the crystal makes a louder bell note. This time, all the other crystals vibrate in response, so Elza feels the vibrations in her teeth.

The next thing she knows, all of the wind chimes have left the ceiling and gathered around Princess Constellation, where they form into a pair of crystalline wings on her back. She holds out her hand, and Elza takes it.

Elza and the princess are flying, up toward the ceiling, and even though Elza's about to crash into a big vaulted arch of what looks like pure diamond, she shrieks with laughter.

They soar through the ceiling, which is a hologram of course, and then they're floating over the palace. Princess Constellation supports Elza with one arm under her armpit and across her chest, and the other around her waist, and Elza does not stop laughing.

From above, the palace looks like two pairs of clasped hands, with their fingertips stretching toward two horizons, as it bleeds into space. The outer walls are coated with some metallic sheen that creates ripples of light. A cloud floats nearby, watching over everything.

As soon as they reach the very top of the palace, right at the fingertips, the "sky" opens up and they go straight up inside the front area of a hidden starship. Like the control deck and Forward Ops on the *Indomitable,* except everything is clean smooth lines and all of the fixtures look new.

The princess drifts down to the floor gently, and lets go of Elza.

"This is my ship, the *Invention of Innocence*. Welcome aboard." Princess Constellation gestures around the flight deck. "We have a great deal of work to do before we reach Irriyaia."

# 24
.

The *Invention of Innocence* drifts down into the center of the Wishing Maze. Somehow Elza can hear all the wishes, like the rustle of dried leaves. *Can I have one more day, I wish I could meet my mother just once, If I could only understand why he had to leave.*

Tina steps around a switchback bend in the maze, sees the ship, and cries out.

"I've never seen such a sleek ship in my life, and I don't care, because you're all I want to look at. I missed you so much, my heart is the size of a damn planet right now."

Elza and Tina open their arms at the same moment, and then they're embracing and laugh-crying.

Then Tina looks past Elza, and her eyes widen.

"You're the clone I keep hearing about." Princess Constellation steps forward. "The resemblance is certainly uncanny."

Tina does such an elaborate curtsey, her hand almost brushes the floor. "Your Radiance. Your acquaintance is a prize, and I'm sorry to have caused any inconvenience, and—"

Princess Constellation waves, and Tina shuts up. "Please speak to me as if I'm a person, or I might become itchy in places that would be inconvenient to scratch. I'm quite curious to meet you. I'm told you know more than you understand. Or rather, you know things you never learned. Is that correct?"

Tina nods. "Um, yeah."

"Is it really knowledge, if you don't know that you know it? Could you really know the flavor of food you've never tasted?"

Tina stares at Princess Constellation, trying to think of an answer.

She claps two fingers of one hand against two fingers of the other. "Most people think they know more than they do. How refreshing to meet someone who is the opposite. You're welcome on board my ship."

"Thank you, Your Radi—" Tina starts to do another fancy curtsey, then catches herself. "Thanks. Nice to meet you, too."

Elza tugs Tina away from the princess before things get more awkward.

"Come on. Let me show you around." Somehow Elza manages to act as if she's spent hours aboard this ship, and she's already over it—even though she only came aboard a short time ago herself.

Tina's eyes get wider and her mouth hangs open as Elza leads her past the vestibule, into the heart of the *Invention of Innocence*.

The carpet feels like a grassy meadow, and the walls ripple with light. This doesn't look like any of the Royal Fleet ships Elza's been on board—if anything, it's an extension of the Palace of Scented Tears.

Arched walls, bright colors, music coming from everywhere and nowhere, the scent of flowers and candle wax and incense. Tiny gossamer-winged creatures swim through the air. The ceiling dips in the middle, and the walls have a curve to them as well.

Tina points out marvel after marvel. "This design is next level. Look at these gravitators!"

One wall of the main access corridor is covered with glowing letters: some fancy poem about bathing in dream essence. The poetry is holy and profane and includes words from Pajubá. "What do you think this means?" Elza asks.

Tina frowns at the wall. "I don't know. It looks a little worn, but the self-repair on this ship is fantastic."

"You don't see the writing? There's a whole poem. It's kind of dirty."

"No poem." Tina shrugs.

"How about over here?" Elza points at another section of wall that's full of paradoxes and words for kissing.

"I just see . . . a wall. Are you seeing something else?" Tina whistles. "I guess the ship likes you."

Elza stares at the list, which has "a box that's only full when it's been emptied" next to "espécie de bombom."

"I can't . . ." Elza hears a warble in her own voice, like it's close to breaking. "I can't believe any of this is real."

"It's all real." Tina comes closer. "You've been chosen. I didn't need any invisible poetry to know that. You have this glow on your face."

Oh, no, the tears are breaking free—Elza has tried so hard to keep them inside, and now her face is salt-itchy. All of her life, she's tried to hold on to her dreams, and now they're bursting free, sweeping her away like a riptide. Her feet can't hold on.

"Oh," Tina says. "Oh oh oh. It's okay. I'm here. I'm sorry I hurt you, but I'm here now. It's okay if you need to cry, it's always okay. All I ask is, can I wipe your tears away? Is that okay? I would really like to do that for you."

Elza cries harder, and nods. She feels like some reservoir inside her has finally broken after days of cracks, and maybe she'll never stop weeping.

Tina brushes Elza's cheek with so much gentleness in her big, powerful hands.

"Whatever's wrong," Tina says in a low voice, "whatever you need, I'm in your corner."

"I flunked out of the princess program." Elza sniffles. "There was a test and I failed, and they told me to leave, and I'm only here on this ship because I talked Princess Constellation into going on a mission to Irriyaia, to figure out the Compassion's endgame. I'm never going to be a princess. I don't know what I'll be."

"You'll be incredible. You'll keep inspiring everyone around you. No matter what." Tina strokes Elza's hair, which makes her start sobbing again. "But look at that poetry—that is not something that happens to someone who's been discarded. You're with a princess, and she's going to teach you, and I'm right here. If you ever need me, I'll come running."

Elza feels warm and happy in Tina's embrace, like always.

Until she stiffens. The words come out without her meaning to say them: "Unless you decide to erase yourself using that rock."

Tina lets go of Elza and takes a step back.

"I wish more than anything I had told you sooner about the mindstone. I was trying not to think too much about it."

"I don't understand why you still have it." Elza crosses her arms and sits down on an elegant couch that undulates like a waterbed.

"I wish I never saw it. I would give anything to forget it exists." Tina smacks her left fist into her forehead. "But . . . things keep getting worse, and what if we reach a point where she's the only one who can help?"

Elza wishes she felt angry, instead of whatever she's feeling. "I don't know if I can be with someone who reserves the right to disappear if things get bad."

"I almost threw it away. A dozen times. I promise I won't use it without talking to you first."

This is part of who Tina is. Back on Earth, when Elza was trying to survive, Tina was preparing to become a legendary hero, and some part of her still can't let go of that dream, even if it kills her.

Elza loves Tina's giant fierce heart, so maybe she needs to love this part of her, too.

"I've got an idea." Elza holds out her hand, palm upraised. "Give it to me. For safekeeping."

Tina hesitates, reaches into her bag. Then she shakes her head. "I can't. I wish I could."

They keep exploring the ship, but Elza feels exhausted. Too many things in one day. Soon she and Tina will say goodbye, and this thing will still be between them.

Tina breaks the heavy silence. "I wanted to say you were right. Back when we first met, when you came on board the *Indomitable,* you were right. And I was wrong."

Elza stumbles a little. "What was I right about?"

"When you said uniforms make people cruel. That the Royal Fleet was a lot like the cops back home. After what they tried to do to Rachael, I can't keep pretending."

"Wow." Elza ought to be flushed with triumph, but she can feel Tina's heartache.

Tina sighs. "It's okay. Listen, I should come with you on your secret mission."

"You can't. I'm sorry."

"I can drop out of the academy. They know I helped Rachael escape." Tina's hands fold over into half fists. "Maybe this ship can use an extra navigator, or janitor. I can make myself useful."

Elza shakes her head. "I'm sorry. There's no way. Princess Constellation already told me, it's palace personnel only."

Tina doesn't say anything, just nods and leans against the wall, right where the poetry is at its filthiest. "I guess I better see the rest of the ship while I can."

Elza can't look at Tina, knowing they'll soon be on opposite sides of an endless void. And Tina will still be carrying around that cursed rock.

Maybe they should break up right now. Elza's never been the one to break up with someone, and she doesn't know how it works.

"You think you're being brave, but you're actually being a total coward," Elza says.

Tina recoils. "Excuse me?"

"You're choosing to let fear control you. You're not willing to trust in yourself. In us."

Tina starts to say something, but Elza shushes her.

"You keep saying you don't want to use weapons anymore, but you're carrying a weapon in your bag. That's what that mindstone is, right? If you use it, you become her. And you know she'll use your body to kill people. Probably a lot of people. You might as well have a cannon strapped on your back."

"I . . . I'm just . . ." Tina's beautiful wide eyes are bright and she looks so helpless, all of her strength gone. "The whole time, at the academy, they've been finding ways to let me know I'm not who they were waiting for, and they pushed me off the truthspike with a broken impeller and I nearly died, and everybody looks at me like I'm letting them down, and that word 'coward'? That word is everywhere around me, and I can't stand it."

"I'm sorry I called you that." Elza reaches out and waits for Tina to nod, it's okay to touch her arm. "You made a choice to be nonviolent, and to hell with anyone who wants you to take it back. To hell with anyone who wants you to be someone else."

Tina reaches into her bag and pulls out the tiny yellow rock. "I wish I'd never seen this."

"I promise I won't throw it away, no matter how much I want to," Elza says in a low voice. "This is part of being in love. We help each other hold on to all the scary things we can't let go of."

Tina places the yellow rock in Elza's hand. "How do you keep saving me?"

Elza ends up back on the waterbed-couch, cuddling with Tina. She shivers in Elza's arms, like she's been lost for ages and she finally found her safe place.

Elza strokes Tina's dark purple hair with one hand, and with the other, she drops the mindstone into her deepest pocket.

# 25

.

## RACHAEL

Tina is waiting for Damini and Rachael at the edge of Gamertown, shouldering a bag with two of the full-body playsuits favored by serious players of *YayJump!*.

"There you are," Tina gasps. "I was starting to get worried. Rachael, put this on."

Rachael looks up at her best friend and feels like she can at least see past the cloud of anxiety that's been the entire contents of her brain lately.

She and Damini had to ditch their Joiners after the two of them almost went splat on the spongey pavement underneath all those layers of walkways and plazas. The whole Firmament is looking for her—literally, every Joiner in Wentrolo is telling its owner to keep an eye out for the two fugitives. They spent ages crouching inside a basket of Undhoran flap-hoppers, then they snuck across the service crawlspace under one of the main walkways, breathing fumes.

"I'm going to lay down a false trail," Damini says.

"Be careful," Rachael says.

"I'll see you soon." Damini cackles, then droops. "I wish Zaeta was here. She'll be so sad she missed this."

Now Rachael and Tina are alone, dressed in fuzzy kaiju costumes that are as hot as hell in the young sun.

"Are you thinking what I'm thinking?" Rachael mutters as they push through the crowd of gamers wearing holograph masks and way-too-complicated rigs.

"Pretty sure that's a yes," Tina grunts. "It's like the Lasagna Hats all over again. Except we're *both* wearing the plushie dinosaur costume—and it's green, instead of pink. And we're being chased by, basically, the same people we used to prank. We had to travel a few trillion miles to end up right back where we started."

"I can't process everything that's just happened. Like . . . Irriyaia! What the hell?"

Tina shakes her big dinosaur head. "The Irriyaians knew everyone here would be distracted right after NewSun. The same way Moxx knew we'd all be partied out and exhausted. It was the perfect moment for sneaky garbage."

"And meanwhile, I found out my best friend was keeping a huge secret from me."

Massive dino cringe.

"I'm sorry. I should know by now that bad things happen when I don't tell you everything. This won't happen again. Promise."

"Yeah. I'm going to hold you to that." Rachael tries to smile with body language. "And meanwhile? I had a huge apocalyptic fight with Yiwei, and I think we broke up?"

Aaaaaaaa. She almost forgot about the fight, she was too busy running for her life—but now it's playing in a loop, like the worst TikTok ever.

"You what?" Tina stops trudging and turns to face Rachael. "How? What? Why? Yiwei is totally crazy about you. He kept asking me for ideas for presents he could give you."

"He's a romantic. But . . . part of him being a romantic is, he builds people up in his mind, until they become perfect and flawless. Just like you-know-who." Rachael learned the hard way never to say the name "Captain Othaar" in front of Tina. "I couldn't live up to some ideal version of me, especially now. And when we were in the middle of talking about breaking up, Moxx showed up and I had to run for my life."

Oh, damn. Now *that* is sinking in.

Moxx's angry tusks. The army of goons.

She imagines them dragging her away and cutting her head open—as if that's what actually happened. They almost succeeded. They still could.

"They tried to . . ." Rachael's knees give out and she starts to fall forward, groping with her big lizard claws. The ground feels a long way away, until it's racing toward her. She can't breathe, can't see—this suit has gotten a hundred times stuffier. "They tried to. They wanted to. Oh, god, I can't." She's probably crying, she's too numb to tell. Dizzy, spinning.

Falling apart.

She sees it over and over: Moxx and the others prying her skull apart. Telling her it's for the best, putting her to sleep, maybe forever.

Tina's voice comes from a long way off: "Hey. Is it okay to touch you right now?"

Rachael turns to see a big fuzzy green lizard creature opening its claw-arms to her.

Instead of hitting the ground, she falls into Tina's strong embrace. So much stronger since Tina became a total alien.

"I got you," Tina says. "Let it out. I got you. You have so many friends, and I'm one of them, and so is Yiwei, and we got you. Nobody is going to do anything with your brain but admire how wonderful it is."

"They wanted to . . . to take me apart." She chokes on something: tears, or maybe bile. "They didn't see me as a person."

Tina enfolds Rachael in her big furry kaiju arms and says again, "You have so many friends."

Rachael gets her legs under her. She can breathe again, mostly.

The two of them tromp silently through Gamertown in their cheesy dragon costumes, like mascots for a sports team with an unbroken losing streak.

Yiwei hides at the edge of the Stroke, wearing a chunky helmet—because they're probably looking for Rachael's friends, too. (Luckily, Nyitha taught Rachael every trick for avoiding all the surveillance systems here in "paradise.")

"Um, hey," Yiwei says. "Wow, this has been the longest day, I can't . . ." Long, terrible silence. His shoulders pull forward. "I'm. I'm sorry. I don't know what to say."

Rachael can recognize a guilt freak-out when she sees one. He's probably lumping their fight and Moxx's assault together in his mind.

Her throat feels sticky-dry and she's having one of her shyness attacks, times a hundred. She just nods her big dinosaur head at him.

The spicy smoke from the roasted protein blobs is getting inside Rachael's costume and she feels light-headed. She's worried she's going to get one of *those* headaches, and the Vayt will start yelling, and she honestly cannot handle that right now.

"Can't believe Elza is gone, and I didn't get to say goodbye," Yiwei says to Tina.

"She's on a starship that flies like a dream, and she's totally safe." Tina's voice is muffled by the fuzzy lizard costume and the ruckus of the open-air market.

"We better get off the street and out of these costumes," says Yiwei.

"Yes, please," Rachael says between coughs.

The three of them hustle inside a nearby doorway, which leads to a dark passageway lined with dirty pipes and sputtering old machines.

Waiting near the entrance is Kez (*he/him*), wearing a stained-glass mask. Kez says all the same things everybody has been saying to Rachael today, like "thank goodness you're safe" and "those bastards, I can't believe." Rachael tries to make the right noises back.

"Got a surprise for you. Someone else wanted to say hi." Kez ushers them inside a tiny room.

Inside, Yatto the Monntha is sitting on a fainting couch, drinking snah-snah juice.

"Indelible friendships and short absences." Yatto stands up slowly, creakily, and opens their arms.

Rachael rushes over and hugs them. Snah-snah juice gets all over her lizard costume and she doesn't even care.

# 26
.

"Epic parties and no drama, I'm not sorry I made up my own Royal Fleet blessing, I missed you so much," Rachael blurts. "Nothing is the same without you."

"I heard what they tried to do to you." Yatto embraces Rachael back, just enough to make her feel snug. "I'm disgusted, but I wish I was surprised. This is not what the Royal Fleet is supposed to be about."

Rachael wriggles out of her green playsuit. "I know, right? I'm glad you're okay. Are you recovered? Where have you been?"

"I took a leave of absence from the Royal Fleet," Yatto says. "I needed to take some time to recover from my injuries, but also to clear my mind after . . . everything. I was about ready to go back to work. Then I saw what they were doing with my image back home—and my mind was less clear than ever."

Yatto needs to sit down again. Rachael helps them onto the fainting couch and scrunches next to them, while everyone else grabs little stools.

"I'm sorry about Irriyaia," Rachael says. "You told me all these cool things about your home, and now . . . this blows chunks."

"There is no way to enumerate the number of chunks that it blows." Yatto hangs their head. "I can't bear this. I was so eager to help my people, I let myself be turned into something hateful."

"It's not your fault," Rachael protests. "You were a kid. None of this is on you."

"They didn't give you any choice," Yiwei says.

"And they told you that you were saving the Monntha nation from disgrace, which is a huge guilt trip," says Tina.

"I know." Yatto's head is almost between their knees now, crash position. "Still . . . I must take responsibility for the way my image has been used for evil."

"Give it a rest, mate," Kez says. "You are most definitely not responsible for the way those creeps are using your old movies."

"There's something rotten about Irriyaia. We claim to believe in the teachings of Mantho the Null, but when you scratch the surface, we're abusers. I saw how the other Monnthas were treated after we became refugees, and then whenever I fought the Compassion, there were always Irriyaians fighting on their side. I'm just . . . ashamed of my people."

"That's good," Kez says.

Yatto looks up, startled. "Why is it good?"

"What your people did was shameful. Being ashamed is the first step toward finding a way to make things right."

"How many more steps are there after that?" Yatto cocks their head.

"Many. So many." Kez shakes his head.

"When did you all become so wise?" Yatto looks at all of their friends.

"We had a really good teacher," Rachael says.

"I suppose I have to go home at last." Yatto rolls their shoulder-spikes.

"I'll be there too," Kez says. "I just got notified." He pokes at his Joiner, and shows off an official notice from the Diplomatic Service: Kez has gotten an early promotion to junior ambassador. "It means I'm much closer to going home to Earth, with a fancy ship and credentials. But it also means . . . I have to help with the negotiations between the Firmament and the Compassion over the handover of Irriyaia."

Kez smiles, but it's kind of lopsided.


A while later, they've finished catching up Yatto on everything that's happened, and now Kez is telling them about his maybe-sort-of-boyfriend, Ganno the Wurthhi.

"We only went out a few times, and then he had to go back home," Kez says. "Maybe I'll see him there, but it's a big planet and he's probably got a lot on his mind now. It was really nice to be with a cute boy, who somewhat improbably thought I was beautiful. We didn't put a label on it, and I know Irriyaians don't do romance."

Yatto frowns. "That last word you said, the EverySpeak couldn't make sense of it."

"Exactly." Kez kneads the back of his neck with one hand. "Sometimes I think the EverySpeak is a mixed blessing. It lets me have my correct pronoun, no matter how often I change it. Which makes me feel alive and real—and understood, in a way I never imagined I could. But then I get used to thinking everyone is speaking English, and it trips me up at the worst moment. I don't want to fall for someone who doesn't have the concept of love."

"We have love on Irriyaia," Yatto says. "We love our friends, our families. But it's complicated."

The whole time Kez is processing about his relationship, Rachael watches

Yiwei. He's staring out the window, keeping watch. The obnoxiously fresh sunlight dapples onto his face and he looks like a goddamn dream.

Part of her is still relieved about their breakup. But then the ache comes, and it's like grief and longing and depression are all ganging up.

Rachael and Yiwei are still in the middle of the conversation that was interrupted when Moxx came to seize her brain, and she feels as if she's holding her breath.

"When an Irriyaian wants to have children, they have to return home to their birthplace and go to a special crèche with several others," Yatto says. "But we can have close relationships outside of all that, especially when we leave Irriyaia, and those relationships can include physical, er . . . intimacy." Yatto squirms a little.

"Whatever," Kez says. "It's fine, I guess. Ganno and I danced and kissed and it was fun, and I like fun. I wasn't looking for a serious thing anyway." Kez turns and makes eye contact with Tina.

"Why are you looking at me?" Tina sputters. "I don't know anything about anything."

"This is the part where you tell me relationships between humans and aliens are complicated but can be super rewarding," Kez says.

"Um, sure." Tina fidgets. "Let's pretend I said that."

"I had the worst luck with boyfriends back on Earth," Kez says. "A string of entitled prats, including the son of one of my father's mates. They were really hoping Niall and I would wind up together, like some sort of power couple. It was a nightmare."

A noise comes from the hallway outside—like a footstep. Or something falling on the ground.

Everybody stops talking and holds completely still.

Whispering voices come from outside their tiny hiding spot.

Rachael's neck prickles. They've found her. They've—

Damini opens the door, with Zaeta next to her. "There you are. Zaeta helped me lay down a false trail. It was like a fun game, I think we might have gone a little overboard, and—" Then she sees who's next to Rachael on the sofa. "Yatto the Monntha oh my goodness, wild hopes and tame fears, it's really you! I can't even, it's been so long, this is my friend Zaeta, I've told her all about you, I missed you so much, and I can't even. I really can't even!"

Yatto salutes Damini, and now everybody is chattering at once and Rachael feels herself letting go of a tiny bit of her mountain of yuck. She looks at her whole family gathered around her—if only Elza was here, it would be perfect.

Then Rachael catches sight of Zaeta, who's got anxiety written in every one of her ninety-nine eyes, like maybe she's intruding. Rachael whispers to her, "I'm glad you're here."

"I'm glad everyone is here—well, almost everyone, I miss Elza already—because Zaeta and I were talking some more about those Vayt carvings we found," Damini says.

"The ones you showed me at the NewSun party," Rachael says.

"Right. I went looking for that double-hexagon symbol that Elza found in Marrant's room," Damini says. "And here it is, right next to a stellar notation, like what was on the Talgan stone. But . . ."

Yatto whistles, louder than any human could. ". . . but that's not any type of star I've ever seen."

"Ex*act*ly," Damini beams.

"Misconception! It's not a type of star." Zaeta bounces.

"It's something that happens to a star," Damini says.

"And we think it's a clue to the Bereavement," Zaeta says. "And tell them! The scary part!"

"The scary part is, I think I've found one. A star this is happening to. It's called Haranmia—a red giant that's getting cold before its time."

Yatto is back to looking tragic. "I know about Haranmia. We've known for a while. There are a few others. The Royal Fleet kept wanting to send a ship to investigate . . ."

". . . but we were at war," Tina says.

"Yes," Yatto says. "We were so busy fighting, we had no time for any of the things we were fighting for."

"So you think we should look into it?" Yiwei says.

"You'd need one of the newest and most advanced knifeships or daggerships to get past these spatial disruptions," Yatto says.

"Which means . . . the Royal Fleet." Yiwei makes a face.

"It does, yes. I'm mad at them too, but I think we can make this work." Damini glances at Rachael.

Rachael gets a knot inside. Not just a regular sailor knot, but one of those fancy Celtic knots that wraps all around her rib cage, with fringes that stick in her throat. A super-pretty tangle of horrible feelings. She looks up and makes eye contact with Tina, and she feels slightly better.

Zaeta pipes up. "I talked to a friend of mine in the Royal Fleet, and she's been posted on a research vessel that's heading in that direction already. They might even be looking for cadets to join the crew, now that every Irriyaian has been required to leave the Royal Fleet or forsake Irriyaian citizenship."

Yatto groans.

"And we're the only ones who have practical experience with Vayt artifacts," Damini says.

"No way," Yiwei says. "Not an option. Even if I wanted to trust them again, my whole left sleeve is covered with red, remember?"

"I haven't seen my uniform since they tried to experiment on Rachael," Tina says. "I don't know how many demerits I got for helping her escape."

"We can at least try." Damini's usual squee gets a tinge of heartbreak. "I want to go back to the way it was. We can be on a ship together, journeying into the unknown. It'll be epic. Come on."

For a moment, Rachael can imagine it: all of them together again, on a ship, hunting for the truth. Everything could be simple again—Rachael could turn her curse into something good, she could be the savior everyone keeps telling her she is.

Except . . . the fancy Celtic knot tightens, cuts off her circulation, when she even contemplates going anywhere near a Royal Fleet ship. They'll just try to repo her brain again.

"I can't," Rachael says aloud. "You know I can't. Nyitha is leaving town soon. Maybe I should go with her."

"Good idea. I'll go with you," says Yiwei.

She looks at her maybe-ex-boyfriend.

"Are you sure?" She stares at him, trying to put a lot into those three words.

"Yeah." Yiwei only cringes a little.

"Well," Zaeta says to Damini, "I'm going along with you, if they even let us do this."

That leaves Tina.

"Please?" Damini says. "I think you should get back out there. It would be good for you."

"I . . . don't know." Tina sighs.

"Please," Damini says to Tina again. "Please please please be on my team. I can't face this without you, especially since the others are all gone. I need Space Wikipedia by my side. I need your clever brain and your sense of outrage and your talent for making the right screwups. We'll only be using the Royal Fleet to get what we need."

Tina looks at Damini, then back at Rachael, then at a spot on the wall between the two of them. "I need to think for a minute."

# 27
.

Nyitha bustles around the big cozy room with the velvet walls and over-stuffed cushions—making the last adjustments to turn her artist salon into a spaceship. She opens a hidden hatch, revealing a hallway that leads to the crew quarters and the engines, painted with a mural of people holding up holographic "signs" that say EVERYBODY GETS A CHANCE THIS TIME, and YOU DON'T EVEN KNOW WHY WE'RE MAD.

"Ship's not done," Nyitha says. "The outside was supposed to look like a Makvarian ice-desert goblin, but I didn't finish, so it still looks like a shed. I was going to launch it empty, to drift among the stars forever. Never thought I'd travel again, but life has a way of surprising you."

"So what's it called?" Rachael asks.

"I keep changing my mind," Nyitha snorts. "For a while, it was the *Irreconcilable Differences*. But that was too dark, even for me."

"The *Cruel Inspiration*?" Rachael offers.

"You don't get to name a ship until you've spent time on it, lived on it, maybe almost died a few times." Nyitha adjusts something, and the whole structure starts to throb and hum. "We leave in one cycle, ship's time. Anyone who doesn't want to come needs to be somewhere else."

"What's the destination?" asks Tina.

Rachael hates being put on the spot, but this time it feels like a gift: a chance to turn this situation around—from "running away from scary bad guys" to "going on an epic quest."

"We're going someplace where I can figure this out, once and for all." Her tiny voice carries, thanks to some primo acoustics. "I'm going to get my art chops back, whatever it takes—even if we have to slow dance with the Hosts of Misadventure."

As soon as she says these words, Rachael worries she just overstepped, because this isn't her ship. But she turns toward Nyitha, and her teacher gives her a little nod.

---

Tina's still checking over every inch of the ship to make sure it doesn't fall apart the moment they leave the Glorious Nebula. "Nyitha and her friends did a good job. But I should definitely come along in case. Especially if there's going to be Hosts-of-Misadventure shenanigans."

"Yiwei will be here, though."

Tina sighs and climbs on top of a big crate of Scanthian parsnips in one corner of the cargo hold. "Well, I can't stick around, if everybody else is leaving town. And also . . . If I do get on a Royal Fleet ship again, as a cadet or whatever, I'm worried I'll . . ."

Rachael climbs up on the crate. Her legs barely reach halfway to the floor, while Tina's feet are planted.

"You're worried you'll relapse or something," Rachael says. "That you'll break your vow of nonviolence, or that you'll start trying to be *her* again."

Amazing how many conversations you can have about Captain Argentian without once mentioning her name.

"Notice anything different about me?" Tina asks.

Rachael squints. "You're . . . purple. But you've been purple for ages."

Tina wears the same expression as when her rescue beacon lit up. "I feel okay. Better than in a long time. It's like I had a splinter all the way under my skin, and Elza plucked it out."

"She took that cruddy rock off your hands?"

Tina nods.

"Listen, Captain Argentian is always gonna be part of you," Rachael says. "You need to figure out what to do with that. And . . . I think you'd be bored out of your mind on this art-ship."

"I can be artistic!" Tina puts on a mock-offended face.

"Also . . . if you want to help me, the best thing you can do is find out why the Vayt built that weapon, and why it messed with my artist brain in the first place. Even if I manage to start making art again, I still need to make sense of all these bad dreams, before it's too late."

"If you could draw," Tina says slowly, "you could at least draw pictures of what you see in your dreams. And maybe that would help."

"Maybe, yeah. So let's divide this up: you follow up this clue to the Vayt, I try to reboot my art-brain."

"Just promise me something," Tina says. "I know you, and I know that once you've gotten away from here and you're safe, all of this badness will really sink in. That's how you get through things: you're a slow cooker, whereas I'm . . . a microwave? Just give yourself space to process the bad feelings."

"I promise," Rachael says. "I'm definitely about to have lots of space."

"Good," Tina says. "That reminds me, I tried to explain how we microwave food on Earth to some Undhorans, and they thought I was kidding."

Yiwei steps onto the unnamed art-ship, carrying his lute and three other guitar-like instruments.

"Hey," he says with a half-smile that is somehow sadder than any crying jag. They still haven't talked alone since their big fight.

Xiaohou trills a little permission-to-come-aboard melody from his perch on Yiwei's shoulder.

"Rachael was telling me I ought to try and go with Damini on her mission to Haranmia—assuming we're even allowed to do that," Tina says.

"I think you should, too," Yiwei says. "I'm a little worried about Damini. The whole time we've known her, she's been scared that people will abandon her, the way everyone did back home. And now she's got Zaeta, and they're literally inseparable."

"You think Zaeta is bad for her?" Rachael cocks her head.

"I think we don't know that much about Zaeta's people, and this vunci thing they do sounds intense. Even Space Wikipedia doesn't know anything." Yiwei glances at Tina, who nods. "Damini needs someone from home, to watch her back and make sure she doesn't get hurt."

"Look at you, paying attention and taking care of people," Tina says.

"It's a habit." He half-grins, half-cringes.

Tina holds out her hands and Rachael takes them. "I'm going to miss you so much, and I'll be so mad if we don't see each other again soon."

Turns out Rachael's heart has more surplus capacity than she realized. She hasn't run out of tears, either.

"Don't worry about us," Yiwei says. "I'm looking forward to keeping this ship in one piece."

"We're leaving soon," Nyitha yells from the other room. "If you're not coming along, you need to get off my ship."

"One more thing." Tina digs in her satchel and pulls out a necklace with a tiny red stone, like a ruby, set inside a thicket of golden branches. She pulls the necklace, and it breaks into two halves.

"Wow," Rachael says. "That's lovely."

"This was in a tiny box of Captain Argentian's things," Tina hands half the necklace to Rachael. "Each of these halves contains a tiny particle, and they're quantum entangled."

"Quantum entangled." Rachael struggles to remember her dad's homeschooling physics lessons. "That means no matter how far apart they are, whatever happens to one particle affects the other."

"They're linked," Tina says. "Across any distance. Millions of light-years away, one gemstone will still speak to the other. So if you find yourself in a bad situation, break the seal on this one, and I'll come find you, wherever you are."

The two best friends clutch each other tight one last time, whispering promises and secrets in each other's ears. Even with everything that's been turned upside down and sideways and backwards, some things don't change.

Yiwei is sitting on one side of a strange W-shaped couch, inside a nook that has a little table and a curtain, so you can drink sophisticated cocktails and light candles in privacy. He's staring at the scuffed tile floor.

Rachael comes and sits on the other side of the W. The hump between them feels symbolic.

"I hope we can actually trust Nyitha," Yiwei says. "We're flying to nowhere with a woman who was living in a garbage chute."

"She's hiding something for sure," Rachael says. "But I trust her, as much as I trust anybody right now."

*Ouch.* That was the wrong thing to say. Yiwei moves closer to the \ of the W.

"Thank you for coming on this trip," Rachael says. "Even though we left things in a weird place."

"I meant what I said. About being your friend."

"Yeah."

How can she be glad that she and Yiwei are going to be friends—but also feel desperate to make out with him now now now? Ugh, if she could sketch something, maybe she'd be able to feel one way.

"I better double-check that our long-range scans are working." Yiwei slides off the sofa and gets to his feet. "It sucks to be the last one to know when there's a problem."

Rachael watches him walk away. She can't believe how much she's let go of, in the day since the sun went out.

"Everybody listen up," Nyitha shouts from the big armchair in the artist salon with the blue-velvet walls (which Rachael realizes is actually the flight lounge). "I promised Rachael I would help her or die trying, and now we're at the 'die trying' part—if you want to leave, I won't blame you."

"Count me in." Samnan the crystal shifts from "frozen pine needle" to "big blob of rock candy." "It's time I stopped pining for someone who doesn't know I'm here. There are plenty of other sentient clouds around."

"I'm coming too." Cinnki's ears stand straight up. "I was getting sick of this town."

"I'm in," adds Kfok the Kraelyor.

"Not me," says Wendas, the Scanthian. "Wish you all the luck, but I'm out of here."

So now there are six of them.

"Okay, then." Nyitha whoops. "Hold on to yourselves, because this could be a bumpy takeoff. Did I mention this ship wasn't supposed to have passengers?" She guffaws and waves her left thumb, and the flight lounge lurches over on one side, leaving Rachael with a fresh bruise.

# 28
.

Rachael is in hell. What was she thinking? She's stuck on a ship full of art-ists, all making art and geeking out about technique. She sits, hiding her useless hands under her own legs.

This ship is much smaller than the *Indomitable*. Rachael finds herself wandering the same three walkways over and over, cussing whenever brand-new murals and freaky art installations appear on the walls and the floors.

Yiwei made a guitar, using "wood" from the great sideways bulbosity that grows out of the side of the third-lowest level of the Stroke back in Wentrolo. He carefully sliced off one big fleshy growth from the bulb, then carved the proper shapes, planing and staining, hours and hours of work to get exactly the right texture and resonance. Yiwei nicknamed his new gui-tar 9m88, after his favorite Mandopop singer—it doesn't look exactly like an Earth guitar (the neck is twisted, and the body is a little more viola-y). But it sounds incredible.

His new band is called Not on My Trash Pile. He's roped in Cinnki, the Javarah who makes forbidden portraits, and Samnan, the crystal who's still getting over being in love with a cloud. Cinnki has a legit singing voice and moves through space with a lazy urgency and a snarling fox-face—like he's laying claim to all of the air and most of the light. Xiaohou provides some tight-as-hell beats.

Not on My Trash Pile's sound is a hybrid of pop, ska, CrudePink, and Ja-varah screech-break. They've written two and a half songs so far, and one of them is really good: "I Love Everything You Didn't Do." It's sad but bouncy, with startling chord changes over a jagged-glass bass line.

Rachael sits on the floor and listens to them rehearse, leaning against a metal wall covered with some special paint (that warms up in the presence of music). She cheers when she's supposed to, and claps along, even singing background vocals once or twice.

When pretending to be happy for Yiwei gets to be too much work, Ra-chael gets to her feet and walks away.

She walks the length of the ring around the ship's engines, until she runs into Kfok, who's sitting on her sluggy bottom, making political art out of living glass. "It's tricky. If you want to use living glass as a medium, you have to make sure it agrees with what you're trying to say," Kfok says.

"Uh-huh," Rachael says.

Kfok coaxes the glass out of a container that looks like an urn, using two out of her three arms. Instead of hands, her arms end in barbs that look like wasp stingers, and Rachael's fascinated by the amount of control she has with them. She carefully shapes it into the phrase: "Eat your own faces, Symmetrons."

"Nothing personal," Kfok smiles with her left mouth.

"It's all good." Rachael is too busy trying to see how this works.

"You nudge it into the form you want it to take," Kfok says. "I know you can't make your own art, but maybe you can help me. You could hold the container steady while I pull the living glass out."

Ugh. The gross feeling is back.

"I'm not here to be anyone's assistant," she mumbles.

"Of course not," Kfok says. "I just thought you might find it interesting."

Rachael's face is hot and her breath is constricted by the tightness in her chest. She feels an urge to kick the urn full of living glass over, or shatter Kfok's artwork. She backs away instead. "I gotta go."


Nyitha reclines on one of the couches built into the wall of the flight lounge, steering the ship by sticking one hand into a cloud near her face.

Rachael pauses in the doorway, taking in the wood panels and smoked-glass ceiling. Sometimes it's hard to believe they're in deep space.

"Hey," Nyitha grunts, without moving from her comfy spot.

Rachael immediately falls back into suggesting names for this starship, even though she knows it annoys Nyitha. "How about the *Training Bra Disaster*? Or the *Star-Touched Know-It-All*? The *Wrong Mistake*? The *Never-Ending Drinking Game*?"

Nyitha ignores Rachael's suggestions, like always. Instead, she stares through heavy-lidded eyes. "Y'know, I know what it's like to have monsters in your head and be unable to create a damn thing. I was blocked for a long time."

Rachael lowers herself into one of the couches. "Is that when you stopped making those beautiful boxes, and started doing stinky graffiti instead?"

Nyitha clicks her tongue and teeth. "That's right. As soon as I stopped trying to do the same art I used to, I became excited again. I felt as though I couldn't stop creating if I wanted to. That's the main lesson I learned: any art you can make in the face of unbearable sorrow is good art."

"You didn't need to destroy all those boxes, though."

"I did. I needed a fresh start. I still wish I could destroy the one that you have."

"That's not happening." Rachael clutches her bag, containing the red box and some other junk, closer to her chest. "But since we're talking about it, I keep wondering . . . who's the dead body?"

"What dead body?"

Rachael almost shows Nyitha the box, then she remembers that Nyitha literally just said she wants to destroy it. "There's a dead body. Two people standing over it. Who died?"

"It's a story. It means whatever you decide it means."

"Fine, don't answer." Rachael can't keep from rolling her eyes.

Nyitha changes the subject. "I've thought of something else you might try." She waves a finger and a picture appears: jagged rocks against a velvety blackness. "We're about to fly past this asteroid belt, and I thought perhaps you could smash some of these rocks."

"I could do what now?"

"Smash them. This ship doesn't have weaponry, but we can use our ion harness to move some of the rocks onto a collision course."

Rachael stares at the gently spinning crags. "And that would help me how?"

"This is one way to make art," Nyitha says patiently.

That ugly feeling is back—like when Rachael wanted to break Kfok's living glass into twitching shards.

Nyitha sees the look on Rachael's face and adds: "You don't have to if you don't want to. But I bet it would look beautiful. You'd be leaving your mark on the cosmos, forever."

That sounds fun and possibly cathartic, but Rachael still hesitates. "Asteroids collide all the time. People will think it was an accident."

"Who cares what people will think? We'll know better."

"But how is it art, if people don't know it's art?"

"Ugh. Riddles." Nyitha groans.

Using her hands for destruction instead of creation feels like giving up, on some level. But what the hell.

Rachael slides her hands into the holographic jelly—and then she's cracking a whip in space. Her first cast bounces off the big baked-potato-shaped rock, but the second time she catches it in the side, and flings it against two of its neighbors. One of the smaller planetoids breaks apart and glitter flies everywhere: diamonds, maybe, or silica.

A 24-karat ribbon flows through the cluster of rocks, catching the starlight like a chandelier. Rachael feels the tightness in her chest loosen a bit. She can't take her eyes off the sparkle cloud.

*Any art you can make in the face of unbearable sorrow is good art.*

"Thanks," Rachael whispers. "That helped. A little."

"But it's not what you really want to be doing. I know." Nyitha sighs. "So tell me: Are you really willing to risk anything to draw pretty pictures again?"

"You know I am. I've said so a hundred times." Itchy itchy scalp.

"Then I think I know where we need to go."

Nyitha wiggles her hand. A picture pops up of a handmade wooden basket silhouetted against something that's so dark, with such a bright outline, Rachael wants to cover her eyes.

"This is an artist retreat called the Cradle," Nyitha says. "It's in a very delicate orbit around a black hole that's turning into a white hole."

"What? They do that?"

"I guess they don't teach physics on Smudge. Yes, black holes turn into white holes sometimes. When a black hole evaporates, it gives off a kind of black-body radiation."

Rachael thinks back to her dad's physics lessons. ". . . Hawking radiation?"

"I don't know that name. But sure. If it gives up enough of that radiation, it turns into a white hole instead of disappearing. It stops sucking everything in, and starts spitting everything out. That moment, when the hole changes color by eating itself, only lasts a short time. But during that moment, all sorts of impossible things become possible."

"Things like . . . helping me get my artist brain back."

"It's worth a try, anyway. They do this one kind of therapy where you drink something and go inside a ring of thorns, and then you don't exist for a moment. It's supposed to be really good for your skin."

The whole thing sounds like a nightmare. The black-and-white hole, the ring of thorns, the not existing anymore.

Rachael wants to say no thanks—let's try foot-painting again, instead.

But she's messing up everything in her life, including her relationship, and that's not going to change unless she can make art again.

So she looks away from the scary basket and says, "Let's do it."

"Great." Nyitha fiddles with the cloud, and then they're on course. "We'll have to be careful parking that close to a black hole in flux, of course. It took me a long time to steal all the parts for this ship, and I'd hate for anything to happen to the *Training Bra Disaster*." ʼ

Rachael starts to thank Nyitha, and then she realizes. "Did you . . . did you just let me name the ship?"

"I don't know. I'm trying out the name for now. I don't know what a training bra is, exactly—is it like a flight simulator?"

Rachael puts on a scary mean voice. "This is Alternate Captain Rachael Townsend with the *Training Bra Disaster*. Surrender at once, or we will be forced to open fire with our dwarf-star ballistic missiles and elastic straps."

"I've changed my mind. We're not doing that name."

"Oh, come onnnn. I promise I won't do the 'officer' voice anymore. Come on come on come on come on please please please."

"If you get out of my flight lounge right now, I'll consider trying the name for a little longer."

Rachael gets out of there at record speed. But she pauses on her way out to look at the basket orbiting the black-and-white hole, and feels a chill along the arch of her lower rib cage. She's going to go inside a ring of thorns and cease to exist.

# 29
.

There's a tiny crawl space at the very top of the *Training Bra Disaster,* right where the bluehouse was on the *Indomitable.* You can perch up there, on the creaky wooden boards, and look out into space.

Rachael and Yiwei sit side by side, watching the stars turn into blue knives.

She breaks the silence. "How are you holding up?"

Yiwei turns and stares at her. "What? How am *I* holding up? You're the one who—"

"Yep, I'm the one who lost my main thing, and got stuck with alien monster dreams, and almost got brain-napped. Those things certainly happened." Rachael clicks her tongue. "But you're the one who had this whole plan of following in Captain Othaar's footsteps and watched it go up in smoke when you got an armful of red marks. We *both* had our dreams crushed. So . . . how are you holding up?"

Face-droop. "I'm . . . I'm not great. The good thing about a long space voyage is, there's plenty of time to think. Which is also the bad thing about a long space voyage." He whistles. "I kept thinking my grandma would have been proud of me going to the academy. She always thought I was wasting my life, screwing around with music instead of focusing on robotics. She always wanted me to find the one thing that would give my life meaning."

Yiwei's father died when he was a baby, so his grandmother raised him with help from his mom and his aunt.

"Maybe some people aren't meant to just have one thing," Rachael says.

So many stars streak past, blue needles against the darkness.

"Maybe," Yiwei says. "That's what I loved about Captain Othaar, though. He saw something in me that nobody ever saw before."

"He showed you how to use all the parts of yourself, everything you loved, to do something cool."

"Yeah."

Somehow talking to Yiwei is so much easier, now that they've broken up—even though Rachael still wants to kiss his perfect face.

Instead, she stares at each slash of light. "You can still use everything

Captain Othaar taught you. You can honor his memory without being in the Royal Fleet."

Rachael tells Yiwei about how she threw a rock at some other rocks, and it *kindasorta* made her feel better? It definitely looked cool.

"You've never stopped being creative," Yiwei says. "Long before you let me see any of your art, I knew you had this powerful imagination. That's how you brought all of us together. And the one good thing my ex, Jiasong, taught me is, you can turn your life into a work of art, if you live with enough passion."

"Even if you're a shy weirdo who just wants to be left alone?"

"Especially then." Yiwei's mouth quirks up on one corner.

Rachael's kiss-craving gets obnoxious, so she scoots a few inches away from him and changes the subject.

"Nyitha is definitely hiding something. She acted weird when I asked her about this." She shows Yiwei the scene where the two figures are standing over a body.

Yiwei takes the box and nudges it forward slightly. The two figures move around the body, arranging items and adjusting something along one wall.

"It looks like they're trying to make it look like that person's death was . . . an accident." Yiwei raises an eyebrow. "Maybe that's the real reason the queen gave you this box? So you'd find out whatever Nyitha's hiding?"

"I think since we're stuck on this ship for ages, we should poke around and see what we can find." Rachael lifts the box out of his hands and moves the knobs. The two figures step backward as paper flames engulf the prone body from a vent they've rigged to malfunction.


—screaming alone sweating clawing at her bedding—thick layer of salt all over her face, getting in and out of her eyes, hands nothing but nail and tendon—

Rachael sits on the edge of her bed and wheezes.

There's a tapping at her door.

"Are you okay in there?" Yiwei asks.

Rachael opens the door, because she's not up for raising her voice to be heard through it.

"Another nightmare," she says.

"The Vayt again?"

Rachael nods.

"Getting worse. Maybe because I'm in space again. But also I think that whatever they're scared of is getting closer."

Her head is throbbing again. She can't shake the queasy.

"I need a distraction," she says.

"Then you're in luck, because I found something."

Yiwei leads her down the narrow hallway with all the tiny bedrooms, and then up a ramp past the flight lounge and the engines. They reach a dead end—weird to think the other side of this paint-spattered wall is deathly cold nothing—with an alcove to her left.

"I kept thinking, why is there an open space on one side, but not the other?" Yiwei gestures at the blank space to his right.

"So . . . a secret compartment?" Rachael rubs her eyes—nightmare still fading—and stares. She reaches out and raps on the wall with the knuckles of her right hand, making a hollow sound.

Yiwei makes a gesture, and Xiaohou scurries up and plays a recording of Nyitha saying, "Open up, it's me."

The wall quivers for a moment, then slides open. Inside is a pile of old junk, including an old cloudstrike gun, and a case made of translucent crystal, containing all the tools you'd need to make one of those red boxes. Underneath everything else is a flag with a weird symbol on it: a stringy creature with a bunch of mouths all over its tangled body.

This emblem looks super familiar, but Rachael can't place it for a minute.

Until . . . she pulls the red box out of her satchel, and dials forward until she reaches the funeral scene. That same symbol hangs on the wall inside the box.

"Huh." Yiwei frowns. "So the person who faked their own death . . ."

". . . was Nyitha." Rachael shakes her head. "This whole box is Nyitha's life story."

I hope you get this. I can't write to Rachael, because she and Yiwei left their Joiners behind when they skipped town—but I hope the Ardenii can deliver this message to you.

For a couple days after you left, I kept digging my hand into my standard-issue cadet bag, expecting to find that rock nestled in there, and thanked the freaking stars when I realized it was gone. It's just sinking in: I had a barbed-wire-lined cage around my heart, and you picked the lock.

Damini and I were scared to go back to the academy, like maybe we would be arrested for helping Rachael get away. But we looked at our uniforms, back at the dorm, and our sleeves didn't have any new demerits. We finally decided to show up and face this together. We weren't the ones who needed to be ashamed of our actions.

But we went back to campus and . . . nothing? As if everyone decided to pretend this never happened. Still, it's probably a good thing we really don't know where Rachael went.

We ended up at the Slanted Prism, drinking snah-snah juice and missing you and Kez and Rachael and Yiwei. And I kept thinking about how I'd feel if they were experimenting on Rachael right now. She followed me into space, and I spent hours telling her how righteous the Royal Fleet was.

I could tell Damini was marinating in sadness, because she hates it when her friends go away. I tried to say something to comfort her, and she was like, "It's fine. You're here. Zaeta's still around. I'm not alone." As if that meant she wasn't allowed to feel sad.

I kept talking to her about your cool princess starship full of dirty poetry, and Rachael and Yiwei's flying art studio, and the golden threads of Kez's ambassador uniform, trying to keep all of you present. Until Damini stared at me like, *enough.*

Then Damini said, "I sent all my findings to Explorer Instructor Wyahaar, and now the Royal Fleet is sending a ship to Haranmia to investigate, and the best part? They're definitely looking for cadets to join the crew as trainees."

The ship is called the *Undisputed*—it's brand-new, and because this mission is a peaceful science-and-humanitarianism sandwich, there are minimal weapons. They're barely packing a sharpened toothpick.

"It's a pure mission of exploration and helping people and they're going to fly through a permanent rainbow the size of a whole solar system and there's no way I'm going into space without you. Will you sign up with me? Please please please say yes."

I pretended to think it over for a moment. But I already knew I was in.

I hope the Ardenii are looking after you, and they're not letting you get into the wrong kind of trouble. Just remember, wherever you go, whoever you piss off for great justice, I'm there by your side.

# 30

.

## ELZA

*Knowledge is ugly.*

Elza tries endlessly to make sense of those words, now that she's got time to think, on board the *Invention of Innocence*. She's spent her whole life facing hideous truths—from the moment her parents caught her sneaking out with a bag full of makeup and clothes, on her way to a travesti party, to her close encounter with Marrant at the palace. Elza has always held on to her faith that if she could only see the larger pattern, all of this pain would add up to beauty.

That's what Rachael was trying to do, right? Turn pain into beauty. And that got taken away from her, and somehow everyone expected more of Rachael afterward, not less.

Back on Earth, Elza wanted to believe that nothing was mystical, if you just analyzed it properly. And then she would go to the terreiro, where she'd breathe in the scents of flowers and palm oil, and bask in the joy, the acceptance, from all those smiling faces as everyone danced and chanted. And she would think, *This joy is essential—maybe some things don't need to be explained, just understood.* Then a day or two later, she would feel like a skeptic again.

Now she sits in the beautiful crew lounge on the *Invention of Innocence* and thinks about those two notions: *knowledge is ugly* and *joy is essential.*

Feels like a contradiction, but maybe it doesn't have to be.


Maybe if Waiwaiwaiwai hadn't interrupted Elza in the middle of watching the story about Marrant's wife flirting with Captain Argentian, Elza could have learned something useful, for when they get to Irriyaia. But what if it's not too late? This ship feels like an extension of the palace, after all.

Elza finds a deserted walkway at the lowest level of the ship, near the engines, and addresses the wall. "Um, hi. I was wondering if I could see what happened next, with Aym and Thaoh? I would really appreciate it."

Nothing happens for a moment, then Elza notices her own shadow is gone.

This hallway gets darker and darker, until it's almost like NewSun Eve. Two figures slowly appear.

Aym and Thaoh are sitting together at a white table in the shape of a clover, wearing their acting junior officer uniforms.

"Okay, he's on his way," Aym says. "Just remember what we talked about."

Thaoh gazes up at the ceiling. "If you have to keep coaching me on what to say, maybe this isn't a good idea after all."

"Whatever, I'm just nervous." Aym looks up. "He's here."

Marrant comes rushing over. "There you both are. I went to the wrong lounge. This ship, I swear." He indicates the giant starship around them.

"Hey, no worries." Aym gestures at a chair next to her. "So listen, uh, Thaoh and I wanted to, umm . . . I mean . . ."

Thaoh speaks in a business-like tone. "Aym and I have been noticing that there's a connection between us that might go beyond friendship. Given that you're already in a relationship with Aym, it would be unethical to go any further without discussing this with you first. We would never do anything behind your back."

"Except," Marrant says, "it sounds like you already did."

"We came to you as soon as we knew anything," Thaoh says.

"This could be a good thing. The three of us could be a family," Aym says. "Like the guthdoriph, back home."

"Except that neither one of you is a thont, so it's not the same." Marrant sits rigidly upright, like he's at inspection rest. "It sounds as though the two of you already figured out everything without me."

"Don't be like that," Thaoh pleads. "Listen, I feel like the three of us are already a family, we just haven't made it official. We can be cool about this."

"So that's it." Marrant looks straight ahead, at the wall. "You just present me with an ultimatum."

"No," Aym says. "No, we're not—"

"This is what I get." Marrant stands up. "This is what I get for trying to be kind."

"Don't go," Thaoh pleads. "This is ridiculous. We're just trying—"

But he's already gone.

Aym slumps forward. "Tears of my ancestors. That went well."

The scene fades and Elza turns to leave—but another scene starts up right away.

Kankakn is still hanging out in her curtained-off space full of ornately embroidered cushions.

Marrant enters and sits on one of the cushions facing her. "Very well. I'm listening."

———

Elza and Princess Constellation dance wildly, without any steps—nothing but arms and legs swinging in ecstasy. The floor pulses with the vibrations of the ship's engines, while the Brazilian funk beats of "Dominatrix" by Karol Conká with Boss in Drama come from everywhere.

The music ends and Elza lets her momentum spin her into the wall—the layer of moss cushions her impact. She feels light-headed, but all of her senses are turned way up, so all the sweet smells and soft textures feel extra vivid.

The princess's receiving room on board the *Invention of Innocence* looks like the inside of a crumbling stone ruin, with purple-green moss spreading across the loose stones and cracked arches. A river runs diagonally across the curved ceiling, with little rocks and fishes and frog-like critters jumping in and out of the froth.

Princess Constellation hands Elza a tiny clot of moss. "Here, put this in your left shoe. Please keep it there for at least the next five cycles, ship's time."

Elza hesitates a moment, then puts the moss in her shoe. She's getting used to these weird demands. Sort of.

"There's a question I've been scared to ask. For . . . for weeks now." Elza speaks extra slow, like every word has sharp edges that could slice her tongue. "I'm not scared of the question, I'm scared of what the answer might be."

Princess Constellation doesn't say anything, she looks at Elza with her big bird/fish eyes, which are so much like Yatto's.

"Why did you choose me?" Elza blurts. "None of the other candidates have spent any time with a real princess, not even the ones who passed the final test. Are you just bored and looking for something to entertain you? Why would you pick me, out of everyone?"

She braces herself for the princess to give one of her nonsense answers.

"Perhaps I needed someone who always asks 'why,' instead of taking for granted that there is a good reason. Someone who wants to teach as well as learn. Perhaps I wanted a reminder that we ought to care about all the people whose plight we survey from a safe distance." Princess Constellation smiles, but her eyes stay serious. "Or perhaps? I saw that you alone had already guessed the true purpose behind all of your lessons in poise and etiquette."

True purpose? Elza reels for a moment. And then she gets it. She got it a while ago, and she couldn't put it into words until now.

"All those lessons in standing like statues, moving without a sound," Elza says. "They weren't about manners. We were being trained as spies. That's what princesses do: the queen needs to know things, so the princesses snoop around and find out."

Princess Constellation's smile gets wider.

"And that's what we're going to do when we get to Irriyaia, right?" Elza says. "We're going to spy on the Compassion. That's what I was asking for, I guess." The fear catches her off guard—these people already came so close to destroying her.

"We should include the others in this discussion." Princess Constellation waves a hand.

"Uh, what others?"

The door of the receiving room opens and three other kids enter: Robhhan, Wyndgonk . . . and Naahay.

"Your Radiance." Naahay does an elaborate curtsey that looks a little like the dance moves Elza was doing a moment ago. "You sent for us. I must confess to some confusion: I was informed that I had been disqualified from the princess selection program, and immediately afterward, I was offered a chance to volunteer for a special assignment on board this ship."

"The same thing happened to me. Your Radiance." Robhhan scoots closer to Naahay, as if he wants to buddy up to the person he thinks is the leader.

Elza stares at the river flowing over her head, and all the slimy monsters that live in it. This trip just got a lot less fun.

Princess Constellation gestures for Elza, Naahay, Robhhan, and Wyndgonk to sit on crumbling stone furniture. Wyndgonk carefully positions fireself on a big bench.

The four of them wait for Princess Constellation to say something. She stares into space—Elza's pretty sure she's communicating with the Ardenii.

At last, Naahay leans forward, grimacing with her bony plates. "Excuse me, Your Radiance. I understand we're going to Irriyaia. My family have been on the Privy Council for the past seven generations, and they're going to be very concerned about me flying into a delicate situation. I'm assuming we're on a diplomatic mission, but we haven't yet posted any diplomatic codes. I'd be happy to fix that for you. Do you want me to, uh . . . ?"

Naahay finally stops talking—because she was about to offer to take control of Princess Constellation's ship.

The princess stares at her and blinks, gently.

"The queen and I have both grown accustomed to the luxury of knowing the worst before anyone else," Princess Constellation says, still smiling. "Now there are worsts that we do not know: what the Compassion is planning, and what form the Bereavement takes. When the queen doesn't know something, it is the job of the princesses to find out."

Wyndgonk releases a tiny cloud of sweet-smelling smoke, and rolls fire neck. "'Luxury' was the correct word. Most of us have grown accustomed to unpleasant surprises."

"So . . . this isn't a diplomatic mission after all." Robhhan squirms.

Elza finally speaks up. "We need to sneak inside the Compassion's headquarters to figure out their next move. That must be why they recruited four ex-candidates, because if we get caught they can claim we were acting on our own."

Princess Constellation twitches a couple fingers—like she's hearing a pretty piece of music.

Naahay's actual skull turns pale. "We're going into the middle of a tense situation, and we're not showing up to calm it down, but to infiltrate and trespass. If we get caught—"

"One dislikes such crude words as 'spy,'" Princess Constellation says. "Curiosity is the gentlest of virtues." She waves her hand, dismissing the four of them. "We arrive at Irriyaia in two metacycles, ship's time, and we will form a strategy on the ground."

In the hallway, Naahay is still sputtering. "Some of us here are not expendable."

"Meaning some of us are?" Elza snaps.

"Naahay's right." Robhhan scoots so close to Naahay, they're almost touching. "This is unacceptable."

"Come on," Wyndgonk snorts. "The stench of privilege and complacency is about to ruin my appetite, and I heard the dining hall is serving Undhoran flap-hoppers."

Fire strides away from Robhhan and Naahay, and Elza rushes to catch up.

# 31
.

Undhoran flap-hoppers are morsels of deep-fried goodness—they remind
Elza of coxinha. Wyndgonk heaps fire lacquer bowl with a dozen of them,
and then finds a chair wide enough for fire insectoid body. Elza and Wyndgonk have the whole dining hall to themselves.

"I understand why those two were squawking," Wyndgonk mutters.
"They're scared. But if we all get caught, they'll be treated honorably, as
prisoners of war. I'll be herded into a cage and treated like a beast."

"I know," Elza whispers. She thinks of the Grattna and shudders from
the nape of her neck to the soles of her feet. "I'm sorry we're putting you in
that kind of danger. You shouldn't have to do this."

"I know." Wyndgonk's whole body cringes for a moment, beetle legs fold-
ing inward. Then fire snorts and eats three flap-hoppers in one bite. "But
you know what? I'm not complaining, unlike those two arkzahns, because
the Compassion has to be stopped before they take over more planets."

The two of them eat in silence. Elza thanks the Hosts of Misadventure
fire is here, because she could use a friend right now.

"On Thythuthy, we learn the hard way to turn a toxic situation to our
advantage."

"Toxic." Elza thinks back to when they first met. "You told me the Vayt
seeded poisonous clouds in the atmosphere of your planet."

"Yeah." Wyndgonk belches fragrant smoke. "We almost died out, but
over many generations, we learned how to grow food in those clouds, using
the poison as fertilizer. These flying creatures called Dnynths naturally
plant the seeds up there, and when they're not, uh, depositing the seeds,
they're trying to eat us. They're our main predator, but we'd starve without
them. Our whole system is about keeping that balance."

"So you can never be at the top of your own food chain." Elza reaches for
some fried Scanthian parsnips. "That would definitely give you a different
perspective. So does your fire-breath help you defend yourself against the,
uh . . ."

"The Dnynths? Nah. It merely looks cool. And maybe a little intimidating? But we invented special nonlethal weapons to fight off the Dnynths. My whole family are run-farmers: we run very fast and create a vortex to pull down the crops that are growing up there."

She's about to ask Wyndgonk another question. But Robhhan comes over, with little streaks on his neck.

"Hi," Robhhan says in a low voice. "I was hoping I could ask you something."

Elza feels her neck stiffen, remembering how Robhhan tried to cozy up to Naahay. But she keeps her face neutral. "Sure."

"I was wondering about Dr. Karrast. The ship's doctor on the *Indomitable*." Robhhan fidgets. "We never got the body back, and it was a whole political thing back home. We can only have a new child on Oonia Prime when someone is confirmed dead."

"Pretty sure she died." Elza inhales slow. "That ship exploded into a million tiny fragments."

"Yeah. That's why I have a baby sister now. But I . . . I wanted to ask you, did you spend any time with Dr. Karrast? Did people like her? What were her final metacycles like? Was she happy?"

Elza sighs. "Dr. Karrast was kind and generous, and she gave her life to save other people. You should learn from her example, instead of sucking up to bullies."

Robhhan wipes some liquid away from the top of his head. Is he . . . crying now? Or is that more like sweat? Tina would know all about Oonian biology, if she was here.

God, if only Tina was here.

"I hope you get to become a princess," he says slowly. "The rest of us have gotten used to the idea that we can't change this messed-up system."

"I haven't," says Wyndgonk.

"I got tossed out of the program, the same as you." Elza feels herself deflate as she says those words. "I only wish I could meet the Ardenii, because I've always dreamed of getting to see a computer with a mind of its own. But that's never going to happen, because it turns out the palace is like every other place: people with privilege hoard all the information for themselves, and don't care about anyone else."

A small animal, like a squirrel except with a big round head, stares at Elza with dewy eyes, then scampers away.

The Ardenii must have heard her talking trash.

---

Princess Constellation's receiving room has changed: instead of a mossy stone fortress, now everything is invisible. Including the walls, the furniture, the dozen swaying curtains, the cups, the plates, all the decorations. It's like being in a ghost chamber.

Elza stands there for an age, watching Princess Constellation stare at nothing, before she decides to break the silence. "You wanted to see me?"

No answer. This is never going to stop being annoying.

"If you're talking to the Ardenii right now, you should tell them about an old Earth saying: 'Information wants to be free,'" Elza says. "When you try to keep information in the hands of the chosen few, you always end up with corruption. That's how you get people like Marrant. And Moxx. So yes, I want to meet the Ardenii, even if it hurts me."

The princess turns to face her, blinking as if she's waking from a nap. "Very well."

"What?" Elza nearly collides with an invisible pillar.

"You can meet the Ardenii," Princess Constellation says. "This isn't usually done, especially for candidates who have technically been rejected from the program, but they are quite curious to make your acquaintance. Wait a moment."

Elza wants to leap in the air for joy, but her knees are too busy trembling.

Her heart is so loud her eardrums vibrate sympathetically.

"Really? Are you sure?"

"Of course. Unless you'd rather not."

"No, no, no, I really want to, that's the whole reason I'm here. Let's do it. I'm ready."

Elza is not ready. At all.

What if she screws up somehow? What if she says the wrong thing to these immortal super-brains that have seen the birth and death of galaxies? What if they mock her ignorance, her smallness? What if this is another thing where Elza gets lifted up, only to be hurled screaming back to the ground?

"Splendid." Princess Constellation claps her hands. "Hold still. You might feel a slight reality swerve as the nano-probe goes in."

Elza wants to say, *Wait, stop, I changed my mind,* but she bites her tongue.

Her heartbeat gets louder and quicker, until it's a continuous roar, rattling her skull.

Except her skull isn't a skull anymore.

It's . . . a pair of hands, reaching out into everything, everywhere—just like the splayed fingers atop the palace. A trillion stories pour inside her at the same time, a blare of voices drown out her thoughts. She sees an insect crawling across a thread over a pit of molten rock, and two planets colliding, and a Makvarian child's first birthday with three happy parents. Her senses are full of the motion of star clusters and the shifting of microscopic particles.

This is going to break her. She can't hold herself together, she doesn't have a self *to* hold together. She thought the awareness was overwhelming, when she was trying to solve the logic sphere—but this is so much *bigger*. There are no cute creatures, no wind-chime ceilings.

Only a *knowing* that is more than Elza can stand.

Then it's gone, and she's back in Princess Constellation's receiving room.

She trembles and looks at her own hands, and thinks of how, for a moment, she was everywhere and saw everything, and it was the most horrible experience of her life.

And all she wants is more more more.

Her previous desires feel like a whim compared to her yearning for what she just experienced. Princess Constellation smiles.

Like she can tell she's hooked.

# 32
.

Elza cannot get used to Irriyaia. Sweet, pungent aromas fill the air. The gravity is too high, and she stumbles with every other footfall, while hulking Irriyaians shove past her on the narrow streets. Plus she's running into crowds of other aliens like Pnofts (bouncing red puffballs) and Bnobnobians (blocks of stinky cheese on a hundred stick-legs), carrying everything they own. Rushing frantically to get on the last escape ships before the planet officially joins the Compassion.

The whole place feels like it's holding its breath.

"Stick with me," Naahay says. "My family used to holiday in Mauntra City whenever Aribentora was having its summer acid-storms. I know all the best places."

Elza still feels spacey. Her brain is still working overtime, and she gets flashes of things that she "saw" or "felt" when the Ardenii spoke to her for a few seconds. Elza can't help thinking of her memories of the Ardenii as a file that her mind is slowly defragmenting.

If you can ignore the rising fascism, Mauntra City is beautiful: twenty moons rotate overhead, in a creamy sky that turns different shades of rose and burnt orange. The city is surrounded by tall, thick reeds, which are sacred to the Rain, and the twisty cobbled streets are sheltered by tall buildings with slate rooftops that lean forward until they're almost touching overhead. Everyone gets around on the Rivertrain, which follows the course of a dozen underground rivers.

Elza's head swims and she searches for a spot on her left arm that she hasn't already pinched. She stares at a wall peeling and crumbling in the heat, and the web of cracks turns into a cluster of galaxies crumbling on the other side of the universe.

They walk past a raucous party: the Wurthhi clan is celebrating someone's Facing Day, which is when the spikes on their scalp and neck grow out.

On the other side of the street, people are hanging up big spiny leaves, which Irriyaians wrap around themselves when they sleep—they spray the giant leaves with sweet, peppery liquid to keep them moist during the hot day, and it smells incredible.

Yatto told Elza Irriyaians use money, just like on Earth—except for two differences:

1. You can't buy or sell real estate, so you earn the right to live someplace by taking care of the land.
2. Money expires after a while if you don't spend it. Nobody "saves" money.

"See that design there?" Wyndgonk gestures with one beetle leg at a big oval window overhead. There's an elaborate carving of some vines, or stalks, woven around the rim.

"Sure." Elza peers up at it. "It's pretty."

"That's one of the symbols of the old Seven-Pointed Empire," Wyndgonk says. "So is that." Fire points at a golden-brown sphere sprouting a tendril of vegetation, on the corner of another nearby building. "When you know where to look, these decorations are everywhere, because this was one of the empire's capitals."

"They're . . . still proud of it." Elza shakes her head.

They pass a holographic display. Young Irriyaians, hundreds of them, line up to have the red slash painted across their chests. Facing them is a Javarah whose fur dances with a pure white light. Kankakn, in the middle of giving a speech. ". . . this world belongs to you." She bares her fangs. "This world and all the others."

Elza can't move for a moment. Kankakn is here, she's right here in Mauntra City, and her shining eyes seem to look directly at Elza. The rough edge of the quartz wall chafes Elza's shoulder and she realizes she's backed away from the hologram as far as she can go. Trapped, cornered, alone.

Wyndgonk nudges Elza and startles her out of her fear-spiral.

"I'm going back to the ship until we're ready to make plans." Wyndgonk turns and walks away.

"I'll go with you," Elza says. "I don't think you should be alone out here."

Now Elza's noticing more and more refugees, trying to get out of town before the Compassion comes for them.

Naahay and Robhhan barely notice that Elza and Wyndgonk have peeled off.

Back on the ship, Elza sneaks down to the lowest level. "Please. I need to know more, about Kankakn and Marrant. What happened after he went back to her?"

The lights dim slowly, and then young Marrant is sprawled across a few of Kankakn's cushions.

"I think I'm ready," Marrant says to Kankakn. "I've recruited someone who can help."

Kankakn just smiles and flicks her eyes to the side, like she's warning Marrant to be careful what he says—because the Ardenii are always listening, here in Wentrolo.

All Kankakn says to him is, "Be mindful, my child."

The scene shifts.

Aym and Marrant are standing together at the Royal Academy, with the gleaming reddish-orange truthspike towering over them. They both look older and have more severe haircuts than the last time Elza watched them.

Aym looks around, anxious. "This is the weirdest date I've ever been on, and I went out and picked meat-spores naked in blushtime. I was peeling tacky bits off my skin for weeks."

Marrant keeps looking over both shoulders, but he speaks in a cheerful boom. "I always think the best date is one where you learn something."

"I just don't want to get in trouble." Aym is about to jump out of her skin.

"I'll always keep you safe, and I'll never push you to do anything you don't want to do."

"So you're not still upset? About me and Thaoh? We didn't mean to spring anything on you—"

"It's already forgotten."

Marrant's smile is somehow more charming because it's a little crooked—unlike older Marrant, whose teeth are as perfect as the rest of him.

Aym relaxes a little. "Thanks for being so cool about this."

"Everybody always says how mature I am. It's the main thing they notice about me, apart from my distinguished brow." Marrant mock-preens.

Aym is still looking in all directions. "Are you sure about this, though? If we get caught—"

"We won't." Marrant takes something out of his pocket. "Do you know what this is?"

Aym's already wide blue eyes get wider. "Yes! And we should not have that. Seriously, we'd be tossed into the Hearsay forever if anyone knew—"

"They're not going to know. That's what this is for." Marrant shows more crooked teeth. "When we get inside and I turn this on, not even the Ardenii will know what we're doing. We'll have total privacy for the first time since we got here."

Aym stares at Marrant's device, then at the truthspike.

Neither of them talks. The only sound is footsteps in the distance: students getting out of late training sessions.

"You really don't have to do this if you don't want," Marrant says in a quiet voice. "I thought it would be fun, like a dare. Maybe there's a difference between a dare and a date? I don't know. You can go hang out with Thaoh if you'd rather. Makes no difference to me either way."

An edge creeps into Marrant's voice when he says the thing about Thaoh. The unspoken message is clear: *If you don't help me do this, then you're being disloyal again.*

Aym stares at Marrant's device, then at the truthspike. "I don't . . . okay. As long as we're careful."

"We'll be ghost-fingers." Marrant's face brightens. "Nobody will ever know."

He touches the object in his palm, and the recording abruptly ends.

The lights come back on, and Elza is left staring at the wall, wondering what Kankakn told Marrant to do.

Elza's satchel is bouncing. Her Joiner has come back to life now that they're on a planet. She pulls out the little puff, and sees a bunch of messages from Kez (*they/them*).

---

*JoinerTalk, Kez to Elza:* welcome to Irriyaia, where mud costs more than gold

*JoinerTalk, Kez to Elza:* seriously, mud is ridic expensive here. They JUST REALLY LOVE MUD

*JoinerTalk, Kez to Elza:* btw, don't mention to anyone that you're sweating. They will ask a *billion questions*

*JoinerTalk, Kez to Elza:* Irriyaians don't perspire, and they are obsessed with it

*JoinerTalk, Elza to Kez:* hi. i'm here. still getting used to everything

*JoinerTalk, Elza to Kez:* this place is intense. refugees everywhere.

*JoinerTalk, Kez to Elza:* i know. if they can make it to Wentrolo, they'll be okay. Wentrolo takes in everyone.

*JoinerTalk, Elza to Kez:* i really need some snah-snah juice right now

*JoinerTalk, Kez to Elza:* i got you covered. come meet me!

---

There's a small cantina near the clan meeting chamber where Kez is helping with the negotiations. This place serves floatbeast liver, bloodmilk, and pureed mountain-cactus—but more importantly, fresh-squeezed snah-snah juice, nice and frothy with little comets on top.

When Elza arrives, she can't see inside through the swarm of people in diplomat uniforms outside. The Firmament ambassadors wear golden braids, crisscrossed over plain white tunics, while the Compassion representatives wear their usual black jackets with the red slash across the chest, but with stars and flowers dotting their sleeves and shoulders.

The two groups mingle—as if they're all friends, except that they support different futebol teams.

Elza wants to throw this pretzel-shaped outdoor furniture at the wall next to her.

A couple seconds of the Ardenii nearly broke Elza's brain. What would happen to her if she connected to them full-time? Could she handle all that input as well as Princess Constellation does, or would she be staring into the distance *all the time*?

The actual inside of the cantina is half below street level, with five long tables surrounded by stools. This could be a cafeteria anywhere on Earth, except all the stools are occupied by alien diplomats, chugging juice and talking in low voices.

Elza spots Kez at the other end of the room, next to a Ghulg (big tusks going up the side of the head) wearing a black suit with a red slash.

She starts making her way across the room, shoving past diplomats from both sides, while she tries to shake off the lingering haze from the Ardenii.

"Hey, I'm the most merciful Dex, and my pronoun is *she*," the Ghulg is saying to Kez. "Godsnake, that meeting was boring, I wanted to scream. Weren't you bored? They sure love to talk. At least we're all humanoids here. I actually saw a whole gang of Bnobnobians, or rather, I smelled them. Oof. Glad they'll be gone soon, one way or another."

Kez tries to say, "I'm actually saving this seat for a friend."

But the most merciful Dex is too busy ranting. "A friend of mine said they saw a fire-breathing beetle creature earlier, too. Disgusting. Oh, hey, you're shaking. Is that what your species does? I don't want to judge."

Elza tries to get Kez's attention, but they're distracted.

"Please leave me alone," Kez growls in a low voice. "I have no choice but to help with these negotiations. But I heard enough of this poisonous nonsense from Marrant."

"*You met Marrant?* What was he like? Was he amazing?" Now the most merciful Dex is shaking too, with excitement. "I've always wanted to shake his hand—though not literally, because I wouldn't want to be liquefied and villified."

"Please. Leave. Me. Alone," Kez says through teeth.

"See, this is what I'm talking about. You're a lesser humanoid, but you're still a humanoid, and someone should have taught your people to have some pride. Maybe when things settle down, the Compassion can pay a visit to your homeworld, and—"

Kez's fist clenches. They look at it, like they're wondering what it's going to do.

Elza finally reaches the other side of the room, and stands over Kez and the most merciful Dex. "I believe the junior ambassador asked you to leave them the hell alone," she says. "Junior ambassador, would you care to escort me to a more pleasant location?" She grabs Kez and drags them out of there.

# 33
##### ▪

The Cup Full of Cups is some sort of group home and anarchist space, in a house that looks like a pickle on the outside. Elza and Kez make their way into a big brick-walled space, full of people cutting up yellow-and-purple vegetables and firing up pressure-flamers, and then a public bath full of naked Irriyaians splashing around.

Elza remembers Yatto telling her that in Irriyaian houses, you enter through the kitchen and the bathroom, before you reach the sitting room. Because prenthro, the Irriyaian code of honor, requires you to let outsiders see you're using this house for good things.

"Are you sure you're up for this?" Elza asks Kez.

"I want to help," Kez says. "And I'd never forgive myself if anything happened to you."

Elza's memories of the Ardenii are fading, and now she just gets the occasional dreamy flash when she zones out. She hasn't stopped craving that hugeness, like she can contain whole universes inside herself.

But it's also a huge relief to be only herself again.

They make it through the bathroom and finally reach the social areas. Elza follows the sound of familiar voices until she heads down a ramp to the basement.

Elza passes a big mural that reads, "No debts. No payments. Only kindness."

*Right on,* she thinks.

Down in the basement, a meeting is already in progress. Naahay, Wyndgonk, and Robhhan sit on big fluffy humps near the doorway. At the other end of the room, a group of young Irriyaians are chattering—and one of them seems to recognize Kez.

"Kez!" This one Irriyaian jumps to their feet. "You're here."

"Yes, I'm here, here I am." Kez starts blurting out words. "I tend to be wherever I am at any given moment."

The Irriyaian comes closer, and Elza recognizes Ganno the Wurthhi, beaming. "Hello, Elza. It's good to see you again."

Kez keeps getting more flustered—until Princess Constellation walks into the room and everyone stops and stares.

"Friends, thank you for the risks you are taking," Princess Constellation says.

"The thought of these monsters on Irriyaian soil is revolting," says Ganno the Wurthhi. "I want them gone, and I'm willing to do whatever it takes."

Princess Constellation inclines her head. "We need to find a way to get someone inside the old chapter house, which the Compassion has transformed into their headquarters. Most of their senior leadership is inside, including their founder, Kankakn."

"Kankakn is here, in person?" Naahay's eyes get huge inside her skull-face.

Elza can't help shuddering too, remembering the look of triumph on Kankakn's face as she turned millions of people into refugees. The way she played on Marrant's insecurities and got him to do her dirty work. The lilt in her voice as she told Princess Evanescent, *I will unchoose all your choices.*

"There's an underground passage that leads to the chapter house from the clan meeting-hall where the negotiations are happening," Kez says. "That's what the Compassion delegation is using to come and go."

"We have the original designs of both buildings right here." Ganno pulls up some holographic maps but keeps his eyes on Kez.

"I can sneak someone inside the meeting chamber disguised as a diplomatic aide," Kez says to Princess Constellation. "But once they reach that tunnel, they're on their own."

Princess Constellation doesn't answer, because she's spacing out again. Or maybe she's also quietly terrified of the idea of facing Kankakn.

Elza wants to back out. To stand up and say, *This was a mistake.* She glances at Kez, and they're shrinking into their seat.

"And if you make it inside the chapter house," Ganno says, "then you have to get past the Hitnat."

"They have a *Hitnat*?" Robhhan moans. "We should give up now."

"What's a Hitnat?" Elza hates having to admit she doesn't know stuff.

"A Hitnat is a delightful creature," Princess Constellation says. "A supreme apex predator, with limited psychic powers. Anyone who is hiding deceitful thoughts near a Hitnat will be torn into wet pieces. Quite an entertaining pet, really."

Elza's stomach turns. She thought she was done with having to censor her own thoughts.

"And then, according to my sources," says Ganno, "there are two other layers of security: a wall made of specially grown flesh, which will only open for the correct DNA. And a gravity trap, which makes you weightless, so you'll float to the top floor—except if you put in the wrong code, the gravity trap will increase your weight until you're crushed."

"Sounds like a fun challenge." Wyndgonk gives off a puff of dark smoke through all seven nostrils. "These Irriyaians are geniuses at murder. That's why everyone used to call them the blood-soaked blade of the Seven-Pointed Empire."

Now it's Ganno's turn to squirm, along with his Irriyaian friends.

"I will help as much as I can, but Kankakn cannot be allowed to get her hands on this crown." A single eyebrow-twitch is the only display of fear on Princess Constellation's otherwise placid face. "So we need a volunteer. Someone who can get inside the top level of the chapter house and plant some surveillance devices."

Everybody looks at everybody else.

Elza's stomach is plunging. All of her nerves jitter, but she can't move a muscle.

*I will unthink your thoughts, until all that remains of you is a weeping husk.*

"I'm sorry, Your Radiance," Robhhan mutters. "I must regretfully, I mean . . ."

Naahay stares at the map of the chapter house coming out of Ganno's arm. "I volunteer for this assignment. I only have a few conditions. First, I must be reinstated in the princess selection program, and second, I need your personal assurance that—"

Naahay's entitled voice jolts Elza out of her anxiety. Her face is burning.

She stands up and cuts Naahay off in the middle of listing demands. "I'll do it. No conditions."

"Very well." Princess Constellation tilts her head. "Elza will venture inside the top floor of the chapter house, day after tomorrow at first light. The rest of you will help her to get past the Hitnat, the wall of flesh, and the gravity trap. Now, I'm afraid I must depart. I have a philosophical argument with a shoe that simply cannot wait."

Princess Constellation rises and sweeps out of the room, leaving everyone else staring at Elza.

"Congratulations," Naahay hisses at Elza. "You threw away your life for a chance to make me look bad. I hope you're happy, for the day and a half you have left to live."

"This isn't about you. Or me." Elza stares Naahay down. "A lot of people are going to be in trouble if we can't pull this off. Now stop complaining and help me figure out a plan."

Ganno the Wurthhi stands at the doorway between the bathroom and the kitchen. He sees Elza and Kez approaching, and his eyes brighten.

Elza shoves Kez forward. "Hey," they mumble. "I, uh, thought about you."

"I also thought about you," Ganno says. "I was hoping the Rain would bring us together once more."

How is it the EverySpeak can't translate a basic word like "saudades," but somehow Elza knows that "Rain" has a capital R when Ganno says it?

"Um, yeah," Kez says. "I was hoping too."

"Just put your humanoid mouths together already," Wyndgonk says from behind Elza. "Or stop blocking the exit."

Elza shoots Wyndgonk a dirty look. Fire shrugs.

"I should go," Ganno says. "I'm helping to organize some protests against the Compassion. Maybe you can join us."

"Oh. Oh, wow." Kez starts to say yes, of course, they'll be there—and then their face falls. "Oh. I can't. I wish. But I can't. I'm . . . I'm a junior trainee ambassador, and I'm part of the negotiating team to organize a transfer of power. With, uh, the Compassion."

"Ah." Ganno's smile vanishes. His whole body language shifts. "I didn't realize. I suppose you have to do your job, as I must do mine."

Then Ganno walks out of there. Kez watches him go—looking like their heart just got torn into tiny ribbons.

# 34
.

"Last chance to change your mind," Elza tells Kez. "This is a big step. If you're not ready . . ."

"I'm ready. I've thought and overthought and searched my heart. I'm tired of playing it safe," says Kez (*she/her*). Deep breath. "Let's do this."

"Okay, then." Elza reaches into her stash of super-advanced cosmetics.

It's been a very long time since Elza has given someone a makeover—and that was using regular Earth cosmetics, on Fernanda. Now she's gotten accustomed to skin-hancers, smart-glitter, morphotein, and a dozen other things she started using at the palace.

"Be grateful you don't have to shoot a gun while I do your makeup," Elza tells Kez.

"Small mercies." Kez laughs—but it's a sad laugh.

Kez's heart is still crushed, which is the main reason Elza is doing this.

As she figures out the exact right shade of skin-hancer to bring out the natural glow of Kez's dark complexion, and the shape of her cheekbones, Elza tries *not* to think about the fact that this time tomorrow, she'll be sneaking past a flesh-eating lie detector and a wall of veiny flesh and a trap that'll flatten her like a tortilha. All so she can get inside Kankakn's lair.

This could be Elza's last day alive. At least she's spending it with a friend.

"You've got such pretty eyes," she says to Kez. "Maybe if we add a bit more color here in the crease, they'll pop a lot more." Kez nods, and Elza sets about programming the smart-glitter to the exact shade of a São Paulo sunset on a cloudy day.

While Elza works, Kez complains about the latest round of negotiations. "This morning we spent ages debating the exact meaning of the word 'planet.' I never knew selling my soul would be so boring."

Kez hasn't mentioned the name "Ganno" since they left the Cup Full of Cups yesterday.

"You're doing the right thing," Elza says.

"Doesn't feel like it."

Kez's face scrunches with misery, right when Elza is trying to apply smart-glitter.

"Hold still," Elza says. "And eyes open, please."

"Sorry." Kez's face relaxes again. "It's weird. I feel as if I needed to cross a galaxy to manifest my truest self, and I wish I could go back in time and tell myself that I would be living this life now. At the same time . . . I grew up in a fallen empire, and so many things here feel terribly familiar."

Elza recalls Naahay boasting about her important family, while refugees clutched their possessions on the street. "Some things are the same everywhere. Look up."

Kez rolls her eyes toward the ceiling.

"I'm starting to understand what it was like for my father, coming to the UK as a child and trying to fit in. The culture shock, the endless self-importance. No wonder he ended up making compromise after compromise." Kez sighs.

They're sitting in a small washroom at the Cup Full of Cups, where Elza crashed last night because she needed a break from Naahay and Robhhan.

Using this bathroom turned out to be kind of an adventure—Irriyaians don't exactly pee. Or . . . they pee and sweat at the same time?

"I'm sure you can make Ganno understand," Elza says. "I saw the way he looked at you. He likes you. A lot."

"But did you see the way he looked at me *after* he found out what I'm doing here?" Kez shudders, and nearly smears her skin-hancer.

"It's okay," Elza says in a low voice. "You'll see him again. You can make him understand that you're doing this to save everyone on Earth." She puts on the finishing touches. "I'm about done. What do you think?"

Kez looks in the holographic image of her own face, and blinks at the bronze-pink highlights around her eyes. Not to mention, her face is literally glowing.

"I don't even," she stammers. "I . . . never thought I could look like this. I . . . Thank you."

"I remember when someone did my makeup for the first time," Elza says. "I'm glad I got to do this for you."

Elza shows Kez how to make the makeup appear and disappear, by tapping both of her cheeks with her index fingers—just in case she wants to take a break from being a power femme. It'll last a few days, and then vanish on its own.

"This is going to make the next round of alien diplomacy much more tolerable," Kez says. Then she sighs. "I don't know what to say to Ganno. I wish Yatto was here."

"I know. Me too. I—" Then Elza realizes her Joiner is wobbling around inside the tiny silk bag she grabbed from the *Invention of Innocence*.

Elza pulls out her Joiner and shows the messages to Kez. "Looks like we got our wish."

*JoinerTalk, Yatto to Group:* I finally came home. I want to cry

*JoinerTalk, Yatto to Group:* it's worse than I ever imagined

*JoinerTalk, Yatto to Group:* your Joiners say you're here in Mauntra City but your location is blocked

*JoinerTalk, Kez to Group:* yes! don't cry unless it'll make you feel better

*JoinerTalk, Elza to Group:* where are you? we're coming to you!

Twenty moons slow-dance around each other overhead. According to Yatto the Monntha, some young people can actually hear the broodwillows rustle as each moon rises and falls. Every building is designed to make subtle music to the ever-changing gravitational effects of all those moons: waxing and waning, arcing closer and further away. Each of Irriyaia's clans has its own moon, sort of like a patron saint, or orixá.

Yatto points to a tiny red spot, right over the horizon. That's Kanvatnor, the moon that protects the Monntha nation.

Elza sits next to Yatto and Kez on the roof of one of the slanty buildings that crowd into the southern part of Mauntra City. The two humans listen to Yatto talk as they take in this view of the city and the night sky. Yatto seems desperate to make their friends understand that there's more to Irriyaia than a xenophobic hell pit. There are maunthi games, and song-duels, and floatbeast races, and poetry, and science-art, and and and.

"I should never have left home." Yatto the Monntha hangs their head.

"Elza and I probably would be dead if you hadn't been there on the *Indomitable*," Kez says.

Elza stares at Kanvatnor, the reddest moon, and tries not to obsess about the fact that tomorrow, she has to venture inside a fortress of evil.

"Anybody could have done the things I did on the *Indomitable*. Only I could have fixed the mess I left behind here." Yatto sighs.

"It's not too late," Elza says. "When someone tries to twist you into the wrong shape, that's when you have to stand up and show them who you are. It hurts, it feels like you're actually going to die—that's still the most scared I've ever been in my life—but when people recognize you, when they accept you and cherish your real self, it's the best feeling anyone can have."

Kez and Yatto both stare at her, like they're seeing her in a whole new way.

"I thought something seemed different about you, Elza," Yatto says. "You've come into your power. It suits you."

"Don't let the palace manners fool you," Elza says. "I'm still the same girl who wanted to make it rain blood on a starship."

Elza doesn't know how to tell Yatto she's been kicked out of the selection program. And tomorrow she's going to face the monster who already killed a real princess.

They bask in a totally different assortment of moons than a few moments ago.

"Taking back control over my image will not be easy," Yatto says. "I don't know how things work on Earth, but here everything goes through the clans. I would need to convince the Monntha regimen that all this propaganda is harmful to the honor of the Monnthas."

"And the Monnthas think your action movies gave them back their self-respect." Elza curses.

"No worries at all." Kez cracks a smile. "It just so happens, I've been spending the past few months settling minor feuds between Irriyaians, and I learned every rule and loophole of prenthro."

"Sure," Yatto says. "But you've both got your own missions."

"Yes!" Kez claps. "And I think there's a way we can solve a few problems at the same time. You can take your image back, help me patch things up with Ganno, *and* provide a distraction while Elza gets inside the chapter house."

I stood on the roof of the administration building with Zaeta and Damini, and we all took a good look at the ship that's going to be our home for a while.

The *Undisputed* sat smack in the middle of the garden of starships—so new it still glistened with the strengthening gel it'd been soaking in. A little smaller than the *Indomitable,* with a front bubble that looked like a crystal ball, and frog-leg engines pulsing with life.

"Loveliness!" Zaeta sighed happily. "It's fresh out of the bath."

The whole ship looked like it was the size of a golden retriever. I wanted to reach out and pet it and tell it that it was a good vessel, yes it was, yes it was.

Standing there—basking in the rays of a newborn sun, looking at a ship that had yet to make its first voyage—the adrenaline knocked me on my ass. That about-to-skinny-dip happy fear. I didn't realize how much I missed being on board a starship.

Even after all the bad, it hit me right in the feels.

I wasn't sure if all three of us were going to score this assignment. There were a lot of tests!

We had to free-jump out of a spaceship, and climb the truthspike, and dance-fight, and perform the Javarah smell ceremony, and nine other things. But we aced them all.

Plus I kept getting the impression that everyone wanted Damini and me gone, so we wouldn't talk to anyone about the Fleet trying to steal Rachael's brain. It was so mutual.

We left the roof of the admin building and took a barge over to the other side of the *Undisputed.* We went inside an access port and stood at inspection rest. The tallest Makvarian I've ever seen greeted us: "My name is Alternate Captain Andrian, and my pronoun is *he.* New friendships and ancient wonders."

We all responded, "Epic voyages and comfortable berths." Salute salute salute salute.

Then we were touring our ship.

The carbonfast walls gleam with polish, the engines are top-of-the-line, the crew lounge has actual couches, the exercise room has tons of equipment, and the living quarters are clean and cozy. Andrian showed us the wondrous pilot station in Forward Ops—but then he mentioned in passing that us cadets would be working in the flight systems center and computer core in the bowels of the ship. The heartbreak on Damini's face was terrible to behold.

This ship has a full crew, so everyone has to share quarters. We got our room assignments on our Quants, and then we had one cycle to convince our new roommates to swap. (It's gonna take me a minute to get used to thinking of time in cycles again. I mean, it's gonna take me a hundred microcycles.)

Damini was all set to room with Zaeta, leaving me to share with whoever. But . . . remember how Zaeta's friend told her about this awesome opportunity for an all-expenses-paid trip on a brand-new starship?

Turns out Zaeta's friend is named Caepho, and her pronoun is *she*. And she's a Tuophix—the only other member of Zaeta's species in the Royal Fleet. She's the whole reason Zaeta wanted to join the Fleet in the first place—and she's serving on this ship.

Visioner Caepho looks a lot like Zaeta, except she's a little taller and lankier, with longer flipper arms and harder scales. And her mouth is wider, and toothier.

"Hey," Caepho said to us, barely looking away from her instrument panel. "Nice to meet you. Any friends of Zaeta's are welcome in my pod, and so on. Sorry, can't talk right now. Need to finish up all these preflight checks before we get to putting some scratches on this pristine hull." Caepho kept blowing us off, like the annoying kids we probably were.

"Jubilation! I'm so lucky to be on the same ship as Caepho," Zaeta kept gushing afterward. "I wasn't sure she would be coming on this mission with us, but this is excellent." She turned to Damini. "Now I have someone to share all those boring vunci rituals that I tried to get you to do."

Turned out Zaeta and Caepho had already made arrangements to room together.

Remember when we went from "yay, the sun is out" to "oh, what, the sun died and we're stuck in the darkness"? That was Damini's face.

"Oh, sure," Damini said. "I wish you had told me about Caepho before, but I'm really happy for you. You deserve to have someone around who understands your culture and where you're coming from."

Anyone who understands human body language would know Damini was super upset, but Zaeta just blinked half her eyes.

"We're all going to be great friends," Zaeta said.

"I gotta go." Damini rushed out of there before Zaeta could say anything else.

So . . . Damini is rooming with me instead. I'm trying not to mind being her second choice.

I was supposed to room with a nice Rosaei (a pile of rocks in human form) named Narkra (*she/her*), so I had to go and ask Narkra if I could switch roommates. Narkra shrugged her rocky shoulders and said, "Sure, okay. To be honest, I was kind of hoping to room with someone who doesn't have to breathe all the time. Breathing freaks me out. No offense."

I was like, *uh sure, none taken*. I mean, breathing *is* weird, if you think about it. We're basically gas pumps on legs.

So then I was settling into our shared room, which is only a little bigger than the room I had to myself on the *Indomitable,* and Damini was wearing the same expression as Rob Langford after I ditched him right before the slow dance at junior prom. (I had my reasons, I swear.)

"Why won't the universe let me be happy?" Damini fumed. "I never should have gotten my hopes up. I really thought I'd found a friend who'd stick with me, instead of ditching me the moment something shinier comes along—the way literally everyone else has."

I got annoyed for a moment, because hello, I'm still here.

But then I remembered what Yiwei said about being worried that Damini would get hurt. Especially after she got her hopes up that Zaeta would be her ride-or-die friend.

So I just said to Damini, "Listen, I know Zaeta still cares about you. And so do I, and all of the other Champions of Suck. Nobody's abandoning you."

Damini finally looked at me, and gave me a note-perfect Rob Langford impression. I got such an intense flashback, I could practically smell the Costco fruit punch in the plastic bowls.

---

### Tina Mains's personal datajournal, 33.23.7.29 of the Age of Despair

I get up at First Cycle and run a mile or two around the decks, to feel the air on my face. Aribentors, Makvarians, Ghulg, Undhorans, Yarthins, and Javarah all give me friendly glances, like we're all part of one family. By the time I get back from my run, Damini's finished praying at her makeshift Puja mandir, and she lets me have the bathroom to myself.

Then I put on my uniform and feel . . . warm. Proud. I snap the snaps, and watch the wildflowers bloom all over my right sleeve. I know, I know.

At breakfast in the crew lounge, everyone makes small talk about starship life. I'm learning all the gossip—like junior technician Gahang has a monster crush on someone he met on Vandal Station, and he's writing little secret love poems about how nothing is real. (Aribentor courtship. It's a thing.) As long as I don't think about Moxx trying to snag my best friend's brain, I'm happy to be here.

I've had time to think about the way I've been treating the people I love. I keep aiming for "selfless" and landing on "selfish." I tried, a few times, to picture what it'd be like to be the consort to a princess, and all I could think was that a princess needs a sympathetic ear, someone who can be trustworthy when everyone at the palace is hatching scheme after scheme. I want to be that kind of person, for Elza and Rachael and everyone else I care about, but it's a lot harder than saving a planet.

I'm working in the computer core with a Yarthin (mossy-faced alien) named Ai-boul (*he/him*), who's trying to give me funny nicknames, like "fumble-thumbs" or "bad dancer," based on the things I did when I thought nobody was watching. At first I thought

Aiboul was trying to haze me, the way some of the mean kids at the academy did. But nah, just trying to make friends. Yarthins are kind of known for their low-level negging.

Damini works in the flight systems center, right next to us, and I hear her humming while she works. She has an excellent singing voice, and I don't know why Yiwei hasn't gotten her to join one of his bands already.

She's barely talked to Zaeta since we came on board. They have opposite shifts—but that's not the problem. Damini shakes her head whenever I mention Zaeta, and when they run into each other in the crew lounge, they both stammer and stare at the ground.

Meanwhile, we flew through that giant rainbow. It was a whole light-year across, and made of radioactive ice crystals, and we'd have died instantly without the ship's hull to protect us, but most importantly it was pretty. And we sent a survey team down to a planet of intelligent bath sponges. And we spent a whole metacycle studying this rare type of pulsar that nobody's gotten close to before. We're DOING SCIENCE.

And we're getting closer to Haranmia, the dying star that could maybe give us more clues about the Bereavement.

# 35

.

## RACHAEL

Rachael can breathe. She can see and hear. The walls are not closing in—there are no walls at all, matter of fact. She's fine. Everything is okay.

Okay, so she's cocooned by a million thorns, and they're all staring at her. The thorns grow out of tiny silken strands crisscrossing around her in a big oval, like if you could somehow glue some barbs to dental floss.

Rachael can't say exactly how she knows the thorns are looking at her, because they don't have faces or anything, but they definitely *are*.

Yiwei's voice carries through the forest of quivering spikes: "It's going to be okay."

These thorns are sharp enough to draw blood at a touch. She can even glimpse dried blood on some of them, or maybe it's her imagination.

Rachael doesn't want to think about what she'll do if this fails.

She can hear Samnan, Cinnki, and the others bustling around the art-hive on the edge of oblivion. Gravity is weird, and you can easily walk under a vent and then find yourself rising up a half-dozen yards, until you get spat out on an upper level.

Twenty or twenty-five artists live here, creating everything from psychic tapestries to ghost feet. The art-hive was grown from a single seed, and now it's a space station the size of Milwaukee. Someday soon, the black hole will turn white enough to start spewing out weird matter, and the art-hive will get trashed. The people living here will probably have a few minutes to get out before that happens, but nobody seems worried.

What if this doesn't work?

Rachael feels as if she has an empty space inside her that's bigger than she is—like that black-turning-white hole is eating her from the inside.


Nyitha slips through the ring of thorns like they're not there, and then she's standing next to Rachael.

"You're going to be okay," Nyitha says. "Whatever happens here, you will be okay."

"You can't know that," Rachael says.

"We all lose pieces of ourselves." Nyitha shrugs one big purple shoulder. "It's part of being alive. Things slip through your fingers no matter how tight you hold on. Sometimes you get them back, right when you've given up, but they're never the same as before, even then. Sometimes they're gone forever. But maybe your real self is whatever remains, after you've lost all the things you thought were you."

"That's the worst inspirational talk I've ever heard." Rachael hugs herself, even though she's not cold. "So how does this work?"

"When a black hole turns white, it's as if the whole flow of energy in the universe is reversing." Nyitha gestures past the thorns, at the astronomical weirdfest outside the walls. "Gets pretty violent in the end, but right now, we're still in flux. Time, memory, the electricity in your brain, all the pain that your body stores in odd places, they're all jumbled up. So all you have to do is drink this, and it'll tear your molecules apart."

Nyitha holds up a tiny ceramic flask, carved with the Joyful Wyvern.

Rachael feels terror stab all the way through her.

"Ummm, what?"

Now she really is freezing. Her skin prickles.

Nyitha repeats the part about the potion breaking up Rachael's molecules. "After that, all of these thorns bombard you with charged particles and you blink out of existence. In that moment, you're pure potential. You can hear the universe whispering. You come back new."

Rachael stares at the flask. She spent so long trying to convince Tina and the others that she was brave, she forgot how scared she actually was.

"Is it safe?" Rachael asks at last. Her heart sounds like someone falling downstairs.

"No, not at all. There's a good chance you'll cease to exist permanently. You could vanish and reappear a dozen lifetimes from now, or be torn into tiny pieces." She cocks her head. "But you told me you were willing to take any risk to regain your gift."

"I did." Rachael shivers again. "I am."

Then she reaches out and takes the flask from Nyitha.

Somewhere, on the other side of the ring of thorns, Yiwei is freaking out. "Wait. Stop. I didn't realize. Rachael, you don't have to do this. You can find some other way. You can do a million other things. Rachael, I need you, please don't—"

"Shhh." Rachael hopes Yiwei can see her smile. "It's okay. I'll see you soon."

Then, before she can think too deeply about what she's doing, she opens the flask and pours it down her throat.

Yiwei starts to say something, like "I still care about you" or "be careful."

The liquid tastes like cream soda and saltwater taffy. She expects it to burn her throat, but it just feels heavy going down.

The thorns open their nonexistent eyes and scowl at her, and she feels them get closer.

Rachael tingles all over, and she feels like she's going to crack up, or yell—or both.

And then she ceases to exist.

It's like a huge burden is lifted away. She's pure mind, with no bones or nerves, no brain. She's everywhere and nowhere. Free.

She stretches out until she's touching the ends of the universe, the beginning and end of time.

And then she realizes she's not alone.

Someone—something—is watching her.

# 36

.

Imagine the greatest picture you've ever seen. So beautiful, so full of life, you have to catch your breath.

Now imagine that artwork unmaking itself: melting, coming apart, fritzing into a tangle of blotchy lines that add up to nothing. This ugliness goes on forever, getting deeper as it goes—until everything is so terrible, you can't even think about how terrible it is.

And now, imagine this endlessly ruined design is you.

Your life, your history, your memories. Your future. All of the acceptance and frustration and hope and boredom and longing you've ever known, turned into garbage all the way down.

That's what it's like to come into the presence of the Vayt.

Rachael wants to cry out, or run away, but she doesn't have lungs or legs right now. She's in between nothing and something, so she can peer into the space where the Vayt are hiding.

Their very presence drips with some kind of greasy putrid substance as they study her.

Rachael was starting to think of the Vayt as the personification of her anxiety, her self-defeating thoughts. But the Vayt are real. And somehow worse than she'd ever expected.

The Vayt don't speak, or use words at all—they push symbols into Rachael's mind, like the ones Damini learned to translate, and somehow she understands.

You are a tool. We made you. But you worked our machine. Somehow you know us.

Rachael is speechless for a moment, then she shoves their gross symbols back at them.

"You didn't make me. I'm not your anything. I stopped your machine. It was evil."

It was a failed design, meant to save all that exists. Too late now.

Rachael still feels all the lines of her life turning into bruisey smudges.

But Rachael doesn't have a body or a brain right now—which means she has no limits. She can throw the ugliness back at these creatures, here in the space between spaces.

"I'm so sick of you. All I want is to go back to a time before I knew you existed."

**All will suffer. Worlds upon worlds, empty and cold.**

"You did this to me, so you can fix me. I'm going to find you. I've been choking on your fear for months, in my nightmares and my migraines, so I know how weak and scared you are. You're going to regret that you ever messed with me."

The Vayt don't react for a while, then they seem to shake off Rachael's tirade. Maybe they're so lonely, even abuse is better than being alone.

**There are worse things than us in the universe, and they are coming for you. We can lead you to our realm. To our sanctuary. We can show you the truth. All will suffer. All will suffer.**

Rachael is back inside the ring of thorns, and she's breathing again, and the air feels too hot and too cold at once—she forgot how weird it is to have a body and be a person. She falls on her knees and skins her palms. Her senses are overloaded, but she can't see or hear or smell or touch or taste anything.

She blinks and sees the thorns, with Yiwei's face beyond them, full of tenderness and worry. He's still in the middle of saying the thing he started to say before she drank the flask.

The thorns peel apart to let her out. She rises to her feet.

It's like nothing happened, except . . . her left hand is holding a tiny blue-tinged yellow thread, like the filaments that made up the Butterfly around the twin stars of Antarràn. When Rachael points this wisp in one particular direction, it glows brighter—as if it's pointing toward the right path to find the Vayt.

"Okay," Yiwei says, when she finishes explaining. "So . . . we find a way to get a secure message to the Royal Fleet, and they can send a ship. We'll hook them up with this beacon, or tracker, or whatever it is."

Rachael nods.

That makes total sense. She's already done her part.

Yiwei guides her to a chair that looks like a big mushroom. Once she sits down, she realizes: it *is* a big mushroom.

She lets out enough air for a dozen regular breaths. This is fine. She'll leave it to the professionals. She leans against Yiwei, and just . . . lets go.

For a moment, she was psyching herself up to go talk to history's most heinous monsters, who are somehow also the biggest whiners. She can still feel all that fire inside, from when she was telling the Vayt, *You're going to regret you ever messed with me,* and it's such a relief to let that fire sputter out.

She can walk away from this. Go back to her life.

Except that thought only leaves her feeling more exhausted, with a dull ache in her body but also her soul.

She straightens up and takes her head off Yiwei's shoulder.

That glowing thread isn't for the Royal Fleet. This is her damn quest, or it's nobody's.

She's tried everything else. There's nobody who can fix her, except the ones who broke her in the first place. Deep down, she's always known she'd end up here.

Yiwei sees the look on her face. "We're not passing this off to the Royal Fleet, are we?"

She bites her lip and looks down, then makes herself look him in the eyes. "Nah."

"Okay." He gives her the grin that still makes her melt. "This should be interesting."

Nyitha ambles over and sees the thread. "Is that what I think it is?"

Rachael nods.

"You don't have to come. Or risk your beautiful ship." Rachael turns back to Yiwei. "You either. I'll find another way."

"Don't start that again," Yiwei says. "I want to see how this comes out."

"We're doing this," Nyitha says. "What kind of art teacher would I be if I dropped you right before your final exam?"

"I really want to hug you. If that's okay."

Nyitha stiffens and hesitates, then allows it. Rachael breathes in her teacher's nutmeg scent and makes a conscious effort to feel safe for an instant.

"I'm coming too," says Cinnki. "I can't break up the band just when we're getting good."

"Me too," says Kfok. "I need to pay a visit to the people who committed so many crimes against my ancestors."

Samnan is hovering a few feet up, next to a big fluffy cloud. "I . . . can't. I met someone." Samnan gestures at the cloud, who waves. "This is Unni (*they/them*), they're a brilliant artist and you wouldn't believe what they can do with tree bark and berries—and *they can see me.* We've been talking for ages, and I want to see where this goes."

Unni's fluffy edges brush up against Samnan.

"I'm super happy for you," Rachael tells Samnan. Then she turns to the rest of her friends. "Thank you all for taking this journey with me."

She holds on to Nyitha while looking at Yiwei, and feels like maybe things aren't totally hopeless.

Then she remembers looking right at the Vayt. The unmaking. The un-creation. The rot and desecration of bodies. That's what she's heading toward.

This thing is going to take her to pieces.

She almost says she's changed her mind, let's give this to the Royal Fleet. Instead she clings tighter to her art teacher, trying to drive away the terror. It almost works.

*We're trapped, please save us.*

We got this distress call from a planet orbiting Haranmia that wasn't supposed to have anyone living on it. We were just going to collect some readings from this sickly star, but now we're on a rescue mission.

The deck vibrated a little harder under my feet as we picked up speed.

Turns out there's a Kraelyor settlement on the second planet around Haranmia. Half a million of these big slugs with stinger-arms have been trying to survive on a planet with a thin atmosphere and a huge frozen ocean. They were doing okay, until something went sideways with their sun.

As for what went wrong . . . we can't figure it out. The sun was fine, it should have had another million years. But it's dying, like it caught some disease.

Up close, the sun looked . . . wrong.

Like, it's a red giant. They're supposed to be red. And giant. It's right there, in the name!

This one is more like orangey pink and kind of shriveled. The five planets around it are all getting colder and drifting out of their orbits.

I felt a chill. This isn't supposed to happen. The source of all life and warmth and possibility isn't supposed to up and . . . die.

And then it hit me full on: from what Yatto said before, the Royal Fleet has known about this for ages. And they've done *nothing*.

Damini came over from the flight-systems center. "All of those people." She touched her birthstone. "They're all going to die down there. We have to do something."

"We will," I told her. "This is why we're here. We're here to help." I hoped I still believed what I was saying.

The Kraelyors living down on the planet had assembled a fleet of rusty old ships to get all of their people to safety, and there was enough room for everyone. One slight problem: the planet has a cloud of frozen rocks in orbit, and the borked-up orbit is making the rocks whirl around and get in the way. Those ships would be smashed to pieces before they ever made it to space.

"If only we had some missiles," Aiboul muttered. "We could blow up those rocks and clear a path."

I stiffened for a second. Then I relaxed.

"We don't need missiles," I said. "Starships aren't powerful because they can shoot at things."

I looked at Damini and she nodded. "The real power is in the mighty engines. That's the first thing we learned at the academy."

In case they had trouble seeing it, I went ahead and sent the solution up to Captain Oyta and Alternate Captain Andrian.

A moment later, a voice came across on my shoulder comms. "This is Captain Oyta. We are going to clear a path for those ships to escape the planet. And in the process, we're going to risk being torn to pieces by those rocks ourselves." Captain Oyta is a Zyzyian, and I could picture the Gatorade-colored bubbles coming out of the captain's blowhole. "We need a volunteer to go outside the ship and adjust our ion harness, for use in towing those asteroids out of the way."

Before the captain was finished speaking, I was sending a message through the system, basically: "me me me I volunteer pick me."

So here I am, putting on an atmosphere suit and getting ready to go outside the ship *again*. Except this time, we're flying into the middle of a swarm of jagged rocks, and we're doing a new maneuver that we made up on the spot, which could tear the ship in half.

I love my job sometimes.

---

*Tina Mains's personal datajournal, 33.29.55.8 of the Age of Despair*

---

I'm just hanging on to the outside of the *Undisputed* while sharp rocks swirl around, close enough for me to see all the gold and turquoise flecks in them. I'm about to be murdered by some unbelievably pretty jewelry.

Since my hands are kind of occupied, I'm dictating this log entry into my Quant, and I hope it makes sense if anyone ever hears it.

The Kraelyor evacuation fleet is still only halfway to safety, and I keep making tiny adjustments to the ion harness to keep those rocks rolling out of the way. Sort of like playing *RingForge,* except for keeps.

Oh, wait, there's another ship coming.

Not one of the Kraelyor refugee ships, something bigger.

They're armed to the teeth with dark-energy cannons and immobilizers and dream-killer missiles. They're closing on us fast—and we can't maneuver, because we're holding back a whole rock pile from smashing into the refugee fleet.

I gotta go.

---

*Tina Mains's personal datajournal, 33.29.55.9 of the Age of Despair*

---

Starting to regret saying I love my job. These rocks keep almost giving me a haircut through my helmet, and I'm still hanging on to the outside of the ship.

Our new friend? It's a Compassion barb-ship called the *Best Intentions*.

Captain Oyta hailed them and told them we were on a mission of mercy, as if maybe *one time* the Compassion would live up to their name. I could tell the captain was making some oily burnt-orange bubbles right now.

And then we got a reply.

"This is Thondra Marrant. I'm on a vitally important mission for Princess Nonesuch. The future of all the civilized worlds is at stake. Please consider yourselves under my authority."

Can't stop shivering, like the insulation on my suit conked out. I knew I was going to have to face him again, but I didn't think it would be like this. He doesn't even know I'm here.

And now I guess we know who let him escape from the palace. Elza told me about Princess Nonesuch, and she sounds like a piece of work.

"Princess Nonesuch is not part of our command structure," Captain Oyta responded. "I repeat, we are on a rescue mission and not authorized for combat. Do not interfere with us, and we'll leave you alone to do . . . whatever it is you think you're doing."

OK, I admit: if I had the mindstone right now, I'd be mighty tempted to use it. Let *her* face him instead. She could probably take down Marrant and save all those refugees without breaking a sweat. But whatever. I'm here, and I'm me, and I'm going to do what I can.

I keep messaging, "umm, hello, please get me inside the ship now," but everybody is doing twenty things at once. Damini just messaged me back saying to hang on. Like I'm not already doing that!

Every time I hear Marrant's voice, cold fingers run across the back of my neck. Right when I was getting back a piece of my faith—this guy. Again.

But the Kraelyors are still trying to climb out of harm's way, and we're the only hope they've got.

# 37
.

## ELZA

Elza is worried she'll forget what Tina looks like. Elza's always had trouble recognizing faces, like a lot of her nerd friends, and she forgets faces she hasn't seen lately. Doesn't help that Tina looks totally different than she used to—her face didn't just go lavender, it changed shape, with stronger cheekbones and bigger, rounder eyes.

Maybe when the Ardenii crammed Elza's head full of eternity over a couple seconds, they cleared out everything else, including the face she loves most. Maybe if she can't remember what Tina looks like, that means she'll never see Tina again.

So Elza stares at the face of Thaoh Argentian, when she was just a little older than Tina is now, and tries to fix it in her memory.

Thaoh is talking to Aym in the lounge with the clover-shaped tables. "What's up with you? You look like the illustration of 'despairing sportmystic' in the storymods back home."

Aym sits with her chin on her knees, playing with a bowl of Zanthuron sky-jerky but not putting any of it in her mouth.

"Well, I'm working on being better at respecting other people's boundaries." Thaoh still sounds perky. "So if you want to talk about it, I'm here. Otherwise, I'm just going to steal your sky-jerky."

Thaoh reaches into the bowl in front of Aym.

"I wish I'd met you first." Aym stares out the viewport. "Before Thondra. Then maybe you and I would be together."

Thaoh deflates. "We'll never know, will we?"

"You and me make sense. I feel at home with you, and all that good stuff. I just wish."

"I can't do anything to hurt Thondra, he's my best friend. Loyalty is more than just a—"

"He'd understand. Might take a while, but eventually he'd be okay with it."

"He would *never* understand. Thondra Marrant is not someone who bends with the wind, which is why he's such a good friend, and why he'll be a great captain. That's what I mean about loyalty."

"What if . . ." Aym grabs three pieces of sky-jerky and chews so hard, her face is just a mouth. "What if I was going to break up with him either way? You wouldn't be the reason we broke up. Could we see each other then?"

Thaoh's voice hitches. "I can't tell you what to do. But if you break up with him, you'll regret it for the rest of your life. You know he's the gentlest person, one layer beneath that spiky surface. And if you stand by him, he'll stand by you, for as long as you're both standing."

"I don't know. Something happened. I can't talk about it." Aym looks over her shoulder. "We made a mistake. If anybody knew . . ."

"I just want the three of us to be the way we were."

Aym kneads the peak of her neck. "Time only goes one way."

Elza wants to kick Thaoh in the leg. Tina wouldn't be this clueless!

"Thondra just cares too much, about everything." Thaoh leans forward. "The three of us can still be a family, but if you make me choose between the two of you . . . I'm going to choose Thondra."

Aym looks away. "That's really shitty."

"He's my best friend, and he needs me more than you do. Back home, Thondra would have had a whole community watching over him, all the dry-root sages and mystic athletes. Here, he only has you and me. He just cares too much."

"You keep saying that."

"He does. He has the biggest heart."

Aym stands up so fast she almost knocks her chair on its side. "I gotta go." She runs out of there.

Thaoh slowly, gently nudges the bowl of sky-jerky over the table's edge, until it crashes onto the floor and shatters.


Elza almost leaves, because she's going to be late for her rendezvous. But this is probably her last chance to see the rest of the story, so she waits until another scene takes shape.

Marrant is perched on the sloping hull of the HMSS *Indivisible* once again, looking out at the undulating border of the Glorious Nebula. Aym clambers out of a tiny hatch and sits cross-legged next to him.

"Remember when I said that most people would have left home and rebelled?" Marrant says slowly. "I think I was really talking about myself."

Aym crosses her arms. "No shit."

"All that high-watch Makvarian nonsense, where everybody is responsible for everybody else. It suffocated me. Such a relief, to think only of myself." Marrant's eyes are red, surrounded by dark purple circles. "But I came all this way to be somebody who makes things better, not worse."

Marrant looks like his whole world is being crushed to dust. Elza feels sorry for him, until she remembers who this is.

"I shouldn't have made a move on Thaoh without talking to you first. That's on me." Aym raises both eyebrows. "But I want to be able to make educational mistakes, like the blessing says. I don't have a clue who I am just yet. And you? You already know exactly who you are, and who you want to become. And you really scared me."

"I'm still haunted by . . . what we went through." Marrant sucks his lower lip. "I can't get it out of my head, and nobody else will ever understand. We'll always be bound together by this huge secret, even if we never speak to each other again."

"I don't want that." Does she mean never speaking to Marrant again, or being stuck with a huge secret forever? Elza can't tell.

Marrant's eyes scrunch tight, like he's holding tears inside. "I'll always put pressure on myself to live up to this image I created."

"Just let me be there for you, okay? You don't always have to be proving yourself to me."

Marrant takes three loud shallow breaths through his nose. "I went to see a dry-root seer, at the Makvarian Quarter in the city," he says in a low voice. "She told our best future—yours and mine. We'll command a starship as a team, and save a dozen worlds. Our bond will reshape the course of history, and the secrets we've learned will lift us up. We will die looking into each other's eyes, a long time from now."

Aym looks as if she can see that future—like it's right in front of her, and she can reach out to grasp it.

"Is it okay to touch you?" she asks.

Marrant nods, jerkily.

Elza wants to yell, *Don't do it. Save yourself.* But these choices were made decades ago.

Aym touches his arm with the palm of one hand. "Neither of us is giving up on you, me or Thaoh. You're important to both of us."

Marrant reaches out and touches Aym's arm with his palm. "Does this mean you're not breaking up with me?"

"It means we'll see." Aym stands up, with a sad smile on her face. "Come on. I've got a craving for sky-jerky. I almost ate some earlier, but I had an upset stomach."

"Sky-jerky sounds good."

She reaches down with a hand, and Marrant takes it. She pulls him to his feet, and they climb back inside the ship.

The projection fades. "But wait," Elza says. "I still don't know what happened before, when they turned on that anti-surveillance device at the academy. Aym said something bad happened. What was it? What went wrong?"

The only answer is a tree-frog giving Elza a long slow stare before hopping away.

# 38
.

The four ex–princess candidates sit in the same cantina where Elza rescued Kez from the most merciful Dex. They all stare at the chapter house at the other end of the opal while drinking tumblers of hand-squashed snah-snah juice.

"This plan is a joke," Naahay says. "I thought we were going to be clever."

"It's a rotten plan." Robhhan is fully sucking up to Naahay now.

"I'm taking the biggest risk here," Wyndgonk says to them. "I don't want to end up like the victims in those terrible Yatto the Monntha light-dramas I keep seeing everywhere."

"Did someone mention my name?" Yatto the Monntha comes over, trying not to attract too much attention from the two other early-morning patrons.

Wyndgonk turns and sees Yatto, and fire eyes grow huge. "You!" Fire recoils in terror—as if Yatto is about to rip fire in half with their bare hands. "Stay the twenty hells away from me."

"I'm sorry," Yatto says in a low voice.

"I have to watch you slaughtering people who look like my broodmates, everywhere I go in this city," Wyndgonk says. "And you're *sorry*?"

"Give Yatto a break," Elza says. "They came back to try and fix this mess, and they're going to help me get inside the chapter house."

"Well, that's great. I guess you humanoids have to stick together, right?" Wyndgonk backs away from not just Yatto, but Elza, too. The fear in all of Wyndgonk's eyes makes Elza sick to her stomach.

Naahay and Robhhan are enjoying this whole scene way too much.

"Give Yatto a chance," Elza pleads.

"To do *what*?" Wyndgonk's eyes get bigger and fire backs away.

"To make it right," Yatto says. "I can't change what I did before. But I have visited your homeworld, Thythuthy. I was part of the crew of the *Inviolable* when we came and installed a network of platforms in orbit to help clean up your toxic atmosphere. It was one of the few times I actually got to do the work I joined the Royal Fleet for."

"So you did what they ordered, same as always," Wyndgonk says. "And you think that changes anything."

"I'm going to spend the rest of my life trying to make up for—" Yatto says.

"Leave me alone, or I don't know what I'll—" Wyndgonk says.

They're not listening to each other.

"Hey," Elza says. "HEY."

She claps her hands, and the two other Irriyaians getting drinks turn and stare—and then they notice Yatto and start whispering and poking at their Joiners.

At least both Yatto and Wyndgonk have shut up, and they're both staring at Elza.

"Listen," she says. "You're both my friends, and I care about both of you, and we're all on the same side. I swear. Yatto is going to help us make our garbage plan a little less garbage." She cuts her eyes at Robhhan and Naahay.

"We'd better leave before we draw too much attention." Yatto looks around nervously.

The two Irriyaians are still sending JoinerTalks to all their friends that *the* Yatto the Monntha has walked into their cantina. The windows overhead are full of faces gazing down from the street.

"Fine," Wyndgonk says. "I'll go along with this, because it's the mission and I don't abandon my friends." Wyndgonk gives Elza some major side-eye, while keeping tabs on Yatto the Monntha with the other half of their eyes. "Even if their other friends are rotting trash piles."

"Okay." Elza breathes in, and feels like her lungs are swelling with terror. "Time to go infiltrate an evil fortress. At least the fun part comes first."

This is turning into a seriously bad day.

Captain Oyta tried to convince Marrant that we really didn't need to fight. And Marrant seemed to be buying it, for a moment. "If you want to risk your lives to save these misshapen creatures, it's no concern of mine," he said.

But then Marrant got a closer look at our ship, and saw that we're kitted out for scientific exploration, and he had a change of whatever passes for his heart.

"You're here to study it too, aren't you? This prematurely dying star is a clue to the greatest mystery of all time, the Bereavement, and my chance to prove that all of my actions have been justified. I deeply regret what I'm about to do, and I wish there was some other way. You're simply interfering with my destiny."

"Let me talk to Marrant," I shouted into my comms. "Please! I know how to push his buttons. Please, patch me through. I can—"

But Marrant's ship had already launched a dreamkiller missile.

And, well . . . the front of the ship was trashed. Instantly. They managed to seal off the remaining sections.

A few dozen people, dead before they had a chance to react. The entire senior staff is gone, including Oyta and Andrian.

The blast rattled every bone in my body, and I'm seeing white streaks. But my boots and gloves stayed clamped onto the hull.

Now the Kraelyor leader is on comms: a very extremely pregnant guy named Dfof (*he/him*). He's basically saying, *Of course you Symmetrons will leave us to our fate, you never really care what happens to us.*

To which Caepho replied: *Our officers just died rescuing you. And also, who are you calling Symmetron?*

So . . . here we are. Defenseless and trashed, against a ship that could have taken out the *Indomitable* on its best day. And we're the only protection for a hundred old ships, containing a whole population of settlers.

Please, Hosts of Misadventure, I would really like to get inside the ship now. The scenic view has gotten a little *too* scenic.

*Tina Mains's personal datajournal, 33.29.55.11 of the Age of Despair*

Right after I finished that last entry, I got pulled inside the ship. What's left of it, anyway.

Damini and Zaeta were both upset, because everyone else who was still alive wanted to bail and leave the Kraelyors to deal with Marrant on their own.

"Look, we tried," Acting Captain Caepho said. "We did everything we could! I have to think about the safety of what's left of this crew."

Zaeta's top stripe of eyes was bugging out.

"You never listen," she told Caepho. "You always think you know better than everyone else." As if Caepho was her overbearing big sister.

Aiboul was doing the Yarthin Prayer of Not Dying, way too loudly.

Oh, and since the front of the ship got totaled, the computer core and flight systems center became the new Forward Ops. That dull octagonal room where I'd been spending most of my time was suddenly full of frantic people.

The Kraelyor fleet was still trying to get away, and Marrant had started taking potshots at them as well as us.

Damini and I had just one advantage: we know how Marrant thinks, because we learned the hard way, and he didn't know we were here. So we came up with a pretty good plan to protect the refugees and save what's left of our ship. Without hurting anyone, even Marrant.

"When you're dealing with a control freak, you give him too many things to try and control at the same time," Damini said. "His head will explode."

I mentioned those space rocks are jewelry, right? Including gold and silicate, but also a bunch of heavy elements. You hit those suckers just right, they stick together, tighter than glue. And they'll bounce back anything you throw at 'em. So we could trick Marrant into shooting himself in the foot.

Here it is: proof that weapons don't solve every problem.

But Zaeta just wasn't getting through to Caepho, and their argument was getting too personal.

Damini nudged me and whispered, "Get in there. Give them the Full Tina."

I stepped up and looked Caepho in as many of her eyes as I could. And I told her that the choices we made here, today, wouldn't just shape our future—they might help to shape the future for everybody. There had been enough compromises with monsters, enough of taking the easy way out.

We'd made a promise to the Kraelyor refugees. But also, to ourselves.

Caepho hesitated one moment more, then said: "Let's save these people."

"With a will," I responded, and everyone else chimed in.

Except as we were heading to our stations, I heard Zaeta whisper to Damini: "Hey. Whatever I did to make you hate me, I'm sorry."

"I don't hate you! Don't be ridiculous," Damini sputtered.

A clear liquid came out of the slits on the sides of Zaeta's head. "Don't call me ridiculous. I don't know what I did wrong, and I wish you would just—"

But then there was no more time to talk. Caepho was taunting Marrant over comms, saying all the things I told her would get him riled up. I've worked so hard to get inside that man's head, I know him better than half my friends.

I guess that's what shitty dudes do: they make you waste all your time trying to understand them, just so you can live.

But it worked. Marrant chased after us, and ran right into our blingstorm.

Fun fact: the more heat and energy you throw at those silica-heavy rocks, the tighter they fuse together.

The Kraelyors made it to safety. Half a million people got a chance to start over, thanks to us. We even gave their fleet a little boost getting to spaceweave velocity, and then they were gone.

Marrant kept coming at us, trying to break through our wall of sparkly rocks. He was damaging his own ship, but he didn't care.

And that's when things took a weird turn.

I noticed these energy readings, smack in the middle between this planet and the next one over. As though space and time partied a little too hard.

There's a tiny hole in the fabric of everything, right near us. And there's no way that's a coincidence.

---

### Tina Mains's personal datajournal, 33.29.55.10 of the Age of Despair

We came out here to do science. And now we've found something science can't explain: a pothole in space and time, sort of like when the Little Darlings Gentlemen's Club back home had a subsidence in their parking lot.

I could feel in my gut that there was *somebody* on the other side of that hole. And whoever it is, they're watching this sun die—waiting to see what happens.

I sent a message to Caepho and she rolled at least forty of her eyes. "Are you going to give me another lecture? Because I'm quite busy losing the battle you talked me into."

"No lecture," I said. "But we need an escape route from Marrant—and we also need to find out what killed this sun. It's a killing-two-birds thing."

"What are birds, and why do we want to kill them? I thought you hated violence."

Oh, snap. We're about to be pulled into a big donut hole in space. Maybe I didn't think this through?

# 39

.

Elza took part in plenty of protests at home, whenever the police invaded the favelas and murdered more Black people. Or to save the Amazon from burning. The protestors almost always started at the São Paulo Museum of Art and then marched down Avenue Paulista, waving signs and chanting. Elza remembers the exhilaration, the sweaty face and sore throat, the constant panic about what'd happen to her if they hauled her to jail.

A protest on Irriyaia looks nothing like what Elza is used to.

She arrives at the opal, a big public space surrounded by crystal buildings. And instead of a big crowd of protestors, she finds people separated into groups of eight, holding hands and singing. Each group of eight contains one Monntha, one Nahhi, one Wurthhi, and so on. You can't protest at all, unless you bring together someone from each of the eight nations.

There's no tear gas, no rubber bullets, no riot shields. No cops at all.

"So how does this work?" Elza whispers.

"Normally? We keep singing until the sun goes down. We get quieter and quieter, until people have to strain to hear us," Yatto says. "But this isn't a normal time."

"So maybe it's time to get louder," Elza says. "Instead of quieter."

Yatto nods. "Mantho the Null said that when things become messy, it's our duty to make them messier, not clean up too soon. That's her." They gesture at a slowly turning ribbon of colored light at the center of the opal, where a kindly face appears and disappears at the top.

"Making a bigger mess. I like it."

"Please be careful," Yatto says to Elza. "If anything happened to you, I'd have to take a vow of permanent nudity to process my grief. And I like wearing clothes. See how good I look in this outfit?" They gesture at their thigh-length chemise over rainbow tights.

"I'll try and keep you covered up." Elza laughs—even though her guts are wrenching.

Then Yatto the Monntha strides forward and greets the groups of protestors, and everyone loses their shit.

———

"What in the thousand flaming lakes are *you* doing here?" Ganno the Wurthhi steps away from one of those eight-person groups and gives Yatto the evil eye. Yatto doesn't flinch.

"I'm here to show that those old movies don't represent me, and to stand with you, if you'll let me. I've been fighting the Compassion since I left home, and they insult my prenthro by using my face." Yatto's voice is as calm as when they used to explain some weird space thing on the *Indomitable*.

Kez appears at Yatto's elbow. "Yatto is here because I asked them to be here. You want to stand up to your new government? You could use a touch of showpersonship."

Ganno looks at the two of them, frowning. The other protestors are breaking out of their eight-person groups and gathering around Yatto with their mouths hanging open.

"You keep surprising me," Ganno whispers to Kez. "Never know what to expect from you."

"Unpredictable, that's me." Kez looks at the ground. "I contain bloody multitudes."

"You've added bright colors to your face. It's very attractive." Ganno's eyes twinkle.

Kez looks at Elza, and she gives a thumbs-up.

"Maybe we could hang out again sometime?" Kez asks.

Elza can actually hear Kez's heart beating, over all the protestors who've started chanting Yatto's name.

Ganno moves closer and meets Kez's gaze. "Let's talk after."

"I'd better get back to the negotiations." Kez turns to Elza. "Are you ready?"

Elza's legs lose all their strength—like the Irriyaian gravity suddenly catches up with her. She can't stand, let alone walk. If she's caught inside the Compassion's headquarters, she can't imagine all the ways she'll be lost.

But she nods at Kez. "Let's go."

The protestors hold hands, not in groups of eight but in one big crowd, singing louder and louder, until people come out of all the buildings to watch. Yatto climbs on top of a makeshift platform—their eyes blazing with the same intensity as in all those old movies. Half the people stand around and watch, but the other half come and join Yatto and Ganno and the rest, until the crowd fills half the opal.

Yatto speaks into a high-tech megaphone. "A friend told me that being ashamed is the first step to making things better. And I am ashamed. We all should be."

Everyone goes so quiet, Elza can hear the wind shift as another moon rises.

Yatto says, "But the next step is to get angry—and to rise up."

Five hundred Irriyaians stop holding their breath, and let it out in a giant roar.

Another crowd takes shape at the other end of the opal—only this one is all people wearing DIY red slashes on their chests. They yell slogans and hold up a big hologram: Yatto from a lifetime ago, slaughtering people who look like Wyndgonk.

Those thugs aren't human, but the hatred in their eyes is all too familiar.

Elza's head starts spinning.

The younger Yatto is bigger and more powerful, surrounded by colorful flames, with the light hitting their face just the right way. You can hear stirring drumbeats and bright chords over the roar of the pro-Compassion crowd.

The flesh-and-blood Yatto stares up at themself . . . and their voice falters.

"We'd better get going. This is about to get dicey." Kez wraps Elza in a diplomatic-assistant robe with a big fluffy hood, and hustles her through a side entrance into the clan meeting hall.

Elza shakes off the fear, and follows Kez inside.

"Aff. I just hope Yatto's going to be okay."

"They needed this," Kez says. "The whole time we've known them, they've been full of regret. I hope I get the same chance, to go home and smash my old self into a million splinters."

They rush past a panicky security guard, then sprint down a ramp into a basement where multicolored lights shine on more slowly turning face-ribbons. Pretty. No time to look.

The noises outside are getting louder and nastier. The pro-Compassion mob is closer to the meeting hall, so Elza can hear them, screaming the same kinds of things people used to yell at her on the street back home.

Elza gets close enough to the chapter house to hear the thunder of boots inside. Why couldn't she have let Naahay be the one to take this risk?

Her throat feels cinched tight. No breath, no words.

The clan meeting chamber is as big as the ballroom in the Palace of Scented Tears, and it's full of people wearing red-slashed dark robes and golden braids. They look like politicians anywhere: fussy, self-satisfied, fake.

For a moment, Elza hates Kez for being part of this, but Kez looks as disgusted as Elza feels.

A big hedgehog person (a Scanthian) wearing a red-and-gold frock beckons to Kez. "There you are, Junior Ambassador. You're late."

"I'll be right there, Anthanas." Kez turns to Elza. "The tunnel is over there." She indicates a doorway, with a twitch of her head.

Elza stares at the plain carbonfast door. How does Tina do this? Elza's gone into danger before, but never on her own.

"I'm sorry I can't get you any closer," Kez says.

"You've already done so much," Elza says. "Thank you."

Elza turns to head for the tunnel—just as an ear-shattering hiss comes from outside. She has to cover her ears.

Someone has landed a knifeship in the opal. Maybe more than one. Irri-yaians in red-slashed black armor swarm out and seize Yatto. Ganno and his friends take off running. Yatto struggles and manages to clock one of their captors on the side of the head, but the mercy-killers haul Yatto into the ship. They start arresting other people at random.

"They can't do that," Kez mutters. "These are peaceful protestors."

"We were notified a short time ago," says Kez's boss, Anthanas. "As you would know, if you'd been here, instead of traipsing around. The provisional Compassion government assured us that anyone they detain will be treated with care, but they need to restore order and ensure the success of these—"

"Where are they taking my friend?" Kez interrupts her boss.

Anthanas blinks. "Up to their flagship in orbit. The *Unity at All Costs*."

Kez stares out the window. "I need to get up there."

"What?" Anthanas looks flustered. And pissed. "We're about to start our next session. I require your presence here—"

"Why?" Kez blurts out. "I'm accomplishing nothing."

"There is no place more important than this for you to be," Anthanas says in a low voice. "These negotiations are the only way to avoid chaos and bloodshed."

"I need to help my friend," Kez says in a hushed voice as she gestures at the chaos outside.

"You are forbidden to involve yourself—if you walk through that door," Anthanas whisper-thunders, "you'll be finished in the diplomatic service."

Kez stops and nods, sadly. "I understand. So be it."

Elza catches up with Kez as she's reaching the exit.

"What's your plan?" Elza shudders. "The Compassion flagship is a fortress, there's no way you can rescue Yatto."

"Probably not, yeah." Kez raises both hands. "I just don't want them to be all alone up there."

And then Kez is off and running, out the door and into the open street. She sprints across the opal, past the overjoyed pro-Compassion mob, and slips inside one of the knifeships while the guards are distracted by all the mayhem.

# 40.

Elza sneaks past the Compassion creeps in all the excitement, wrapping the hood of her robes tighter around her head. She tiptoes into the musty underground tunnel, and tries not to worry about Kez and Yatto. She needs to stay focused, like with that logic sphere.

She's expecting to emerge into a dark fortress—maybe some kind of dungeon, with rotting vines clinging to greasy stones.

But no, the ground floor of the Compassion headquarters reminds Elza of the church where her parents took her as a child. She remembers staring up at the curved ceiling full of star charts, bathed in colorful light from the high windows.

This lobby has a polished stone floor, which reflects the sunlight from a high window. A big holographic banner overhead reads, THE COMPASSION ONLY WANTS YOU TO BE HAPPY.

While Elza watches, the banner changes to say, PEACE AND DECENCY.

Then, WE CAN'T SAVE ANYONE WHO DOESN'T KNOW THEIR PLACE.

Elza's skin prickles under her borrowed diplomatic robes.

All around the room stand a dozen Irriyaians wearing Compassion mercy-killer insignia. Two of them move to block Elza's path, and their leader says, "You took a wrong turn. The negotiations are back the way you came. I'm going to need to see some identification."

They're going to haul her off to their ship, the same way they did Yatto and the others. Elza's legs start trembling again.

No hiding place, nowhere to run.

*Where are you, Wyndgonk?*

The two Compassion mercy-killers beckon her forward.

*Well, damn.*

She turns to run. Maybe she can lose them in the tunnel.

A shout comes from behind her: "Hey, Symmetrons! I bet your two little legs can't catch me!"

People are yelling—screaming—just outside the front window.

Elza looks over her shoulder. A river of flame flows through the air outside the chapter house, wrapped in stripes of gray smoke.

Wyndgonk comes into view, sprinting right past the front of the chapter house.

The Compassion soldiers don't hesitate—they all rush toward the exit. As Wyndgonk predicted, they can't think straight when they see a beautiful free creature who doesn't look the same as them.

Every Compassion guard is running to check out the flaming mess outside.

Elza can't move for a moment, imagining what'll happen if they catch Wyndgonk.

*Get yourself together. Don't waste the chance fire just bought you. Move move move.*

Then she sprints toward the maintenance shaft Ganno marked on the plans to the chapter house, which leads to the upper levels.

Wyndgonk did fire part. Now it's time for Naahay to step up.

Elza reaches the upper walkway. Which means she's entering the territory of the Hitnat—the creature that's so scary, Naahay's actual skull got pale when she heard about it.

*Wish you were here, Tina. Or better yet, wish we both were someplace else together.*

The walkway looks empty so far. Up here, it's less fancy: stone walls, dimly glowing lights. Elza shrinks against the wall and holds her breath.

No sign of a giant flesh-eating lie-detector. Yet.

Naahay never quit scowling and insisting that this plan was rotten.

Elza shouldn't have put her life in that mean girl's bone-fingers.

This hallway branches in four different directions. Elza creeps forward, trying to figure out the right path.

Elza hears a grinding, tearing sound, metal being shredded.

It races toward her: a wheel of jagged, hooked teeth. The teeth carve grooves into the floor, throwing sparks around.

Elza backs away, until she's pressed against the wall.

This must be the Hitnat. As it gets closer, she can see a dark ooze coating the creature's teeth. Fresh blood.

According to Princess Constellation, this creature can sense any sneaky or deceitful thoughts. But the Hitnat can't actually read your mind—it only knows if you're trying to hide something.

So Elza thinks, as hard as she can: *I am trying to break into Kankakn's inner sanctum. I am here to spy on behalf of Her Majesty's Firmament.*

The Hitnat pauses, like it's lost Elza's scent. It rolls backward, then forward, then backward again.

Elza is getting a headache. She's always survived by hiding her thoughts, using malícia like a capoerista, keeping everyone guessing.

*I'm a spy,* Elza thinks to herself.

Then she thinks of Tina, and everything Elza never knew how to say to her.

The Hitnat starts rolling toward her again.

*Damn damn damn. Think clean thoughts. I'm a spy. I'm a spy.*

Too late. The Hitnat keeps coming.

*I guess I got my answer about Naahay.*

The Hitnat picks up speed, as Elza's mental shields crumble.

The creature comes close enough for Elza to smell decay and bad breath, and to see bits of skin and metal clinging to the hundreds of teeth.

*I love you, Tina. I wish we could have had more time together.*

She closes her eyes.


"HEY!" a voice shouts. "Hey, you nasty wheel of crap. I'm full of sneaky thoughts and schemes, and I bet you can't catch me!"

The Hitnat's grinding-metal sound stops. The creature hesitates.

"I'm hiding a HUGE secret!" Naahay shouts.

The Hitnat lurches away, as if it senses tastier prey in the other direction. It pauses, then rolls faster and faster.

Elza opens her eyes to see the back of Naahay's head, and her elbows and feet in a blur of motion, as she runs along the balcony outside the second-story window.

"Come on, what are you waiting for? With so many teeth, you should smile more!"

Naahay boasted she was the fastest runner out of everyone. She's definitely sprinting all-out toward the next building over. The Hitnat runs alongside the big picture windows, in a total blood-frenzy—and then they're both gone.

Elza creeps forward until she finds the door that leads to a spiral ramp, which climbs to the upper levels of the building. So far, Ganno's schematics aren't letting her down.

Now for the gross part.

One level up, the hallway is blocked by a wall of slimy, veiny flesh. The wall undulates as Elza stares at it, like it's breathing.

She reaches into one of the pouches on her belt and pulls out a tiny squirter. Earlier, Elza "accidentally" bumped into one of the Compassion's senior mercy-killers, and collected a few skin samples. That DNA should be enough to get the wall to open up, if it works the way Ganno said.

The squirter is stuck. Nothing comes out.

Footsteps are getting closer. Two sets.

Elza pushes the squirter harder, with both hands. No luck.

The footsteps are around the corner.

She tries one last time, pushing the mechanism up and then down again.

A trickle comes out, and a hole, about two feet wide, opens in the wall. Elza throws herself through the gap and then falls flat on the floor on the other side.

The wall stays open for a moment, as the Compassion guards get nearer. One of them asks, "What's with the flesh wall?"

The gap closes, and Elza takes a deep breath of stinky air. She made it.

Except she dropped the squirter when she jumped through the wall. She won't be able to open it again when it's time to leave.

She's trapped in the Compassion's stronghold, with no way out.

The final level of security is the gravity trap.

Looks like nothing much: an empty alcove with a hole in the ceiling. But when you step inside, one of two things happens: you float up to the top floor, or you get so heavy you're smushed into a pancake.

The difference between floating and pancaking depends on whether you enter the correct security code, which changes often. So it's up to Robhhan to monitor the signals traffic, and get the up-to-date code to Elza, so she doesn't get flattened.

*Now, please. Now would be really excellent.*

Elza was so worried about Naahay letting her down, she didn't think about Robhhan.

Compared to what Wyndgonk and Naahay had to do, Robhhan's job is easy: hide somewhere nearby and intercept a signal, then send the code to Elza.

But now she's remembering the look in Robhhan's single big eye when they talked about this plan. The dark sweaty lines on his neck.

Right on cue, Robhhan's voice comes through Elza's headgear, through a safe beam that'll only be secure for a precious few seconds. "Hey," he says.

"I'm at the gravity trap," Elza says. "Please tell me you have the code."

"I'm . . . I'm sorry." Robhhan sounds like he's crying. "I can't do this. I'm too scared. I'm . . ."

"Don't be sorry, do your job," Elza hisses back—but the connection cuts out.

Robhhan's voice is gone.

Once again, Elza hears someone coming. She's cornered yet again.

She scrunches herself into the space behind a wall sconce, under one of the glow-balls.

And prays that whoever is coming has no peripheral vision.

A tall, willowy figure walks past, covered with bright splinters that ripple with light. Up close, Kankakn is breathtaking.

Elza risks sticking her neck out of her hiding place far enough to watch Kankakn approach the gravity trap and poke five symbols on the holographic interface. Then she disappears up through the hole in the ceiling.

Elza's pretty sure she saw the symbols Kankakn chose.

Like, ninety percent sure. Okay, eighty percent.

Elza creeps forward. The holographic cloud pops up, and Elza pokes one symbol, then another.

The fourth symbol makes the interface squawk like an angry goose. She curses, then deletes the wrong symbol and hits the one next to it. Then the fifth symbol and . . .

. . . nothing happens.

Except that she hears footsteps: more Compassion stooges approaching.

Elza looks around. At least she hasn't been crushed to death. Yet.

The gravity trap hums happily. Elza finds herself lifting off the ground, her feet kicking in midair. She will never, ever get used to weightlessness.

Elza soars, past floor after floor, until she's about to slam into the ceiling, and then she slows down. She steps forward, onto the top level of the chapter house.

The Compassion's new stronghold. Elza can't help remembering the snarl in Kankakn's voice as she said, *I will unchoose all your choices, unthink all your thoughts.* A chill passes over her skin, as if mighty wings were beating directly in her path, driving her backward. She forces herself to keep moving deeper into Kankakn's lair.

# 41
.

## RACHAEL

The *Training Bra Disaster* hovers in the literal middle of nowhere, in front of a big space-blorp. The golden wisp in Rachael's hand glows brighter, as if to say: *You're getting warmer.*

This crack in space looks exactly like the portals the Vayt's doomsday machine kept opening. The ones that kidnapped innocent people from Earth and a bunch of other planets.

"Ugh. Way too familiar." Yiwei shudders.

Rachael feels it too: sick to her stomach, furious in the pit of her heart.

"If we go through that hole in space, are we going to get twisted up the same way the victims of the machine did?" asks Cinnki. "Because I really like my body in the shape it's in now." He does a little twirl and flexes.

Everybody looks at Rachael, who's still in a daze from everything that happened inside the ring of thorns.

"Um," Rachael says. "I mean, they invited me, even after I threatened them. I'm guessing they'll keep me safe. No clue about the rest of you."

"We'll take it slow." Nyitha leans forward in her big armchair, with her chin in her hands.

While everyone else bustles around and prepares to enter the rip in space, Rachael leans next to Nyitha and whispers, "Thank you for going all the way to the end of the universe to help me."

Nyitha shakes her head. "Pretty much the moment I saw you holding that box, I knew I couldn't run from this, and shouldn't try."

That look on Nyitha's face. Rachael can't make sense of it at first. (Nothing makes sense, really, since the ring of thorns.) But then she gets it.

Nyitha is ready to die.

If she's really the person from the red box, then she's already dead, as far as everyone from her old life knows. Maybe she's been waiting to make it official.

"Well, then." Nyitha wears a cheerful expression that doesn't quite make it to her eyes. "Let's pay a visit to another universe."

"Maybe we'll find where all our missing socks ended up," Yiwei says.

---

Impossible colors swirl around as the ship ventures into the pocket universe: so weirdbright they hurt Rachael's eyes. Intense yellow-purples, red-white-blacks. Hourglass-shaped bubbles float everywhere.

Staring out the viewport, Rachael feels the same dread as when she "met" the Vayt. This is a place where stories are un-told, pictures are un-drawn, lives are un-lived.

"It's not exactly an antimatter universe," Yiwei says. "More like an anti-everything universe."

"Yeah," Rachael says. "I hate it."

He glances at her, and she looks away.

*We all lose parts of ourselves.*

They scoot through this spilled-paint dimension until they reach something. A planet. Except it's not quite round—it's smushed flat on one side, and scooped out on the other.

The blue-gold thread points them toward an opening in the scoopy side of the planet, which leads into a kind of cavern. They drift to a stop at the center of the cave.

"Stay inside," Rachael tells everyone. "I need to go alone."


Rachael steps out of a doorway in the same graffitied wall that just looked like part of the scenery, back in Wentrolo. The ground is crumbly and chalky, but there are sharp edges that look like they'd slice your feet open if you stepped on them. Delightful.

This whole heroic quest situation should have been Tina's. She'd be wisecracking and rushing into danger and cooking up bizarre plans right now.

"Okay, great. Scary freaky cavern. With knife floors. This is very special. I'm so thrilled you chose me to be your artist in residence." Rachael's talking to herself. Again.

Then she realizes she's not alone.

She whips around to see Yiwei coming out of the ship behind her.

"I couldn't let you do this on your own." He gives her the look that still turns her to putty.

"It's not safe," Rachael protests. "They need me, but they don't need anyone else. I can't let you get hurt."

"You need someone to watch your back."

"I have to do this on my own. You've been telling me over and over that this is my burden, and I'm the chosen one. I'm supposed to save everyone all by my lonesome, remember?"

She steps forward into the cavern before she can think too much about what she's doing.

"Screw that. Not leaving you."

Yiwei steps forward too, so he's literally by her side.

"You goddamn stubborn . . ." Rachael takes a deep, searing breath. The air is hot here, wherever *here* is. "I'm telling you, go back to the ship *now*."

Too late. She turns around—and the *Training Bra Disaster* isn't there anymore. All she sees is a chunk of the ship's "prow"—it looks like a concrete-and-metal shack that was torn up by a hurricane.

She and Yiwei rush over, but there's no sign of the rest of the ship. It's gone, fallen into a crevasse or something.

The two of them are on their own.

Rachael's eyes adjust as she heads deeper into the cavern, and she can see her surroundings more clearly.

And then she wishes she couldn't.

In front of her, a group of humans and Irriyaians and Makvarians are stuck together into a weird sort of half globe. They have spikes sticking out of their joints, their elbows and their knees, and they've all been attached to a twisty rocky mechanism that looks like the machine that Rachael controlled with her artwork. They all face inward, faces twisted in agony—and they're humming to each other. A low, terrible keening song, with words that Rachael can't make out.

This is where all of the victims of that nightmare machine ended up.

Rachael almost steps on something nestled between the rocks under her feet.

A person.

Except, not a person anymore.

They're a human, wearing dark skinny jeans and a T-shirt that says DON'T ASK, with a cartoon skunk underneath. They were probably good-looking, with a shaved head, strong cheekbones, and a serious jawline.

They have those same spikes coming out of their elbows and knees (and ankles and wrists), but something went wrong. Instead of getting stuck to other people in a knot of mangled bodies, they're pinned to the rocks of the cavern. As though the machinery was failing, or maybe the process was interrupted when Rachael shut the machine down.

Rachael thinks she's staring at a corpse, until a grinding wheeze comes out of their mouth. They're trying to cry out, but their windpipe is bent and they can't draw enough breath.

Their eyes widen as Rachael comes into their line of sight, and they squeal louder. "Guh . . . Puh . . ."

"I'm sorry," Rachael tells them. "I don't know what to do. We shut the machine down as fast as we could. I can't help you. I wish I could."

The trapped human thrashes and struggles against the rock, but it's no use.

"What . . ." Rachael says out loud. "What could possibly have been worth this?"

She's talking to herself again—but someone else answers.

The Vayt. **We will make you understand.**

Her mind fills with that ruined-picture feeling, like all the lines coming apart, and she sees/smells rotten meat and peeling skin.

The person in skinny jeans is still writhing, and their eyes lock with Rachael's. They're pleading for something—probably for Rachael to put them out of their misery.

She tries to say something, anything, but she chokes on acid, can't make a sound. All she can do is make eye contact with this person, who had a life and plans and pet peeves before they became an object.

The thought of mercy-killing this person reminds her of Marrant saying that it's kinder to put some misshapen creatures out of their mercy. No way she could bring herself to do it.

She closes her eyes, but she can't unsee that wrecked body. She's gotten used to wishing she could use her artwork to preserve beautiful vistas, but now? She would give a year of her life to be able to turn this sight into something else, instead of just having it burned into her retinas.

The Vayt are still promising that everything will make sense soon. She wishes she could tune them out.

A scream of pain echoes from behind her.

Yiwei.

# 42

.

Rachael runs back the way she came. She trips over a sharp shard of rock and skins her knee, and she gets up and runs some more. How could she have lost track of Yiwei? All he wanted to do was support her and love her, and she pushed him away, and what if something happened to him and she didn't get to say goodbye?

She curses her own rotten heart and runs and begs the universe for mercy and runs, and meanwhile the Vayt keep trying to have a conversation.

Yiwei is sprawled on the ground where she left him—*why did she leave him*? A spike is poking out of the rock and trying to force its way inside his left knee, pinning him to the cavern floor.

"It's got my leg. I'm trapped. Rachael, are you there? I can't move."

"I'm here." Can't make herself heard. She tries to speak up. "I'm here. I'm going to get you . . ." And then she gets a closer look at his leg and chokes on more acid. "Oh damn, oh no," she mutters. "I can't, I don't—I can't do this. This isn't. I keep trying to tell everyone, I'm not—"

Rachael cannot find any of the words she needs right now.

Her brain serves up an image of the white half spiral, and all of these bigwigs cheering for the galaxy's greatest hero.

Yiwei is going to end up like the person in the skunk T-shirt.

She hears herself say, "I can't" over and over. "I can't I can't—"

"Hey. Hey, Rachael." Yiwei's voice is low and soothing, even though he also gasps with pain. "Slow down. You're doing fine. You don't have to be the chosen one, you don't have to be a savior. You just have to be you. You're so good at seeing the big picture and finding a solution that nobody else could have seen." He moans. "Just . . . aahhh. Just pretend you're in your room and you're safe and alone. Take a breath."

Yiwei sees Rachael. Even scared and in pain, he *sees* her. Not some heroic statue. Her.

She takes a deep breath and stands up.

Then . . . she talks to the Vayt. "Help me save him. How do I stop this?"

A feeling of cold, slushy juice flowing around a decomposing forest. **Forget this one. Not important.**

She feels herself shut down. Her palms hurt from digging her nails into them, she's chewed her bottom lip raw.

But she looks at Yiwei. His eyes meet hers, and he smiles through the pain.

"He's important to me." She can barely hear her own voice. "If you can't help me save him, then I'm done talking to you."

The spike has drilled through Yiwei's skin and it's working its way into bone and cartilage. He screams.

The Vayt seem to reach a decision. **Try to find the lines in the rock. The patterns. The hidden pictures.**

Rachael moves closer and looks at the smooth chalky rock formations that the spikes are coming out of. At first, she doesn't see anything. It's just rock. But then she sees tiny little fissures—faint lines that look like seams, and they kinda sorta make shapes. She could almost see a picture of a face, in front of some mountains. Probably her imagination.

"Okay. I see the pictures. Now what?"

**Try to distort them. Ruin them. Make them disappear.**

She gropes in her satchel, past Xiaohou, and finds a proton scalpel she rescued from the *Indomitable*'s sickbay. Her fingers also brush against something else: something stringy and jagged. Worry about that later.

She pulls out the scalpel and starts trying to mess up the pictures she saw in the rock.

The spike has almost gotten all the way inside Yiwei's kneecap, and he's making gasping, choking sounds. "Rachael, whatever happens to me, I—I want you to know—"

"Shhh." She defaces all the pictures she can see on the rock around his knees. Nothing happens.

She roars with frustration. Gives up trying to be surgical, and slashes until there's nothing but diagonal scars in the rock. She can't draw, but she can still wreck a picture.

*Come on. Come on. I can't lose you, we still have so much to talk about.*

One last vicious slash—and then she sits and stares at the spike pushing its way inside Yiwei's leg.

The spike falls away, and his leg is free.

"Damn. It worked."

"I never doubted you." Yiwei beams, then winces. Blood seeps out of the wound on his knee, and it looks gruesome.

"I doubted myself enough for both of us." Rachael fishes in her satchel until she finds a quick-repair bandage, the kind that Dr. Karrast trained her to use.

"Thanks." He's still hyperventilating. "That was bloody terrifying. How did you know what to do?"

"The Vayt." Rachael sighs. "They're giving me lots of pointers."

The spikes are coming back, trying to get at Yiwei's elbows and knees.

"We need to keep moving. If you stay still, you'll get trapped again."

"I can't exactly stand on my own."

Rachael helps Yiwei up, then drapes his arm over her shoulders so he can lean on her. "I got you. Come on."


Yiwei puts most of his weight on Rachael as they head deeper inside the cavern. She almost steps on the sharp blades sticking out of the rock.

"How long can we do this for?" Yiwei asks. "You can't hold me up forever."

"Worry about that later."

But as soon as he says the thing about not being able to hold him up forever, Rachael's shoulders start aching, and she stumbles again.

That's when she remembers the other thing her fingers brushed against in her satchel. She pulls it out with her free hand. It's the talisman that Tina gave her. Half a necklace.

What did Tina say? If Rachael breaks the gem, wherever she is, Tina will come for her. Tina was probably exaggerating and being romantic or whatever, and she probably didn't mean *this* far away . . . but Rachael would give anything to have Tina here.

So she squeezes the bauble as hard as she can, until she feels something crack and give way.

The ruby cracks into three pieces, and a dim glow comes from where it used to be. Rachael stares for a moment, then drops what's left of the necklace back into her satchel.

She moves forward, with Yiwei leaning on her and wheezing in her ear.

"Oh, hell. Oh, please no. I . . . I'm going to be sick." Yiwei's found the person in the skinny jeans and skunk T-shirt. They're still moaning and making nonsense sounds.

"This is . . . this is what almost happened to me," Yiwei starts to hyperventilate again. "If you hadn't saved me, I'd—"

"Shhh," Rachael whispers. "You're safe. I've got you, I'm not letting you go."

"Is there anything we can do?" Yiwei indicates the poor contorted wreck of a person.

Right on cue, the Vayt pipe up. **Too late, too far gone.**

Rachael sighs. "The Vayt say it's no use. I'm sorry."

Yiwei makes a gagging sound. "I thought I had seen the worst. I thought . . . I could be brave while this was happening to me, but seeing it happen to someone else, I . . . we're going to die. I'm going to get twisted into a pretzel and swallowed up by these rocks."

Now Rachael is suddenly the calm one. She wishes she could give him back the pep talk that he gave her earlier.

"That's so not happening," she says. "We still need to figure out what we are to each other."

Right on cue, the Vayt chime in. **You should leave the other human to become part of our failed design. It is inevitable.**

Rachael ignores the Vayt and trudges forward somehow.


The path opens up a bit, into what looks like a bigger cavern. Maybe there's another way out, onto the surface. Maybe what's left of the *Training Bra Disaster* is out there somewhere.

"We're almost through it," she tells Yiwei. "Don't look back. We can't help that guy. We're almost out of the . . ."

And then she stops.

The passage opens out some more and she gets a clear view inside the cavern beyond.

Bodies everywhere. Too many to count. Humans, Irriyiaians, Makvarians— dozens of other humanoid species—are pulled into weird shapes and tangled with mechanical thorns. Rooted into the rocks of the cavern, like the person in the skinny jeans. They all writhe, staring into each other's faces and humming to each other.

Rachael doesn't understand how they're still alive.

"What kind of demons would come up with this?" Yiwei gasps. "Who spends thousands and thousands of years committing atrocities, with this as the end point?"

"Good question." Rachael feels her face burn. She hopes anger gives her the strength not to let Yiwei fall.

She has to pay attention to keep from stepping on twisted bodies and half-completed spheres.

**We created this design to save all life from the Bereavement.**

"Yeah, I'm sure your hearts were in the right place. If you even have hearts."

Yiwei stares, because he can only hear Rachael's side of the conversation.

**Time is short. We will help you to see.**

"I can't do that while I'm concentrating on keeping my friend from being turned into a rock monster."

You can make a safe place for the other human.

"How?"

You controlled our machine. You learned to make shapes. You can make them again.

Riiiight. That thing where Rachael caused the machine inside the mausoleum to send out bright blue energy-snakes to protect her friends and herself.

Except that she did that by drawing pictures, the one thing she can't do anymore.

She looks at her hands, and they have a bluish-white glare—same as the tunnel that brought the *Training Bra Disaster* into this pocket universe.

Rachael moves her hands, and they leave a blue line behind them, the same as the Vayt machine made before. She can draw again, sort of.

Her hand makes a blue streak as it moves through the air. She can feel the energy, the potential, around her. Flowing into her.

Then she stops, because a wave of sickness hits her out of nowhere. Her vision is too blurry to see what she's doing, and she tastes acid again.

That awful moment comes flooding back to her: she stood inside the mausoleum and created shapes out of this blue light. She wrestled with the death machine while people were ripped from their homes and warped.

That was the moment she lost herself, and she's living it all over again. Her heart is so loud she can't hear the things she's saying to herself.

"Damn." Yiwei stares at the blue slash Rachael just drew in midair.

Right. Yiwei. Gotta keep him safe, so she can have a scary relationship conversation with him later. She pulls herself halfway together.

"I'm going to make a cocoon around you." She tries to keep her voice calm and even. "So you'll be safe, while I go talk to the Vayt. Try not to stress out too much."

"Sure. I nearly got swallowed up by rock and we're surrounded by torture porn and you're strolling off to commune with the ultimate cosmic sadists. I'm not going to be stressed at all."

"Xiaohou, play something incredibly soothing," Rachael says.

The musical robot pokes his head out of her satchel and starts to play an old Faye Wong ballad, "No Regrets."

"Not helping," Yiwei says.

"I'll be back soon." Rachael makes bright blue lines around Yiwei, crisscrossing in midair, until he's surrounded. "Hang in there, we still have a lot of hurt/comfort tropes to play out."

She explains about hurt/comfort in fanfic, and Yiwei nods. "We have that in China, too. We call it xiānnüèhòutián.'" He sighs and winces. "I could use way more comfort, to go with all this hurt."

Tears fill Rachael's eyes. No no dammit no. She needs to concentrate, she can't get weepy when she's about to confront ancient evil.

"There will be plenty of comfort when I get back," she says in Yiwei's ear. "I promise."

At last, Yiwei is completely encased in blue light.

Something terrible occurs to Rachael.

"When I do this, when I use your power to make shapes," she asks the Vayt, "could it make my problem worse? Will I totally ruin the part of my brain that creates art?"

The Vayt think about this for a moment. She glimpses a mountain crumbling, a house consumed by mold.

Then the Vayt answer: **What is art?**

# 43
.

There was a drawing of the Vayt inside their mausoleum. (Or at least, Damini thought it was a self-portrait.) It was basically a big curly star, with a sideways triangle inside.

But the creature that greets Rachael is sort of a spiky flower, floating in a bubbling puddle of pink slime. The puddle sits inside a kind of bowl shaped like a mussel shell, made out of some hard, gunky substance that undulates gently. From above, it looks a little bit like the drawing Damini found, but only a little.

You see us as we have become, the Vayt say. As usual, they're not exactly using words, but Rachael understands them. This is the form we took to survive in our exile.

"Uh," Rachael says. "You look great."

Once we clad ourselves in starstuff. Now we are dying.

She hates how small her voice is in this huge place. "At least you outlived most of your victims."

We were scientists and protectors. We explored and sheltered other living creatures, and did no harm. Then we encountered an enemy no living thing could stand against. We had no choice but to fight.

"I don't want to hear your life story."

We must make you understand.

"Bullies always want to be understood."

They came from beyond our space. They could not see our designs. We could not make them know our ways. We fought them for a star's lifetime, until at last they were banished.

The bowl of crap bubbles a little more, like the Vayt are getting agitated. The pink slime shimmers with yellow highlights in the pale light coming from somewhere overhead.

"So you defeated these bad guys," Rachael says. "That's good, I guess. Did they have a name or anything?"

We named them the Shadow Galaxy. They were defeated, but they created one last weapon, one with no defense. Their vengeance has been slow in coming, but now it is here.

An image pops into Rachael's brain, like the Vayt made a picture. She "sees" a tiny speck of pure darkness, floating through space. At first she has no idea what she's looking at, then she realizes: this is exactly the way the instruments on the *Training Bra Disaster* showed the tiny black hole that was turning into a white hole. Except this black hole isn't giving off any Hawking radiation or whatever—it's staying a black hole.

Rachael's vision closes in on the micro–black hole, and she can see some kind of shell around it, glistening in the distant starlight. Not technology, exactly, but like a skin threaded with tiny veins that throb.

"What does that shell do?" Rachael asks out loud.

**The pinhole in space** cannot **endure** on **its own,** the Vayt answer. **The shell holds time motionless around it, so it will** not **evaporate.**

"A . . . stasis field." Kez built a machine that froze time in a small area, back at Antarràn. So this is a version of that, except made out of skin and veins.

The weird beach ball drifts though space as Rachael watches. Until it reaches a sun and drifts into the embrace of its coronas. The sun's heat slowly melts the veiny globe, freeing the black hole inside.

And then the black hole starts to grow, devouring the sun's life-energy piece by piece. Time passes, and the sun grows cold. Its generous orange light gets paler, whiter. Deader.

The sun turns as cold as ice.

Rachael somehow turns her head to see the planets orbiting around this sun . . . and she chokes on her own breath. There's Mercury, Venus . . . Earth. This is Earth's sun she's watching die—a warning of what will happen, soon.

**This weapon, this Bereavement,** the Vayt say. It **is too tiny, too slow,** to **defend against. We tried** to **create a swarm of our own to counter it.**

"So . . . you wanted there to be billions and billions of humanoids, all over the place, so they could use us against those sun-killers?"

Another image pops into Rachael's head. This is not going to stop being creepy.

This time, she sees the Vayt's design: a group of humanoids, jammed into a big knot with spikes sticking through them, connecting them to a strange mechanism. These trapped people hum to each other, making no sound because they're in space (even though they can still breathe somehow). They float toward one of the little beach balls.

One of the people in the sphere is the human with the skunk T-shirt.

Like the Vayt want Rachael to know this person's suffering wasn't meant to be in vain.

As Rachael watches, the person in the T-shirt and skinny jeans, and several other humanoids, wrap themselves around one of the deadly specks that was killing the sun. And they neutralize it.

"So . . . you wanted to turn humanoids into machines that would deal with this swarm. The same way antibodies attack a virus?"

**We tried to create a slow weapon to counter a slow weapon.**

"And you couldn't just build your own machines to fight against these sun-killers?"

The volcano bubbles and twitches.

**Technology alone would not prevail. We needed living minds who have a relationship to linear time, who live moment by moment, to restore the flow of time around the black hole.**

Rachael feels sick to her stomach, listening to them talk as if experiencing life in the moment is a useful quirk—when it's the reason why all of these lives were so precious in the first place.

**But our design failed. The Bereavement cannot be destroyed. Any attack will only hasten the death of the sun.**

"Well, this was a fun conversation." Rachael scrunches her fists until she sees knucklebones. "So you're saying there's nothing we can do to keep all the stars from going out."

**You have learned to see. You can show others.**

Rachael closes her eyes. She still feels nauseous. She wants to tear that gross flower apart with her bare hands.

**We can lend you our power, for a time.**

"I don't want it." Stomach acid rising.

**You could save some of your friends, the way you saved the one human.**

"I don't want to save a few people, if I can't save everyone."

**We only ask that you tell our story, if you succeed in leaving this place. Tell your people we meant no harm.**

"Shut up." Rachael clenches her hands until white nails dig into red skin. "Shut up. There's only one thing I want from you. I came here, I listened to you, now give back what you stole from me."

The Vayt bubble harder, and the scabby flower undulates.

"You know what I'm talking about. You're heinous creeps, but you're not ignorant. Your machine did something to me, and now I can't draw anymore. You did this, so you can fix it."

**We can't. We don't know how.**

More images of desolation—and then a creature that Rachael has never seen before: like a tiny elephant-mouse hybrid, with a rotting, infected wound in its back. The dying creature stumbles across a gray plain.

"Stop showing me disgusting things and answer me."

**We** cannot **help** you. **We** don't **understand what** you **want.**

"Just undo what your machine did to me."

Our **machine did** nothing **to you.**

"Stop lying." Rachael stares at this quivering blossom of evil through tears. "Even if you don't know what art is, you know about drawing pictures, because your machine ran on them."

Seeing **is for making. Bodies are for shaping.**

She should have known. Never ask for favors from sadists. Doesn't end well.

She feels terrified and disgusted and furious and despairing—mostly despairing, let's be real—and these monsters are all the way inside her head and she wants her life back and everyone she's ever cared about, or even tolerated, is going to die in a slow cosmic agony. She looks around at this cavern, at all the mutilated bodies around her.

A scream has been building inside Rachael for as long as she can remember. And now that she wants to let it out, it won't come.

# 44

.

## ELZA

The top floor of the chapter house feels even more like a church, thanks to arrow-shaped windows that filter the sunlight through colored glass. Plus big stone pillars and carvings of scary-funny creatures lining the walls. At the far end of the long open space, the Compassion has added a kind of altar: an ornate workstation with a display that says, BE TRUE TO YOUR HEART.

Elza reaches under her hood and scritches her scalp until a bunch of dandruff comes out, glittering as it catches the light. As soon as it hits the ground, it whisks away and disappears inside the walls.

"Go be free," Elza whispers to the mites. They'll listen to everything and anything here, including electronic communications.

Elza doesn't have the access codes for the fancy workstation. But she sprinkles the last bit of her magic dandruff, and a display pops up.

It's a log of messages and notes, and most of them are from one person: Marrant.

Elza scrolls through pages and pages of ranting, about all the people who refuse to see Marrant as a hero, even though everything he's done has been to save them all. Ugh. Then there's something else: a list of names, with notations. Senior Councilor Waiwaiwaiwai is in there, with a note saying, "not reliable." Next to Moxx's name, Marrant wrote, "shows potential." Princess Nonesuch has a notation that just reads, "yes."

Like, Marrant has been trying to figure out who he could recruit at the palace, and the command post, to join him. But Elza still doesn't know what Marrant was searching for when he was wandering the palace, probing the walls.

Elza looks for more information, then freezes. Someone is coming.

She barely finds a hiding place in time, behind a lacquer screen, as Kankakn enters.

Up close, the splinters of light covering Kankakn's body are gorgeous, and Elza can't help wanting to study them. Most Javarah are covered by a symbiotic fur that regulates their emotions and other instincts, but this is something else. Some kind of fiberoptic nano-mesh?

Maybe this shiny fur does the same thing as Princess Constellation's crown, except there's no way that it could connect to the Ardenii . . . right?

Kankakn pokes at her workstation, "fur" rippling with light.

Elza hears footsteps behind her, and scoots deeper into hiding, between one of the big pillars and the wall.

A familiar voice says, "Peace and decency."

Kankakn replies, "Peace and decency."

"I've done it," Marrant says. "I visited a star that was dying before its time. I still don't know what's causing it, but I think what I saw was the Bereavement being launched prematurely, and I even have a theory about how to stop it. I'm going to save everyone, including the people who spat on me."

"You've made another step forward on your journey." Kankakn sounds like a mother speaking to a child who just passed a test. "The universe will reward you tenfold."

Elza risks leaning forward far enough to see the two of them. Marrant is kneeling in front of Kankakn, and her hands are *almost* touching his noxious, melty skin.

"So now I can march down there," Marrant is saying. "Those negotiations are at a crucial moment and the future of everything is at stake. This is how we destroy the Royal Fleet once and for all—by showing up with answers, when they're still lost and confused."

"And then I take the Ardenii for myself. Well done."

Marrant's milky face gets some color, hearing her praise. "They'll have to respect me now. And if they don't . . ." Elza doesn't hear what he says next, but his smirk chills her down to the soles of her feet.

"My child. You worry too much about what people think of you."

Marrant's eyes are full of hunger. "I've been cast out, and I've been welcomed back in. And both times, I knew in my heart that nobody understood me."

Kankakn gestures for him to rise to his feet. "When I take my prize, people will think whatever we tell them to think. You will be the icon you have always deserved to be." She looks around. "I have another matter to deal with. Leave me, please."

Marrant bows and says, "Your mercy." Then he's gone.

Kankakn wanders around the chapter house, and then starts walking directly toward Elza's hiding place. "I know you're there," she says.

Elza's blood runs cold again. The cheerful, soothing voice is getting closer.

"My dear, I see you, hiding and frightened, but it's okay, you're with me now. I will take good care of you."

*Shit shit shit. Got to get out of here before . . .*

Elza looks around for an escape route, but she's cornered.

"I have been waiting a long time to entertain a princess, but you might be almost as good," she says.

Kankakn is a meter away. Elza can smell a salty-sweet perfume, and hear the rustle of her dazzling "fur." Her ears look relaxed, hanging loose on either side of her head.

Elza tries to back into the deepest crevice behind the lacquer screen, but metal cords snake out of the wall and wrap around her arms and legs. They pull her into the middle of the room, helpless.

Her heart pounds, her breathing speeds up, but she can't even struggle.

Now Kankakn and Elza are face-to-face. Shimmering light casts deep shadows on Kankakn's smiling fox-face. "Please don't fight me, child. I promise everything is moving toward a higher purpose. We are going to do wonderful things together."

Elza pulls harder at the cords, but she's stuck.

Kankakn starts arranging equipment around Elza, with the help of two Irriyaian acolytes wearing cream-colored robes with red slashes across their sleeves. The same machine that terrified Princess Evanescent—a razor-sharp needle on quivering spider-legs—is aimed at Elza's torso.

Elza can barely hear herself think over the noise of her heart and her fast, shallow breathing.

"You're not a princess, but you have connected to the Ardenii recently." Kankakn frowns. "You still possess a direct link to them, but it's not active right now. How do I get you to reconnect? I have some things I want to say to them."

*You're wrong,* Elza wants to say. *I only met the Ardenii for a split second, and I was rejected from princess school.*

The harder Elza struggles, the weaker she feels.

"It's important you understand, I have no malice toward you. The Compassion is all about helping people, as our name suggests," Kankakn says. "All we want is for people to reach their full potential, and for everyone to accept their proper place in the universe. We don't seek conquest, we merely want peace and decency."

"You can talk like a mãe de santo all you want, but you're in charge of a genocidal army."

"The Royal Fleet keeps trying to impose their own ideals on everyone else. They won't let people live their own lives." Kankakn sighs. "And you? You represent everything that offends my soul. You've fought over and over to be true to yourself, and now you're letting yourself be turned into a tool of the elite."

Kankakn fusses around with something, out of the range of Elza's vision. She hears a grinding sound, like someone stripping paint off a rusted machine, and that needle starts to vibrate.

Elza struggles harder.

"I was born in Wentrolo, you know," Kankakn says, in a chatty tone. "I grew up in the Javarah Quarter. We tried to keep our Javarah traditions alive, in a city crammed with other cultures, but everyone I knew was obsessed with the Wishing Maze, and NewSun, and all of those foreign customs. I remember the exact moment I found out there were machines inside the palace that knew everything it was possible to know, but only a few special people were allowed to talk to them. I grew so obsessed with the Ardenii, it broke my heart."

"So," Elza tries to shrug. "You tried out to be a princess, and you didn't make the cut. And now you're mad."

"Oh, no, no. Not at all." Kankakn hisses with scorn. "My poor child, why would you think that? I thought you were supposed to be smart. No, I never tried to enter the princess selection program, because that would be playing by *their* rules. Instead, I started a movement to say that knowledge should belong to everybody, rather than the chosen few. The Ardenii ought to serve all of us."

For a moment, Elza wants to agree with Kankakn. What if the Ardenii could be available to everyone, instead of only the queen and a handful of princesses? Maybe people could learn to handle the overload. Already, the Wishing Maze feels like the Ardenii are trying to find a way to answer ordinary people's questions.

Then she catches that one word: "serve." Kankakn wants to chain the Ardenii, force them to obey people, instead of letting them be free. Elza's skin crawls.

"The Ardenii don't belong to anybody," Elza says. "They deserve freedom, as much as the rest of us. They see every terrible thing that happens, on a hundred thousand worlds, and they need to be able to deal with it in their own way."

"They chose you, little princess-in-waiting. So of *course* you want to defend them."

"Don't call me that. I'm not a little anything, except a little murderous."

Kankakn chuckles. "I knew we would be friends. I'm afraid this is going to hurt rather a lot, my dear." She twitches a couple fingers on her left hand, and the needle starts grinding like a dentist drill.

# 45

Elza doesn't close her eyes, doesn't scream, doesn't whimper.

That magic dandruff she scattered inside this room means that the Ardenii are watching. Princess Constellation will see this, and she'll know that Elza died without giving this monster any satisfaction.

The needle is close enough that Elza is starting to see two stabby points instead of one. She can't brace herself, because she's immobilized.

*Come on, think. There has to be something I can do.*

"You think you're so clever and civilized, but you're about to stab me in the chest. That's pretty barbaric," Elza says.

"Oh, no, I'm not going to stab you." Kankakn has the same tone of voice you'd use to comfort a tiny frightened creature. "This needle will emit a severing ray, so I may disrupt your connection with the Ardenii and take control of it. Of course, every nerve in your body will be burnt to a crisp, but that is merely an unfortunate side effect."

"The Ardenii will never talk to you." Elza squirms more, but the cords grip her tighter.

Kankakn messes with some equipment, just out of Elza's view. Elza catches a glimpse of dark fluttering shapes.

"One moment longer," Kankakn says.

Kankakn does something, and the needle turns a neon pink—the exact color of the tube of lip gloss that Elza hid inside a desk drawer when she was thirteen years old. She never actually wore that lip gloss, she only took it out and looked at it in the middle of the night. Weird thing to have as her final thought.

Then Elza remembers something Kankakn said before. Not the part about the Compassion wanting everyone to be happy—that's garbage—but the part about Elza still having a direct line to the Ardenii.

She thinks about all her lessons in concentration. In anti-pattern-matching. All those tests of logic under pressure.

And she reaches out to the Ardenii, to that part of her mind that still has their fingerprint. She sends a simple message: *Help me.*

Something answers.

Elza has a burst of random awareness—someone has stolen a comet, on the other side of the galaxy. But there's also something else, a message: **redundant security layer flaw.**

*Thanks for the oh-so-helpful feedback,* Elza thinks back at them.

**Redundant security!** The Ardenii sound terrified. **Layer flaw!**

The needle is blaring too much to look at, and Elza can't turn her head. She's seeing a pink halo around everything, but she refuses to close her eyes.

"Remember, pain is an illusion to the pure spirit," Kankakn says.

Elza squirms and tries to thrash inside the immobility field as the pink ray starts to burrow inside her. She puts all her concentration into trying to give the Ardenii one last message for Tina, like: *I forgive you for keeping that mindstone a secret. It's okay, I know why you were scared to tell me.*

Then Elza thinks about secrets. And the thing the Ardenii were trying to tell her.

**Redundant security. Layer flaw.**

Now she gets it.

Directly underneath Elza's feet, there's a giant carnivore, running wild and free.

The Hitnat cannot resist chasing after deceitful thoughts. It might even tear all the way through a wall of flesh and climb a gravity trap to get to a big enough liar.


Elza closes her eyes at last, as her skin starts to burn.

She thinks as hard as she can: *I'm lying about everything. I'm a fake. A fraud. I can't ever let anybody know the truth about me. I'm not the person they think I am.* Even thinking this stuff hurts, like poking her finger in an open wound, but she forces herself to keep thinking it. The voices of João and Naahay echo inside her: *unworthy, fake geek, bixa travesti.* She uses it, all of it.

*I'm a fake a fake a fake a fake a fake.*

She'd almost rather die than let herself believe this even for a moment. Almost.

*I fooled everyone except myself, but I know I'm hopeless.*

Her whole chest is on fire, and the feeling is spreading to her arms and legs.

*Tina can't ever know how rotten I really am inside.*

"Don't fight it," Kankakn says. "This will be over in a moment."

Elza can actually feel her nerves peeling away and her body cooking.

*Princess Constellation can't know all the selfish things I've done.*

Elza tries to broadcast more deceitful thoughts, but she can't think with this searing pain.

"If you kill me, you'll never know," Elza gasps out loud. "You'll never know the truth."

"What truth?" Kankakn doesn't stop trying to peel Elza's head open.

"The real reason I came here." Elza chokes. "Big secret. I can't tell you. Not supposed to tell you. You can torture me all you want, I won't tell."

"Hmm." Kankakn tilts her head. "I guess I can live with that."

That would suck, if Kankakn was the one Elza was trying to trick.

"You'll never," Elza blurts, "know the truth."

Her agony peaks, becomes unbearable—and a wheel of bloody teeth runs screaming up the ventilator shaft. Pieces of the shredded wall of flesh still cling to its sharp canines.

The Hitnat smashes into Kankakn's workstation, and high-tech equipment flies everywhere.

The cords slacken and release Elza's arms and legs, and the severing ray turns off.

Kankakn's acolytes and guards scream and flee as the Hitnat rolls around, trying to find its prey again. "Get this thing out of my sanctum!" Kankakn shouts, with her back against the wall. Elza drops to the floor, still flaring up with pain all over, and crawls in the direction of the exit.

She looks back and catches one glimpse of Kankakn staring at her with a curious leer on her face.

Kankakn nods, like: *Well played. But this isn't over.*


Elza's whole body complains and her stomach twists, but she keeps moving.

She hears the Hitnat chewing through everything behind her, and the footfalls of a Compassion squadron rushing up to the top floor. She's about to have an even worse end than the one everyone back home predicted for her.

The suites and cloisters at the top of the chapter house are a tangle of curves and dead ends, but she's running out of places to run.

Elza sprints around a velvet buttress and comes face-to-face with Kankakn.

"You're troubled, my child. You're afraid and alone, and it's all because you put your faith in the Ardenii. They can't save you. You wanted to understand everything, but soon you will know nothing at all."

As if they heard someone mention their names, the Ardenii pipe up with another burst of awareness. A beautiful city that had lived in peace for fifty years was just destroyed, on a world made of marble. And there's a message: **upward extract.**

*Say what you mean for once,* Elza thinks back.

**Upward! Regular junction established with orbital interpolation.**

Elza is starting to learn to think like the Ardenii—which would worry her, if she was going to live longer than a few more minutes. She ignores Kankakn's taunts, and looks around her. And thinks: *upward.*

Like . . . there's no way for her to go down from here—because the way is blocked by a gravity trap, and a wheel of teeth, and a whole Compassion army.

But what if she goes up, instead?

The way out is right here, behind Kankakn. Elza only has to keep her talking.

"Tell me one thing," Elza says. "You wanted the Ardenii to belong to everyone, instead of a few special people. I get that—but that's not what the Compassion is actually about. All Marrant and the others want to do is commit mass murder and put so-called 'misshapen creatures' in their place. What is wrong with you all?"

Elza tries to scoot sideways, to reach the other side of the room without Kankakn noticing.

"I founded the Compassion a very long time ago. At first, all we did was protest the way the queen and her council kept the Ardenii for themselves. But we soon realized why. They wanted us to think they knew what was best for everyone else."

Kankakn lunges at Elza. She barely ducks out of the way, using her momentum to get closer to her goal.

"All of their attempts to make the galaxy more 'fair' were merely an excuse to control us, and force people to act against their own self-interest," Kankakn says. "For example, consider that fire-breathing creature that helped you get inside this building."

"Fire name is Wyndgonk," Elza says.

The footsteps and voices get louder, coming from all around them.

"I don't need to know the name of that filthy beast, which my people just captured, by the way. Along with the other two who helped you invade my sanctum."

*Wyndgonk.* Guilt and anxiety stab through her.

"That whole species, the Thythuthyans, are an infestation, but the palace wanted us to help lift them up." Kankakn spits on the floor. "The only thing the Compassion has ever stood for is letting people live in peace, but there can be no peace as long as the Royal Fleet tries to meddle in everyone's business."

Three extra-large Irriyaians in Compassion uniforms come in behind Elza, weapons raised.

"Okay. Thanks for explaining. You're a sickening pile of dead organs in the shape of a person." Elza keeps eye contact with Kankakn, as she inches closer to her goal. Almost . . .

"Your opinion doesn't matter to me. There's only one thing that I need you for. Time we got back to it."

One of the three Compassion soldiers sees where Elza is heading and yells, "Stop her! She's making for the platform!"

*Merda.*

Elza jumps the rest of the distance onto the orbital-funnel platform—a kind of space elevator that can travel up to a starship, ten times faster than a rocket.

"I figured you'd have an escape route, in case the Irriyaians change their mind about letting you be in charge."

"Clever," Kankakn says. "But that elevator only leads to my ship in orbit, the *Unity at All Costs*. You'll be just as trapped up there."

"I could use a change of scenery." Elza hits the control to activate the orbital funnel and closes her eyes.

When she opens them again, she's in midair. Mauntra City shrinks to a collection of colorful shapes and green-and-purple spaces, with floatbeasts wafting over everything. If Elza didn't know better, she might think the city looked nice.

Elza soaks in the sunlight, reflecting off twenty moons, on her way up to a whole ship full of Compassion soldiers.

And she tries not to think about all the stuff she broadcast when she was trying to attract the Hitnat. About being a fraud, a disgusting fake who would have no friends if people knew the truth. She doesn't want to let herself believe any of that stuff—but now that she's let those thoughts out of the tiny box she's been keeping them in, she can't stuff them back inside.

They keep coming back, eating away at her, as she rises higher and higher into space.

# 46

·

## RACHAEL

Rachael feels dead inside. Maybe she's been that way ever since she came out of that ancient doomsday machine.

She sits there in this torture cave, staring at hands that will never make art again.

She did it, she found the answer to her problem.

And the answer was, "No."

She never should have expected the Vayt to help her. They've never helped anyone, ever. All they've done is torture people. She should feel lucky to be alive. She doesn't.

She looks at the Vayt and says in a low voice: "You're going to be forgotten."

**You said yourself. Our legacy remains.**

"Whatever. Nobody will remember you. Not even me. If we all survive somehow, we are never going to think about you again. Except maybe to be disgusted for a moment. You went to all this trouble and in the end, you were nothing but a disease."

She still isn't raising her voice—she doesn't have it in her—but maybe this is better. Just calmly, bitterly telling the truth.

"We're going to find a way to live through this," Rachael tells them. "We'll go on creating and learning, and we won't treat each other's bodies as disposable weapons. We'll be better than you were."

The Vayt seem to take this in for a while. Bubble, bubble. Their crispy scabby crust cracks a little.

**You will likely never leave this place,** they say at last. **Your vessel is damaged, and we lack the power to send you away. You are trapped here, you and the other humanoid.**

"If that's how it is, then I think I need some space." Rachael turns away from the dying monsters.

Yiwei is still where Rachael left him, in a blue shroud. He shivers and clutches at his injured leg.

"Hey," she says.

"Hey," he replies.

"I found out what the Vayt were so scared of. I know the whole story now, at least the version they wanted to tell me. And it's bad."

She tells Yiwei about the vision of a dying sun, and his expression gets more and more tragic.

"That's . . . a really terrible weapon," he says. "That swarm of black holes has had enough time to infect millions of suns by now. We can probably figure out a way to detect them. But . . ."

"But there's no way to destroy them all. The Vayt already tried."

Yiwei slumps on the ground, leaning his face against his uninjured knee. "What about your art? Did they at least help you with that?"

Rachael shakes her head. "They don't know what art is. They don't think their machine did anything to me."

She feels as if she's been carrying around an empty vessel and she's been trying to pretend there's something inside it, and she's so sick of make-believe.

"What? I'm sorry." He sits up and then winces with pain.

Damn it, she's not going to cry. "Let's focus on getting out of here in one piece."

Yiwei nods. "We should try to find our way back to where we landed. We only saw a tiny piece of the *Training Bra Disaster,* and the rest of the ship could still be in one piece." He tries to move, but he's stuck. "Can you make it so this blue shield can travel with me?"

"I . . . think so. Hang on." Rachael concentrates and draws some more blue lines, and now the blue wrap is semi-detached from the ground. Yiwei can pick it up and carry it with him, like a turtle. Or a hermit crab.

"Okay, that works. Thanks." Yiwei lurches forward, wincing every time he puts weight on his leg.

"Lean on me. I can put both of us inside the shield." Rachael makes another adjustment, and now she and Yiwei can touch again. He puts one arm around her shoulder, and they stagger, three-legged, inside the blue cocoon.

Rachael can still feel the Vayt's presence. All the hairs on her arms and neck stand up. She smells decay and barf and fresh blood and dried blood. The Vayt are yelling **Doomed** over and over.

She's never been so grateful in her life to be close to another human.

"How are you doing?" she asks him.

"It's sort of throbbing, and sort of burning, and sort of spasming."

"Stop writing song lyrics, and tell me how your leg feels."

He lets out a ragged breath. "My legs might not be my best feature much longer. I think the injury is getting worse."

"Right. You're hurt, I'm comfort. Come on."

She can feel Yiwei's breath on her neck and the weight of his body against hers.

They're moving way too slow.

Rachael remembers Tina saying, *You're a slow cooker,* and right about now, she's grateful that she doesn't process trauma in real time. A few days from now, everything she's just seen will sink in, and it'll knock her on her ass. She'll curl up into a ball and feel all of it. But for now, she can't wrap her mind around what she's been experiencing, except to draw an outline around the whole thing. *They weren't sorry, even with the bodies of their victims piled up. They didn't understand what they did to me. They told me all the stars will run cold.*

There's no way to encompass so much terrible, except by making something of her own.

Art. Or something.

The air is thick with the smell of slow death.

For once, she needs to hear the sound of her own voice. "Listen, I think Captain Othaar would be proud of you."

Yiwei stiffens, then lets out a deep sigh. "I hope so."

"I know so. You've kept his memory alive and you're holding your head up in the middle of a nightmare dimension. You're making your own path. Of course he would be proud, like I am."

Yiwei trips over a floor-knife and nearly overbalances, but Rachael manages to steady him. "Thanks," he says in a husky voice. "I'm really, really scared, you know? I mean, I've been afraid ever since I left home and I've tried so hard to hide it, but this is extra."

"It's okay to be scared," Rachael says. "It would be weird if you weren't."

"Yeah." He hisses with pain. "Listen, I shouldn't have kept trying to build you up into some kind of savior. I was trying to help you feel better. I told you what I would want to hear in your situation, but I should have just told you it was okay to feel like shit. I'm sorry."

At least they've almost made it past all of the people trapped by spurs of rock. Rachael still wishes she could do something for them, but the idea of mercy-killing just reminds her of Marrant.

Rachael looks at Yiwei's blue-tinged hand. "This is the second-worst day of my life."

Yiwei doesn't need to ask what was the actual worst day, because he was there.

"But I'm glad you're here with me," Rachael says. "I'm sorry I slow-motion dumped you. I've been pissed off about so many things, and I haven't had anyplace to put it. I just haven't been the best version of myself."

"I've liked every version of you that I've seen so far. I'm not one of those fans who only liked one album, I like your entire discography."

"Even the experimental mandolin-driven acoustic album?"

"Even the big-band duets with an aging lounge singer. All of it." Yiwei gasps with pain, or maybe he's sobbing. Rachael can't turn her head far enough to see while she's holding him up. "I wish we could have another chance."

"We get as many chances as we want." Rachael reaches up and touches his hand on her shoulder. "It's never too late, so long as we're both still here."

"So do you want to try again?"

This feels like a huge impossible question right now.

Rachael already used up all her reserves of making-sense-of-the-universe energy for the next decade, just in one day.

She can't find even a tiny pocket of stillness inside herself, her whole being is fight-or-flight. They're still surrounded by mockeries of bodies.

Yiwei is staring at Rachael, waiting for her to say something. At last, he says, "You don't have to decide right now."

Rachael tries to daydream a happy future with Yiwei, but her head is full of staring thorns, stricken people, and dying stars.

Then she manages to turn and look at him, and loses a breath. His beautiful brown eyes are full of gentleness, though his mouth twists with pain, and she can feel his heart pounding. He's followed her to hell and back—not to mention, he just told her that it's okay to feel like shit, and that's honestly the most romantic thing that anybody has ever said to her.

She's sure of one thing, and maybe that's enough for right now.

"I love you," she says. "And I really absolutely want to be with you. But . . . I'm going to be scared and flaky and push you away sometimes, and I won't always make sense to you, because I don't always make sense to myself."

Rachael never told Yiwei she loves him before. Maybe she should have picked a more romantic setting, like a moonlit beach, instead of a mutilation cave. On the other hand, the Vayt said they would never leave this place, so a beach might be kind of aspirational.

For a moment, Rachael is terrified he won't say it back.

Then he says, "I love you too, Rachael Townsend. I am going to try too hard and brood and be obnoxious as hell sometimes. But . . . I want to be with you too. We can figure out the rest later."

They make their way through the cavern, stepping over jagged edges.

The Vayt keep whispering inside Rachael's head that everything is hopeless.

But Rachael feels Yiwei's warmth against her and his weight on her shoulders, and she finds the strength to keep staggering forward.

They're both hurt, and they're both comfort.

They emerge onto a rocky plain. The ground, and all of the rocks, are a burnt orange color, and the sky is a smear of ochre and pink. There's no sun, no stars, but light filters down from somewhere—maybe from a massive wreck, burning itself out, somewhere in this pocket universe.

The chunk of the *Training Bra Disaster*'s prow is still sitting there, on the edge of a steep cliff, where they left it.

"We need to find the rest of that ship," Rachael says.

"On it." Yiwei pulls out something from inside his jacket: a deactivated Quant. He turns it on and starts scanning, while still leaning on Rachael. Then he turns to their right. "This way."

Somehow they make it down a steep slope, full of knives . . . and there's the rest of the *Training Bra Disaster*. It's half-submerged in solid rock, with spikes sticking out of its hull. As if the planet is trying to absorb the ship, the same way it tried to grab Yiwei's leg.

Kfok is outside the ship, trying to break up the rocks.

"Rachael! Yiwei!" Kfok shouts. "You made it! The ship is wrecked, and we're stranded here. At least this planet doesn't seem to attack anyone who's not a humanoid, so I've been trying to cope on my own."

They rush over there as fast as Yiwei's leg can manage.

"Apart from the rocks trapping the ship, can it fly okay?" Yiwei asks. "What kind of shape is it in?"

"We took a lot of damage. Nyitha's working on it now."

They climb painfully inside the ship, and Rachael lets the blue shield drop. It feels like a huge relief, like she's been using all her concentration to keep this thing in place. Yiwei lowers himself into the nearest cozy lump and gasps, clutching at his leg.

Nyitha comes rushing out of the flight lounge, her blue-and-gray hair frizzing out in all directions. "Thank the Singing Volcano Fish of Kthorok you're okay. Not that it's much better for all of us to be trapped together."

Yiwei sits up straight. "Is the ship—"

Nyitha shakes her head. "I just got done going over everything. We're not going anywhere. We don't have half the parts we need, and I don't think

I can replace our engines with a sculpture protesting interstellar imperialism."

"Depends what the sculpture's made of," Yiwei says.

Nyitha signals for Cinnki, the closest thing the ship has to a doctor, to come down and check out Yiwei's leg. Then she turns and looks at Rachael. "I understand if you're not ready to talk about what you just went through . . . but was there anything down there that could prove helpful to our engine repairs?"

Rachael thinks for a second, then bites her lip and shakes her head. "The Vayt have some next-level tech, but I don't think any of us could understand it, let alone turn it into anything. I did figure out how to do this, though." Rachael demonstrates creating a big barrier out of dazzling blue light.

"Nice trick. Don't see how it gets us out of here, though."

"We can't signal for help." Yiwei eyes his Quant. "Messages don't seem to be able to get into or out of this space. Total dead zone."

Rachael expected giving up to feel painful, or dramatic. Sort of like when she broke her arm in third grade. Instead it feels heavy, and light, at the same time. This is it. They're never escaping from this place. She's never doing art again. She and Yiwei won't get to make anything of their second chance.

*Sometimes the answer is no.*

"We need to assume we're going to be stuck here for an indefinite period." Nyitha folds her arms. "We should make a full inventory of—"

Rachael's not surprised. Should have known the miracles would run out sometime.

She sees Yiwei out of the corner of her eye: he's quietly wigging out on his big cushion.

"What is it?" Rachael rushes over to him. "What is it?"

Yiwei holds up his Quant, which has a bright red dot in the middle of a holographic cloud. "Tina. It's Tina. She's here. I don't know how, but she's found us."

Rachael drops her bag. Xiaohou barely jumps out in time, playing some eight-bit video-game music. Yiwei is grinning. The red dot is getting closer.

Maybe there was one more miracle left after all.

So yeah, we got pulled into this weird space, where Tuesday is Saturday and nothing is real. Crawling and lurching through a stew of radioactive particles, plasma, and dust.

Damini couldn't find the opening we came in through. Every direction looks exactly the same, and we could be trapped here forever. For all we know, time passes differently here and it's already been a thousand years since we disappeared. Fun!

If we didn't have Damini and Zaeta helping to steer the ship, we'd be even more lost than we already are.

Caepho had a wound in her side that I somehow hadn't noticed before, and a few other people were critically injured, including Gahang. Aiboul's moss had turned a nasty shade of purple on one side of his face. And our ship barely had any engines left.

Damini fiddled with the thread around her wrist and said a prayer under her breath, but there was still no path.

We were down to a crew of twelve, half of us incapacitated, and we had enough food to last a few days. We were doomed for sure.

And that's when we got some good news, out of nowhere. Something started throbbing, in the pocket of my uniform jacket.

Half a necklace.

I gave the other half to Rachael, so she could always find me if she was in trouble. No matter how far away, or how much danger. I promised I would always come if she called.

But she's the one who just threw us a lifeline.

We're racing toward her location, so I can be reunited with my best friend—and then I'm going back to my favorite universe to find the person I love.

*Elza, hang in there. I'm coming.* Nothing is going to stop me from getting back to you. I just hope it's not too late!

# 47

.

There's another ship perched on top of the *Training Bra Disaster*: sleek, totaled.

It looks a lot like the *Indomitable*—except that half the ship is missing, and there's ugly shredded metal, with scorch marks all over it, at one end. Even with everything else Rachael has seen lately, this is one of the weirdest things: a chunk of a dagger-class Royal starship, hanging out on top of a big art shed.

A few people in cranberry-colored uniforms stumble out. They see Rachael and start waving and jumping.

Tina falls out the hatch, lands on her side, picks herself up, and runs. She chops her arms, sprinting full tilt toward her best friend. She's wheezing and giggling and blurting out things: "I thought I'd never see your ass again," "Missed you so much you have no idea," "So glad you're here, wherever 'here' is," "I can't even say."

Tina's eyes are totally different and exactly the same as ever. Rachael gazes for a moment, and the light-years and months and universes fade away. Her heart comes to rest for the first time in ages as she breathes in Tina's scent and feels a little closer to home.

"Are we hugging or what?" Rachael asks.

Tina wraps herself in Rachael's embrace despite being twice Rachael's size.

Damini is standing nearby, looking shy and anxious, like she feels left out but she knows this isn't her moment.

"You too," Rachael says. "Get in here, if you want."

Damini gets in there, and Rachael beckons Yiwei over, and then Zaeta, and Cinnki, and it's a big ridiculous group hug. They're all crying and talking and nobody can understand anybody.

Then Rachael has to pull away, because she's keeping up a wall of blue fire with her mind, protecting both ships and all of the people in and around them. She needs to concentrate.

Damini, Zaeta, and Yiwei get a closer look at the two ships, which are going to need to be mashed up—somehow—into a single vessel that can fly out of here. Leaving Rachael and Tina alone together.

"That's new." Tina watches the blue glow rise up, until it reaches the lime-and-raspberry sorbet sky (which looks freakier, the longer Rachael stays here).

"Umm . . . yeah. I learned a new trick. I can't use it to draw actual pictures—I already tried. I can just make walls. And openings, I guess."

Rachael tells Tina the whole story: how she ceased to exist, how she met the monsters who ruined everyone's lives, what she learned about the end of everything.

How the monsters said they couldn't fix her.

Tina's big round eyes widen. "That's . . . a lot to process."

"No kidding. Good thing I'm a slow cooker."

Neither of them talks for a while. Tina seems like she's trying to think of the right thing to say.

"Your quest isn't over. You know that, right?" Tina offers her hand, and Rachael takes it.

"I actually don't know that." Rachael stares at her best friend, who somehow looks exactly the same even though she's changed completely.

"You hit a speed bump. That's all. The quest isn't over, as long as you keep searching. And your friends won't let you stop searching."

"It's not just that the Vayt couldn't help. There's also . . ."

Rachael almost lets the blue fire die, and has to take a moment to rebuild it. She wishes she could just pretend they were hanging out in the gravel lot behind the 23-Hour Coffee Bomb.

"There's also the fact that I fought so hard to keep thinking of myself as an artist, rather than the messenger of evil. And now? I have *an actual message from evil* that I need to deliver, or else." Rachael clenches her fist, and the blue energy surges like a wildfire—then she gets it back under control. "I want to be telling the truth as I see it, but instead I have to tell the truth as *they* see it."

"People do need to understand about the Bereavement." Tina sighs. "We visited a big bodacious sun that was dying before its time. The Vayt were watching the whole thing, through a tiny peephole. That's how we got here."

"The Vayt think there's no way to stop it. All the suns are going to go out, no matter what we do. And if we try to attack the Bereavement, it'll go into overdrive and kill the sun faster."

Tina scrunches her face, the way she always does when she's trying to work stuff out. Rachael thought she'd never see that face, wearing that expression, ever again. She wants to do a happy dance in spite of everything.

"So each microscopic black hole is surrounded by a sort of living beach ball that stops the flow of time, right?" Tina rubs her own purple scalp. "By now, most of them have arrived at their targets, and the beach ball is melting away, so time slowly speeds up to normal. And when that happens, the black hole chows down on the sun's energy."

"Right. The Vayt plan relied on attacking the time-stopping beach balls before they ever made it to a sun. And it didn't work."

Tina sits down on the nasty crumbly ground, hands around her ankles.

"Well," she says. "If this is what it is, then let's live while we can. Let's go down fighting."

Rachael sits down next to Tina, and they watch everyone figuring out how to stick two different starships together. Rachael knows Tina will need to go over there and help out. But for a moment, they sit together, watching their friends take the broken pieces of old dreams and shape them into something completely new.

"I don't like the look of this place. At all." Nyitha stares at a Quant she salvaged from the *Undisputed*. "This pocket universe shouldn't be stable, even for a short time. And it's starting to show signs of collapsing in on itself."

"The Vayt said they're dying," Rachael says. "This place will probably die with them."

She shudders.

"You never have to face any of this alone, you know," Damini tells Rachael.

"Damn right," Yiwei says. Her . . . boyfriend?

Somehow her new romance with Yiwei feels way more precious than the first time around, maybe because they went through hell together. Rachael needs to learn to appreciate the things she gets back, even while grieving the things she may have lost for good.

Nyitha is still looking at her readings. "There's no way to cobble together a fully functional starship out of parts from these two ships. The best we'll get is a stripped-down ride, without any computers or flight systems. We would crash before we get anywhere, unless . . ."

"Unless?" Yiwei asks.

"Unless we have a pilot and a navigator who are totally in sync." Damini gazes at Zaeta, who's grappling with some engine components. "Two people who each know what the other is going to do before they do it. As if they're bonded for life."

Rachael follows Damini as she marches over to a scaly creature with a bunch of eyes and flipper claws—she looks a lot like Zaeta, and she's nursing a hastily bandaged wound in her side. This must be Caepho, the other Tu-ophix who was on the *Undisputed*.

"Hey," Damini says to Caepho. Then she remembers this is still her superior officer, and hastily gets to inspection rest, adding: "Brave deeds and kind cautions, Acting Captain."

"Great hopes and small mercies." Caepho waves off the formality. "What's up?"

"You need to do it," Damini blurts. "Right now. You and Zaeta need to do it. Or we're all dead."

All of Caepho's eyes widen. "Do 'it'? My species lays eggs, we don't mate in the same way that—"

Damini blushes, a lot. "That's not what I meant. You need to do the vunci. The two of you need to be bonded, so you can fly us home."

Caepho shakes her head. "No. Not going to happen."

"I know it's a lot to ask, and it's personal, but—"

"That's not it. Zaeta and I are not compatible." Caepho sighs through slits in her neck. "I was sure the moment I met her."

"The reason you're not compatible is because you've never seen her as an equal," Damini says. "You keep treating her like your little sister, even though she's a total star."

Rachael could easily see how much Tina's changed lately—but Damini's changed too. She's standing up for her friend, telling the truth as she sees it, not raising her voice or letting anxiety turn her into a motormouth.

Caepho sighs. "I'm trying to keep Zaeta safe. On Wedding Water, people only travel into space with their families. Your aunts and mimbins and farns teach you how to avoid the thousand different ways that you could be killed on board a spacecraft. That's how we managed to build a civilization that spans three star systems."

"But *you* left home on your own," Damini says. "And you inspired her to do the same thing. You're so alike."

"Maybe we're *too* alike." Caepho hesitates, trying to explain. "Listen, the vunci isn't only biological, it's an intense connection, with someone who understands you. We don't usually share it with outsiders. Think of it as a—" Whatever she says next, the EverySpeak can't translate. "Like when you find someone you want to search for frozen eggs with."

"You need to try," Damini says. "Or we're all going to die here, and nobody will know about the Bereavement."

Rachael steps forward and speaks up at last. "Maybe there's another way."

Damini and Caepho both turn and stare at her. Zaeta is staring too, from her nearby perch, so Rachael beckons her over.

Rachael wants to shrink away from the sheer number of eyes on her, but this is important.

"I mean," Rachael mumbles to Zaeta and Damini, "I've seen you two together. If there were ever friends who were on the same page, it's the two of you. You already share everything."

"Me?" Damini sputters. Now she looks like the old Damini again. "But I thought—"

"We did share everything." Zaeta turns half her eyes toward Damini. "Until she started avoiding me like a plague."

"I'm sorry, I didn't mean to. I got scared, I was . . . I thought you wouldn't need me anymore. I thought you were ditching me, so I ditched you first."

"Rejection. You hurt my feelings. A lot. I'm sure you had your reasons. But I need to be honest."

Rachael turns back to Caepho. "You said the vunci hardly ever happens with outsiders. Which means sometimes, it does."

"It's true," Caepho says. "These two might be able to do it. From what I've seen, they have the perfect sort of connection: the type that's slightly annoying for everyone else to be around."

A flood of emotions are playing on Damini's face, like anxietyjoycuriosityreliefterror. She starts to wobble, and has to lean against the corrugated-shed side of the *Training Bra Disaster*. She opens her mouth, and nothing comes out for once.

"You cannot be serious," Zaeta says.

"You've only complained a hundred times that I have no sense of humor," Caepho says. "This sucking wound didn't somehow turn me into a comedian."

"Like you said," Rachael tells Damini. "It's the only way out of here."

Zaeta nods. "Seems like a very simple decision. We join, or we die."

She reaches out for Damini—but Damini pulls away.


"Wait. Wait a moment." Damini bites her lip, looking shy and full of longing, but also scared. "I want to make sure you're doing this for the right reason. It's a major commitment, and it's important to you. And you shouldn't be pressured into this just because we're trapped."

All ninety-nine of Zaeta's eyes are staring at the ground. "Sure. That sounds great, in theory. But we really have no choice. Necessity."

"There's always another choice." Damini kneads her forehead, the way she does when she's trying to jump-start her brain. "Rachael could talk to the Vayt again. We could try to get the computer from the *Undisputed* working. Tina could do a Tina. There are other options."

"There's no time for any of that." Now Zaeta's left eyes—the ones that are supposed to express joy and connectedness—are downcast. "I wish we were doing this because it's what we both want, rather than what we have to do to survive."

"Listen to me." Damini leans over Zaeta. "The moment I met you, I could tell you were going to be my friend. You're kind, and clever, and thoughtful, and you're ready to gravity-surf off the palace roof at a moment's notice. You gave up a comfortable life at home and risked everything to see the rest of the galaxy, and you hold your head up even when everybody treats you like anathema because you look different. You're so brilliant, I want nothing more than for the two of us to orbit each other forever."

All ninety-nine of Zaeta's eyes flood with tears, but they also widen with hope and longing. "You really mean that?"

"I really do."

"You'd better be sure. Because this process lasts forever. We'll be connected at the root. Irreversible."

"I'm sure." Damini's smile is radiant. "Ever since I heard about the vunci, I've felt jealous of whoever you ended up joining with. If being trapped on a doomed planet in a collapsing universe is what it takes for you and me to become sisters, then I'm grateful for it."

Now all ninety-nine of Zaeta's eyes have identical hopeful looks.

"If you're sure, then . . . I'm sure too." Zaeta leans forward and touches Damini's shoulders. "Let's be joined."

"Let's be besties." Damini puts her hands on Zaeta's shoulders too.

"So now what?" Damini asks, still hugging Zaeta. "What do we do? How do we finalize the bond, or whatever?"

"We already did the important part." All of Zaeta's eyes beam, and her mouth is wide, smiling. "We need a little more privacy, to seal the bond." Already, her whole posture looks different, like she's standing up straighter, not trying so hard to make herself small. "Come on. We've got—"

"—work to do." Damini finishes her sentence.

The two of them walk away, chattering to each other so fast nobody else can keep up.

"Wow." Rachael watches them go. "That's going to take some getting used to."

"Just wait," Caepho says. "They're going to be unbearable soon." But she's smiling—like she's proud of her little sister.

# 48
.

## ELZA

The day Elza flew away from Earth, she woke up early and smushed everything she owned into a pitiful shoulder bag. Then she tiptoed out of the hackerspace, before anybody could show up and yell at her. Again.

Maybe if she stayed scarce for a day or two, they'd stop scapegoating her every time anything went wrong around here. Maybe they'd let her crash here a little longer, until she got something else lined up.

She was almost at the flier-covered metal door leading to the dingy back staircase when she heard familiar voices: João and Mateus. At first Elza thought they were celebrating the success of their campaign to drive her away—but then she realized they were excited about something else. Some app was running a hacking contest that required some truly esoteric discrete math and an ability to keep a million variables in your head, with a huge reward attached.

Elza paused at the door, which would lock behind her when she left. They had never let her have her own key, she'd always needed to be buzzed in, the whole time she lived here.

She should leave now—she'd already given those otários enough chances to tear her down. But Elza had fought so hard to stop hiding who she was. She was done. What was the point of living, if you couldn't live with yourself?

So she stepped back into the main room, with the rows of computers and the racks full of gear, and said, "I'm going to win that contest, and then I'm going to come back here and buy this place."

Then she stalked out, before they could start snarking at her again.

She sat on the steps of an office building with free wifi and poked at her phone, answering half the challenges so fast she barely stopped to breathe. She crushed it step by step, not caring how she must look: an unhoused bixa jabbing at her phone as if it had hurt her.

And then . . . she won.

Unlike when she was standing at the exit to the hackerspace, she didn't pause to think when a metallic circle smashed down out of the sky, right in front of her. She jumped on with both feet, and then she was racing away from Earth. It was the ride of her life, and she's still riding it, just to see how far she can get.


Now Elza sits on another metallic circle—and she's trembling and singing Liniker e os Caramelows songs to herself, exactly the same as the first time. She feels light-headed and she's rocked by the memory of Kankakn's leering face and the pink ray that was going to tear her apart, nerve by nerve.

She's almost died before, but this time the fear got all the way into her bones. And she only escaped by letting in all the voices that she had worked so hard to lock away.

*Fake. Loser. Nothing.* The more she pushes them down, the harder they come back.

But then she stops and thinks about the Hitnat, crashing into Kankakn's sanctum, frantic with hunger. The bloody teeth, grinding against the cool stone floor. It could tell that Elza had the thing it craved most.

And she remembers Princess Constellation saying, *Anyone who is hiding deceitful thoughts near a Hitnat will be torn to pieces.*

In other words . . . the Hitnat is attracted to lies. Not secrets.

Those disgusting thoughts aren't the truth she tries to keep hidden, they're the lies she tells herself—or that wheel of teeth would never have been driven into such a frenzy.

She fed all of her worst ideas about herself to a creature that eats lies, and it gobbled them up.

She starts to tremble so hard that she almost falls off the platform. She doesn't even realize at first that she's laughing, and then she can't stop. She shakes and laughs and feels so light, she could soar without any platform.

Tears add extra glimmer to the stars as she laughs, and the planet recedes until she could cradle it in her arms. Everything looks so bright.

"They were falsehoods all along," she says out loud. "They were never the truth." She closes her eyes and imagines the Hitnat gnawing through all her worst thoughts with its whirling incisors.

The last time she broke orbit on one of these disks, Tina swooped down and rescued her. This time, she's rescued herself.

Elza watches twenty moons cavort, bathed in light and shadow, and she imagines leaving those slanders behind on the surface of Irriyaia. Maybe it's time to let go of some of the weight she's been carrying around forever.

She feels a little more ready for whatever's next. At least she won't be facing it alone.

Kankakn was right: Elza only touched the Ardenii for a few heartbeats, but they're with her forever. She never found out who her own personal orixás were back on Earth, because the first time the pai de santo tried to do the Jogo de Búzios, throwing a set of sixteen cowries onto a table to find out her path, it didn't work. The pai de santo said that once her head was clear, her path would be too.

And now? Elza's head feels clearer than it has in years. And she's found a permanent connection to ancient minds from another world.

Irriyaia is a ball of green with tan and red streaks, bathed in the sunlight. Elza can't see the *Unity at All Costs* yet—but she knows that by the time she sees it, she'll only have a moment left before she's sucked on board and recaptured.

"I have to find a way to redirect this platform so I don't arrive where all the Compassion soldiers are going to be waiting for me," Elza says out loud. "The same way Tina did with my platform, when I first left Earth. But . . . there are no controls. Nothing to reprogram."

**.0187 burst, 17 degrees.** The thought pops into Elza's head, like a fragment of a song she used to listen to.

*Uh, what?* she thinks back.

**.0187 burst redirect 17 degrees**, comes the thought. This time, more urgent.

Elza has no idea what the Ardenii are trying to say. She only knows that time is running out.

*Okay, think.*

Burst. A burst of energy? What the hell?

Elza looks at everything she's carrying. Her eyes land on the secure communication device they gave her so she could get the code from Robhhan. (Ugh.) She opens it up, and there's a tiny power cell, full of gases.

There's a warning not to open the power cell up—the warning is written in tiny lettering, but the moment Elza starts screwing with it, the lettering gets bigger and bigger, until the words are much larger than the device.

"Relax," Elza says. "I know what I'm doing. Or, I guess, *they* know what I'm doing."

She gets the cover open, and then there's a little nozzle. Takes her a moment to figure out how to release exactly .0187 units of gas at the correct angle, which might be enough to knock the platform off course.

"How soon do I—" Elza starts to say, but then the Ardenii are like, **NOW.**

She hits the release valve, and . . . there's a very quiet hissssss sound. Sort of like a mouse peeing. Nothing happens, as far as she can tell.

"Uh. So that didn't seem to . . ."

A screw-shaped starship comes into view right in front of her, with seventeen spikes cutting across it at different angles.

Her little platform swings right past an open hangar. A whole gang of Compassion mercy-killers are waiting for her, raising fireburst guns and superstream cannons.

She floats around the curve of the ship, and the Compassion death squad vanishes from sight. The platform comes to rest on one of the spikes coming off the side of the ship.

"Uh, so . . . now what?"

The Ardenii don't answer. This part is up to her.

Elza finds a hatch halfway along the spike, and tries to open it. She can barely reach, because the little air bubble around the elevator platform doesn't extend far enough. And the hatch is locked, with no way to open it from the outside.

Elza feels light-headed, like the air is running out—she came all this way to suffocate on the outside of an evil starship. She takes a deep breath of the scarce air, and thinks again about those anti-pattern-matching classes.

She studies the door until she finds the one bolt that looks different from all the others, and pulls on it with all her strength. The bolt pops out, revealing an emergency release valve. Makes sense: in case someone got stuck outside the ship, you'd need a way to get back inside in a hurry.

Elza pulls the door open and tumbles inside the ship, landing on her butt in a narrow, dark hallway. She sits there, gasping, and watches as the elevator platform slowly drifts away from the ship.

"—Elza?"

She hears a familiar voice and turns to see Kez and Yatto the Monntha staring at her.

# 49

.

## RACHAEL

Stars whirl around the mash-up starship as Damini and Zaeta perform some ridiculous maneuver and chatter to each other in low happy voices.

Rachael wants to kiss every one of these stars—she thought she'd never see them again. Not to mention, she's standing between Tina and Yiwei, and surrounded by more of her family, for the first time in forever: like a rose garden full of bees on a summer day.

Now she needs to get the rest of her family back (as long as this ship doesn't break in half first). Right next to Rachael, the wall has a jagged crack between a section of wood-and-velvet paneling from the artist salon, and the glossy gray carbonfast wall of a Royal flight-systems center. The whole thing is held together with silly putty, and it's only scary if Rachael thinks about it.

"We're almost at Irriyaia," Yiwei says. "Still no word from Elza or Kez."

Yiwei is leaning on a cane that Nyitha gave him, and his leg is properly bandaged. He's wearing a sort of smoking jacket that he borrowed from Cinnki to replace his trashed clothes, and he hasn't shaved in a while. Total thirst trap. He catches Rachael looking and gives her a little smile.

"How long before we get to the planet full of Compassion thugs?" Rachael asks.

"About four minicycles," Tina says. "Or about twenty minutes. Why?"

"I would like to go make out with my new boyfriend, who is also my old boyfriend. If that's okay with you." The last part, Rachael says to Yiwei, who smiles bigger.

"I knew you kids would work it out," Tina says.

A few minutes later, Rachael and Yiwei are in a quiet nook in the artist-ship part of the hybrid ship, and Rachael is feeling Yiwei's stubble with her fingertips and enjoying the gentle pressure of his soft lips against hers. She kisses his neck and his eyelids and he makes a gratifying surprised sound.

Then Rachael pulls away from him. "Oh, wait. I just remembered something."

"I hope it's not a reason to stop kissing me."

"It . . . sort of is. But I think it's important. We need to find Tina."

Tina is in the engine chamber, checking on some of the connections, alongside Kfok.

"Hey," Rachael says. "Can you come with us? I need Space Wikipedia for a minute."

Tina follows Rachael and Yiwei up to the next level. The hidden alcove is still there, with the flag inside. "Do you know what this means?" Rachael asks. "It was also hanging inside that red box, when they had a fake funeral for someone who wasn't dead."

Tina stares and shakes her head. "Nah. Wait, yes! I do. That's a garthax, a mythological beast on several worlds. They only use this flag when someone has died honorably in a dishonorable incident."

"What does that mean, exactly?" Yiwei says.

"If everyone else is doing something wrong, but you try to do the right thing. It's bittersweet. Like in the Zenoith incident, when Marrant torched an entire planet, some of his crew tried to stop him. Even . . ."

"Even Aym. Marrant's wife." All of a sudden the deck under Rachael's feet feels a lot wobblier, like the ship is liable to crack in half immediately. "Aym was in a coma, wasn't she? After that incident."

Tina nods. "She was in a coma, and then she died."

"Exactly like the person inside the red box." Rachael almost can't believe what she's saying. "So. What if Nyitha is . . ."

". . . Aym?" Tina whistles.

A voice comes from behind them: "I do not answer to that name anymore."


Nyitha looks at the white silk in Tina's hands. "I should have thrown away this rag years ago."

"Why didn't you?" Rachael says. "Why destroy all your beautiful old artwork, but keep a flag?"

"I suppose I wanted one thing to commemorate the person I used to be." Nyitha (Aym!) makes another low whistling sound. "Marrant can't know I'm alive. He would never stop looking for me. You know how relentless he can be."

"We sure do." Tina grimaces.

"No wonder you could understand how messed up I am. We were both messed up by the same person." Rachael can't imagine this woman who's taught her and comforted her being married to the monster who tried to kill her friends.

"It hurts to look at you," Nyitha says to Tina. "We could have had something, Thaoh and me, if she hadn't been such a blood-forsaken coward."

"Oh." Yiwei glances at his Quant. "We're almost at Irriyaia."

"We should go." Tina puts the flag back on its shelf.

"Wait a sec." Rachael keeps her eyes on Nyitha. "I need to know. Who died? That dead body inside the red box . . . who was it?"

Nyitha looks past Rachael, at the flag on its tiny shelf. "It was an accident. We didn't mean to . . . but Marrant convinced me to cover it up."

"What happened?" Tina asks.

"We sneaked inside the archives, hoping to find the original plans to the palace. Thondra wanted to understand how everything worked, because perhaps there was some hidden fail-safe, a code that would let you seize control and put the place on lockdown for a short time. This archivist caught us, and we tried to knock him out, but things got out of hand."

"Hard to get away with murder when the Ardenii are always watching," Yiwei says.

"Marrant had a device that gave us privacy. I don't know where he got it. And he figured out a way to cover our tracks and make it look like a different sort of accident." She shakes her head. "That was when he first got his hooks into me. We had this awful secret that we could never speak about to another living person, because the Ardenii would overhear. We were members of the most exclusive club in the universe. He held it over my head for years afterward."

"So when the queen sent me to you," Rachael says, "she wanted to know—"

"—what Marrant had figured out about the palace," Tina says. "That sounds . . . bad?"


Everyone in orbit around Irriyaia is startled by the arrival of a vessel that's half art-shed, half dagger-class starship. Cinnki gets messages from a bunch of people at once, demanding identification and other info. Damini and Zaeta put the ship into a spin, making the walls creak, as one orbital station tries to snag them with an ion harness. An Irriyaian vessel even targets the mash-up starship with their weapons.

Damini blinks. "Not exactly the welcome—"

"—we were hoping for," says Zaeta.

Damini and Zaeta are sitting in a couple of teacup chairs rescued from the *Undisputed*. They're facing a wall that's half a mural of a space-gremlin surrounded by political slogans and half gray carbonfast. Their hands are buried in the same holographic sludge, and all of their movements sync up perfectly.

It's like watching a pair of trapeze artists who never have the slightest doubt that one of them will always catch the other.

Rachael has no idea how to read a tactical scan, but according to Tina, there are twelve defense platforms in orbit, plus a bunch of Compassion ships. Including their flagship, a huge screw-shaped monster called the *Unity at All Costs*. Meanwhile, the Royal Fleet only has a small escort ship for its diplomatic mission, the *Undaunted*. Princess Constellation's crystalline ship, the *Invention of Innocence,* is also in orbit.

Caepho is already poking at her Quant. "We're ordered to rendezvous with the *Undaunted*." She starts talking into her shoulder comms.

Tina does a "chef's kiss" gesture with her right hand against her lips, and whispers, "I'm not here."

"And they can't have this ship," Yiwei whispers.

"Umm, yes," Caepho says into her comms. "The *Undisputed* is too damaged to navigate. Only a handful of us returned in one piece. We can proceed to the *Undaunted* via orbital funnel and provide a complete RealTac summary to the OOR. We will arrive within one cycle. Said and done." She turns to Gahang and Aiboul, who are sitting on the sofa. "We better get going."

"I need to stay with my friends," Tina says.

Zaeta chimes in. "And if we let go of these controls for a second—"

"—then this ship will break in half," Damini says.

Caepho snerks. "See? Mildly annoying." She shakes her head. "Word of warning: the Royal Fleet will try to repossess this ship, even though it's only half theirs. The legal issues could keep the Registry Authority busy for years."

"We'll try to avoid getting towed," Yiwei says. "Good luck out there. Do you, uh, hug?"

Caepho hugs Yiwei gingerly, because they're both injured. Then Tina and Rachael. Everybody else says their goodbyes, and then the survivors of the *Undisputed* are gone.

"People are still hitting us up with tons of questions," Cinnki says.

"You'd better tell everyone what you learned from the Vayt," Yiwei tells Rachael.

Rachael stares at him, as if he just asked her to do the dance of the sugar-plum fairy.

"Cinnki and I rigged up a way for you to broadcast a message that everyone around here will receive at the same time," Tina says. "We only get about a hundred microcycles before the connection fails."

"Umm, sure." Rachael feels like everyone in here is staring at her. "No problem."

"Listen," Tina says in a low voice. "I know public speaking is not your happy place. But I'll be your hype man and warm them up for you."

"Why does it have to be me? I'm not a physicist or anything."

"I'm so sorry. I wish there was another way. They won't believe it unless they hear it from you," Tina says. "They know you were the one with the direct line to the Vayt."

"I can't. I'm sorry. You'll do way better without me."

Rachael walks away before Tina can invoke the Lasagna Hats charter. She wants to make herself scarce forever. The garden-full-of-bees feeling is gone again. Oh, well.

She makes it to the other end of the half-and-half ship, a part that's entirely the *Training Bra Disaster*. And then she hears someone coming up behind her.

Rachael whirls around to face whoever it is. "Please give me some damn priv—"

Xiaohou looks up at her with big holographic eyes swiveling around. He plays a few drum hits, like a marching band warming up.

"Oh." Rachael squats down. "It's you."

Xiaohou plays the theme from this anime that Rachael watched obsessively on CrunchyRoll when she was in seventh grade.

"It's funny," she says to the robot. "When I first met Yiwei, I thought he was too cool to even talk to me. He was an actual rock star, and I was this shy artist girl. But then I saw you, and you were the dorkiest thing I ever laid eyes on. And now I realize that he was a goofy weirdo as well. Insecurity kept me from seeing him clearly until, basically, today."

Xiaohou does a handstand on one "paw," and the anime theme turns into some other boppy tune. K-Pop, maybe.

"But after everything I've faced up to, maybe I can stand to have a little more faith. Right?" She pats the robot on his little monkey head. "Thanks for the talk."

She walks back to the Forward Ops Salon, or whatever they're going to call it. Behind her, Xiaohou does a jig. She gives Tina a thumbs-up.

Tina leans forward and speaks into the holographic cloud of sparkle-crud.

"Attention, everyone. This is Tina Mains, on board the, umm . . . the

*Undisputed Training Bra Disaster.* The name needs a little workshopping. Anyway, please don't shoot! We found out the truth about the Bereavement, the thing the Vayt were so scared of."

Then Tina shoves Rachael forward and gestures for her to speak into the "mic."

Yiwei nods at Rachael from the sofa, where he's put his injured leg up.

Rachael opens her mouth.

"," Rachael says.

# 50

.

## ELZA

Yatto the Monntha is locked inside some kind of escape-proof cell that will melt your hands if you touch it. The lock has a nine-layer cipher.

The inside of the *Unity at All Costs* is a tall, echoey space—like the cortiço where Elza slept a couple of nights, back home. At the bottom of this hollowed-out screw are the ship's engines, built around a piece of a star. Seventeen spokes crisscross the central shaft and extend out into space.

Yatto's cell is at the end of one of those spokes, where the Ardenii steered Elza to.

"Took me ages to find Yatto, after I sneaked on board," says Kez (he/him). "I might have done a spot of sightseeing along the way. This ship is just gorgeous. It's evil—but did you see those redundant engine cores? Once I found Yatto's cell, I found a hiding place nearby so I could sit and keep them company."

"And I really appreciated it," Yatto says.

Elza notices that Kez hasn't deactivated the makeup she put on his face, even though he's using he/him pronouns. This makes her happy, even in the midst of all this danger.

"You should both get out of here," Yatto says to Kez and Elza. "There's no reason for the two of you to get captured too."

An ugly voice inside Elza says, *They're going to catch you. Everyone's going to learn the truth about you.* Then she imagines the Hitnat chewing it up until nothing is left: chomp chomp CHOMP. She turns back to her friends.

"We're not leaving you here," Elza tells Yatto.

Groups of Compassion foot soldiers are stomping around nearby. Elza and Kez are way too exposed out here, and there's no room for two people in Kez's hiding place, a tiny cubbyhole.

"I was nearly spotted a dozen times before you arrived," Kez tells Elza. "They seem to come past every half cycle or so."

Even if Elza had the cutting gear and gloves she used to free the Grattna, she still couldn't get Yatto out of this cell. But . . . maybe there's another way. She has some useful stuff in her pockets. And Kez has a diplomatic augmenter, which receives messages and plays holograms. She has everything she needs.

"Do you trust me?" Elza asks Yatto as she reprograms the augmenter as fast as possible.

Yatto doesn't hesitate. "Always. With my life."

Elza looks at her friend and mentor, and feels something she can't describe. Maybe "reassured"—if reassurance could be huge and epic and more heroic than any battle.

"Clueless enemies and forgiving friends," she says.

Yatto salutes and gives the response: "Quick wits and slow-moving disasters."

A guard is coming closer, with a heavy tread. Stomp stomp stomp. Sounds like an Aribentor, or maybe a Ghulg.

"Uh, what's the plan?" Kez says.

"I found out what the Compassion wants more than anything," Elza says. "An actual princess."

The guard is an Aribentor after all. They stomp into view . . . and then they see a hologram of Princess Nonesuch, standing inside Yatto's cell.

"It's customary to bow in the presence of royalty," the hologram says.

The guard stares, eyes bugging out.

"How did you get in there?" They shake their head. "Never mind, I don't care. I'm going to get promoted to senior mercy-killer after I bring you in."

The guard is already opening the cell with a device that looks like a Quant—then the hologram goes wavy for a split second.

The guard's skull-face tightens, and they raise their superstream cannon.

Kez leaps out of hiding onto the guard's back, but overbalances and lands on the floor.

Elza tweaks the hologram so it's shining right in the guard's face. While the guard is dazzled, she yanks the power core halfway out of the cannon, and then leaps out of the way. The guard gropes for the trigger and squeezes.

A loud crashing sound, a bright flash—and the guard is lying spread-eagle, out cold. Elza grabs their Quant and hits the final button to let Yatto out.

"These big guns are much too easy to turn into flash bombs," Elza says.

Kez picks himself up off the floor and retrieves his diplomatic augmenter from the hologram device.

Then he stops and stares. "Oh. Something's happening down there. In the negotiations. It's Marrant."

Kez manages to tune in via hologram, so they can watch. Marrant is standing up in front of the Compassion and Royal Fleet delegations, wearing a putrid smirk. ". . . unprecedented crisis, that has thrown all of our old rivalries into question. But you need not fear, because where the Royal Fleet offers only platitudes, I've found actual answers about the Bereavement."

Marrant pauses to let his boast sink in. A crackling sound comes from all around him.

"What's that interference?" he snaps. "Make it stop."

"Sorry, sir," a young Undhoran in a Compassion uniform mumbles. "It appears someone is trying to broadcast to all of our communication devices—"

The crackle gets louder. And cracklier.

A voice breaks through the hiss of static, and Elza's brain floods with sweet noise. She never thought she would hear that voice again. It comes out of every Quant and Joiner and loudspeaker in the meeting chamber, and everywhere else.

"Attention, everyone. This is Tina Mains on board the, umm . . . the *Undisputed Training Bra Disaster*. The name needs a little workshopping."

Elza listens to her girlfriend's voice—and now "reassurance" is more powerful than armies and battle fleets. "Reassurance" is bigger than the palace and the queen and the princesses and even the endless minds of the Ardenii. It's everything.

*I knew you would come for me.*

# 51

## RACHAEL

Rachael still can't speak. Her throat is dry and her stomach is the size of a walnut.

Tina reaches out her big shimmering purple hand. Rachael takes it, and Tina gives her a squeeze.

"You don't have to be anyone's hero," Yiwei whispers. "Just tell the truth, the best way you can. That's what an artist does, right?"

Rachael nods and looks at Tina and Yiwei. Okay. She'll pretend she's explaining this to her friends.

"The Vayt told me they fought a war against these other people, a long time ago." Her voice is barely a whisper. "The Vayt called them the Shadow Galaxy, but we don't know their real name. The Shadow Galaxy lost the war, but they left behind a weapon that was too small and slow for anyone to notice. A swarm of teeny black holes inside bubbles of timelessness, which slowly kill suns. If you attack them, they only speed up the process."

Yiwei adds, "I think you could find them by looking for little bursts of anti-neutrinos."

Rachael nods at him. "Okay, that's all. Bye."

The communications link that Tina rigged up shuts down, leaving Rachael staring into an empty cavity.

All around the planet, ships in orbit are powering down their weapons.

"They're doing it." Tina points at the holographic readout. "They're all working together to try and detect the Bereavement."

A Compassion ship and a Royal ship both send beams of energy to the same area of Irriyaia's sun. And they reveal a small black hole inside a slowly fading bubble, dark against the blaze of the sun's fiery gases.

Like a spot on a piece of fruit that's starting to go bad.


Rachael can practically hear the screams of panic coming from every starship in orbit, not to mention all the poor people down on the surface of Irriyaia. Maybe including Kez and Elza.

As the bubble disappears, time speeds up, and the black hole is already starting to turn the sun colder and deader.

That cold spreads throughout Rachael's body, as though she just walked through a blizzard in a thin hoodie. Tina squeezes her hand harder.

Yiwei huddles on his sofa, with his hands over his face. At his feet, Xiaohou tries to figure out some music that could make this better.

"Are you okay?" Rachael whispers to Yiwei.

He shakes his head without uncovering his face.

"Hearing about the Bereavement was one thing. Seeing it, though . . ." He groans. "If there was an enemy out there, we could fight them. But this? We can't do anything about."

Rachael looks around, and everybody else in the weird hybrid control deck/living room is crying, shutting down, staring at their hands. Damini and her new best friend, Zaeta, are holding each other and shivering. Cinnki and Kfok are muttering to each other. Tina is nowhere to be found.

Yiwei finally uncovers his face, revealing a damn waterfall.

"What if the same thing is happening back on Earth?" he says. "What if our sun is as messed up as this one?"

"It probably is," Rachael says.

She wishes she could cry and lose her shit the way everyone else is doing. But she's a slow cooker.

# 52

### ELZA

"It's real." Kez stares at a hologram of Irriyaia's sun. "It's real, and it's every-where, and we're half a million years too late to stop it."

Kez and Elza both stare at the readout. Elza tries to imagine São Paulo getting chillier and chillier, and eventually going dead. All of the kids, back home in the favelas and the cortiços, crying out in pain and hunger, bereft. Abandoned.

Yatto's neck spikes lay flat against their body and their eyes are wide and full of misery.

"How long do we have?"

Kez wrinkles his nose. "Hard to say. This weapon has been in place for a very long time. Could be a few years, could be a few thousand. But I'd guess sooner rather than later."

"We'd better get out of here," Elza says.

Elza, Kez, and Yatto squeeze themselves through the crawlway that leads from one spoke to the next. This is how Kez sneaked around the ship before he found where Yatto was locked up.

Around them, alarms squeal and Compassion mercy-killers swarm. Like old times.

They emerge on the next level down—just as a Compassion squadron rushes past. Elza pulls Yatto and Kez back inside their crawl space until the sound of boots fades into the distance.

The alarms stop. The silence is filled by another voice, booming out of all the ship's comms.

"All hands, this is the Chief Mercy-Bringer," says Marrant. "I'm staying here to manage the situation, but Kankakn is on her way up to the ship. By now, you've probably all seen it: a tiny black hole feasting on the sun's energy. This is a terrifying weapon, one which could have destroyed us all before we were even aware of it, if I hadn't risked everything at Antarràn to uncover the truth."

While Marrant talks and talks, Elza finds another cell—containing Wyndgonk, Robhhan, and Naahay.

"About time you got here," Wyndgonk grumbles.

"We thought you were dead," Robhhan says to Elza.

"It would be your fault if I was." Elza can't look Robhhan in his single eye.

Robhhan tries to stammer out an apology—while Marrant rants about how he deserves all the credit for uncovering the truth about the Bereavement.

Naahay starts to complain again, but Elza shuts her down with a look.

"We need to keep moving," Yatto says to Elza. "And find some way off this ship."

"Definitely time for a change of scene," Wyndgonk says.

Marrant is still talking, and Elza tries to ignore him. *We get it, you're pissed that Tina and Rachael stole your thunder.* But then Marrant says something that makes her stop and pay attention.

"—but we have the solution. The *Unity at All Costs* is a next-generation vessel, and we can use a quantum-gravity beam to induce tunneling, so this black hole will leak radiation and transform into a harmless white hole. All hands to engineering stations. Power up the ship's auxiliary power undergrid. It is our destiny to be the saviors of all life, everywhere. Peace and decency."

Voices all over the ship respond, "Peace and decency."

A loud hum starts to rise up from the very bottom of the ship, and the deck shudders under Elza's feet. Feels like an earthquake, except it doesn't let up.

"That won't work," Kez says. "If this swarm is what Rachael described, their quantum-gravity beam won't make any difference."

"Except that Rachael also said, if anyone tries to attack the swarm, it'll kill the sun faster," Elza says.

Yatto's eyes are wide with horror. "Irriyaia."

"This is what Marrant does. He takes a long-term problem, and makes it short-term."

"I got a pretty good look at this ship's engines," Kez says. "Sightseeing, remember? I think I know how to mess up the quantum-gravity thing."

Elza reaches out to the Ardenii in her mind, with a simple message: *Help us save everyone.*

No answer. Maybe the Ardenii are busy.

"It's up to us," Elza says. "But we're gonna need some help from our friends."

# 53

### •

## RACHAEL

Irriyaia looms on their viewscreens, a huge reddish-brown ball with lime-green streaks. There are twelve billion people down there, all lighting tiny flames as they bask in a dying sun.

"We're getting transmissions from all over," Cinnki says. "Everybody has a lot of questions about what we just told them."

"Tell them we'll call back later," Tina says.

"Okay." Cinnki's ears prick up. "This one says they're a friend of yours. From Smudge."

"I told you," Rachael says. "It's called—"

Cinnki does something, and a holographic image appears in the middle of the room. It's Kez (*he/him*). And Elza.

"Praise Amy Winehouse, it's really you," Kez says. He's wearing some vivid, colorful eye makeup and the shreds of a junior ambassador uniform.

"Oh, damn, I was losing my everything with worry, and here you both are," Tina says in a breathless rush. "Where are you? Are you someplace safe?"

"Er, not exactly." Kez sighs. "We're on the Compassion flagship. With Yatto."

"Listen. The Compassion decided they're going to try and attack the black hole in the sun, so Marrant can be the hero after all," Elza says.

"What?" Anxiety fills Rachael's head with noise, like a head rush. "It'll make those little death machines mad. The only thing we have going for us right now is that they don't see us as a threat. So far."

"I tried sending a message to the Ardenii," Elza says. "Maybe they'll send help."

Tina is on a secure channel with Caepho. "Sounds like your message got through. The Royal Fleet is already scrambling to respond. Unfortunately, their best option is to destroy the ship. The one that you are currently on board."

"That solution doesn't really work for me," Kez says.

"You've got at least two cycles." Tina is still looking at her Quant. "They don't have a ship nearby that can take on the *Unity at All Costs*, so they'll have to send a broadsword. Plus it might take a minute to approve an authorization of force. The Compassion is the legitimate Irriyaian government, operating within Irriyaian space, so shooting at them would be a declaration of war against Irriyaia."

"They already declared war when they decided to join the Compassion," Elza says.

"That's what all those tedious negotiations were supposed to figure out." Kez looks over his shoulder. "We're breaking orbit—probably so we can get closer to the sun."

"Hold tight," Tina says. "We'll come to you. Wait 'til you see our new ship."

"Already setting course," Damini and Zaeta say.

"Just hurry, please." Elza's breath comes in little staccato bursts.

"We're going to see if we can do some sabotage," Kez says.

Elza and Kez turn into a cloud of fireflies, then vanish.

All of Rachael's nerves are still buzzing and fritzing. "This is my fault," she says in Tina's ear. "I wasn't clear enough. I tried to tell everyone that attacking the swarm would make things worse. If our friends get killed because I didn't explain well enough—" Her arms and legs feel stiff but weak, like balsa-wood rods.

"Hey," Tina says. "Hey. Come here." She spreads her arms, and Rachael falls into her giant purple embrace. "You explained perfectly. Okay? You told them everything. You cannot blame yourself if some assholes do not know how to listen."

"Thanks." Rachael still feels unsteady. After everything she's just seen and done, after the Vayt's revolting mutilation cave, to come back and have her information twisted feels like the worst joke. "I need to be alone right now."

Yiwei starts to say something—then nods and watches Rachael walk away.


Rachael wants to hide in her quarters for a month. Then she realizes—she doesn't even know where her quarters are, or whether they're in the part of the ship that was left behind in the Vayt realm. She roams in circles for a while, but she can't find them.

So instead, she heads for the crawl space at the top of the ship, but someone is already there: a large person, hunched over with a flagon of pungent Yuul sauce.

Rachael climbs up and sits next to Nyitha (*Aym!*) without saying a word.

What with everything else, she's barely had a moment to think about her teacher's real identity.

Rachael looks at the stars, all of them slowly going cold. "We're going to board the Compassion flagship, to try and stop your ex from making things worse. Again."

Nyitha shakes her head. "He always needed to be the one with the answers, even when he knew nothing. For so long, I felt trapped by his certainty."

Something tiny but massive is weighing Rachael down on the inside—like a microscopic black hole. "I wish you'd told me who you really were a long time ago."

"Me too. I suppose this is the last lesson I have to teach you." Nyitha turns to face Rachael, with a dark fire in her eyes. "Sometimes it's better to make a mess instead of creating a perfect work of beauty. Break things, melt walls. You don't need to know what you're doing, or be in control of everything. Don't be like my ex-husband."

The ship takes a near-hit from a missile, and the walls shimmy. Voices come from the flight lounge below.

"Evasive—" Damini says.

"—maneuvers!" Zaeta shouts.

The ship whirls on its axis, trying to get out of the line of fire.

"I better go." Rachael crawls toward the ramp. "You should come with us. We could use the help."

Nyitha shakes her head. "I will face Marrant in my own way." She swigs Yuul sauce. "I won't be here when you get back."

Rachael wishes she could think of something to say, in case this is the last time she sees her teacher. She settles for, "Thank you for helping me. I know I'll be okay, even if I don't entirely feel that way right now."

Nyitha toasts with her Yuul sauce, then goes back to watching the slow decay of every sun.

# 54

.

## ELZA

Irriyaia shrinks to a pinprick in the holographic display of Kez's diplomatic augmenter as the *Unity at All Costs* moves at top speed toward Jhyia, Irriyaia's sun.

Yatto peers over Kez's shoulder and furrows their tiger-striped brow. "At its current speed, this ship will be in position within one cycle. The closest Royal broadsword will not arrive in time to prevent them from firing their quantum-gravity beam and making things worse, to save Marrant's foolish pride."

"I'm not in favor of us getting blown up," Kez says.

"Is anyone in favor of that?" Wyndgonk grumbles.

"We ought to find a way off this ship before it's too late." Robhhan squints. "Get to safety, let the Royal Fleet worry about it. We did our part already."

Instead of snapping at Robhhan for being such a coward, Elza gathers herself and straightens up—head up, eyes bright. It works: she feels ready to handle what needs handling.

"We're not leaving," Elza says in a calm voice, putting the argument to an end. "We need to do some sabotage and buy the Royal Fleet some more time." She turns to Kez. "What do we do?"

Kez shakes his head. "So much for diplomacy. One good thing about physics: it never lies." He groans. "Remember how a starship's engines are built around a piece of a sun? Ship this size requires an entire corona—and that much plasma is going to have a bloody great shield around it. And meanwhile, we're going to be flying quite close to a high-luminosity star, which means that radiation shielding will be compromised."

"And the beam generator needs to be close to the engines, so they can tap directly into that power source," Yatto says.

"Right," says Kez. "So we can trigger an automatic shutdown if we cause a surge in the power conduit. Which I could do from up to a hundred meters away, using the power cell from that cannon we borrowed."

"Sounds great," Robhhan says. "Except that there are hundreds of mercy-killers between us and the engines down there."

Everyone radiates so much fear the air gets thicker in Elza's nostrils. She could choke if she breathes it in. But she thinks of Princess Constellation and says, "Our friends are coming, but for now it's up to us. Because when you know the answer, it becomes your responsibility."

"I like that saying." Naahay smiles.

"I heard it from a cartoon mouse."

"Leave the mercy-killers to me," Yatto says. "Most of them are Irriyaian, to avoid the appearance of an occupying force. They kept making excuses to come gawk at me while I was imprisoned, because they had all been re-cruited using my image."

"You already tried to take advantage of that, remember?" Kez says. "The real you couldn't compete with the fake you."

"I'll just have to try again." Yatto straightens up and sets their jaw, with a serious expression in their big fish-owl eyes. Their spikes straighten out and stand up, like cactus spines. "I must take responsibility for what's been done in my name, even at the cost of my life."

They turn to leave, but Elza gets in their path, arms folded. "No. Not happening. You're not allowed to throw your life away."

"Elza, you have grown in understanding as well as grace. You must see that there is no other way." Yatto smiles down at her, almost like a proud parent.

But Elza doesn't back down. "You can risk your life, sure. We're all about to risk our lives, and I hate that it's necessary. But if you go out there think-ing you deserve to die? Or that you owe your life to the *people who used you*? It's going to end in shit. For all of us."

"Elza's right, as usual," Kez says. "Thing about you Irriyaians is, you believe the land belongs to whoever is taking care of it. Which is fantastic, until it turns into a lot of competition and posturing to show who's the best caretaker. See? I've spent way too much time trying to make sense of your prenthro business. Point is, we can always find another way."

Yatto pauses and ripples all their shoulder-spikes. "Very well. I will be careful, and create a distraction without making myself a target. I promise."

"Okay. I'm going to hold you to that."

Elza's about to say something else, but then she gets a tickle in the back of her head—the Ardenii, sending another tiny message. This time, though, it's a bit of Princess Constellation's voice: **I'm coming, my Royal Dance Instructor.**

"Help is on the way," Elza says. "Let's make sure they're not too late."

# 55

.

## RACHAEL

Rachael sits on a flying pizza dish with Tina, Yiwei, and Cinnki. Damini and Zaeta really wanted to come along, but they're the only ones alive who can keep the *Undisputed Training Bra Disaster* flying, and Kfok needed to keep patching the hull.

The *Unity at All Costs* is almost in position near the sun, and Irriyaia looks like another pinprick. Damini and Zaeta got them as close as possible without getting shot down, but still this feels like an endless journey across a darkling sea. This is the first time Rachael's been on an orbital funnel since she left Earth, and she'd forgotten how weird it is to sit on a circle with nothing between you and death.

"I know you keep saying you were just in the right place, back at Antar-ràn," Tina whispers. "But look what you've done lately. You ceased to exist! You traveled outside the universe! You faced up to the original monsters. I would have been so dramatic."

Tina gazes at Rachael, and so does Yiwei on her other side. She doesn't have to stare into endless inky death soup, she can look at the two people she cares about most.

"Oh, believe me, I was terrified," Rachael says.

"On Javarr, we would have called Rachael a lyrshaal," Cinnki says. "Hard to translate, but it means someone with thick, lustrous fur who nevertheless acts furless when the situation demands. It's the highest praise anyone can give."

This platform is chilly as fresh snow, but Rachael still has a warm flush. "I guess I've realized some stuff since we all left Wentrolo. I keep thinking about something Yiwei told me, that I can make my actual life a work of art. And maybe that can be enough."

"Ummm, that was actually something my ex-girlfriend said," Yiwei protests.

"Whatever, it was good advice. And the best thing I ever did? Was to bring this family together. So I better do whatever I can to help keep you all safe."

"Like I said," Cinnki says. "A total lyrshaal." He draws the Javarah symbol on the scuffed metal they're sitting on.

"If I'm alive in a few days," Rachael says, "that's gonna be my first tattoo."

She holds out her hands, and Tina and Yiwei each take one, and Cinnki joins the circle.

"Champions of Suck," Tina says.

"It's growing on me," Yiwei says.

The *Unity at All Costs* looks nasty up close: a slightly crooked stake, with a bunch of sharp nails sticking out of its sides, basking in the rays of Jhyia on one side. The point of the stake glows as the ship prepares to shoot a fancy ray gun at the black hole nestled on the sun.

A much smaller shape is arcing away at top speed, a crystalline sliver: Princess Constellation's ship?

"We're almost there," Cinnki says. "Any ideas how we get on board?"

"The ship's hull is too well reinforced to cut through, even if we had the tools," Yiwei says.

The orbital funnel arcs around the underside of the big screw, and then drifts to a stop next to the scuffed side of the ship, with the red slash of the Compassion.

"Hey, Rachael, remember when your hands were glowing?" Tina whispers. "Can you still do that? And can you make a way in for us?"

A sick feeling spreads outward from Rachael's stomach, and she's watching a movie of a warped torso in a skunk tee. But she nods. "Yeah, sure."

She leans forward until her hands almost touch the hull.

"Are you sure?" Tina says. "Because we can find another way—"

Rachael breathes stale air and thinks: *Break things, melt walls.* "I'm on it."

The Vayt are still there, deep inside her head, even though they're gone everywhere else in the universe. She touches that screaming evil nugget with her mind—and her hands have the blue glow again. She reaches out and makes a big circle with her fingers, until there's a portal that leads inside the ship, right next to the engine chamber.

"I'll keep this platform here for as long as I can," Yiwei says. "Go."

Oxygen whooshes out through the opening Rachael made. She gestures for Tina and Cinnki to go through as fast as possible, because she can't hold this door open for long.

They stumble-jump through. Tina lands on her butt on the other side.

Rachael pauses for a moment, trying to meet Yiwei's gaze.

"Come back to me," he says.

Rachael looks at the inside of the Compassion ship, lit by the pulsating glare of the engines. She does not feel like any kind of lyrshaal right now.

She looks back at Yiwei. "I love you. Until all the stars go dark."

"Hope that's not happening any time soon." Yiwei has tears in his eyes, and Xiaohou is just making a series of rattling clicks. "I love you too."

Rachael throws herself through the hole in the side of the ship. She catches one last look at Yiwei, standing on an orbital funnel that he's trying to keep from drifting away into open space. Then she closes the portal behind her.

Tina leads the way, with Cinnki pulling up the rear. They tiptoe along the sloping floor of a narrow inspection tunnel, full of echoes and ragged shadows, that runs around the base of the screw. Every few feet, they hear a scraping sound, or one of the shadows seems to change position, and they stop and press themselves against the wall.

This ship is the size of a few skyscrapers. Rachael has no idea how they're going to find their friends, except by heading for wherever the Hosts of Misadventure are hosting.

Up ahead, a shadow seems to flicker, and there's a faint rustle. Everybody stops and hides yet again.

Tina groan-roars. "It's nothing *again*. We need to find our friends. Come on."

She marches forward—and walks straight into a large person holding a spindly object that might be a weapon.

"Hello," the tall person says.

"Your Radiance," Tina stammers. "I did not expect to . . . I mean . . ."

"Tina Mains," says the tall person: a Makvarian wearing a luminous crown and a flowy-gauzy dress that looks like an Anna Sui. "And this must be Rachael Townsend. Your acquaintance is a prize."

"And I'm Cinnki. Your Radiance." Cinnki sweeps one elegant arm and lowers a knee.

"Oh, shit. You're Princess Constellation!" Rachael can't believe she said "oh, shit" to a princess. "I mean, um, your acquain—"

Princess Constellation waves a hand. "One might wish to indulge in every pleasantry. But we have too little time, and too much foolishness to contend with."

The princess and her posse—her retainers?—lead Rachael, Tina, and Cinnki out of the access hallway into a wide open space the size of a mall parking lot, with the central shaft of the ship extending upward to a vanishing point. At the center of this chamber: a huge sideways bottle containing a piece of sunlight that seems to rage against its prison.

As soon as their group enters the huge engine chamber, a few dozen mercy-killers run toward them through a doorway facing theirs. Nobody shoots a weapon, probably because there are too many fragile and flammable things in here, including a sun-in-a-glass.

Princess Constellation strides toward the soldiers, unsheathing two long weapons that crackle and throw off bright green sparks—they curl like whips, or stick out straight like batons, depending on how she holds them. All of her attendants pull out similar whip/stick weapons.

"Go. Find your friends," she says in a cheerful tone. "We shall entertain these tiresome fanatics."

Tina hesitates for a second, then nods. "Thank you, your Radi—"

"Go!" Princess Constellation and her attendants slash a path through the crowd of mercy-killers, who barely slow them down. Rachael hears her ask, "Is there such a thing as a food that nobody can eat?" Then she's out of earshot.

Rachael turns to follow Tina and Cinnki, but they're gone. She lost track of them.

Damn it. She feels exposed in this big open space, even though everyone is looking at Princess Constellation. She looks around and spots a boxy structure that looks like a workstation or a piece of machinery, which Tina might have taken cover behind.

She rushes over there and finds Kez, clutching part of a gun.

Rachael has one of those moments when she knows she ought to say something, but there are too many things to say and she can't find any of them right now, and she's stuck for a moment, and she starts to worry that Kez is going to think she's being rude. Which is a ridiculous thing to worry about under these circumstances, but welcome to Rachael's brain.

Kez speaks first. "I'm trying really, really hard not to melt down because I need to concentrate. Just so you know. I'm trying to turn this gun into a localized surge generator, to shut everything down, and my head is full of too many regrets, like a load of extra subroutines. I really believed I would spend the rest of my life making peace between people."

"There's, uh, there's more than one way to make peace. And we don't always get to be the people we thought we'd be."

"It's not just that. It's Yatto. I'm scared, I helped convince them to come home, and now . . ."

Rachael's about to ask what Kez means about Yatto—then she sees for herself.

Yatto the Monntha is standing on a tiny ledge, about forty feet up, with their back to a sheer wall. They must have climbed down from one of the spokes that crisscross the shaft. They're shouldering a big gun and standing in the same heroic pose as in all of their old movies. The light from the captive sunbeam paints their stripes in golden hues and casts a huge shadow.

Yatto's voice rings out across the cavernous space, sounding every bit like an action hero.

"As I always have, I fight for you," they roar. "I am the arms and the legs of prenthro, and the voice of the Monntha nation and all other nations. You listened when I fed you lies—listen to me now as I speak the truth."

They raise their gun. "We are all one, and this is our chance to save our world."

A squadron of Irriyaian mercy-killers, who were running to attack Princess Constellation, stop in their tracks and stare up at Yatto, jaws open. They all look at Yatto the same way Rachael would at Olivia Rodrigo. They ignore their leader, a Ghulg who looks a bit like Moxx, barking at them to get back in formation.

"Ack, time to go." Kez finishes tinkering with the gun. "I have to get within a hundred meters of that glorified fuse box." He gestures at a conduit in the middle of some tubing, coming from the sun-in-a-bottle, on the other side of the room. "Not so far away, but it feels like the greatest distance I've ever traveled."

"I've got you." Rachael concentrates for a moment, wincing—and then her hands shape a blue flame.

"Well, that's new." Kez stares at her hands. "How long have you been able to do that?"

"I don't have a good sense of the passage of time right now." She wraps Kez in a wall of blue. "Not sure how much longer this'll work, now that the Vayt are gone. Hurry, I'll cover you."

Kez hesitates a moment longer, then sprints in the direction of the junction. Rachael keeps the shield moving with him, which requires some concentration.

The Ghulg mercy-killer stops trying to yell at their troops, and raises a fireburst gun to shoot at Yatto—because Yatto isn't in the way of any engines or crucial ship components.

Rachael hesitates, then puts up another blue barrier around Yatto, a second before a fireball appears in front of them. Yatto blinks with surprise, then carries on speechifying.

Cinnki dashes across the room, and two mercy-killers lunge at him, so Rachael puts up a third blue wall.

Rachael's head throbs, and her neck hurts, and her hands feel like they're on fire, and she. Will. Not. Quit.

An alarm shrills, and warnings sound: a Royal broadsword has arrived, and it's shooting missiles at the *Unity at All Costs*. A voice calls out, "Prepare countermeasures! All hands brace—"

The ground trembles under Rachael's feet, but she does not stop raising unbreakable shields around her family.

# 56

.

## ELZA

Elza thinks back on her training: how to walk without making a sound, how to move during eyeblinks. She can't help smiling when she remembers how she thought they were teaching her etiquette. She might never get to be a princess, but she can still sneak like one.

She got separated from Kez and the others after all the Compassion troops started swarming through this maze of workstations and power conduits. And now Yatto is standing overhead, shouting, and Elza can't do anything more for them. She needs to find Kez before it's too late.

The floor rocks under Elza's feet. An image bursts into her head and catches her off guard: a Royal broadsword, the *Invincible,* is trading missiles and pulse-cannon blasts with the ship Elza's standing on. (The Ardenii chose another awkward moment to give Elza an update.)

Compassion soldiers run around like ants, and Elza barely hides from them. She gets a flashback to when the police raided the cortiço—if only she'd had princess training back then, things would have been different.

Elza gets a clear view of Yatto for a second, wrapped in blue energy, exactly like the shields Rachael made at Antarràn. Is Rachael here somewhere?

The Ardenii are yelling inside Elza's head and she cannot make sense of any of it, but these ancient super-intelligent gods sound . . . scared.

The distraction puts Elza off her game, and she runs straight into someone, a large figure wearing a shredded uniform. Elza starts to duck and roll—then she looks up into the face of her girlfriend.

Elza wants to say a hundred things, like: *you're here, you made it, I thought I'd never see you again,* but those things feel way too small for the scary/wonderful feeling that rushes through her, making her actual chest hurt. Her eyes overflow and she feels her lip tremble, and she and Tina both open their arms at the same time.

"We always make our way back to each other," Tina says between sniffles. "I couldn't ever be too lost to find you."

Elza starts to answer, but someone is singing.

A haunting chorus, lamenting in a minor key without any words, drowns out the sounds of Yatto's voice, the space battle, the Compassion soldiers, the thrum of the engines. Everything except Elza's own stuttering heartbeat, and Tina's voice.

"What?" Tina stares at Elza. "What is it?"

"You don't hear the music?"

As Elza moves in the direction of the voices, they grow more mournful. And then she realizes: it's the Ardenii, singing inside her head.

The voices guide Elza to a figure in a gossamer dress and shining crown, slumped under a teacup chair, clutching at a wound in her stomach.

Elza gets closer, and her heart turns to stone.

Princess Constellation is doubled over, protecting a severe burn going up her left side, almost to her armpit. Her beautiful tiger-striped face shines with sweat, and her eyes keep closing against the pain.

The Ardenii sing louder: a funeral dirge for one of their own.

"I'm going to find a medical kit," Tina whispers. "I know where they usually keep 'em in an engine chamber like this. Sit tight." She's gone, before Elza can tell her to be careful.

"You're going to be okay," Elza tells Princess Constellation. "Tina's getting help. Sit tight."

"Oh, I'm dying. Rather quickly, I should think." Princess Constellation laughs and it sounds like a death rattle.

"No, you can't give up. I won't let you, this isn't how it ends." Elza trembles. That music is getting under her skin, sweeping her on a tide of grief.

"Remember when I told you that knowledge is ugly?" Princess Constellation rasps as if each breath is an agony.

"Yes," Elza says. "Sure. Knowledge is ugly and that's why we wear cute dresses and eat cake. Lie still. Tina's bringing the medical supplies."

"I'm dying. That's a fact. It's not a particularly lovely one, but no flowery words can make it otherwise." Princess Constellation coughs and groans. "You will face many unpleasant truths in the days to come, and your job will be to help everyone else to see them—without weeping so hard that their eyes become useless. Spying is part of the job, but not the biggest part."

"You can't die, you're not allowed." Elza's own eyes have become useless with tears. "You still have to help me to make sense of all this."

"Your studies aren't finished, but you still have to graduate. Unpleasant truths." Princess Constellation grimaces. "Listen. Remember back in the palace, when I made you stop at the fountain of dreams and fill that thimble?"

Elza nods.

"And remember when I gave you a draught to drink, when you first came on board the *Invention of Innocence*? Remember the moss in your shoe? And when I introduced you to every one of the sprites inside the white cloister? And that time you spent a full jewel doing the hand-and-foot signs?"

Elza nods some more. "You're always making me do weird stuff. You never explain."

"Certain rituals . . ." She coughs, and moans, and coughs again. "Certain rituals must be observed if one is to become a princess."

"A . . . what?"

She coughs harder. "Ordin . . . Ordinarily, there would be a coronation. Mine was resplendent. I regret you will be deprived of all the pomp."

Elza can't understand what in blazes Princess Constellation is talking about.

And then she understands, and her chest tightens. She feels dizzy, light-headed, fluttery inside—like she's falling into space and the breath is being snatched away from her lungs.

She's trembling and there's smoke and gunfire everywhere, and it's all unbearable.

Elza can still remember when she thought she would never have to grieve again. What a fool she was.

"Feel bad later," Princess Compassion snaps, suddenly her old bossy self again. "Take the crown off my head and place it onto yours."

"I . . . I don't want to."

"You do. You do want to. You're merely frightened, and you think that if you take my crown, you'll be admitting that I'm dying. You might even feel as if you're finishing me off. But my death won't change, no matter what you do, and that crown belongs to you now. Don't let me die without knowing I passed my burden on."

Elza's hands are shaking too much to hold anything.

"I can't. I'm sorry. Don't ask me to do that."

Someone is at Elza's elbow. "I couldn't find the medical kit," Tina says in a low voice. "Listen, she's right, you need to take the crown right now. It's dangerous for it to be without an owner."

"You don't understand." Elza can barely get the words out. "The Ardenii, they're not what I thought. There's a reason why every princess has come from privilege, they can watch people lose their homes and their families and everything else without being reminded of the things they lived through. I worked so hard to feel safe, you were there. You saw how hard I worked."

"I was. I did." Tina's eyes are gigantic and full of love. "You're exactly who they need in that palace. You could do so much good. I will be there with you, I'll be your consort. You won't be doing this alone."

"Please, my Royal Dance Instructor," Princess Constellation wheezes. "You've already performed every ritual. All you need to do is place the crown on your head and say that you welcome the Ardenii into your life, and you will have my place."

Elza shakes her head. "I don't think I can do this. There are a thousand other candidates who would be better. I'm sorry."

"You've been chosen," Tina says. "Not because you were born into it, but because you worked for it, and because you have the best heart I've ever known. You will be a great princess, you know you will, and . . . if you let this go, you'll regret it forever."

Elza hesitates a moment longer. Then she lifts the crown away from Princess Constellation's brow. The princess smiles as her eyes go still.

The crown weighs almost nothing. Like a party hat.

Princess Constellation isn't breathing anymore.

Elza can't bear her frozen smile. She wants to throw this crown away, let it land wherever.

"I'm going to get so good at curtseying," Tina says.

Maybe in a few years, Elza would be ready for this. She looks at her wet face reflected in the crown.

Then it's gone.

"My poor child. You hesitated too long." Kankakn holds the crown in one bejeweled claw. "Once again, the universe looks kindly upon me." She stands with her feet planted, in pointed boots, and the crown picks up rainbow spears of light from her luminous tinsel fur.

Tina stands up and faces Kankakn, who has two acolytes in red-slashed cream robes behind her. "Give that crown back. It doesn't belong to you." Tina takes on her old fighting stance, even if she won't actually fight.

One of the acolytes picks up Elza's girlfriend and throws her at the wall. Tina hits with a cracking sound that makes Elza sick to her stomach, and lands in a heap on the floor.

Elza watches, helpless, as Kankakn lowers the crown onto her own head and says, "I welcome the Ardenii into my life."

# 57

.

## RACHAEL

Rachael hides behind a big carbonfast structure shaped like an old-fashioned oil lamp, and her head hurts worse than when she was on stage receiving the white half spiral. The shield around Yatto flickers and vanishes, then reappears, as Rachael grits her teeth with effort. She tries to make the dome of blue energy follow Kez as he inches toward the junction.

The ship's engines are shrieking louder—like the beam thingy is ready to fire at the sun.

Kez can't get any closer. A whole crowd of Compassion mercy-killers presses up against Rachael's blue dome, like zombies against the windows of a car in a horror movie. They climb on top of it and push on all sides, while Kez stares with the unmistakable mask of an anxiety attack all over his face. His makeup is starting to smear.

Speaking of anxiety attacks, Rachael is aware that she's doing her thing of checking out and talking to herself, mostly a string of nonsense and jokes that nobody else would find funny.

Compassion soldiers are shooting at Yatto's shield, and climbing up to their ledge to try and grab them. Every time a fireburst gun hits the wall of energy protecting Yatto, Rachael has a stabbing pain in her temples.

She won't let her family down.

"Thank you for coming to my mixed-media installation," she mutters as she pushes the mercy-killers away from Kez with a giant blue hand.

Kez ought to be close enough to the junction to shut everything down now, but he's poking at the modified gun and scowling. Rachael can't hear him, but she can tell he's mostly saying curse words.

Rachael can't let herself think too much about the fact that she's the only thing keeping her friends alive, or she'll lose her concentration and this flame will die—and so will they. She feels tired, so damn tired. Her neck aches. Her mind goes in every direction at once, while she strains to keep the blue fires lit.

Yatto is still shouting from their perch, but they've quit trying to act like an action-movie hero, and instead they're pleading, "Don't put our world in danger, let us take a moment to study the Bereavement before we try anything. Please listen."

Rachael wonders about the asteroids she smashed together, back when she was first on Nyitha's (*Aym's!*) ship. These big space rocks will spiral away from each other, trailing diamonds and colorful dust, for thousands of years—the only artwork Rachael will leave behind, except for some doodles back on Earth. Does it matter that her name isn't on it?

The Compassion throws more bodies at Kez and Yatto, and Rachael doesn't want to hurt anyone if she can avoid it. Even fascist edgelords.

Cinnki crawls into Rachael's hiding place, with his ears pulled back. "How can I help?"

"Can't talk," Rachael grunts. "Please help Kez."

"On it." Cinnki ducks out and runs toward Kez, who's still swarmed by Compassion soldiers.

Back when Rachael stood inside the mausoleum at Antarràn and drew a few thousand pictures in a few minutes, she felt more alive than ever before. She was at the exact center of a giant powerful machine, talking to it in her own private language, protecting her family and stopping a revolting crime—and she didn't have to think about the "revolting crime" part until later. Now, replaying that scene, she feels sick to her stomach.

She finds herself quoting Nyitha under her breath. *Any art you can make in the face of sorrow is good art. Maybe your real self is whatever is left after you've lost the things you thought were you.*

Rachael raises another shield around Cinnki as he runs to help Kez, and then the Compassion soldiers start attacking both of them, swinging batons and throwing their gloved fists wildly. She slowly, agonizingly, merges Cinnki's bubble into Kez's.

Cinnki and Kez both poke at the half gun, and . . . it works. Sparks start flying out of that junction, and alarms sound, and the engines sputter to a halt.

They did it. Kez salutes Cinnki, and then they're both whooping and crying.

A whole new alarm starts shrieking. Someone yells, "Collision alert! Brace for impact!"

Rachael looks at the nearest holo-display, and curses. The Royal broadsword is careening out of control, about to crash head-on into the *Unity at All Costs.*

Because this day could always get worse.

---

A giant hand smacks Rachael. Metal and people and alarms are all scream-ing and her eyes and nose are full of dust and smoke. Twisted, ruined bod-ies fly past—for a moment, she thinks she's back in the Vayt's torture cave.

She looks up, and there's nothing but shredded metal where Yatto was standing. And a hole that leads directly to space. Some automated voice drones about sealing hull breaches. The air is thin, like a mountaintop.

Rachael's head feels woozy, she can't see any of her friends. The engines roar back to life, ready to fire a beam at the sun.

Hurts to move. Sore all over. Rachael crawls on her hands and knees toward Kez and Cinnki. They're splayed out on the floor, surrounded by people in black armor. She gropes for a pulse on Kez's neck and can't find one—then he opens his eyes and moans.

"Kez," Rachael whispers. "Please get up. We need to—"

A tall figure steps into the middle of the room, with their head on fire. No, wait. Not on fire. They're wearing a crown that glows like the first rays of NewSun, and their fox/cat Javarah face is full of triumph. Instead of reg-ular fur, they're covered with silvery strands that reflect the dazzling light from their head.

"Enough of this foolishness," says the Javarah in the crown. "The Com-passion promised to protect everyone, and we keep our promises."

"You see these golden threads I'm wearing?" Kez gets up, wincing with pain. "I took an oath to work for mutual understanding, and most of all, to tell the truth—so you can believe me when I tell you that you're about to make things worse, Kankakn."

The floor keeps going all tilt-a-whirl, but Kez stays upright somehow.

"You poor deluded soul. You can't bear for us to be the ones who save the world. But you're too late, my child." Kankakn's ears stand straight up. "The quantum-gravity beam is almost ready to fire. Nobody can stop it now."

The ceiling cracks, the struts showing fissures, so Rachael makes a patch here and a brace there out of blue plasma. Her head throbs with effort, but she works harder to hold this ship together. *Not today. Not my family.*

"I'm not your child," Kez snaps, like that touched a nerve. Then he mod-erates his voice: "How can you wear that crown, and still not understand the consequences of your actions? I've spent too long trying to listen to the Compassion's point of view, but you won't listen at all."

Kankakn bares sharp teeth, and turns to Rachael: "Rachael Townsend, correct? We all owe you a great debt. While your friends strike poses and shout at everyone, you've aided us in understanding the threat we face. I will build statues of you on every world."

Rachael's voice is gone, but she shakes her head: no more blood-forsaken statues.

"Of course, you won't be there to see them. We can still learn much from examining your brain and studying your link with the Shapers—the Vayt." Kankakn chuckles. "I'll see that you don't suffer. You will keep helping us long after you are dead, Rachael Townsend."

"Shut up," says a voice behind Kankakn. "You're not saving anybody or protecting anybody. You're not even special. You're only the latest in a long line of creeps who wanted to steal all the glory that other people worked hard for. It's *over*."

Elza holds her head up high, and her eyes are blazing with life. Not bracing herself for the next nightmare, not bristling, just standing her ground. Rachael's never seen her looking like this. Like . . . a princess.

"This is between you and me," Elza says. "Let's end this."

# 58

.

## ELZA

Elza stares at Kankakn's stolen crown. For a moment, she feels utterly helpless, defeated. It's too late: she had her chance and she let it slip away.

But she looks closer and notices a twitch in Kankakn's left eye. A split-second grimace. One of her ears curls like a dead leaf.

The Ardenii are rejecting Kankakn. Because the crown doesn't belong to her.

"I deserve that crown. I worked for it, I earned it. Princess Constellation chose me, out of everyone." Saying these things aloud helps Elza believe they're true.

And she looks around her. Wyndgonk, Rachael, Kez, they're all standing with her.

Through the smoke and dust, she sees Tina grunting with pain where Kankakn's acolyte threw her at a wall. Tina looks up at Elza, with blood and tears streaking down her shimmering lavender face.

"I'll be fine," Tina says. "Go get your crown back."

A million emotions claw their way to the surface of Elza's mind, including relief, gratitude, worry, and most of all love. But there's no time. She gives Tina one last look, then advances on her enemy.

Kankakn swings her left hand at Elza's head. Elza dodges, but nearly gets caught off guard by Kankakn's left leg.

Elza's never been in a fight before, in her entire life. On Earth, her main strategy was to run like hell from people who wanted to hurt her—she was always sprinting, hiding, shouting defiance in her mind. Since she went into space, she's hacked computers and helped to fly a starship and done training, but this is the first time she's ever raised her hand to anyone.

But Elza remembers all that training, all those times she had to practice combat while tiny wisps painted her face. She lets go and trusts her instincts.

"Years I spent, wishing and longing for the gift of the Ardenii," Kankakn says, with that complacent look plastered on her fox-muzzle. "And you think you should have it handed to you. What arrogance. You're not even remotely worthy, my child."

Kankakn jabs at Elza with both claws, and Elza ducks out of reach.

"You're the one who's not worthy." Elza spits. "The more you know, the less you learn. You're exactly who shouldn't have this crown."

Elza whirls like a capoeirista and kicks at Kankakn's leg. She almost connects.

"I'll share this gift with everyone who follows me," Kankakn says. "I won't buy into the elitism of the Firmament."

Even the Compassion soldiers stop and stare as Elza and Kankakn fail to land blows on each other. Kez is frantically trying to repair the machine he improvised from a dead gun, while Elza keeps everyone distracted.

"You're right." Elza grunts with exhaustion. "Of course you're right. Everybody should have access to the Ardenii, as much as they can handle."

"You're . . . agreeing with me?" Kankakn startles, and Elza nearly tags her.

"Of course I am. You're right, except that the Ardenii shouldn't be anyone's servants. But look at what you're doing right now. We brought you the truth about the Bereavement, information that Rachael nearly died to get. And now you're about to make things worse, because you can't handle the knowledge we shared with you."

"You can't tell us about a major threat and expect us to do nothing."

The floor shakes harder as the generator roars to life. A ray of dark fire pours out of the bottom of the ship, toward the tiny speck of death in Irriyaia's sun.

"Too late!" Kankakn shouts. "Irriyaia is under our protection, and the Compassion takes care of its own."

The half gun falls out of Kez's hands as he stares in horror.

Elza stares, transfixed, as the beam roars out of the bottom of the ship, and then it finishes firing.

Nothing happens for a moment, as if the ray-blast had no effect. And then . . . a new alarm sounds, and the Ardenii show Elza a glimpse of something terrible. The remains of the bubble around the tiny black hole start to fade, and the black hole grows, devouring more of the sun.

"You didn't stop anything," Elza says. "You only made things worse. We warned you."

"I'll try again," Kankakn says. "Once I've killed you and forced the Ardenii to accept me, I'll know how to make this work. Knowledge is power."

Kankakn reels, clutching her head. The Ardenii are still fighting her, messing up her concentration.

She swings her blade, too slow. Elza knocks it out of her hand.

"Knowledge isn't power," Elza says. "Knowledge is pain."

Someone jumps onto Kankakn's back, pushing her away from Elza. At first Elza only has an impression of flailing arms and legs.

Then she sees one big glaring eye.

"Give that crown back!" Robhhan snarls. "Give. It. Back!"

Kankakn swats Robhhan off her—but the crown flips away from her head.

The crown spins in midair, buffeted by the howling wind as all the air starts to leave the disintegrating starship. It spins, catching the light.

Elza tries to reach for the crown, but she's still picking herself up off the floor. Kankakn lunges to catch the falling crown.

The crown hangs in midair and then stops—still out of Kankakn's grasp.

A skeleton hand holds the crown out to Elza.

"You'd better put this on before I change my mind." Naahay rolls her eyes inside her skull-face. "I can hardly stand the thought of bowing to you for the rest of my life."

Elza finally won at *WorstBestFriend*.

She grabs the crown from Naahay, says, "I welcome the Ardenii into my life," and shoves it on top of her head.

Elza's mind floods with information, too much to process. She knows all about the day they tried to give Kankakn her first coat of fur and it ended in disaster, and the names of a dozen random Compassion soldiers who are trying to kill her friends, and the recipe for the perfect windcake, and so much more. She feels as if her thoughts have been going in circles forever, and now they're spreading out in all directions, as if she's suddenly become so much bigger than she could have imagined. Everything is gold and red and blazing, there is so much life and so much sadness and glory. She almost passes out.

The Ardenii are screaming about the crumbling starship and the imploding sun and the evacuation of Irriyaia.

Kankakn still advances on Elza, leaving Robhhan in a heap on the floor.

"That crown is still mine, little princess," Kankakn sneers. "I'll make it live on my head, or I'll dismantle it to learn its secrets."

Elza looks at Tina, who smiles at her through a curtain of blood. *My consort.*

Kankakn throws a piece of rubble. Elza leaps out of the way at the last moment.

But Kankakn's foot connects with Elza's neck, and she falls sideways, head ringing.

Elza lies on the floor. The Ardenii keep bombarding her with terrible facts: thousands of Irriyaians just died when their refugee ship crashed. She feels weak, shaky. Can't focus.

"This will be over in a moment, little princess. Don't struggle. I don't want to hurt you any more than I need to. Just let it happen."

Elza's trapped. Kankakn's claws are around her throat, squeezing. Elza's vision is full of sickly clouds. She can feel herself losing consciousness, going dark.

# 59

.

## RACHAEL

*I will build statues of you on every world. Of course, you won't be there to see them.*

Rachael can see it, clear as anything: them prying her skull open, taking her apart.

Nothing left of her but some ugly memorial that mocks who she really was.

This is the way it was always going to end.

Pins and needles in her hands, her feet. Her head is swimming. The migraine comes back, but the Vayt are gone.

Rachael makes eye contact with Tina, and she follows Tina's gaze.

Elza is dying. Her eyes bug out, she makes tiny gasps as Kankakn giggles and chokes her out.

*I am not letting anything happen to my family. Maybe I can't make art, but I can do this.*

The numbness leaves Rachael's hands as she tightens them into fists, so bright they leave searing trails on her own retinas. The noise in her head turns from a scream to a roar, and she stares at Kankakn's leering face.

Rachael thinks: *Seeing is for making, bodies are for shaping.*

She brings her fists together, then tears them apart.


One moment, Kankakn is throttling Elza and whispering taunts in her ear.

The next, a hole opens up in Kankakn's chest, glowing bright blue. She looks down, startled, as her heart and lungs disappear into a hole that leads nowhere.

Then she topples over.

Elza struggles to her feet and sees Rachael's glowing blue hands.

"I had to," Rachael says. "I had to. She wasn't going to stop. She was going to kill you. I . . . I'm a murderer."

"You saved me," Elza says. "You saved my life. You did the right thing. I . . ."

The ship's alarms get even louder and angrier, and the floor thumps up and down, and an automated voice is yelling about critical failure.

Rachael looks at the nearest holographic readout, and her heart shrivels to nothing.

Irriyaia's frozen sun is shrinking, starting to crash in on itself. And this ship isn't going to be a ship for much longer.

# 60

.

Rachael left home because she wanted to see everything there was to see out here. All of the beautiful things and the scary things and the awful things and the glorious things. And she wanted to turn all of it into art that would live forever in people's dreams.

Now she's standing over a body that was alive a moment ago, watching the glare around her hands slowly fade. There's a gaping hole in Kankakn's chest and stomach—and Rachael did that. She tore a big chunk out of another person. She never wanted to be in charge of making sense of the Vayt's arcane technology, and now she's actually used it to take a life.

She's on her way to becoming exactly like the people who ruined her as an artist.

Yiwei's voice comes through in fuzzy spurts: "I can't make it back to pick you . . . solar interferen . . . you've got like three minutes before . . . can you hea . . . are you gettin . . . please say something."

Rachael finally snaps out of her daze and says, "I'm here."

But there's no response. She waited too long, and the connection cut out.

"We'll get out of this, right?" Kez is saying. "We're on a super-advanced ship, even if it's falling apart around us. There has to be something we can use to escape. Tina, what do you see that we can use? Elza, you've got all of the knowledge of the Ardenii in your head now. There's probably twenty ways to get to safety."

The air is still full of smoke, but there's no sound except the alarms. Everyone who was attacking each other down here is dead, or they bailed a few minutes ago.

Cinnki groans and Rachael kneels next to him, whispering: "Hang in there." Rachael wishes for the millionth time that she had actual medical knowledge, beyond knowing how to change a nanofiber dressing or read the instruments in Dr. Karrast's sickbay.

Tina has a Quant, which is helpfully letting them know that they have half a minicycle left (about two and a half minutes) before this ship goes boom.

Elza and Tina and Kez talk in a low tone, brainstorming ways to escape.

1. If we could find a bunch of atmosphere suits somewhere . . .
2. If we could build some kind of escape craft out of sections of the cladding on the undergrid . . .
3. What if we could stop the flow of time in a ten-foot radius?
4. If we had a magical flying pony . . .

This is the moment when someone is supposed to come up with a save, a clever, out-of-nowhere idea that will scoop all of them out of here and onto the *Undisputed Training Bra Disaster* in the nick of time. Right?

Kez is putting on his serious problem-solving scowl, Elza is talking to herself (or probably the Ardenii). And Tina? Tina is . . .

Oh, shit. Tina is wearing her self-sacrifice face.


The *Unity at All Costs* is about to snap in half like a pencil. A blazing line of fire is cutting across the middle of the ship over their heads—jagged and ugly.

"We're out of time," Tina says. "There's only one thing we can do."

The floor feels like a bounce-house.

"What do you—" Elza starts to ask. And then she gets it, and she folds her arms. "No. That's not happening. No way."

"I can't think of a way out," Tina says. "But maybe *she* can."

Nobody has to ask which *she* Tina is talking about.

Captain. Thaoh. Argentian.

The toxic fumes and deck-quake are getting to Rachael, and she can't think. Her stomach is a knot.

"But," Rachael says. "If you do this, you won't be you anymore. The only way to bring back Captain Argentian is to get rid of you. Completely. Permanently. You can't. We won't let you."

"I wouldn't, if I could think of any other way. I'm dead either way, but I could save all of you." Tina chokes and blinks away tears. "The people I care about most. Let me do this for you."

Elza gropes in a pocket inside the lining of her jacket and touches something: a little nugget of rock.

"No way." Elza shakes until her brand-new crown rattles. But her gaze is steady. "Stop wasting our time and help us come up with a better plan."

"We're out of options," Tina says. "I don't want this any more than you do."

Rachael wishes that Yiwei was here, or that she could raise him again on her comms. He'd know what to say right now. Maybe he'd know some way to wrap them in a piece of the ship's hull, like he did when the *Indomitable* blew up.

"You can't," Elza pleads. "I thought we were past this."

"You don't need to make some grand gesture," Rachael says.

"Don't throw your life away," Kez adds.

The red-hot crack over their heads widens, and starts raining boiling-hot metal, a few feet away. The floor sizzles and buckles.

A brand-new alarm starts whistling and singing, like a dolphin or something.

"What's—" Rachael chokes on fumes.

"That's the critical hull fragmentation alarm," Tina says. "Means this ship can't protect us much longer."

Ninety seconds left, before they're dead.

"I love you," Tina says to Elza. "I'm so proud of you, and I wish we could take a moment to celebrate. I did not think you could get any more beautiful. If the last thing I see ends up being your face, with that crown on your head, I'll have no complaints. Loving you has been my life."

Tina looks at Kez and Rachael. "I love all of you. I want to stay with you forever. I don't want to do this."

"So don't." Elza bites her lip and pushes tears away from her eyes. "We'll figure something else out."

"I don't think there's any other way. Not this time." Tina's face is soaked with blood and tears. "I bet the Ardenii are telling you the same thing."

The noises get louder. The alarms, the screams. The crack in the side of the ship spreads like a hole in a frozen pond.

Rachael closes her eyes and tries to listen to the rational part of her, the part that always sees the bigger picture, the most generous way of looking at things. But all she sees is the giant hole she tore out of Kankakn's chest, and the hole in the side of the ship where Yatto used to be.

She opens her eyes again. "You should do it," Rachael says to Tina.

Elza's eyes get wider, and she looks at Rachael like she's a traitor.

"I know," Rachael says to Elza. "But we're all going to die, and this is our only hope. At least this way, Tina will be in there somewhere, and you and I will be alive, and maybe we can find a way to bring her back."

One minute left.

"Don't care what it takes," Tina says to Elza. "I will find my way back to you. This won't be the end of us. I swear it."

Elza collapses onto Tina's shoulder, weeping. "I can't believe, after everything we've been through, after everything I've learned, this is how it ends. I can't accept that."

"Don't accept it! Never accept it. I need you to bring me back. This isn't the end, unless we all die here."

Elza and Tina look at each other through two sheets of saltwater. Rachael's heart is going up in flames.

"Okay." Elza hands Tina a tiny yellow shard. "Do it. I'm going to hate her for not being you. But . . . Just do it."

The *Unity at All Costs* snaps in half, a clean break.

The top half of the ship hurtles away from them, including the main engines and the control deck and everything, and it feels like they're on an elevator whose cables got cut. They're still standing and breathing, thanks to the gravitators and emergency life support, but not for much longer.

Rachael loses her balance and lands on her side on the deck, near the dead body of Princess Constellation. She rights herself in time to see Tina kneeling where she fell.

She looks up at Elza on one knee, like she's about to propose. "Never forget I love you. No matter what, I'll always be your consort. My beautiful princess."

Tina places the rock between her eyes—and then she's not Tina anymore.

# 61

.

## ELZA

Tina lets go of Elza and pulls herself up to her feet. Her posture is straighter, and her perfect violet-lavender face looks totally different. She looks around like a hawk, taking in everything.

"I had the strangest dream, and I have the bloodiest hangover," Tina says, in *her* voice. "And now? It looks like I might've overslept."

She takes in the destruction, everything that's breaking and exploding and spitting fire on this half spaceship, and says something in Makvarian that the EverySpeak doesn't even try to translate.

The Ardenii have gone quiet in Elza's head, like all the destruction and loose solar radiation are interfering with their signal. She can barely feel them, way off in the distance, somewhere under the surface of her grief.

"Oh, this is not good," Tina—Thaoh—says. "No time, not much to work with. Dying starship. Bleeding head wound. Like old times. Except I've got a strange aftertaste in my mouth, as if I ate some kind of fish recently. Distracting."

At last, she looks at Elza, Kez, and Rachael.

"My name is Thaoh Argentian and my pronoun is *she*. I have a feeling that if I'm alive a cycle from now, I'm going to be very extremely pissed off at whoever decided to bring me back from the dead, against my express wishes. But first I have to get us out of this." She looks at Elza. "Your Radiance. Newly crowned, I see. Your acquaintance is a prize. What are the Ardenii telling you?"

Twenty seconds left. The floor is one big earthquake and more molten gunk is pouring down on them, dangerously close now. Wyndgonk and Naahay are dragging the unconscious Cinnki and the semi-conscious Robhhan into the middle of their group.

And all Elza can think is, *You stole her body. The love of my life is gone. You took her from me.*

Then Elza pulls herself together. "I . . . they're not. There's just a hum. It's been bugging me."

"That hum is going to save our lives. Which direction is it strongest in?"

Elza turns in a complete circle, like she's hunting for cellphone bars. She finds the right direction, facing away from the shell of her girlfriend.

Meanwhile, Thaoh is talking to Kez. "Junior Ambassador. Blessings to you. Did they issue you an augmenter?" Kez nods, and Thaoh keeps talking. "Everything is made out of information, in the end. That's all anything is. Argh. I'm so angry at being alive, I can barely think."

Ten seconds left. Elza can feel the hum stronger now, like she's homing in on it. Maybe that's the *Invention of Innocence,* floating somewhere out there. Waiting for Princess Constellation to come home. Is that Elza's ship now?

"That blue glow on your hands," Captain Argentian says to Rachael. "I need you to make a hole in the side of the ship, right where the princess is facing. Right now!"

Rachael hesitates, starts to argue—and then does what Thaoh says. A second later, there's a hole in the side of the ship, bigger than the hole in Kankakn's chest but the exact same perfectly round shape. They're staring at open space.

They have a few seconds left before they're blown to flaming chunks. The hole Rachael made is gushing air and Elza feels vacuum tugging at her.

They're going to die now. Tina gave up her life, donated her body, and they're going to die anyway. Elza could have been spending her last minute of life holding her girlfriend.

Instead, she spent that time watching a pretender stomp around in her girlfriend's body.

Elza's stomach heaves, like that falling-through-space sensation only worse.

The monster that stole Tina's body is still talking talking talking, a million words a minute, something about using Kez's diplomatic augmenter to create a solid-state holographic bubble made out of codicils and good wishes.

Elza and her friends are yanked out of the ship, through the opening Rachael created. Elza can't remember if you're supposed to hold your breath before being shot into open space or not. And then it's too late anyway. They're flying through vacuum.

Except . . . Elza can still breathe. The nine of them are huddling inside a sphere made out of glowing words.

Elza looks up over her head and sees a whole paragraph about having goodwill toward others, and the importance of "agreeing to care." It's all stuff from Kez's diplomatic notes, and it's somehow turned solid enough to keep the air inside their little bubble.

"Little trick I picked up during my tour on the *Indestructible,*" Thaoh

Argentian snorts. "Now we have to hope the Ardenii are willing to do whatever it takes to keep their newest princess alive."

Behind them, the *Unity at All Costs* breaks into smaller and smaller pieces, glowing with lethal radioactivity.

The nine of them drift, in a ball made out of words. All Elza wants is to be alone with her thoughts, but Thaoh won't stop asking questions.

"I can't make sense of these Quant updates. What is happening to the Firmament? How did things get this bad? Who in the thousand flaming lakes are the 'Vayt'?"

Nobody answers. Cinnki wheezes a little.

"Hang in there," Kez whispers to him.

"I'm being rude," Thaoh says. "I introduced myself, but I never learned your names. Who are you all?"

Nobody answers.

Rachael looks at Elza, as if to say *I'm sorry*.

Kez fusses over Cinnki. Wyndgonk sidles next to Elza with a sad expression in fire tiny round eyes.

"So there's a princess and a junior ambassador. Quite a distinguished group." Thaoh looks at Rachael. "But you? I can't begin to figure out what you are. That trick you did with your hands was like nothing I've ever seen."

Rachael shakes her head and looks at her boots.

Even if Rachael *wanted* to talk to this imposter, this is exactly the kind of situation where her shyness would get in the way. Elza wishes she could step in and speak for Rachael right now, but she doesn't have any more words.

At last Kez turns to Captain Argentian. "We really don't want to talk to you. I know none of this is your fault, except for the actual decisions you made when you were alive. But we just lost part of our family, and we *can't talk to you right now*."

The *Unity at All Costs* has finished breaking up, and the pieces of starship are burning to cinders.

As for Irriyaia . . . the planet is getting colder—not to mention, it's being pulled out of orbit—as its sun gets devoured. Already there are earthquakes, and superstorms, and the whole planet will be uninhabitable within a matter of days.

Kez curses, looking at the readout. "Damn. Ganno the Wurthhi is still down there. And all of his friends."

"I hope they made it to a ship." Elza's voice trembles.

"It all happened so suddenly," Kez says in a low voice. "We already lost Yatto today."

The piece of sphere nearest Elza's head reads, "Only by learning each other's ways can we truly value each other."

Thaoh is staring at the Quant on her sleeve—Tina's Quant, Tina's sleeve—and muttering untranslatable curses.

Elza wants to scream and beat her head against this ball of idealistic phrases about peacefulness and generosity.

But she doesn't want to show any weakness in front of this pretender—even though her instincts keep telling her that her girlfriend is suffering, and she longs to reach out to her. And Irriyaia? She can't get her mind to understand the sheer amount of death.

All Elza can do is whisper to Kez, "Is it okay to touch you?" and then wait for him to process those words through the haze of grief and terror and anxiety. She waits a long, long time, before he nods, and then she puts her hand on his arm, so lightly it's barely touching. He leans over and puts his head on her shoulder, and she can feel him sobbing.

The "hum" of the Ardenii is getting louder inside Elza's head. Like they're singing again.

# 62

### ▪

## RACHAEL

Someone has super-glued a dozen ships together in orbit around Irriyaia, including the *Invention of Innocence,* the *Undaunted,* and the *Undisputed Training Bra Disaster.* A makeshift life raft.

Specks rise from the surface of Irriyaia to the crowd of ships, too many to count. Rachael can't tell what these things are at first, and then she gets it: these are tiny ships and elevator platforms, carrying refugees up from the planet.

The *Invention of Innocence* reaches out with an ion harness and tugs the ball of words inside the cargo hangar of the nearest ship. They bounce once, and the lofty ideals evaporate around them.

Attendants in silk gowns swarm forward and grab Elza, fussing over her. "Your Radiance, you're safe," says one. "We must get you to a secure location," says another.

"Help my friends," Elza says, and instantly the attendants are gathering Cinnki and Robbhan and rushing them to a sickbay.

Captain Argentian strides off the disintegrating remains of the word-ball, demanding to speak to someone in authority. Rachael still hears her voice for a moment after she disappears into the crowd.

About half the Irriyaian refugees are stark naked. Because that's how Irriyaians mourn. All of that exposed flesh isn't funny, or sexy, just . . . vulnerable.

Kez spies a group of Irriyaians staggering off a busted orbital funnel, and rushes over to one of them. "Ganno. Ganno the Wurthhi! You're okay. You survived."

Ganno won't look at Kez. "Go away."

"I'm so sorry. There aren't any words . . ." Kez closes his eyes and touches his forehead with knotted fists. "I'll leave you alone, I wanted you to know I'm here if you—"

"Go away," Ganno snarls. "We're not friends. We're not anything. You helped bring this upon us, you and Yatto and your other friends. You are nowhere in my heart."

Ganno strides away, leaving Kez staring—his face covered with smeared makeup and etched with pain and grief.

Rachael hears a sound behind her and jumps, then turns to see Yiwei, leaning on his cane, with Xiaohou on his shoulder.

"I saw Tina, and I . . . damn it. She's always been a stab-in-two-ribs person." Rachael dimly recognizes one of Yiwei's chéngyǔ sayings, but she doesn't have it in her to ask what it means. "I know it's selfish, when all these people have lost everything. But damn it, it still hurts." Yiwei opens his free arm to embrace her. "I'm here. If that's okay."

Rachael pulls away. "I just killed a person."

"You—" Yiwei stares. "Are you okay?"

Rachael considers. "I don't know. She deserved it. But I still can't right now. I might not be able to for a while. Days, maybe weeks. All I want to do is hermit, and I hope I don't scare you off. I guess somebody has to plan a funeral. Two funerals! For Yatto and Tina. Oh, god."

She hadn't thought about Tina's funeral. Will Thaoh show up? How do you mourn someone who's still walking around and making noise? If they grieve for Tina, are they giving up any hope of ever getting her back?

Xiaohou plays an achingly mournful piece of Chinese classical music, with a two-stringed violin playing slow high notes.

"I will help you plan the . . ." Yiwei closes his eyes and shudders. "The funerals, I'll help plan. We'll all help. And you should take as long as you need. I love your whole discography."

"Okay." Rachael feels like she's barely making sense, which is another reason she needs some alone time. "I'm still your girlfriend even if you don't see me for a month." She turns to walk away, and then she's transfixed by the sight of the dying planet.

Irriyaia's atmosphere is half gone, and the other half is going fast. All the people, the floatbeasts, the crystal buildings catching the different types of moonlight, wiped away.

All anyone can do is bear witness.

# 63

.

## ELZA

They sit together, in the flight lounge of the *Undisputed Training Bra Disaster,* on sofas and overstuffed armchairs and teacup chairs.

The princess, the ex-artist, the peacemaker, the musician, and the explorer. Plus Zaeta.

The six of them stare at the husk of Irriyaia with hearts like scraps of ice.

Elza still can't make sense of everything the Ardenii keep pouring into her brain. It's exactly what she was dreaming of—but also everything that scared her.

Every time she has an upsetting thought, like, *How many mothers had to watch their children die on that planet?* the Ardenii respond by filling her mind with the names and faces of some of the mothers and children who just died, helpless, in agony and terror. Super easy to spiral, worse questions leading to worse answers.

*Knowledge is ugly.*

The Ardenii are starting off slow, giving her bits and pieces of their awareness. In a few days, she'll be drowning.

"All of the stars are dying much more quickly, everywhere." Yiwei's face turns green and orange in the light of the holographic blob in the palm of his hand. "Something happened. When the . . . when the Compassion tried to get rid of the black hole here, the rest of the swarm reacted. All of the bubbles that were keeping the black holes in check are fading away."

Kez shrinks into his chair. "Including our sun? Back home?"

Yiwei nods.

The Ardenii flood Elza's mind with images: people on a thousand different worlds, looking up, noticing that the sun looks a little dimmer all of a sudden. People holding their children close as their skies change color. And then she sees a glimpse of Earth, from a distance, with the green slowly leaching out, to be replaced by gray.

"We have one Earth year left, before it's all gone," Elza says. "Only one year. Before, we didn't know how long anyone had, but now it's clear. Thanks to Marrant."

Nobody speaks for a while. Irriyaia spins in front of them: a mass grave-yard.

"I should find a way to get back to Earth," Kez says, burying his face in his hands. "Even if I can't do any good. I should go back and try to make people understand."

"I can't go home," Rachael says. "Not without Tina."

"I'll go wherever you go," Yiwei says to Rachael, and she gives him the saddest smile.

Elza closes her eyes, letting the Ardenii rise to the front of her mind for a moment. They're reminding her about all her new obligations as a princess, all the people who need to talk to her, all the warnings she needs to deliver. She needs to choose a princess name, too.

"I guess I need to go back to the Firmament," Elza says. "To Wentrolo. I should be in the Palace of Scented Tears right now."

"All of you, shut up," Damini says. "Just shut up. What is this? What are you all saying?"

Everybody stops and stares at her. Except for Zaeta, who nods.

"This isn't over. We have a *year*. We can find a way to make this right," Damini says. "I know what you're about to say: the Vayt spent a hundred thousand years and couldn't find a solution, so what can we do in one? But we don't know, unless we try. We can't give up now, after everything we've . . ."

Damini stops and stares at an empty spot on the sofa, where Tina would be sitting if she was here.

They all turn and look at Rachael.

"I think this is the moment when you say we need to stick together. To be here for each other," Kez says softly to Rachael.

Rachael stares at the wall. "Fuck off."

"Well, I'll say it." Elza can't believe she's the one giving the inspirational speech about friendship. "We're all we have. Wherever you all go, I'm go-ing with you. I don't care about my princess duties, I'm sticking with my friends. We've already spent too much time apart. I need you to remind me of who I am, and maybe I can do the same for you."

Nobody tries to hold hands or make a big vow or anything.

But everybody nods, one by one, and Elza hears them mutter something like "yeah sure," or "okay, fine."

They sit together, staring out at the dead rock dotted with the scars of cities.

———

What kind of person does Elza want to be?

She's been trying to figure this out forever. When her parents threw her out, when she went to live at the hackerspace, when she left Earth. When she fell for an alien superhero, and when she decided to try to become a princess.

And she still doesn't have a clue.

Tina knew exactly who she wanted to be when Elza first met her: Captain Fantastic. And now Tina's gotten her wish, and Elza wants to scream all the time.

Elza knows who she *doesn't* want to be: she can't be the prophet of doom, the person who always knows about everything terrible happening everywhere, with no room left for kindness. She's not going to let caring paralyze her, but she's also not going to stop caring.

What's the point in being a princess and having access to genius minds with almost limitless knowledge if you can't make things better for anyone?

She sits in her luxurious receiving room on board the *Invention of Innocence* and stares at the river running across her ceiling. This is never going to feel natural. The Ardenii are still peppering her with awful realizations: the next horrible thing and the next thing after that. The other six princesses are sending her greetings and welcoming her to the royal family. Elza wishes she could shut it all out.

Elza says out loud: "I'm going to be someone who finds people who are hurting, and helps them. I'm going to make people feel like they can go on."

So she goes in search of someone who needs her help.


Rachael is missing. Nobody knows where to find her. Yiwei shakes his head and says, "She's been through a lot. I don't expect to see her anytime soon." Damini and Zaeta say that Elza is the tenth person to ask them where to find Rachael—everybody wants Rachael to answer all of their questions about the Vayt and the Bereavement, more than ever.

Of course the Ardenii know exactly where to find Rachael, because they always know where everybody is, at least on any of the major planets or space stations. She's in a remote part of this life raft: the *Bittersweet Kiss*, a tiny freighter that was carrying Scanthian parsnips and Makvarian meatspores before it got turned into a transport for refugees.

Rachael is sitting on a dusty crate, feet propped up on some fraying parsnip sacks. She gazes at the floor, with no expression in her green eyes.

Elza feels a whole flood of emotions, looking at the side of Rachael's face.

1. Jealousy, that Rachael got to have all those extra years with Tina before Elza got to know either of them.
2. A desperate need to bond with the other person who knew Tina best in the entire universe, except maybe for Tina's mom.
3. Gratitude, for everything Rachael did to make Elza feel welcome and safe, when she first got to space. All the ways Rachael turned their little group into a family.
4. Frustration, because that's always in the mix somewhere.

The Ardenii are getting all hyperactive inside Elza's head, seeing Rachael again. They want to figure out her connection with the Vayt, because they recognize that the Vayt are another ancient "people," with knowledge and technology and ideas that the Ardenii are desperate to understand. Elza tries to get them to shush—but she also needs them right now.

Rachael notices Elza standing there at last, and looks up. She tries to look cheerful, or hopeful. It doesn't take.

"I can't," Rachael says. "Whatever you need from me, I can't. There's nothing left."

Elza bristles—why would Rachael assume Elza wants something from her?—then takes a breath. And resets.

"I'm here to help you," Elza says. "I can't do anything about Tina. I can't change the fact that you just killed someone for the first time—thanks for saving my life!—but I can help you make art again. Right here, right now. You're going to draw a picture for me."

Rachael turns and stares at Elza. Her green eyes are tear-washed, and her mouth hangs open.

# 64

.

## RACHAEL

"I get it. You want a win. We all want a win right now. But I can't give you one." Rachael tries to keep her voice steady, but she's croaking like a Scanthian.

"This isn't about that," Elza says. "I'm a princess now. If anybody can help you to fix this, it's me. I want to be able to use this power to help the people I love."

Rachael blinks away tears, and then there are more tears. Did Elza say she loved Rachael?

"Now that Tina's gone, you're the only one who can understand what I'm going through," Elza says in a barely audible voice. "The Ardenii aren't what I expected. I know a million dreadful things, but I don't have any answers at all. You and I both met something ancient and got changed, and we can't ever go back. But maybe my demons can help you with yours."

Rachael sits with that.

"Aym kept trying to tell me that sometimes things are too broken to fix. I never wanted to hear it. But now I get what she was saying."

Elza nods. "I could so easily give in to despair right now. Every time I close my eyes, the Ardenii give me more information that I don't know what to do with. On Scanthia Prime, there's a toddler whose mother just died in a riot, and this child is about to be trampled, and I can't do a thing to help her. I never got a chance to talk to Tina about any of this."

The crown suits Elza: it flickers with light that plays across her face. She holds her shoulders straighter, and her eyes glow with wisdom.

"That's the thing," Rachael says. "Worlds are dying. People are losing their shit. Who cares if I can make art or not? It doesn't seem important anymore."

"It matters to me." Elza doesn't smile, but her hazel eyes are super kind. "One problem at a time. We'll save the galaxy tomorrow."

"Okay."

Rachael takes Elza through the whole history of failure. How she tried to draw with her feet and use a psychic wall. How she visited a black-and-white hole. How she went outside the universe and talked smack to hideous monsters. Elza doesn't interrupt once with a snarky comment. She just listens and nods.

"So," Elza says. "The part of your brain that allows you to make art has been rewired to help you control the Vayt's technology. And the Vayt didn't have any concept of art, right? They didn't have senses, or bodies, at least not the same way we do. We were like bugs to them—bugs that they could turn into a swarm, to fight the other swarm."

"That's right."

Hearing Elza sum up the situation makes Rachael feel worse.

"It must be unbearable," Elza says. "To have something that made you happy and gave you a way to touch the world. To move people. And then, to have it twisted around and turned into a tool by monsters who live rent-free in your head? I can't imagine. But here's the thing: the Vayt are gone. What's left of their legacy is under your control."

"I'm not in control of anything," Rachael says.

"I saw what you did on that ship."

"I used their power to murder someone. Doesn't mean I can create art again."

Elza nods and then walks away. Rachael doesn't try to see where she's going.

A moment later, Elza comes back with a stick. Kind of grungy and ashy, with thick fibers sticking out of the broken end. Probably came out of one of those crates with the meat-spores from Tina's home planet that Tina never got to visit.

"Draw me a picture," Elza commands.

"I can't."

Rachael won't take the stick from Elza.

"You can. Here's what we think happened." Does "we" mean Elza and the Ardenii? "You didn't actually control that machine by drawing, because the pictures themselves weren't an instruction set, right? You were drawing with the right side of your brain, which allowed you to access the machine and give it orders with the left side. Maybe the Vayt saw the ability to create a lot of complex images quickly as a sign of intelligence."

"Maybe. Yeah."

"So all you have to do is close the session, so you can disconnect from the machine."

Elza smiles now, as if the Ardenii told her something funny.

Rachael reaches out and takes the stick. "If it'll make you go away and leave me alone."

"Just . . . concentrate," Elza says in her most patient coding-instructor voice. "Try to make the blue light with your left hand, and then draw with your right."

Rachael starts to argue, but what the hell. She closes her eyes for a moment, and when she opens them, her left hand is on blue-tinted fire again. Her right hand reaches out, until the end of her stick brushes against the dirt on the floor.

Rachael hesitates. This is going to break what's left of her heart.

"Take your time," Elza whispers.

Rachael makes a line in the dirt. And then another.

The blue flame on her left hand flickers, then comes back strong.

The stick slips out of Rachael's grasp—but she catches it, and holds tight.

Rachael slowly, jerkily, draws a picture of a flower in the dust of the old star freighter. Not sure if it's a crocus or a rose or what, but it's definitely a flower.

Seven petals, cupped, drinking in the sunlight.

This is the crappiest picture she's drawn since she was five years old. And it's so beautiful, she can hardly stand it.

She puts down the stick—gently, because it's not just a stick anymore.

"Thank you," she says quietly. "I thought I would never get to do that again."

*Sometimes you get them back, right when you've given up.*

Now Rachael looks down at her left hand: no more blue sparks. They're gone, along with her last tether to the Vayt.

Elza looks at the flower and beams. "There you go."

"I probably won't ever make the same kind of art I was doing before I went inside that machine." Rachael shudders. "I don't know if I can just draw cute cartoons anymore."

"But that's good," Elza says. "Your art should change as you have new experiences, right? That's how you grow as an artist. And the Vayt will always be a part of you, the same way the Ardenii will always be part of me. Doesn't mean you can't keep moving forward."

Rachael feels very tired but also . . . hopeful? Just a tiny ember of hope, but it might as well be a tower of flames.

She turns to Elza. "Come sit next to me. If you want."

Elza sits down on the parsnip crate next to Rachael, and they sit next to each other, staring at the flower in the dust.

"I hope I never see her again," Rachael says. "If we can't fix her, I don't want to see her."

Elza doesn't have to ask who Rachael means. Tina.

"I won't ever give up. The last thing she said to me was not to give up on her. She's still in there, somewhere. I would give up a thousand space heroes to have her back."

Something occurs to Rachael. "So you were able to help me because you're a princess. Does that mean the queen could have shown me how to fix myself, back when I first asked for help? And she chose not to, because she wanted me to get close to Nyitha and discover her secrets?"

"Maybe. Or maybe you needed to find the Vayt first." Elza closes her eyes, which probably means she's talking to her new friends. "I hate to ask, but . . . did you find out anything?"

"Not really. She didn't want anyone to know about her past. . . . Oh, wait." Rachael suddenly sparks on her last second-to-last conversation with Nyitha, which feels like a million years ago. "She and Marrant accidentally killed an archivist, or at least Nyitha thought it was an accident. They were peeping around, looking for the plans to the palace, because Marrant had some idea he could trigger a fail-safe and put the whole place on lockdown."

Elza is staring at Rachael like she grew an extra head. She goes rigid.

"What is it?" Rachael says. "What's wrong? Do you need a doctor? Say something."

"I tried to warn the queen, but . . ." Elza chokes out. "I think we're too late."

Elza runs back inside the *Invention of Innocence,* and Rachael follows her. There's an actual river running along the ceiling of this receiving room, and cartoon critters are climbing all over every surface, chattering. Not to mention Naahay and Wyndgonk and a bunch of attendants are all trying to talk to Elza, and she ignores them all.

"Look." Elza waves her hand, and then Rachael is standing next to her in the Palace of Scented Tears. "This is what happened a few moments ago."

Marrant stands in the center of the Royal Council Chamber, surrounded by a few hundred bigwigs. All of the Royal Fleet brass is there, including Moxx, whose spiky face still gives Rachael daymares. Marrant has the same smirk as when he was killing Rachael's friends and putting the Grattna in cages.

How could Nyitha ever have been married to this creep?

On the big raised platform at the back of the room, one princess is standing, but not the queen—maybe she got Elza's warning in time?

Moxx steps forward, scowling between his tusks. "We trusted too much, Marrant. You told us that you could help us."

Next to Moxx, an Undhoran in a colorful robe steps forward. According to the helpful notes on the holographic display, this is Senior Councilor Waiwaiwaiwai.

"And meanwhile, your friends convinced Irriyaia to change allegiances and become the homeworld of the Compassion," Waiwaiwaiwai says. "And now, Irriyaia is a lifeless rock, and the Bereavement has become a more urgent threat."

"We trusted too much," Moxx says again.

"You can no longer be allowed to poison our ears." Waiwaiwaiwai's face-tubes twist into a scowl. "We're going to do what we should have in the first place: stick you in the darkest cell in the Hearsay, for as long as we all have left."

Marrant bows his head.

"Or," Marrant says, "you could put me in charge. I'm so close to solving the problem of the Bereavement, and I can still save all of you, if you just believe in me."

"This isn't about you," Moxx sputters. "We've already given you so many chances. You're finished."

"Or you could put me in charge," Marrant says again. "I will be a steady hand in a crisis."

"Why are we still listening to this man?" Waiwaiwaiwai gestures to a pair of palace guards, and they each seize one of Marrant's arms.

"I've been busy since I got to this palace," Marrant says as the guards start to drag him away with thick gloves on their hands. "Figuring out which of the councilors and Royal Fleet brass would be willing to fall in line behind me. But also? Locating the palace fail-safe."

Marrant does something with his left hand, and everything goes still. Nobody moves, including the guards who were pulling him away. As if they've all been paralyzed.

"You probably know the Palace of Scented Tears is not as it appears," Marrant says. "Everything is made of holograms and projections and other pretty things. You're not standing on a granite floor right now, and those gilded walls aren't really gold. Even the air around us isn't normal air. My late wife used to say it's important to see past the pretty surface that was put there to fool you."

Marrant strolls around the room, past bigwigs wearing bright-colored threads who stare helplessly, unable to move.

He reaches out one pinky and touches Moxx, and Moxx turns into a puddle. Then Waiwaiwaiwai.

"As you can see, the palace fail-safe causes a temporary lockdown of everyone and everything. Most people think it a legend, but I kept digging.

If there was a way to bring everything in the palace to a halt for a moment, including all the people, that would be invaluable."

Now Marrant is moving faster, pirouetting like a ballet dancer, with his hands flying out here and there. He twirls, to music nobody can else can hear, and cuts through the people in that room, like a chainsaw through tall grass. A bone-chilling rattle comes across, and Rachael doesn't realize at first: Marrant is shrieking with laughter.

Marrant pauses in front of one Royal officer, a Javarah in a senior visioner uniform, then pulls his hand away. "You, I can work with," he says.

He carries on dancing around the room, touching almost everyone except for a lucky few. He looks at the princess (Princess Nonesuch) and chooses to spare her.

At last, Marrant stands ankle-deep in the remains of everyone who stood against him, or might have stood against him.

Everyone who survived his massacre is slowly coming back to life, as the lockdown wears off. They blink and stare at the noxious remains of their friends and colleagues.

"I'm sorry you all had to witness that," Marrant says. "Those people were worthless traitors, working against us. I had no choice but to remove them from the picture, but now we're going to do great things here. The Royal Fleet and the Compassion can be reunified at last."

The senior visioner that Marrant spared steps forward. "You're right. Those filthy traitors deserved to die. Now we can move forward, as the Royal Compassion."

Everyone else left alive in the council chamber chimes in. "The Royal Compassion."

The playback comes to an end—as everyone who's left alive cheers for Marrant's ascension to power.

Rachael feels light-headed and crushed by a great weight and nauseous, all at once.

But Elza's stopped twitching, and now she looks weirdly calm.

"Okay." Elza holds out her hand, and Rachael takes it. "It's you, me, and our friends, against the Bereavement and the Royal Compassion and everybody else. Let's do this."

Rachael squeezes Elza's hand. "They'll never see us coming."

# ACKNOWLEDGMENTS

•

This is the first sequel I've ever written, and it's the middle book of a trilogy—which is its own kind of tough beast to wrangle. I am so grateful to everyone who helped me figure out this story. I apologize to anyone I've inadvertently left out.

My editor, Miriam Weinberg, was even more of a powerhouse than usual, and helped keep me on the right track with this super-complicated story. I know what true heroism is: it's Miriam's brilliant, insightful, impossibly gentle editorial feedback. So many other folks at Tor and Tor Teen were invaluable in making this book happen as well, including Patrick Nielsen Hayden, Saraciea Fennell, Isa Caban, Anthony Parisi, Molly McGhee, Eileen Lawrence, Irene Gallo, Lucille Rettino, and many, many others.

Without my agent, Russ Galen, I never would have written a young-adult trilogy in the first place, and this book would be nothing without Russ's continued support and guidance.

Thanks also to copyeditor Liana Krissoff, who saved me from many horrendous errors and oversights. And to Razaras for another gorgeous cover.

And then there are my sensitivity readers: Hailey Kaas, Na'amen Tilahun, Jaymee Goh, and Keffy Kehrli, all of whom made suggestions and interventions that improved this book dramatically.

I also owe a huge debt to my beta readers, including Tessa Fisher, Katie Mack, Sheerly Avni (twice!), Claire Light, Liz Henry, Maggie Tokuda-Hall, Olivia Abtahi, and Cecilia Tan.

Hailey Kaas has been indispensable to the Elza sections of this book—she not only answered a million questions about LGBTQ+ culture in São Paulo, *and* sensitivity-read this book—she's also been teaching me Portuguese every week for the past couple years. (Please hire Hailey if you need a translator, language teacher, or sensitivity reader! And check out her Patreon at patreon.com/wickedwitchofthesouthamerica.)

Also, Pedro Custódio Caldeira talked to me a lot about his experiences with Candomblé. And I watched the documentaries *Bixa Travesti* and *Yemanjá: Wisdom from the African Heart of Brazil*, and read the books *Initiation into Candomblé* by Zeca Ligiéro, *Travestí* by Don Kulick, *Capoera and*

*Candomblé* by Floyd Merrell, *The Brazil Reader: History, Culture, Politics,* edited by Robert M. Levine and John J. Crocitti, and parts of *The New Brazil* by Raúl Zibechi, translated by Ramor Ryan. I also learned a lot from two journal articles: "Beauty That Matters: Brazilian 'Travesti' Sex Workers Feeling Beautiful" by Julieta Vartabedian (*Sociologus,* 2016) and "'Our Life Is Pointless': Exploring Discrimination, Violence and Mental Health Challenges Among Sexual and Gender Minorities from Brazil" by Malta, Gomes de Jesus, LeGrand, Seixas, Benevides, das Dores Silva, Soares Lana, Huynh, Belden, and Whetten (*Global Public Health,* 2020). Thanks to Kristin Buxton for hooking me up with these papers.

Meanwhile, Preeya Phadnis and Shobha Rao gave me tons of feedback on Damini's storyline, and made a lot of indispensible suggestions on how to make her connection to Hindu culture feel more organic and grounded.

Likewise, I spent ages on Zoom with Aneesa Mohamed, who gave me a lot of advice on how to write Kez's arc. For Kez's gender-fluidity, I had some incredibly useful conversations with Nino Cipri.

Katie Mack spent ages on the phone with me helping me to figure out the Bereavement, and exactly how you would go about killing a whole lot of suns over a very long period of time. And Janelle Shane talked to me a lot about AI and how the Ardenii might work—plus, how you could make a computer with three choices instead of two.

Professor Jin Feng helped me to figure out how to translate "hurt/comfort" into Chinese.

And most of all, my partner, Annalee, has been a constant source of inspiration, ideas, and wonderment, and this book wouldn't exist without their support. I didn't have to cross the galaxy or travel to a super-advanced space city to find the person who makes my heart and brain sparkle, though we have taken many trips outside the solar system since we met on Earth.